GUARDIAN OF THE DARK PATHS

SUSAN E TROMBLEY

Copyright © 2021 by Susan Trombley

All rights reserved.

No part of this book may be reproduced in any form or by any electronic or mechanical means, including information storage and retrieval systems, without written permission from the author, except for the use of brief quotations in a book review.

Disclaimer:

This is a work of fiction. All of the characters, names, incidents, organizations, and dialogue in this novel are either the products of the author's imagination or are used fictitiously. References to ancient civilizations, myths, and mythical characters are not intended to be historically accurate. Alien character biology may not align completely with the terrestrial biological inspiration in function or terms.

Book cover design by Kasmit Covers

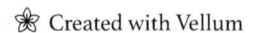

❀ Created with Vellum

1

Sarah shivered when she heard the sound of a car door slamming just outside her townhome. She finished stuffing her sweat-soaked bedding into the washing machine, still shaken by the nightmares that had plagued her last night and left her exhausted. A couple of wash pods and some scent boost later and she slammed the washing machine door just in time to hear her doorbell ring.

Before she could even reach the door, a loud banging started. She jerked it open to catch Bethany with her hand up in the air, ready to pound on the door a second time. Matt stood beside her. He was a few years younger than her, at only twenty, and he was an avid gym rat, as his well-toned, muscular body could attest. Still, something was off-putting to her when it came to Matt.

Bethany smiled her Instagram smile. It seemed very fake to Sarah, but she knew that beneath Beth's obsession with "going viral" and becoming a social media celebrity, she was still the painfully shy girl Sarah had grown up with. She and Beth had suffered through puberty hell together, fast friends who reassured each other that even with braces, bad acne, and baby fat, they were still beautiful and would someday prove to the world how amazing they were.

The social media mask was how Beth dealt with the world and its disappointments. Sarah used escapism with video games and books instead. She hadn't come out of puberty as a beautiful swan like Beth had.

"I thought you were going to chicken out on us," Beth said, flipping her long, blond extensions over her shoulder.

Sarah stepped aside and motioned them into the house. "I still think this is a bad idea, but I made you a promise and I intend to keep it." She gestured to the hallway of the little townhouse. "If you need to use the restroom before we go, it's down that hall."

The gesture was meant for Matt, who'd never been to her home, but Beth was the one who answered as Matt glanced around, a sharp look in his blue eyes as they caught on the gaming system set up in her living room.

"Yes, mother," Beth said with amusement in her voice. "We already went potty and got a drink and washed our hands. We're all ready for our trip. Now, quit stalling. We're burning daylight."

"Sweet system," Matt said, stepping closer to her living room to get a better look at her gaming rig, the lights on her tower glowing the same color as her headset that was propped on its charger.

Beth caught the back of his shirt, tugging him back through suggestion rather than force, since the muscles exposed by the thin fabric tightening over them wouldn't have been challenged by Beth's petite, slender frame.

"We don't have time for video games," she snapped, the amused tone from earlier evaporating as she glared at Matt. "You can pester Sarah about her little hobby later. Afterwards." She put stress on the last word as Matt pulled free of her grasp on his shirt and smoothed his hands down the front of it.

"Fine," he said with a petulant bite to his tone. He followed that up by lifting a hand to pat at his golden blonde hair, as if to insure that it hadn't been mussed by the short interaction.

Sarah shook her head at his obvious vanity. He was a social media "rising star" according to Beth, though Sarah had tried to watch one of his videos and found his channel boring and infantile. She never could understand the whole "pranking" videos fad that people seemed to love so much that they went viral all the time. Some of the pranks were just plain cruel, all to get some likes and shares and comments in the hopes of getting internet famous.

Beth ignored his clear irritation, turning her own slight frown on Sarah. "Seriously, girl. It's time to go. We have a ways to drive and I don't want to get there too late to really explore."

Sarah sucked in a deep breath, closing her eyes as she turned her back on them. She released it slowly, trying to push her anxiety out with the air. It never seemed to work the way the meditation books promised. She still felt the nervous energy tightening her muscles until her hand trembled as she reached for her small backpack.

"You got flashlights? And extra batteries?"

Beth rolled her eyes. "Yes, for the last time! And we have our cameras, which have their own lights as well. With extra batteries," she ground out, waving for Sarah to hurry up. "Let's go!"

Delaying tactics failing, Sarah followed reluctantly in Matt's footsteps as he trailed Beth out her front door. He tossed one last, longing glance at her gaming rig before meeting her eyes and giving her a smile he probably thought was charming.

Sarah was unimpressed. She'd seen enough of his fake smile on the one video she'd tried to watch of his. She had no idea why Beth kept hanging around him, though to be fair, Beth's videos were no more substantive in their content.

Beth was hoping to elevate her profile by doing something more profound and different than she'd been doing. Instead of fashion reviews, makeup tutorials, and unboxing videos to go along with her Instagram modeling profile, she wanted to add some exploration videos, in the hopes of entering a new market that wasn't oversaturated with beautiful blonde girls.

Sarah really wanted to help Beth follow her dreams and become famous, but she'd been uncertain about her best friend's current plan since Beth had suggested it. Neither of them knew much about exploring caves in the middle of the Arizona desert. Matt was going along for extra muscle and camera operation, but he wasn't exactly an expert either.

"We're not going too deep inside this cave?" Sarah asked, as they arrived at their destination. It was the first time she'd spoken since they'd hopped into Beth's Jeep. Her mind had been too preoccupied with worry after her nightmares, most of which she'd instantly forgotten upon waking, but the dread had remained.

Beth broke off her conversation with Matt, who was driving her Jeep and rattling on and on about the recent social media convention they'd attended. He'd dropped a ton of names during that conversation that Sarah didn't even recognize. A few of the video gamer channels registered with her, though she generally preferred to play the games rather than watch others play them in videos.

Matt put the Jeep in park as Beth turned to face Sarah, who sat in the cramped back seat. Her knees felt sore from slamming repeatedly into the back of the driver's seat as they'd bounced over every bump and dip on the unimproved desert road.

"Sarah, we'll be fine! I don't know why you're worrying so much! I'm trying to get you out of your house so you can have a real adventure instead of just running around in a video game world. This will be fun!" She reached back to pat Sarah's bruised knee. "You'll see."

"It's just... risky, don't you think?"

"Come on, Sarah," Matt said as he threw open his door and climbed out. He popped his head back inside to peer back at Sarah, "don't be such a coward."

They had to hike to their destination, and Sarah had to admit she was glad Beth had pushed them to get moving, because even in the early hours of the morning, the desert heat had ratcheted up to over ninety degrees. The scrubby mesquite trees with twisted trunks squatting low to the ground did little to add shade, and the ocotillo stabbed into the sky like thorned pikes left behind on a battlefield after some long distant war, barely casting a decent shadow.

The landscape appeared alien and unforgiving, cruel and uncompromising. Even the air was harsh, dry as a bone and burning with each inhale, as if every breath of it stole some of her water away from her. Sarah preferred thick forests with towering trees and deep shadowed glades to this relentless bright light and crippling heat.

The sight of their destination finally appeared like a mirage on the horizon. It did not endear Sarah any further to the arid landscape. The looming mountain may have promised shade, but that tight hole at the base of it, barely visible behind a cluster of large boulders, did not promise safety. Quite the opposite. It looked like it would crush anyone foolish enough to try to crawl inside. The twisted metal grating that had been pulled from the cave entrance and tossed to one side made the impression of danger worse.

"Oh hell no!" Sarah said, stopping in her tracks as Beth and Matt moved closer to the cave entrance. "There is no way I'm going through that hole."

Beth chuckled as she dropped her pack to dig out her mining hat. "Come on, Sarah, you're not that big." She eyed Sarah's generous hips, chewing on her filler-plumped bottom lip. "I mean, if Matt can fit his shoulders through the opening, you should be able to fit your butt through there."

If Sarah's cheeks weren't already on fire from the heat, they would now be burning with embarrassment as she avoided looking in Matt's direction. She'd heard his laugh just fine. She had no response to Beth's offhanded comment. Her friend hadn't meant any harm by it. They had both struggled with their weight when they were in school. Beth had grown out of her chubbiness, but she knew how much it hurt to deal with the jokes and jibes, so she was usually careful with what she said to Sarah. This time, she was obviously too excited about this little venture to be careful of Sarah's feelings.

They were both now staring at her, waiting for her to agree to crawl into that cave opening with them. A quick glance at Matt showed that he had his mining hat on, and a rope already looped around his shoulder. His camera was already strapped to his chest. Sarah had a sinking suspicion he was recording everything, including the big butt comment and her reaction.

"I could just wait out here," she said, allowing her pack to slide off her shoulder, bending with it to slow its descent to the ground. She unzipped it and pulled out her phone. "Someone needs to be outside where we can get a decent signal, in case of emergency."

Beth propped her hands on her hips. "That wasn't the deal, Sarah. You said you would go into the cave with us. Come on. Don't let me down now!" She pointed a finger at Sarah. "You owe me, girl."

Sarah bowed her head, unable to meet Beth's eyes any longer. She did owe Beth. She'd been the one to come to Sarah's rescue when she found out she was pregnant at fifteen and left home.

She had never gone back to her parents after that. They'd been happy to let her remain living with Beth and her mom at the time. She hadn't even bothered to contact them when Beth's mom got a new boyfriend and Sarah had to move out. Beth had helped her buy a beat up old van that she ended up living in. She'd also given Sarah food and supplies to keep her going.

Beth had been the best friend a girl could have. Sarah hadn't had the chance to repay her. This was a small sacrifice to make up for all Beth had done for her.

Without more protest, Sarah pulled out the mining hat they'd given her and set it on her head, strapping it under her chin. She sucked in a few more arid breaths that scorched her lungs and did little to quell a stomach queasy with nerves. Then she made her way to the cave entrance where Matt was already low-crawling his way through.

Beth gestured for Sarah to follow Matt, promising to bring up the rear. Sarah swallowed her fear, nodding, aware now that they were filming. She wanted to watch every word she uttered so it wasn't caught on camera.

She managed to avoid a sudden onset of claustrophobia only by focusing on Matt's feet ahead of her as she crawled behind him. She felt the rock above her catching on her pack, tugging it, restraining her as the straps tightened around her arms. After a short bout of panic, she realized she could twist and turn to break her pack free, flinching every time a chunk of rock clattered down with their passage.

Then, Matt climbed to his hands and knees ahead of her. He crawled for another half dozen feet before he was able to stand. Seeing him climb to his feet had Sarah moving faster, eager to get out of the tight space of the tunnel into a more open part.

Once she stood on her feet, able to straighten up to her full height, she started sucking in desperate breaths, realizing that she'd been holding her breath for far too long. Now, the drafts of air she pulled in were thick with must, the stench redolent of stale air, vermin, and long dead things. She turned to face the tunnel entrance, seeing nothing but Beth coming up behind her. The light from the opening was so faint as to be barely perceptible with their headlamps and the camera lights on.

Sarah was surprised by how far they'd managed to crawl. She turned back to look at the rest of the tunnel and noted something immediately. "This is a manmade tunnel."

Matt brushed dirt off his shirt and jeans. Even the gym-rat was breathing a little heavier from crawling through the beginning of the tunnel. "It's a horizontal shaft into an abandoned mine. The entrance was caved in at some point and that hole dug out of it again, but the rest of the shaft is solid."

Sarah glanced at him in surprise, then looked back at Beth, who had already brushed off her clothes. She had taken out a mirror to check her face, and was now wiping at a smudge of dirt on her cheek.

"You *knew* this was an abandoned mine?" Sarah spotted a portion of the old mine cart track peeking out from a pile of dirt and rubble. "Why didn't you just say so? I think that's a hell of a lot more interesting than a simple cave."

Beth snapped her mirror closed and tucked it into the pocket of her shirt. She shrugged as she met Sarah's eyes. "Technically, we're not supposed to be here. I wasn't sure you'd want to break the law, so I told you it was just a cave." She turned to regard the dark shaft ahead of them.

"Dammit, Beth!" Sarah bit her lip to keep more frustrated words from spilling forth, reminding herself they were on camera still. "What is this place?"

Beth shrugged again. "An abandoned mine. That's all." She jerked her chin towards the darkness that their lights couldn't penetrate. "Let's keep going since we're already this far in."

With a sigh, Sarah followed in Matt's footsteps, listening to the echo of his voice as he began to narrate for the camera. She found his overacting and his constant references to potential ghosts and spooky mine-monsters eye rolling but kept her comments to herself. This was apparently his show, though he gave Beth a few chances to speak as well. That was yet another fact Beth had misrepresented. Sarah wouldn't have been so willing to come here if she'd known it was for Matt rather than Beth.

The two were probably disappointed as they headed deeper into the shaft, finding nothing very interesting along the way, except for a handful of rusted old cans. There were several offshoots of the main tunnel, but they ended in such short distances that their lights were able to reveal the far walls without them further exploring those areas. Sarah was about to call the exploration a bust. She felt a bit disappointed herself now that she had come this far only to view walls of uninteresting rock scarred by pickaxes and a couple of rusted cans.

Then they arrived at a vertical shaft. On one side was the elevator shaft, with the cables still dangling, but no sign of an elevator. On the other side was the manway, a series of ladders leading down into impenetrable darkness.

Matt told his camera they were going to head down those ladders, and that was the first time Sarah spoke up, interrupting him. "Are you crazy? That wood could be rotted through. We step on it and we go crashing down to our deaths!"

"Relax, Sarah," Beth said from behind her. "The wood will hold. We'll be fine. Besides, you know you want to see what's down there."

Matt turned to face her, getting Sarah's face fully on camera. She flinched away from the bright light coming off his hat and camera, lifting a hand to block it from shining in her face. "My friends have already checked out this mine shaft. The ladders are solid."

"Please, Sarah," Beth said, giving her a dusty hug from behind. "Pretty please with sugar on top. Go down there with us."

Sarah kept her hand up, blocking her face from the camera as she stepped a bit closer to the shaft. She leaned just enough to peer over the edge, seeing the ladders descending beyond where her light could penetrate. "This is madness, you guys. It's not safe. There's a reason we aren't supposed to be here."

"That's because this shaft leads into a secret government facility," Matt said, speaking for the benefit of his audience, clearly, since he was dropping a line of total bullshit.

Sarah shook her head, swiping her sweating palms on her dirty shirt. "There's enough to be scared of just in the threat of collapsing rock walls. I don't think you need to add government conspiracies into it, Matt."

"Come on, Sarah," Beth hissed in a low voice behind her. "Play it up! This is for the camera. Try to look scared."

"I *am* scared, dammit," Sarah said out of the corner of her mouth, taking a step back from the vertical shaft. "I think you're both crazy, and I can't believe I let you talk me into this."

Beth clasped her hands together in a prayer pose, her eyes pleading, her fake eyelashes fluttering in what she probably hoped was a winsome way.

Sarah sighed, then lowered her hand so the camera could capture her expression. She made sure to widen her eyes and flare her nostrils, Blair Witch movie style. "I-I'm so afraid there might be ghosties and goblins down below."

Matt smirked. "I'll keep you safe, Sare Bear."

Sarah made a face, turning away in the hopes that the camera didn't catch it. Not that Matt couldn't edit it out later.

Was he calling her a bear because she had a thick, stocky build? Or was it her plain brown hair and unplucked brows that might be just a little overgrown that made him think of a hairy animal? And why did he make it sound flirtatious? Like it was an endearment?

She gagged a little, turning completely away from them both to face the shaft again. "All right, who goes first?"

"I'll go first," Matt said, flashing her a look she supposed he intended to be sultry. She thought he just looked sleepy—or high. "I'll keep you all safe by fighting any monsters down there." He climbed onto the first ladder, then leaned precariously towards Sarah. "Can I get a kiss for good luck?" He puckered his lips.

Sarah crossed her arms over her chest, shaking her head. "I really hope you aren't serious."

Matt grinned, but there was something mean in the smile as he opened his eyes wide in a falsely innocent expression. "Look at you, Sarah. You think a guy like me can resist you?"

"Matt," Beth snapped, censure in her tone. "Cut it out, now, or we quit filming and head back to the Jeep."

Matt's smile dropped away and he shrugged. "Fine. I was just trying to make her feel better about herself. Isn't that what you're always doing. Tiptoeing around her feelings because she's so touchy about her appearance?" Before Beth could respond with anything more than a gasp, Matt started down the ladder, once again narrating for the benefit of the camera.

They heard a crunch as he stopped on the first tier. "There's a lot of animal bones down here. I'll take some footage for the video, then you can head down."

"I'm sorry, Sarah," Beth whispered as Sarah turned her back on the descending figure of Matt, debating just leaving the asshole in that shaft to head back to the Jeep on her own. Maybe she could convince Beth to come too.

"Why do you even hang out with that douchebag?" For Beth's sake, Sarah kept her voice at a whisper, so the jerk couldn't hear the question.

Beth shook her head, glancing towards the shaft, where they could hear the sound of Matt's voice fading as he climbed further downwards. "He's got a ton of followers, Sarah! Networking is *everything* for my career. He can promote my videos to his subscribers and make me famous a lot faster than if I try to grow my audience on my own."

Sarah regarded Beth with concern. "You're so much better

than this, Bethie. Sometimes, I don't even recognize you anymore."

Beth's lips tightened, flattening out a bit, though not much because of the fillers. "You can get off your high horse, Sarah. You think you're so much better than me because you work with computer software and you're using your *precious* brain. I know that's how you see it, but you have no idea how hard I work at editing my videos and coming up with new content. I work my brain just as much, if not more, than you do. I don't need you judging me all the time."

Sarah was shocked by Beth's words. She'd never considered that Beth might take her comments the way that she had. Then she had to admit to herself that she *was* condescending towards Beth's "career." She still had a difficult time taking it seriously, even though she could see Beth's point. No doubt her friend worked hard on content creation, but she'd also grown so shallow in pursuit of internet fame.

She put her hand on Beth's shoulder. "I'm sorry. I didn't mean to sound—"

Beth brushed her hand off impatiently, then tossed her head so the low ponytail she'd put her hair into on the way to the cave bounced against her shirt. "I sacrificed my teen years looking after you, because you couldn't keep your legs closed when the first boy came sniffing around you. You needed me, and I was there for you. The lies I told, the things I did, to keep *your* secrets, kept me from living my own life. And now, you can't even do this one thing for me and play along so I can get some goddamned video footage to create a spooky mine exploration video." Beth held up one finger in front of her face. "*One* damned thing is all I've ever asked of you, Sarah!"

Stung from Beth's biting words, Sarah faced the shaft again, blinking back the sudden tears that rose to her eyes. She couldn't see Matt's lights anymore. It was time for her to start heading down. "I didn't realize I was such a burden to you, Beth."

"Shit," Beth muttered under her breath, but Sarah still heard her in the stifling silence of the mine. Louder, she said, "Look, I'm... I didn't mean that. I mean, not in that way. That was pretty harsh. It's just that you're always so fucking condescending to me when it comes to my work. It pisses me off, because I feel like I did everything to help you out when we were in high school, and you still think you're better than me."

"I don't think I'm better than you, Beth," Sarah said in a low voice, then without another word, climbed onto the ladder.

"Sarah," Beth took a step closer to the shaft opening.

Sarah didn't bother to turn her head to look at Beth as she started down the ladder. The fear she'd had about heading into the darkness had disappeared. Now she wanted to escape this painful conversation, fighting the tears that threatened to blind her to the wooden rungs in front of her. She also felt confused and shaken by Beth's revelations. She'd never known how much Beth resented her for what happened during high school. She'd also never realized that Beth had picked up on her disdain for the social media madness that seemed to infect Beth.

As she descended, her breaths growing short and labored from the effort, she wondered what she could do to repair their friendship after this. She also wondered if perhaps they had both passed a point where it couldn't be repaired.

2

The emotional upheaval that came from her argument with Beth wasn't enough to completely block her anxiety over what they were doing. The ancient wood beneath her feet creaked as she stepped down each slat of the ladders. The walls of the shaft felt like they were closing in on her, and the dust kicked up by Matt's passage floated in the still air like a choking cloud, illuminated by her headlamp.

Matt was many ladders down, probably even nearing the bottom of the shaft, though she still caught flashes of his lights and heard the echo of his voice as he narrated for the benefit of his video. Above her, she heard Beth climbing onto the first ladder. Dust and splinters rained down onto the boards that supported the ladder on which she stood.

She climbed further down, tensing with nerves as she settled her weight on each ladder, fearing that one of them was bound to give way, or the narrow boards that supported them would suddenly snap, sending her down the shaft the fast—and fatal—way. The ominous creaking of old wood and the crunch of animal bones beneath her boots every time she stepped on a supporting board raked over her nerves, until it was impossible to look downwards at the dark, narrow rectangle of the next level and the ladder that disappeared down into it. She also couldn't look upwards without feeling a dizzying sense of disorientation, or getting a face full of fallen dust and crushed bone and desiccated fur from Beth's movements above her.

Instead, Sarah stared straight ahead at the ladder in front of her, only glancing down briefly at each stop to find her footing on the next ladder. In what seemed like an interminable time, she ran out of ladders, and her boots met a stone floor, earning a gasp of relief from her. Finally on a solid, dependable surface, she tore her gaze away from the last ladder and turned to find a camera in her face.

"You're looking pretty spooked there, Sarah," Matt said with a chuckle. "Maybe you should take a rest and drink some water. You sound out of breath."

She resisted the urge to punch the camera that probably cost thousands of dollars and turned her back on him, unwilling to give him any more footage for his video. She had no doubt her face was white as a sheet after that descent, and she was out of breath, and not just from exertion. She'd almost forgotten to breathe as she'd climbed down, as if she was afraid that the weight of that extra air in her lungs would be the final straw for the ancient wooden slats.

Beth arrived not long after that, which was a good thing, because it distracted Matt from trying to urge Sarah to answer inane questions for the camera.

The two had a little session where they spoke for the sake of the video, talking about the "scary" mine shaft as if they didn't really think it was. Their cringy overacting was almost painful to watch, but it did have the benefit of calming her own nerves. Their obvious lack of concern gave her reassurance.

When they finally finished their act, Matt trained his lights on the drift that snaked away from the shaft. It meandered one way then another without much in the way of interesting sights along the way. There were offshoots everywhere, but the main tunnel was clearly the most developed. The miners must have found a promising vein and followed it deep into the ground.

Occasionally, they found evidence of the long gone miners, in the abandoned and rusted cans, broken gun powder barrels, and even an intact pickaxe, the tip of the rusted head still buried in a chunk of rock. After that landmark, the tunnel changed, growing larger. It also looked smoother, as if, instead of merely picking at the rock, someone had cleaned it up to remove any potential head smashing hazards.

The air changed at that point as well, growing fresher. It also carried moisture from somewhere deeper within the mine, hidden by the unrelenting darkness that filled every tunnel. It was a darkness that their lights seemed to struggle to push back.

Once again, they found cart tracks as they followed the new tunnel until it bisected an even larger one. This time, the tracks were cleared of debris and disappeared on both sides of the tunnel. These tracks were free of rust and even looked like they'd been oiled and had been used more recently.

"Is this part of the mine still active?" Sarah wondered aloud, interrupting Beth's monologue at the camera Matt held.

Beth shrugged, flashing Sarah an irritated glance before turning back towards the camera with a fake smile and wide eyes, her false lashes fluttering as she pretended to be spooked out.

After a few minutes of them talking for their audience while Sarah wandered around the larger tunnel, never straying too far from them, but staying out of the sight of the camera, they finally finished up their little dialogue with a future audience. Matt turned to point his camera towards one end of the tunnel.

"Let's head down that way. I think that's where the secret

military installation is," he said, his tone taking on a serious note filled with excitement, as if they really were about to find some underground bunker with aliens or creepy science experiments—both possibilities had been suggested to the camera during their earlier exposition.

Sarah sighed, but she was already this deep into the mine. After the harrowing trip down the shaft, she figured she might as well make the most of this exploration. As much as she hated to admit it after their argument, Beth might have been right about dragging her out of her house to experience this. It was out of her comfort zone, breaking her out of a rut that she'd initially been grateful for, after spending her teen years living in so much uncertainty. Her current schedule had dug deep grooves in her life, giving her a sense of stability that she'd desperately needed, but it also kept her from experiencing things beyond the virtual worlds of her video games or the four walls of her office.

Now she was curious about what hid behind the darkness at the end of the tunnel, so she didn't argue when Matt and Beth headed in that direction. She followed on their heels, rolling her eyes at their constant commentary and pretend startled yelps as they delved deeper into this new area.

Matt spun an improbable tale of gray aliens being held as experiments as they went along, his tone growing more and more tense with excitement. Beth threw in plenty of gasps and expressions of fear to add to the atmosphere they were trying to create. Sarah just wished they'd shut up long enough to appreciate the genuinely creepy environment as their shadows bounced along the walls with each step they took.

She was about to suggest they take a break from speaking long enough to record the spooky silence in the tunnel, when it opened up wider as the tracks they'd been following veered off to the left. Ahead of them stretched a concrete barrier that took up the entire wall of the larger tunnel.

"What the hell is that doing here?" Sarah asked, walking closer to inspect the wall. The previous parts of the mine had probably been built in the late 1800s or early 1900s. This concrete looked far newer.

"It's the government facility," Matt whispered, his eyes wide, his mouth remaining agape after he finished speaking.

Beth reached for his arm, clutching at his dusty sleeve. "I'm scared now," she said in a quavering voice.

Sarah was about to dismiss their fears, though she felt the hair standing up on the back of her neck. A soft dragging sound caused them all to stiffen, cutting off the words she'd been about to speak.

They moved to stand together in a cluster. Even Sarah debated clinging onto someone's sleeve. They stared towards where the sound had come from, seeing only the impenetrable darkness.

"I'm gonna go check it out." Matt aimed his camera in that direction and took a few steps closer to that end of the tunnel. Beth still clung to him, following in his shuffling, hesitant steps.

"Are you crazy?" Sarah hissed, reaching out to capture Beth's arm. "You have no idea what made that sound. It could be some kind of animal. It might be rabid!"

Beth shrugged her off, tossing a glance at Sarah over her shoulder. "You stay here then. We're going to check it out."

Sarah ground her teeth to cut off her angry retort, still painfully aware that the camera was always rolling and she didn't want to provide actual drama for their video. "Fine." She crossed her arms over her chest. "You want to do something stupid, go right ahead. I'll wait right here."

Without another comment, Beth flipped her ponytail and then turned to follow Matt, who took more confident steps towards that end of the tunnel after no more sounds came from the darkness.

Sarah watched them, every muscle in her body tense as she

strained to listen for any new sound. It was difficult because they made so much noise with their loud, shuffling steps and their constant chattering for the sake of the camera.

Their lights reached the area where the sound had come from. Sarah expected to see the glowing eyes of some poor, lost animal, or perhaps a rabid one. Instead, she jumped as Beth screamed and Matt abruptly backed away from the area.

Their lights had just barely captured the hunched form of some terrifying humanoid creature. They'd moved so quickly that she didn't have the chance to make any details out, but she was already shaking her head, backing quickly towards the other end of the tunnel. She pulled her flashlight from her pack and clicked it on to add some more light to the situation, her headlamp not being bright enough to penetrate that far into the tunnel.

She gripped the flashlight with a white-knuckled hand that trembled so much the beam danced wildly over Matt and Beth's frightened faces as they scrambled back towards her.

Before they could reach her, something grabbed Sarah from behind, hard arms banding around her waist, pinning her arms to her sides.

She screamed, lifting her foot to slam it down on her attacker's foot as she felt the creature closing in behind her. Her booted heel impacted with her full weight behind it. The thing grunted in pain, its hold loosening around her.

Sarah took that opportunity to ram her elbow backwards into the gut of the creature. With a pained gasp, it fully released her. She spun around on her other foot and struck the creature in its gray, pale face with the heel of her open palm.

The dolphin gray, slender monster with the oversized head and huge black eyes had bent over from the strike to its gut. Her strike to its face had a lot of force behind it, causing the creature's overlarge head to snap backwards, hanging crookedly like its neck was broken as it staggered several steps away from her.

Sarah snarled as she followed it, raising the flashlight. The solid weight of it felt like a small club as she prepared to bring it down onto the sagging head of the creature.

"Sarah! No!" Beth yelled, jumping in front of the creature while Matt rushed Sarah from behind to grab her arm.

Sarah kicked backwards, her foot striking Matt in the knee. He instantly released her forearm, gagging with pain as his knee hyperextended. He collapsed to the ground, howling as he clutched the injured joint. His eyes filled with tears of pain as he looked up at her, glaring as if she'd attacked him, instead of the other way around.

"You really are a bear, you crazy bitch!" he gasped out between pained breaths as he rocked side to side.

"What the fuck?" Sarah shouted, turning back to Beth and the creature, only to see that it had transformed into a young man in a rubber alien costume.

Realization struck her all at once as she stared at the attractive but clearly young man who she'd nearly brained with her heavy flashlight. He was still partially hunched over, moaning in pain as one hand clutched his stomach and the other rubbed his chin. He stood with his weight mostly on the foot she hadn't stomped on.

"It was just a little prank," Beth whispered, her eyes wide as she met Sarah's accusing glare. "We only wanted some good footage for the video. We didn't think you'd try to kill Wes. What the hell is *wrong* with you!"

Sarah gasped in outrage, her fingers once again tightening around the flashlight until her knuckles turned white. "What's wrong with *me*? Are you fucking kidding me? You scared the *shit* out of me and you want to know what's wrong with *me*? All for a fucking internet video?"

"We could have gone viral, man," the youth apparently

named Wes grunted. "I spent hours down here waiting for you guys, and you let this bitch nearly kill me."

"Dude, we can still go viral," Matt said to him, his tone excited as he completely ignored Sarah's furious glare. With obvious pain, he pushed himself back to his feet, favoring his wounded knee. "I got it all on camera. Sarah totally kicked your ass! It turned out even better than our original plan."

Wes groaned, straightening to his full height, which was well over six feet, leaving Sarah feeling dwarfed at only five foot five. "Worked out for you maybe. I think I need to go to the hospital. I swear she burst my spleen or something."

Matt chuckled, walking towards the youth with a limping step to clap a hand on his shoulder. "It'll be worth it, man. You'll see."

Sarah completely lost her temper when she spotted another humanoid shadow moving closer to the light they were all casting. "Just tell your other goddamned friend that the gig is up! I swear to god, I will beat the shit out of all of you if he has the nerve to touch me again!"

All three of them turned to stare at her as if they'd forgotten she was there and she'd suddenly just popped into existence.

"What other friend?" Matt asked, feigning ignorance a lot better than his previous acting had been.

Sarah propped her hand on her hip, gesturing with her flashlight. "The one right behind you, Matt. You idiots just don't quit, do you?"

"The fuck!" Matt said, spinning around to face the other "creature" as it rose to its full height.

Like Wes, this one stood over six feet. Only this new guy appeared to be in a furry suit. A high quality one that looked like some movie monster genius had built the costume. It had a beastly, rubbery face that looked like a cross between a cat and a bat. Huge, batlike ears tilted towards them. The body looked lean, though muscles rippled under the coarse brown fur, almost like real muscles might. It was a very convincing costume. If they hadn't already tried to scare her with the party store alien costume, she would have been terrified by it.

Matt shrieked like a girl in a horror movie, and Sarah shook her head at the theatrics "Give it *up*, man. You aren't getting any more footage out of scaring me."

The new arrival swung its arm, claws extending on the end of its hand in a very realistic way as it swiped at Matt.

Something wet and warm splattered Sarah's face. She stared at Matt as he spun around from the momentum of the attack, his throat slashed open. Blood spurted everywhere.

Someone else screamed in a high pitch. The additional lights from Beth's lamp disappeared in the wake of receding footsteps.

A quick glance showed that both Beth and Wes had run from the suddenly very realistic creature that Sarah was still struggling to process.

It growled at her, lifting its bloodied claws to its mouth. A human looking tongue darted from between its beastly lips, revealing a row of sharp teeth, framed by long, vampiric-like fangs. Tasting the blood, its black eyes lifted from Matt's still-twitching body to pin Sarah.

Sarah spun around and took off running in the same direction as the others, heading towards the tunnels that led back to the shaft. The creature's footfalls behind her caught up to her as it shrieked in a sound that made her cry out in terror. The bouncing light from the headlamp caught its shadowy form as it leaped to the wall and started scaling the stone like a spider. It climbed rapidly along the wall around her path, moving upwards until it hung upside down above her. She skidded to a halt as it suddenly dropped down in front of her to block her escape.

It could have captured her at any time. It was so much faster than her. She realized in that moment that it was enjoying the chase. Like a housecat with a mouse, it wanted to play before it killed. She spun around and took off in the opposite direction, running deeper down the tunnel that passed the concrete barrier as the thing shrieked again. This time, she heard the excitement in the sound. The anticipation of the hunt.

She had no idea where she was going, or how she could possibly escape the creature, but a primal need to survive filled her. It drove her steps forward, pumping adrenaline through her blood. The fact that the thing wanted to draw out the chase might just serve to give her a fighting chance. Her rational mind told her there was no way she was getting out alive, but she wouldn't quit trying until she was dead.

Her headlamp cast wild shadows as she ran, illuminating side tunnels only when she was too close to them to change direction. There could be safety in those offshoots, but most likely, they were dead ends. In this case, that would be quite literal.

The creature would occasionally shriek behind her as if to goad her on. Sometimes, the sound would be distant, and other times, terrifyingly close, just beyond the darkness that she left in her wake. At this point, she had no doubt that it was playing, running her like dogs chasing a fox. Reveling in her terror and panic.

Suddenly, the stone beneath her disappeared as her footsteps thudded over wood. The hollow sound gave her a clue of what that change meant, but not before the rotting wood collapsed beneath her weight.

She screamed with a new terror as the boards covering a vertical shaft shattered, sending her crashing down onto the platform that supported the first ladder of the manway. She'd been lucky enough to fall through on this side of the shaft, rather than down the elevator side. Her luck didn't hold as the narrow platform cracked beneath her weight while she struggled to climb to her feet.

It snapped in half, sending her smashing into the ladder below. The first ladder kept falling to bust apart the next platform.

Sarah's screams mixed with the sounds of breaking wood and the thuds of her body against ladder and platform. She grabbed desperately for the wood slats that formed the collar of the shaft as she struck one platform or ladder after another, each one more rotted and fragile than the last. Not one held on her way down, but they broke her fall enough to slow her descent to a survivable speed.

Survivable, if she didn't get crushed by the debris falling around her, much of it striking her body in places that she would certainly feel later when the adrenaline wore off.

Finally, her desperate grasp caught onto a collar board, stopping her plummet. The sudden halt in her momentum jerked at her arm as it was forced to support her weight. Her nails tore on the soft rock behind the collar slat. Even with the adrenaline still flowing, her hand felt like it was on fire and her arm like it was being slowly ripped off.

Then the creature's shriek sounded from above her as she dangled in the shaft, a pile of shattered, rotten wood below her, splintered ends jutting upwards like spikes.

She kicked her foot, desperately seeking purchase on a slat to support her weight before her fingers gave out. Her panicked breaths sucked in musty air clogged with dust from her fall. Sweat poured down her face, running in rivulets through the coating of dirt that masked her.

She whimpered as she heard the sounds of the creature's claws clicking on wood. Those sounds grew closer as her foot finally caught on a lower slat. Her heart pounding so loud it nearly deafened her, she was able to push herself upwards enough to capture the slat above her with her free hand.

Finally, able to brace all four limbs, her entire body trembling from reaction, adrenaline, and the effort it took to support herself in that fashion, she started climbing downwards. She heard the creature above her rapidly descending.

It released short shrieks and huffing and snuffling sounds, as if it were excited. Or as if it was sniffing her out, still able to detect her despite the clouds of dust particles that slowly drifted in the still air in the wake of the manway's collapse.

Though Sarah was climbing down as fast as she could, it felt like it was taking forever. She could hear the creature's claws digging into the slats right above her head when the slat beneath her foot snapped in two.

She'd been reaching for a lower slat at that moment, which forced the weakened board to take most of her weight. That left her off balance.

She screamed as she fell backwards, closing her eyes to avoid seeing the creature above her being illuminated by her headlamp as she plummeted to her death.

She must have been further down the shaft than she thought because she struck ground with a hard impact that stole her breath, but didn't shatter her bones. Shivering in reaction, she turned her head to see that she had fallen into the pile of broken wooden platforms and ladders. Just above her, the boards of the collar buckled beneath the pressure of the soft stone they held back.

The shaft was on the brink of collapsing completely at the lowest level, and her fall had not helped. The already strained collar boards had splintered from the passage of the masses of wood that had come down before her. She felt the soft brush of cleaner air from the drift that was hidden behind the crumpled pile of fallen wood.

She had to get out of there quickly. At the same time, any rash movement could slam more debris into those weakened boards and cause a collapse of the shaft.

Still, the creature approached, apparently unfazed by any fears of getting crushed by tons of rock.

Scrabbling backwards towards the cooler air that indicated the drift, she slowly turned her head until the light of her headlamp crept up past the buckling boards to fix on the hideous face of the creature.

As soon as the light struck it, it shrieked as if in rage. It flinched back, lifting a clawed hand to block its face. Then it shoved away from the collar, dropping downwards.

Sarah kicked her feet to move herself backwards faster, flailing her uninjured arm above her head to push aside enough of the debris to crawl through.

She was just rolling onto her stomach when the creature struck.

It's shrieks vibrated the air as its claws slashed in her direction. She could feel the tug on her pack as it tried to hook her with its claws.

Beneath the hideous sounds of the creature's screaming was a wet, squishy sound, like someone squeezing a raw steak. Sarah wasn't going to look back, determined to escape through that tiny opening she'd made before the creature could tear her apart.

Yet it had a hold on her pack. She couldn't release the pack without rolling back onto her side.

That was when she saw it, her light bright on the creature's face. The malleable features had fallen eerily still now, hovering only a couple of feet away from her own.

The black eyes were glassy and lifeless.

She gasped and pulled herself towards the hole, unsnapping her pack with her injured hand, still sluggishly bleeding from her torn skin and nails.

The creature's claws were buried deep into the material of her pack. Even in death, it hadn't relaxed its grip.

It seemed to be very dead, impaled on a splintered spike of wood that had once been part of a ladder. The wood had apparently shifted from her desperate kicking to escape as the monster jumped down on her, positioning it perfectly to stab through the creature.

Sarah, unwilling to relax until the corpse was well behind her and she was out of the crumbling shaft, kept her eyes on the monstrosity until she crawled through the opening she'd dug out. She had to leave her pack behind, as chunks of stone started to rain down from above, and the wooden collar creaked ominously in multiple places. There was no time to untangle the fabric of her pack from the creature's lifeless grip.

She slipped through the hole like a baby being born, sliding out of the choking dust and the rising stench of meat and freshly spilled blood into air that was still musty but much fresher. She crawled several feet into the drift before climbing to her hands and knees. Her legs shook from reaction as the adrenaline burst began to wane, leaving all her aches and pains to rise to the surface.

Her entire body ached. She felt like she'd gone ten rounds with a champion boxer. With her as the punching bag. Sharp pains throughout her body hinted at splintered wood that had found its way through her clothing to dig into her flesh. Though she was sure by this point that she hadn't broken anything, every joint and tendon and sinew felt like it had been battered and twisted. Much of her bared skin was covered with scrapes and cuts.

She looked back at the hole, now dark and even more ominous since she knew what was beyond it. She slowly backed away from it, not just because she still worried about a collapse, but because she couldn't believe the monstrous creature was actually dead. She feared it would somehow come back to life again and burst out of the darkness to tear her throat out.

She walked backward deep into the drift, casting glances over her shoulder to illuminate where she was going before turning her attention back towards that hole. Finally, she rounded a corner and it was out of her sight. Only then was she able to focus on what lay ahead of her.

She faced the darkness, her lamp barely seeming to make a dent without the aid of her flashlight, which she'd lost during her plummet. The dimmer headlamp created only a small bubble of light in front of her. She didn't want to walk into that unknown place. She had no idea where it led, and she feared there might be more monsters. She also knew there was no going back the way she'd come. Even though the collar had yet to collapse, it was close. Any attempt to climb back out through that shaft would see her crushed by rock as the boards completely buckled.

Her only choice was going forward. Deeper into this mountain. Deeper into the darkness.

3

The mind is a funny thing. Sarah believed, despite all evidence to the contrary, that she could still survive. She refused to acknowledge the logical realization that she was a dead woman walking. Perhaps it was because of all the video games she played. There was always an escape for the protagonist. Always some secret door or hidden tunnel. Always a way out, if she was smart enough to figure out the puzzle.

Or maybe it was something more primal. Maybe it was simply the human will to survive, despite all odds being against her. After all, even humans in the real world sometimes clung to life when logic said they should have long ago given up.

Whatever the reason, Sarah knew she was already dead, but she didn't let that stop her from trying to survive. Her entire body hurt and each new step was a struggle, earning a pained grunt when she didn't have the strength to bite it back as the fall of her foot against the stone floor jarred everything in her body.

The only encouragement she got from delving deeper into the drift was the fact that it didn't seem to end. This mine was massive. Far more so than a wildcat mine should be. But then again, perhaps she wasn't in a mine anymore, though the stone walls of the tunnel still looked like they'd been worked by tools. Most likely primitive ones. The tunnel still meandered as if following a vein. There were still offshoots that suggested tangential drifts, but she decided to remain in the largest, main drift, hoping for another vertical shaft heading upwards.

Instead, she felt as if she were traveling further downwards, as the tunnel had a slight slope that grew more pronounced the deeper she went. She felt it pulling her forward with each step, as if the void of darkness dragged her towards it like a lodestone.

The sound of her shuffling steps growing more labored with each movement was the only sound she heard in the deathly stillness of the tunnel. When she kicked a loose chunk of rock after what felt like hours of endless walking, she jumped as it rolled away with a loud clatter that ended in a soft thud a short distance past the light bubble cast by her headlamp.

She dreaded the moment the battery pack failed and she lost that precious light, which was the only comfort she had left.

She took a few more steps forward. The light preceding her revealed yet more stone floors and walls. Then it settled on a layer of soft sand, signaling an abrupt shift in the tunnel's appearance. The seam between the worked stone and what appeared to be a natural cavern was so dramatic that it was like looking at a glitch in a video game world.

The sand remained on one side of the path, lying in a straight line along the edge of the worked stone. She stepped over the line, straddling both sides as she bent to get a closer look, aiming her light at the seam.

It was after she passed that seam that she first caught scent of something different in the air. The cave air was fresher, and held more moisture. Yet she hadn't smelled that until she stepped over the line. There was also the taint of a scent that was unnerving. A sickly smell that reminded her of a dead mouse rotting away behind a wall.

She stood straight to look around at the cave. The ceiling was so high that her meager lamp only illuminated the occasional stalactite hanging low enough to dip into the bubble of light. The cave was also so large that it stretched off into darkness in every direction. She caught the sound of water dripping, softly echoing, somewhere in the distance.

With a sense of fatalism and a growing bit of hope, she made her way deeper into the new cave, leaving the seamed area and the mine tunnels behind. A quick glance back had her gasping, then rushing back to where the seam had been.

Now it was only a cave wall. She ran her hands over the uneven stone that had been shaped by geological forces rather than tools, panic filling her. Then she pounded her fists on it, her efforts fruitless, only serving to remind her that she was a mass of aches and pains and various splinters that were now probably buried so deep in her skin they would have to be cut out.

She screamed in a combination of fear and frustration, with fear overtaking the lead at the end until her scream rose to a shriek. The sound was returned on a terrible echo that snapped her out of her panic. She staggered away from the cavern wall, desperately searching for a way back into the mine. There was no sign of the seam. No sign of any kind of tunnel heading back the way she'd come. Her foot twisted as she stepped on the rock she'd kicked into the sand.

Bending down, she slowly picked it up and studied it as if she could comprehend what was happening.

A faint sound of sand shifting behind her had her stiffening, her head jerking upwards as she spun around. The rock dropped from her nerveless fingers as she slowly turned her head, her lamp illuminating only a short distance in front of her.

There was nothing there but darkness, but her thudding heartbeat told her otherwise, as did the raised hairs on the back of her neck.

As she stood there staring in the direction she thought the sound had come from, her eyes desperately strained to see something beyond the cone of light. The shadows seemed to coalesce into a shape. A massive, humanoid shape formed from the darkness that stepped into the edge of the light.

It had to be over seven feet tall, and unlike the slender, bat-cat creature she'd survived through luck alone, she knew she wasn't going to escape this monster. A huge body covered by some kind of armor might weigh it down enough to make it slower than her, but she had nowhere to run. Her only escape had disappeared at her back and this creature stood between her and the rest of the cavern.

It straightened from a slightly hunched position, and she swallowed through a dry throat as it stepped further into her light, revealing a face covered by scales, thin lips pulled back to bare two rows of sharp teeth. Reptilian eyes glared at her, narrowed in a humanoid face. Two slitted nostrils beneath a nearly flat nose widened as a long, forked tongue flicked out from between the sharp teeth.

The creature had no visible ears, but it did have a crown of what looked like spines on its head that seemed to twitch as it approached her. She stood frozen in horror, her jaw slackening until her mouth gaped open as the creature moved closer to her. Close enough for her to smell the odd, leathery scent of it tinged by some kind of indefinable musk. Close enough for her to hear its angry hiss rising in its chest. Close enough to see the shadow of a long, crocodile-like tail whipping behind its legs.

Close enough to recognize the necklace of human teeth and fingerbones hanging around its neck.

She screamed again, then turned to the side, her light darting away from the creature as she took off at an oblique angle.

She ran as if she had even the ghost of a chance, unable to hear if the monster pursued her through her own footsteps and pounding heart. It moved far more silently than her if it did, but the alien scent of it seemed to fill every desperate breath she took to fuel her mad dash.

The light bounced erratically as she ran, the wild shadows making it difficult to see the path in front of her. When one step came down on empty air, she tumbled forward, falling face first into a pile of sticks that reeked of rotting things. She flailed, her fingers closing around one of the sticks, dragging it closer as if her paltry weapon would have any chance against the creature.

She rolled onto her back, adrenaline once again blocking her pain and focusing her panic. Her lamp revealed the horrors of the pit she'd fallen into.

They weren't sticks. The round bulge digging into her thigh wasn't a smooth rock. The rotting scent was from the corpses that stared blankly at her, in various stages of decomposition. Most of them were nothing but bones and tattered rags.

Some of them appeared to be wearing military uniforms and broken-toothed grins exposed by a few remaining tatters of torn flesh.

From what she could see as panic threatened to overwhelm her again, they were all humans.

She turned back on her stomach, crawling towards the rock wall that surrounded the pit, her breath coming in short, harsh bursts through her mouth to avoid sucking in most of the stench. She tasted the death and decay and it made her want to vomit, but terror kept her moving.

Digging through the bones to pull herself forward, she felt something beneath a pile. Her fingers closed around the butt of a rifle. She cried out in triumph, stopping her crawl long enough to quickly excavate it from the mass of reeking death.

It finally broke free, the weight of it heavy with a loaded magazine. The M16 wasn't a new weapon and had clearly lain in this pile for some time, but it was the most beautiful thing she'd ever seen in that moment.

With newfound hope, she finished her crawl to the edge of the pit. She shouldered the weapon and began her short climb out.

As soon as she rose above the edge of the pit, the leather-musk scent of the creature drifted to her on some moist cavern breeze. She pulled herself out of the pit and climbed to her feet, swinging the M16 off her shoulder to hold it ready in front of her.

She had no idea how to use a weapon in real life, though she'd become an expert at video game shooters. She knew where the safety was, and saw that it was off. She knew, theoretically, how to use the weapon. She released the magazine, and a quick check showed her that it still held some ammo. She clicked it back into place and pulled the charging handle.

Once the weapon was ready to fire, she turned, searching the cavern with her head lamp. The barrel of the rifle trembled in front of her as she turned first one way, then the other. She was well aware that this wasn't a game. The weight of the unfamiliar weapon helped steady her muscles, but not enough that she was certain her aim would be true if the creature came at her.

It charged her with barely a sound. If her ears weren't straining to pick up any noise other than the shift of bones in the pit and the steady drip of water somewhere within the cavern, she wouldn't have heard the slight crunch of sand that told her it was coming from behind her.

She spun around, her finger reflexively squeezing the trigger.

The sharp retort of the weapon almost deafened her to the pained growl of the creature as it darted back into the shadows. It left a wet spatter of blood that shined in the light as she glanced down at it.

A sense of elation filled her. She finally had the upper hand. If it came at her again, she would blow its brains out.

Something staggered her as it struck her arm, pain and a growing numbness in that limb following the sharp impact. The weapon fell from her hands to thud uselessly in the sand.

Shock delayed her reaction to the dart sticking out of her arm, as some kind of poison burned through her blood. The dart wasn't that large, but it was the toxin that threatened her.

It had never even occurred to her that the monster had projectile weapons of its own, rendering her newfound rifle completely useless as it struck at her from shadows her light couldn't penetrate. No wonder the rifle had ended up in a pit of corpses.

She supposed she would join that pile. An unnatural lassitude filled her and her knees buckled, dropping her to the sand to roll onto her back. She stared upwards at the tips of stalactites pointing down at her like the swords of Damocles. She wondered what was on the other side of life. She didn't have the comfort of religion to soothe her as the creature appeared, blocking her view. It stood over her, staring down at her, sharp teeth bared and spines raised.

It's clawed hand extended towards her just as she lost consciousness.

4

Jotaha cursed the Ajda, the elder gods, roundly as he stared down at the slumbering form of the nixir. Invader. Betrayer of the treaty. Enemy.

And now, apparently, his mate.

This wasn't supposed to happen. Not here. Not now. He and Farona had decided that they wanted to begin a family. He'd gone to the priest of Seta Zul and asked for the mating seal, certain that the goddess would bind him to Farona. Certain that the desire of his heart would guide the goddess' choice. After the seal was painted on his body, he'd had to rush out of the temple before he could seek out Farona to have her activate it. He had to return to his post in the hunting grounds at the boundary, because the urvak zayul—cave spirits—sensed danger approaching, in their enigmatic way. Their growing unease drew him back to his duty, when he was supposed to be preparing to retire his role.

There had been no time to prepare and initiate one of the jotahs to take his place. In fact, he'd moved so quickly to return to the urvaka that he hadn't noticed that the mating gift he'd intended to give to Farona as soon as his seal activated for her was still in his pack, buried beneath the food and supplies he'd quickly stuffed in there. He'd unthinkingly carried a fortune in kivan into the dank caves of the urvaka. Perhaps Seta Zul had a hand in that lapse of memory. He would put nothing past the goddess.

He glared down at the softly glowing seal now visible over his groin since he'd removed his armor. Seta Zul's blood mark had reacted to the presence of the nixir female, as if her alien pheromones had awakened it. He'd felt the warmth of it as soon as he caught the scent of her, following her screams to the boundary. The proof of her role was unmistakable. The fact that he hated her people and hunted them as Jotaha was irrelevant. It wasn't wise to defy the will of the Ajda.

He despised this fleshy creature. He hated the lightly furred, weak flesh of the nixirs, the flat, pointless teeth, the blunt, soft claws, the dark-blind eyes. Yet somehow, these monsters had prevailed and had stolen yara-bralva—the home world of Gaia—from the yan-kanat—the inferno-blessed.

Still snarling at the treaty breaker he'd laid out on a fur after carrying her to his campsite, he withdrew a packet of henac powder from his pouch and crouched down by his small inferno stone pile to dump some of it into the boiling vandiz that bubbled in a crock upon the largest stone.

Removing the container from the heat, he set it on a stone beside his seat, stirring the powder and vandiz until it thickened into a paste. While it cooled, he cleaned the wound made by the nixir's weapon, which had only grazed his arm. The metal projectile had dislodged a band from his pauldron to slice through his scales beneath. The damage seemed prophetic, since that lost band was the only one that Farona had personally crafted for him, her skill and artistry adding beauty to his utilitarian protection.

Yet another reason to despise the fragile creature before him. Though she didn't wear the clothing of the other trespassers, and had found her weapon among their discarded carcasses, she had turned upon him with as much viciousness as any of the nixirs. Eager to kill the moment she had the advantage of her weapon.

The nixirs were creatures of hatred and violence. He felt no remorse for killing them to defend his people and the land gifted to them by the Ajda, after they escaped the purge of their kind by fleeing underground.

He had done so much for his people, spent so much time in the darkness to protect them from nixir incursions that shouldn't have happened after the latest treaty was signed. Yet, this female of the enemy was how the Ajda chose to repay him. He could barely look upon her smooth, scaleless face without feeling seething hatred for everything she was. He had no idea how he could ever endure the sata-drahi'at—first mating —with her.

He left the female only long enough to retrieve the band, tucking the bloodstained, lacquered leather into his pouch. A part of him wanted to keep walking in the opposite direction of his camp after picking up the fallen band, abandoning the nixir in the dark to return to Farona.

The seal would not let him walk away. The further he moved from his drahi—his mate—the more the mark would burn into his scales, until it ate into his flesh, eventually destroying his salavik—mating spine.

Cycles of agony and a lifetime of celibacy and dishonor among his people, or the nixir female as a lifelong partner.

It was a difficult choice.

The fact that he returned and carefully pulled the dart from her arm, settling her more comfortably on the fur, showed that he had made it.

After spreading the healing paste over his wound, he cleaned the crock and refilled it from his vandiz skin, placing it back over the stones to heat so that he could make xirak—

healing tea—for the nixir. The silok venom would take time to dissipate from her blood, leaving her groggy and nauseous. The steeped leaves would speed up the process. Though, if she had not attempted to kill him, as was the way of her people, he would not have been forced to dart her.

Fresh irritation sparked through him as he regarded the female, trying to accustom himself to the sight of her, as his body was already growing accustomed to the scent of her.

Too accustomed. He might hate how she looked, but his salavik already shifted beneath his scales, growing more eager for her with each flick of his tongue.

Her face lay slack, her mouth slightly agape to expose the flat edges of her teeth. He fingered the trophy necklace that hung around his neck. He'd taken much comfort from it over the passings spent in the dark, hunting the invaders that threatened his people. He'd nearly lost his own life so many times to their weapons—their lights blinding, their armor difficult to pierce. They always traveled in groups, so their numbers alone sometimes made battles against them difficult. The cave spirits helped lure them away from each other, but some nixirs were intelligent enough to remain close to their companions, despite the disorienting lures.

Except for this female. She'd been alone. She wore no armor, and her head covering was much weaker than the material used by the other nixirs. Hers had easily shattered when he slammed it against the stone to destroy the light after detaching it from her head.

Her clothing was soft material, even softer than the clothing the others wore under their armor pieces. It hadn't offered much protection, as her body was heavily colored with ugly marks beneath her smooth skin. He knew enough about nixir flesh to recognize the marks as damage. Like she'd been beaten.

The idea made him growl as he slowly removed each item of her clothing to expose more damaged flesh. The inferno stones cast a mellow glow over the pale skin. The dark blotches that decorated it looked alarming and unhealthy.

He could see slivers of wood rippling the flesh on her limbs. He picked them out as he came across them, careful not to further damage her fragile skin with his claws unless he had no choice when digging out the splinters.

Perhaps there was a reason she'd attacked him so desperately. Something had done this damage to her before she'd passed the boundary and trespassed in violation of the treaty. He'd scented her terror when she'd confronted him. He had believed it had been because of him, and most of it probably was, but he hadn't done this to her.

A new fury filled him that overwhelmed his anger at being forced to take her as his mate. If someone had hurt this female, he would find them and destroy them. Their corpse would not go into the pit. He would put it on a pike beyond the boundary in nixir land, so that they would know never to harm what belonged to the yan-kanat. Least of all, the Jotaha's mate.

She was not clothed like the others, nor was she hard with muscle like them. Like the yan-kanat, the nixirs did not appear to send their females into battle—a rare point of agreement between the two species. The others he'd killed had been clearly male—in the open and vulgar way of the nixirs. Though this female had tried to fight him, she had not had the air of a nixir warrior. Nor the body of one.

As he exposed more of that body to determine the extent of her wounds, he discovered that she was soft and round. The muscle beneath that layer of softness was barely defined, making her so different from the others that she could have belonged to another species. Though her scent told him that was wishful thinking.

He had no idea where this one had come from, but it was not from the warrior ranks of the others. Perhaps they had allowed one of their shatazurans to stray from their enclosures.

How else could a female who clearly enjoyed a life of leisure and excess have found her way into the dark tunnels of the nixir underground?

If she was a shataz, then she was far more valuable than nixir warriors. Some nixir males would undoubtedly be on her trail, eager to reclaim their soft-skilled female.

There were tales of ancient yan-kanat raiding nixir lands to steal away the plump shataz from the nixirs to mate them, back before the vile nixirs chased the yan-kanat underground. Perhaps those raids had contributed to the increased anger and violence of the nixirs, but they only began after the nixirs started their war against the yan-kanat, slaughtering many females and nestlings as readily as they did yan-kanat warrior males.

The shataz were trained by the nixirs and kept for passionate encounters. According to legend, their skills were so prized that they made the females valuable to nixir and yan-kanat males alike.

No matter what the background of this female nixir, he suspected his time with her would be challenging. His salavik was already eager to discover if she possessed shataz skills, but the likelihood of her warming to him as his seal warmed for her was not high. Nixir females did not experience love like the yan-kanat, because they were like their coldhearted and vicious males, incapable of such tender emotions.

After completing his examination of her body, ignoring the intriguing scent that rose from her oddly positioned seam that made his tongue flick in anticipation of tasting her deeper, he covered her with another fur and returned to making the tea. He tried to focus on Farona, reminding himself of their love and the commitment they had planned together. He knew his heart, but his body seemed to agree with Seta Zul, already desiring this female as much as he'd ever desired his lover.

It didn't take long for the xirak to fully steep in the hot

vandiz, but he left the drink to cool for a bit longer. Given the condition of her body, even the unnatural sleep caused by the venom would be better for her than to be alert and aware while clearly damaged enough to cause her considerable pain.

He watched her sleep, her breaths shallow, the mounds on her chest barely shifting the heavy fur lying over her.

He couldn't leave his sleeping mate to return to the temple and demand the removal of the seal, even if he were willing to accept the consequences of defying Seta Zul's will. Not only would his body burn for the nixir the more distance he put between them, but his own honor wouldn't allow it. As much as he wished for his beloved, his life now belonged to this creature before him. This female of the enemy.

The most hated enemy of the yan-kanat.

5

Sarah dreamed about being held, and that dream brought tears to her eyes, though whether they were real tears or the ephemeral ones of a dream she couldn't say. She did know that it had been a very long time since someone had held her in their arms, the way someone was holding her now. She had missed that feeling of being cherished, and realized that there had never been a time in her life where it was true.

A warm, firm surface touched her lips as her dream cuddler pulled her further against a strong, solid chest. Her naked back pressed against firm muscles and, oddly enough, a scaly surface —like the person holding her wore an alligator skin vest.

The liquid that splashed her lips was hotter than the surface of what must have been a cup. She jerked away instinctively, feeling it dribble down her chin to splash onto her bare collarbone.

"*Vaka-iv, nixir. Zarken anzha xirak.*"

The hissing sounds whispered past her ear, barely spoken aloud, but still with enough volume to jar her. The grip of her dream companion tightened around her as one hand reached to encircle her throat.

Her eyelids fluttered as that hand tilted her head back towards the mug, settling it against her lips. As groggy as she felt, and as blurry and surreal as her surroundings were when she opened her eyes fully, she now suspected this was no dream.

"Zarken, nixir."

The one holding her must have felt her tension as awareness slowly returned. The earlier hissing that might have been words, since they followed a pattern, shifted to softer sounds with no discernible pattern. They sounded more like the shushing, soothing noises someone would make to a wounded animal as they slowly backed away.

Sarah certainly felt wounded. With increasing clarity, her body sent a thousand messages to her brain and most of them transmitted pain. She ached everywhere, though the stabbing of splinters seemed to be gone, leaving behind only dull embers where sharp fires had once burned.

Despite the softer tone, the grip of the other person remained firm, pressing the mug against her lips. The hand tightened slightly around her throat as she tried to turn her head again. This time, hard, long fingers gripped her jaw to hold her in place.

The strength of that grip worried her enough to obediently swallow whatever was in the mug. She had little choice, since the hand on her throat massaged it as soon as the liquid passed her lips.

The liquid tasted like a strong tea with a hint of a floral flavor. It wasn't terrible, despite lacking the sugar she usually added to her tea, but she feared what might be in it.

"Who are you?" she asked after taking a second swallow.

She tried to shift away from that firm body at her back, her awareness growing sharper with each moment as the liquid warmed her empty belly.

"*Kiv'as shir, nixir. Zarken.*" These words, if that was what they were, were followed by the mug tilting against her lips more persistently, as if to silence further questions.

"Niche-ear?" She'd heard those sounds said together each time the stranger had spoken, if that was what he was doing. She assumed he was male because despite the low volume of his voice, it was deep enough to rumble in her ears.

At her repetition of the sounds, the one holding her stiffened, drawing the mug away from her mouth for a moment, as if to give her a chance to speak further now that she was making sounds he understood.

"What does niche-ear mean?"

"*Nixir*," he said, saying the word slightly different than she had, adding a hiss somehow that she couldn't replicate.

This time his voice came from higher above her head, rather than next to her ear, as if he'd straightened behind her. He sat much taller than she did, despite the fact that she was now leaning against him in almost a full sitting position. A heavy fur covered her nudity from the front, but her naked back lay against his chest. Strangely, that chest felt cooler than her own body temperature, almost as if she was feverish.

Before she could speak again, he said, "*Iv-olar nixir.*"

"Eve ol our niche-ear?" Her head was muddled with her grogginess, and it felt like she was trying to shove aside a mountain of cotton balls just to think straight. Things about her current situation were starting to make her nervous as she struggled to recall how she'd gotten into this position.

She blinked rapidly as if she could clear the blurriness from her vision faster.

"*Ris, Ir-olan yan-kanat. Iv-olar nixir.*"

Though the words were alien—and that in itself put an unnerving dent in her cotton ball brain haven—she picked up a sound of impatience in the deep voice of the one holding her. It was something about the fact that the drawled hiss from the previous words was bitten short this time.

She'd picked up a word, or at least she thought she did, but simply repeating whatever he said wasn't helping her understand any better, and it was clear he was growing impatient. Based on the strength in his hold, she didn't want to try her chances against him. Certainly not in this state. Her arms and legs tingled painfully as if they'd been asleep, reminding her only too clearly about how much damage she'd suffered falling through the rotten manway.

Her thoughts were growing sharper as well. Memories returning, first the manway, the furry bat-cat monster that had nearly killed her, then her desperate exploration deep into the mine.

Then there was the seam.

Her breath came in shallow bursts, her heart thudding in her chest as she clutched the fur covering her in one fist. The final memories came creeping in like assassins. The seven foot monster, the pit of dead bodies, the rifle, the dart.

The mug was at her lips again, pressing, demanding she drink.

"*Zarken.*" The bitten off sound of that possible word came as the grip of the creature tightened on her jaw.

She was no longer under any illusion about what cradled her against its chest. It had her in its grip, and instead of adding her immediately to its collection of dead bodies, it wanted her to drink first. Perhaps it drugged its victims. Then it would cook her over what must be a small fire that cast enough muted light to show her they were in a cozy cave.

She was probably already dead, because there was no way she would be able to break away from a creature whose casual grip was so strong she couldn't move her head. Yet she was determined that she wouldn't go out without a fight.

As she obediently took the next swallow, the grip on her chin loosened. When the mug was pulled away a bit to let her swallow, she tucked her chin and buried her teeth in the clawed hand that had been holding it.

She ground down as hard as possible, sawing her teeth back and forth to cut through the hard scales.

Enraged and pained sounds, like rapid cursing, came from behind her as the creature shoved her away. It flicked its hand out of her grip, tearing some of its scales off in the process. Sarah spat them on the rock in front of her as she rolled away from it, clinging desperately to the fur to cover as much of her nudity as possible.

She scrambled backwards, scraping her naked behind on the stone floor as she stared up at the monster. He had risen to his feet and now glared down at her with cold, reptilian eyes. His bitten hand hung open at his side, red blood welling from the bite mark. His other hand curled into a fist. His crocodile tail lashed behind him. His sharp teeth were fully bared by a snarl as if to show her his bite would be much worse.

A quick glance around to find an escape route revealed that the light in the cave came from what looked like glowing coals within a fire ring. Yet, it suddenly grew a lot brighter inside the cave as the creature's scales lit up like a blue flame. That glow contrasted sharply with the much softer orange glow of an elaborate circular tattoo covering the scales of its pelvis, where a groin might be on a human male.

Now the creature's entire body blazed with what appeared to be some kind of bioluminescence, altering the color of the lighting in the cave. Even the quivering spines that stuck out from the top of its head glowed blue.

"Vauteg, nixirs olar creta!" The sounds were spat from his thin lips as he held up his injured hand as if to show her the damage she'd done. His other hand lifted to finger the necklace of human teeth. "Creta," he snarled, upper lip curling. An angry hiss followed that sound that she didn't think was a word at all.

"If you think you're gonna eat me without a fight, you got another think coming, you monster! At least *I* got the first bite in!" The dreamlike quality that had put her head in a fuzz was now almost completely dissipated, though she still felt groggy and nauseous, as she had when coming out of sedation after getting her tonsils removed as a child.

He studied her for a moment after she spoke, his body still glowing like an underwater sea creature. As she scooted further away from him, he growled, lifting his uninjured hand to smooth the spines on his head, pressing them flat. They popped back up after the first pass of his hand, but as he turned his back on her, the second swipe succeeded in keeping them flattened.

His body glow dimmed dramatically, until his scales barely glimmered with bioluminescence. It was enough to highlight the thickened, ridged scales that covered his massive back.

Sarah had no idea why he'd turned away, but she wasn't about to miss this opportunity. She'd spotted a tunnel leading out of the cave. She'd take her chances on the run over sitting there waiting for him to kill her.

He was muttering something to himself, she suspected, because she detected a pattern to the sounds and heard the same "niche-ear" word repeated several times as she slowly rose to her feet, careful not to make a sound.

To her relief, he paced away from her, his movements restless as he seemed to hold an argument with himself. His injured hand lifted to his neck. She figured he continued to touch that ghastly trophy necklace, while his other hand reached to smooth his spines again as they bristled.

She spotted her clothes and hiking boots piled up at one side of the cave, but he stood between her and them, so she gave up hope of reclaiming them.

The lack of light would be a problem in making her escape, but it might also make it easier to hide from him. Surely, he couldn't actually see in complete darkness. She'd had a light on her head before, basically making herself an easy target. Hopefully, she could use touch to find her way to an escape route.

No matter what the obstacles were out there though, she didn't want to die while lying on the ground, covered only in a fur. She would die on her feet, dammit.

She crept towards the tunnel opening, careful to keep her steps silent. Once there, she turned to face the darkness, still hearing his angry muttering behind her.

She cast a glance over her shoulder as he suddenly fell silent.

Her heart nearly stopped when she saw him facing her, watching her, arms crossed over his chest. His facial features weren't that different from human because she suspected that the quirk of his thin lips appeared to be a slight smirk, as if he were amused by her delusion of escaping him.

"Hako ivkiv janata, nixir?" His tone rose at the end, as if he asked a question. His smirk widened when she remained silent, showing the hint of sharp teeth.

"Nata," he finally said, gesturing to her with his injured hand. He narrowed his eyes when he glanced at it. "Creta," he muttered, turning his glare back to her. His smirk disappeared as his upper lip curled in what seemed to be disgust.

Sarah lifted her chin and forced her own smile, baring her teeth. They were probably still stained by some of his blood, since she could taste the irony flavor of it on her tongue. "You get what you deserve," she snapped, pleased that she was able to keep the trembling of fear out of her voice. Her gaze shifted to the necklace of teeth and bones. "At least someone got a chance to bite you back."

He seemed to note the direction of her gaze and paused his movement towards a leather lump that might have been his pack. His injured hand lifted to the necklace, his fingers stroking the length of it.

With a hard glare at her, he gripped the necklace and yanked it off his neck. He tossed it at her feet.

She jumped backwards at the unexpected motion, her heartbeat pounding. He turned his back on her at that moment, continuing towards his pack as if he'd dismissed her presence. His incoherent muttering started up again as he crouched to dig in his pack.

After staring at him long enough to reassure herself that he wasn't going to jump on her and rip out her intestines as soon as she lowered her guard, she turned her attention to the macabre trophy lying on the stone.

Making a sound of disgust, she kicked it away from her with her bare foot. "I have no idea why you threw that thing at me, but I don't want it. It should be buried, along with all those poor people you left to rot in that pit."

The only response from him was a flick upwards of his head spines, then they settled against his head again. His blue glow had completely receded. Only the orange, circular tattoo at his groin remained softly glowing as he rose back to his feet and turned around to face her again.

He held something in his uninjured hand. As he approached her, he lifted it up as if to present it to her, though his glare was even harder and more intimidating than when he'd flung the necklace at her.

Her gaze flicked from his terrifying reptilian eyes that looked like he wanted to tear her into pieces to the item in his hand.

She caught her breath as the muted light from the round coals of the fire sparkled on the rainbow sheen of mother of pearl. Flat shells, each no larger than a quarter, were sewn in a fish scale pattern onto a length of fabric the color of a tropical ocean.

The creature thrust it towards her as soon as he stood within arm's length, as if he didn't want to step any closer.

He might be some kind of alien monster, but she could still detect the resentment coming off of him, as if the last thing he wanted to do was hand her this beautiful thing. Some of his body language came off as very human—especially the rigid tension in his upper body and the grim line of his lips.

"Nata, iv tega drahi harzek." He pushed the decorated fabric towards her. "Tega!"

Like his body language, she sensed something in his tone that made her certain he wasn't asking her, but *demanding* she take the material.

When she hesitated, he snarled and took one step closer. His shadow fell over her, reminding her of exactly how tall the creature was. His head just cleared the ceiling of the cave when he stood to his full height.

"Tega," he said in a low, menacing growl.

This time, she snatched the material from his hand as soon as he pushed it towards her. It didn't seem smart to antagonize him when he was close enough to disembowel her and add her bones to his pit.

She clutched the shelled fabric to her chest with one hand, noting the substantial weight of it, her other still holding the fur against her. Slowly, she backed away from him, towards the tunnel, though she realized now that any hope of escape from the creature was futile. For now, he didn't seem to want to kill her, so it would be smarter to wait for a better opportunity to escape him, rather than just run to her certain death.

"Drahi harzek," he scowled, lips peeling back as he shifted his glare from her face to the crumpled fabric in her hand. Then he touched his chest. "Jotaha."

When she stared silently at the spot where the necklace had once hung, where he'd touched his chest, he seemed to grow impatient. "Jo-ta-ha," he repeated, tapping his chest with each syllable of the alien word.

He waited for a response, his expression growing more dour with each second that passed as his brows lowered over his angry eyes.

He shifted towards her again, and Sarah backed up a few more steps, nearly through the exit of the cave now.

"Jotaha," she dutifully repeated, suspecting that was what he wanted.

"Jotaha," he said, tapping his chest again.

Insight told her he was telling her his name, not talking about the hideous necklace. "Jotaha." She pointed at him with the fabric he'd given her. "You're Jotaha?"

He cocked his head to one side, his head spines twitching. He studied her for an unnerving moment before dipping his head, once, low enough that his chin nearly touched his chest. "Jotaha."

Then he pointed at her, but said nothing.

"S-Sarah! I'm Sarah." If he wanted her name, maybe he didn't intend to eat her. At the very least, she might be able to convince him not to by humanizing herself. Although, recalling the necklace, she realized that perhaps being a human in his eyes wasn't a positive.

"Ssarah," he repeated, adding the extra S in a drawn-out hiss. "Ssarah, drahi."

Again, she detected what sounded like bitterness in his tone, as he bit off the alien word and his brows lowered even further, until his yellow, slit-pupil eyes were cast fully in the shadow of his spiny, ridged brow.

"Draw he?" She shook her head because he didn't seem to like that word and she didn't think she wanted to be associated with something he didn't like. "No, not draw he. Human."

Instead of making him less angry looking, her response only seemed to agitate him. His spines rose, brushing the ceiling as he bared his teeth. She yelped when he suddenly grabbed her arm and pulled her closer to him. He lowered his head until his face was just above her own. The shadows of the cave retreated as his bio-luminescence returned to a blinding degree. It cast macabre shadows over his face, making him look even more alien and terrifying than he already did.

"Ssarah drahi," he snarled, his breath smelling like the tea he'd forced her to consume earlier. Herbal, with a slightly floral tinge.

"S-sure, Sarah draw he," she said, fighting to get the words out through her panicked breaths as she struggled in his hard grip.

She couldn't even shift his hold on her. He was as unmoved by her struggle as a tiger would be with a kitten struggling in its jaws.

He released her, straightening again to his full height. His glow dimmed, but didn't completely disappear. Instead of stepping away from her, he tapped the fabric in her hand. "Drahi harzek. Iv hachek ver."

As she stared at him, her body trembling, unable to comprehend his words but too afraid to piss him off again, he seemed to soften, the tension leaving his hard muscles. He plucked the fabric from her slack grip and opened it up to reveal what appeared to be a dress, covered by the mother of pearl shells that flowed down the entire length of the garment. With each movement of the fabric, they rippled along its length and shimmered in the cool light cast by his body and the warmer light cast by the round coals.

Again, he pushed the fabric towards her. "Hachek ver."

She took it wordlessly, her hand shaking. This time, she thought she understood what he was demanding of her. She was to wear the dress. It looked like it would be tight fit, but she'd do her darndest to put it on to avoid him getting angry again.

"Um, could you turn around?" she said, without much hope that he'd understand, or even comply.

Again, he cocked his head as if considering her words. Then he gestured towards the flameless firepit.

She recognized his command, even if he didn't bother to express it verbally, perhaps growing frustrated by her lack of understanding.

She made her way to the firepit, biting her lip as she considered what to do next. It was clear by his nudity that he wasn't concerned about modesty. Perhaps he didn't expect her to be, either. And, after all, he'd already seen her naked. He'd undressed her.

She shivered as an idea occurred to her that she wanted to quickly dismiss. A glance at his groin showed that he had no visible genitalia. Only that strange, circular glowing tattoo. It looked impressive and was probably not a tattoo at all, but some extension of his bio-luminescence. Yet it didn't seem threatening in a "I'm about to be probed by an alien" kind of way. If he was even male, then everything was tucked up neat inside, or it was non-existent. At any rate, he didn't appear to be interested in her in a sexual way.

Sucking in a bracing breath, she let the fur drop, despite feeling Jotaha's eyes on her. If he was ogling her nudity, there was nothing she could do about it. Instead, she focused on pulling the dress over her head, moaning in pain as all her aches came to the fore. She'd been so distracted by her fear that she'd forgotten her pain.

The sounds she made were answered by low growls from him. She shuddered at the menace in those sounds, biting harder on her lower lip to keep silent as she struggled into the fitted dress.

It barely made it over her chest and hips, stretching so tightly in those areas that the scales hardly moved, and some stuck straight out instead of hanging down neatly. The dress felt heavy from all the shells, but the fabric was soft and sleek, like silk. It hung more loosely against her legs, and barely brushed her calves like a soft breeze, pooling over her feet. A slit in the back, right above the crack of her ass, gaped open, the material below it stretching tight to accommodate her generous hips.

Sarah looked down at herself, acknowledging that the dress was the most beautiful thing she'd ever worn, even if it didn't fit properly. Then she glanced over at Jotaha to find his gaze intently fixed on her, his entire body still, like he'd been frozen in place. Even his ever-moving tail had paused.

He might be an alien monster, but there was no confusing his body language. Sarah's heart thudded against her chest as she quickly looked away from him. She swallowed through a thick knot that formed in her throat. She no longer suspected he planned to kill her and was biding his time. Now, she suspected her fate might end up being much worse.

6

Jotaha reined in his frustration as the nixir named Ssarah shied away from him whenever he approached her. This was his drahi—his mate for life. They were supposed to grow old together and bring each other comfort in their last moments. They were supposed to have nestlings together, which he knew the nixir could provide for the yan-kanat, rare as such pairings were.

Now, she wore the sitak, the robe he'd had made for his drahi, and she looked surprisingly appealing in it. It had been made to hang loosely on Farona's slender form, but it clung to Ssarah's alien curves in a way that stoked an unwanted desire in him that felt deviant.

She didn't seem in the least bit impressed by the harzek— the treasure—he'd given her. Any more than she'd been impressed by the glowing seal he'd revealed for her sake. He felt vulnerable and far too exposed being fully nude in front of her. Her lack of interest in his form stung, especially when he was beginning to see the appeal of hers.

Now, she wouldn't meet his eyes, turning her body sideways

as he stalked her around the inferno stones. It was a clear sign of submission, making herself appear smaller than she really was by presenting only her side. It was also clearly the sign of prey, guarding the most vulnerable areas of their body.

His nixir did seem more like a creta—animal—than a yan-kanat. She had tried to gnaw his hand off, her flat teeth boasting surprisingly sharp and painful edges that had torn his flesh. Now, that ferocity had melted away and she looked meek. He found her submission suspicious.

Then she seemed to give up on retreating from him and crouched down, bowing her head and lifting her arms to cover it. "Please, don't hurt me. Don't... touch me."

He had no idea what she was saying, but her body language was unmistakable, as was the snuffling sounds she made after speaking. She kept her face turned away from him.

It was rare for a yan-kanat female to weep, but it did happen when they were in pain—or very afraid.

His drahi was shivering, the fortune sewn onto her sitak quivering with her movement, flashing the beautiful colors of the kivan he'd been collecting since he was a nestling. When she'd crouched, he'd heard seams tear, and suspected that parts of her sitak would need to be mended.

He'd stopped advancing on her when she dropped into her crouch, hiding her head. At first, he suspected she still felt pain from her wounds, though the venom would have lingering effects to dull that pain. Then he realized she was terrified.

If she had been yan-kanat, her fear would not have made sense. No honorable yan-kanat male would hurt a yan-kanat female. He'd been so wrapped up in his own anger over discovering that she was his mate that he hadn't paid attention to her body language.

Her fear would not be unwarranted in any other situation. Normally, a nixir would have everything to fear from him if they passed over the boundary. He was Jotaha, Guardian of the Dark Paths, and it was his duty to hunt and slay those who broke the treaty. If she hadn't been his drahi, she would not be alive now—despite being a female of her species.

It was clear she recognized how dangerous he was, but remained unaware of what she meant to him. Her gaze had fallen on his trophies, forcing him to abandon them when her disgust became clear. He could no longer wear the bones and teeth of her people and expect her to welcome him in her bed.

He'd been angry even then, bitter and resentful as he'd cast them down at her feet. Now, he felt a sense of growing shame, as the fear his drahi felt became unmistakable. With the venom wearing off thanks to the drink he'd given her—though her vicious bite had kept him from giving it all to her—she would be sharper and more aware of her surroundings, and her situation—or at least, what she believed was her situation.

She remained in a crouch, shuffling away from him in an odd position to put as much distance between them as possible. Her shivering increased, her entire body shuddering visibly so the shells bounced against the strained silk of the sitak.

Her weeping grew louder and she began to frantically scrub at her face with one hand as if trying to wipe something away.

He'd already cleaned her face while she was unconscious, removing the thick coating of dust and blood that had covered it like a mask. Perhaps she was unaware that it was clean, but her movements were jerky, like she was growing more panicked by the second.

"This is real," she said, rubbing harder at her soft skin until it turned an alarming red shade that was almost as bad as the black and blue colors that covered most of her body. "This is really happening to me. It's not some nightmare. Oh...god... the blood. The *blood!*"

He had no idea what to do for her. Her words made no

sense to him, but the rising volume of her voice spoke of growing hysteria.

When she collapsed from her crouch onto her generous, tailless rump, he stepped closer to her, deeply concerned now because her behavior was growing more erratic. He actually preferred her fighting back by biting him or trying to escape, though she would not have gotten far.

This... this was frightening. His drahi was breaking down, and he could say nothing to soothe her. Nothing that she would understand. He watched her rock back and forth, her arms wrapped around her legs, rending the seams of the sitak even further until the material flapped open to expose the damaged flesh of her side.

Another slow, careful step towards her had her jerking her gaze upwards to stare at him, her eyes open so wide he saw the strange whiteness completely surrounding her eyes. Her equally strange round pupils were so dilated they nearly blotted out the dark brown color of her eyes.

She flinched and scooted further from him when he leaned forward, reaching out a hand to her, hoping she might see the move as the soothing gesture he intended, rather than as another opportunity to chomp on him.

"Don't touch me," she whispered, shaking her head violently from side to side. "Don't touch me!" Her whispered alien words turned to a loud shriek that appeared to repeat the same pattern. Her hand scrubbed at her face again. "It's there. I can feel it. I can smell it! I can taste it. It's... it's everywhere. Mine will be next. My blood will be everywhere!"

"Vaka-iv," he said in a low voice that he hoped would be comforting to her. She undoubtedly didn't understand that he wanted her to calm herself, but it was an automatic response to a panicking yan-kanat. "Vaka, drahi."

She huddled into a tighter ball, pulling her legs so hard

against her chest that he wondered how it didn't hurt her, given her wounds. His attempt at calming her only caused her to rock faster, turning her head so he couldn't see her face.

He backed away several steps and noticed that the tension in her body relaxed slightly, her arms loosening around her legs, but her shivering continued.

Though the temperature of the cave was comfortable to him, she might be too cold, despite putting out so much heat from her body that he wanted to hold her against his scales to soak up that warmth. He used the nixirs' body heat to track them in complete darkness, but he had never realized how good that warmth felt when pressed against his own body, until he'd held his drahi.

He retreated from her until he stood on the other side of the inferno stones, grabbing up his crock. He quickly rinsed the dregs of the xirak from the container and splashed in some more vandiz to set it on the stones. As it rapidly warmed, he dug out a pouch of yanhiss, the fungus powder that warmed the insides and soothed the spirit when drunk. The Ajda had given the yan-kanat the gift of yanhiss, since they did not have the yan—inferno—of the gods inside them to keep them warm in the cold.

He prayed to the Ajda that the yanhiss would put an end to his drahi's shivering and calm her nerves as it did for the yan-kanat.

Even with the heat of the stones, it seemed to take forever for the draught to fully steep, dissolving the powder completely into a dark, greenish liquid that smelled of mushrooms. He added a few drops of *ane* tree sap to soften the bitterness of the yanhiss. It was his preference for that bit of sweetness to make the drink palatable that he hoped his drahi shared, since he could not ask her if she wanted him to flavor her drink.

As he made the drink, his drahi sat on the other side of the stone ring, rocking and muttering to herself in her language.

Occasionally, she would rub her face, but her movements had already grown less frantic when he'd backed off and given her space.

With the drink prepared, he rose to his feet to carry it to her. He paused in a crouched position that he might use for the low tunnels, when he noted her tense up again. Her wide-eyed, damp gaze shot to him, before darting away as she seemed to curl in upon herself.

He sank deep into his crouch, tilting his head so he could still see her, but was not meeting her eyes or looking directly at her. Though it went against everything in him to do so, he bared his neck and brought his shoulders inwards, careful to keep his spines flattened in submission and his tail tucked tightly. Then he shuffled towards her, awkwardly folding his body nearly in half to keep his head lower than hers as he approached her.

It was humiliating to show submission to anyone. To a nixir, most of all. But this was no armored creature, carrying an alien weapon and a desire to kill. This was a fragile, soft female, as delicate as a newly opened blossom. This was his drahi, and there would never be another, even if he dishonored himself by rejecting Seta Zul's will in order to be with Farona. If he handled this wrong, due to his own pride, then he would lose her forever. His bitterness and resentment had already driven her to this point as he'd failed to notice the signs that she was breaking down until it was too late.

When she flinched, even at his submissive approach, her body tightening up again, he immediately set the crock down in front of him. Then he slid it towards her with two fingers, barely touching it. He kept as much of his body away from her as possible.

"Zarken, Ssarah," he said in the softest voice he could manage. "Vaka-iv. Zarken."

Her wary gaze shifted from him to the crock, then she

turned her head away again. Though frustration filled him and he wanted to simply grab her and force her to drink the yanhiss, his still throbbing hand told him that would only cause more problems with his drahi. Instead, he backed away, maintaining his low crouch and submissive posture.

It wasn't until he was on the other side of the stone ring that she finally turned to look at the crock again, shooting suspicious glances his way as he sat as still as possible on the other side. With cautious, yet still jerky movements, she reached down and picked up the crock. Slowly, she lifted it towards her mouth, pausing with it hovering in front of her face.

The delicate nostrils below her jutting nose flared several times, and her mouth twisted in a look that he suspected was distaste. The shivering in her body was so bad now that the liquid sloshed over the lip of the crock.

"If bad things are going to happen to me," she said in a quivering voice, "then I'd rather be drugged than be alert when I suffer them." Then she took a cautious sip.

He suspected she'd spoken a prayer to her gods before taking a sip of a drink that had to be unknown to her. No doubt she was dehydrated, and the yanhiss would help with that too.

"Not as bad as it smells," she muttered, then took a larger drink.

Relief filled him as she continued to drink, no longer speaking her incomprehensible words. One of the elder priests might recognize and even speak her language—most likely Elder Arokiv—but he would not know for certain until he returned with her to the temple to complete his mating quest, now that he had discovered the nixir that was making the urvak zayul uneasy.

The yanhiss worked quickly on yan-kanat, and seemed to do the same for his drahi. Her shivering finally ceased and she drank more greedily from the crock with each swallow of the liquid. The tension in her body loosened and she stopped rocking. A sigh escaped her that he hoped meant she was releasing even more of her tension.

"S'good," she said, once she finished the drink.

The hiss at the beginning of her speech almost sounded like the flourish of his own language, but he still didn't comprehend any of her words. He had to let her body language guide him.

"I feel good," she said, stretching her arms with a low groan that sounded less like pain and more like relief, if he was reading her right. "Warm." She rubbed her belly, the shells covering it making a soft clacking sound as they bumped into each other.

She smacked her lips and turned a heavy lidded gaze on him. "Fine. You got your way. Not like I could fight you." She waved a hand languidly, vaguely gesturing in his direction. "Do what you will. I'm floating right now, so I don't give a damn." Her mouth gaped in an alarming way, baring two rows of nixir teeth that made him think of his trophy necklace.

He glanced over to where it lay, abandoned and nearly forgotten on the stone floor after she'd kicked it away from her. The thought of her teeth adorning that cord made him sick, and he realized that this female could have crossed any of the other boundaries and encountered any of the other Jotahas, and they would have killed her without hesitation. If she hadn't activated his seal, he would have too, and perhaps even added her teeth to his necklace.

If she was attempting to show a threat to him by gaping her mouth at him, she seemed to give up after a few brief moments, lifting her hand to cover her mouth as her other arm stretched towards the cave ceiling.

Then she lowered both arms and turned her body to sit with her legs crossed in front of her, facing the stone ring. Her heels were tucked close into her body, concealing her seam from him.

Her gaze sought his as he sat across from her. "Well, what now, lizard-man? What are you, anyway? A reptoid? Some alien from outer space, hiding in our mines?" She made a soft sound, accompanied by bared teeth. It didn't seem threatening—more like she was amused.

He let her ramble, not trying to discern a pattern in her mutterings. There seemed to be little point in it. The elders would have an answer for communicating with her when he brought her to the temple. He had to believe that.

"There really are lizard people, aren't there? All those conspiracy theories are probably right, then." She shook her head side to side, slowly this time, her teeth still bared. "Can you shapeshift? Take on a human face so you can infiltrate the governments of our world?" She closed her eyes and allowed her head to fall back, releasing another long sigh.

"Ah, I don't even *care* right now. Whatever you gave me makes me feel so... relaxed. It's like Ambien, only better. I don't even feel tired. Just... mellow." She lifted her head and turned her gaze back on him. "And I'm super warm, like I've been tucked into a bed with a big, fluffy blanket pile lying on top of me. This stuff is gold, seriously. You could make a fortune with it."

He remained very still, though it appeared the yanhiss worked on her even better than on the yan-kanat. Not only did she stop shivering, but her body now sagged with relaxation. Though her words remained incomprehensible, her tone was far calmer, no longer rising with panic.

"I saw a man get his throat ripped out today." She cocked her head, one hand lifting to stroke her own cheek, still reddened by her earlier furious scrubbing. "Or was it today? I wonder how long it's been since we went into that mine."

He remained silent, merely watching, content to let her

speak as long as she remained calm and relaxed. He realized he couldn't be impatient with his drahi. He couldn't rush her into accepting her role. Perhaps, if one of the elder priests spoke her alien language, they could explain to her, but for now, he simply needed to earn her trust enough to lead her back to the temple.

"Matt was a jerk," she said, blinking rapidly, "but he didn't deserve to die like that." She shook her head hard, as if to fling some thought from it.

Jotaha worried that the yanhiss wasn't working as fully as he'd thought when the furry brows over her strange eyes drew together in an expression that mimicked a yan-kanat's concerned frown.

"Beth left me. She left me to die like Matt."

Then the tension that had slowly reappeared as she spoke dissipated, the yanhiss winning out as her shoulders slumped and her bared teeth returned. "Never mind. You don't know what I'm saying, and probably couldn't care less." She gazed at him with her strange, dilated pupils. "Welp, let's get this show on the road, as our Boomers would say." She cocked her head to the side, her gaze still fixed on him. "You gonna probe me, or put an alien lizard baby in my belly?"

Whatever she was saying caused another shift in her demeanor, a slight, temporary return to her earlier distress. Like before, the yanhiss won out and she relaxed again, though her teeth baring expression disappeared, her lips now flat and closed.

"Wouldn't be the first baby I had to give up," she murmured, turning her gaze away from him to stare into the stone ring. She suddenly made another chuffing sound, and her teeth baring expression returned, though the upward tilt of her lips appeared shallower.

"This is good therapy, ironically. You're not interrupting me when I'm trying to talk things out, not adding your own two cents or giving me advice I never asked for. In fact, you can't understand a thing I'm saying, so you're not even taking offense, and I don't have to consider your feelings. And right now, I'm so damned relaxed that I couldn't care less that you're a reptilian alien that wears human teeth and bones around your neck."

7

Sarah felt remarkably good, given her situation. She couldn't recall the last time she'd been so free of anxiety. The minor blips in her state of serenity had barely lasted against the strength of whatever drug the reptilian had given her. The fact that she had been drugged should, in itself, be deeply disturbing to her. Instead, she felt sanguine.

The fact that he sat, unmoving, on the other side of the strange, glowing round coals, probably helped keep her anxiety down. Whatever he had planned for her, he apparently wasn't in any kind of hurry. He watched her, his unnerving eyes following her movements whenever she shifted position, but he remained silent. He was listening, but it was clear he didn't understand her, any more than she understood him.

Despite the drug, her mind still felt sharp enough to consider her situation, unlike earlier, where she'd been groggy and the surroundings had felt surreal, as if she was disconnected from reality. Now, she was more than aware of the cave, the coals that probably weren't coals at all, but somehow still glowed and put off heat, the beautiful dress she'd torn that still constrained her, and most of all, her unusual new companion.

Though calling him a companion might be overly optimistic. She felt optimistic at the moment. When her earlier fears and horror tried to trickle through, she felt insulated from it, able to consider it, without suffering another breakdown.

She was also able to consider his actions, and how she might have misinterpreted them. Though he'd given her a drug that made her calm and happy, he hadn't made any move to take advantage of her. In fact, other than that first moment after she'd put on the dress and caught his fixed stare at her body straining the silky fabric, he'd shown no other sexual interest in her. If that had even been what he was showing then. She could have easily misread him, given his alien features.

He also didn't seem keen on killing her, though the disgusting necklace showed that he held no qualms about killing humans. Perhaps it had something to do with aggression. The other bodies in the pit had all been wearing uniforms, from what she'd seen, and there had probably been more weapons in the gruesome pile than the one she'd found. Maybe he only killed humans who threatened him.

She wished she could ask him questions that he could comprehend and answer. If nothing else, finding some commonalities between them and building a rapport with him could end up saving her life if he still had some intention of killing her. The drug he'd given her would undoubtedly wear off, leaving her belly feeling empty and bereft of the warmth that now filled it, and her mind capable of straying back to the dark places it had been trapped in when he'd presented the mug of liquid. He'd done so in a bizarrely twisted position that had him crouching towards her sideways with his head turned away and his neck exposed.

There had to be some significance to that strange behavior. She'd noticed, even in the state she'd been in, that he'd approached her with caution, slowly, like she was a wild animal. She didn't think her vicious bite had made him feel that threatened. Certainly not given the size disparity between them and the fact that he had natural weapons in his teeth, claws, and spines, in addition to whatever dart gun he'd used to take her down initially.

He hadn't ripped her head off after she bit him, an act she now recognized as incredibly stupid, but she'd been in a fog at the time. She'd still been confused and delusional about her chances of escaping him. Now, she was calm enough to understand that she would have to temper her natural fight or flight instinct, and put more consideration into how she acted around him. Miscommunications could get her killed.

And misinterpreting his intent could land her in an even worse fate.

"Jotaha," she said, noting the way his focus on her somehow grew more alert, his head spines half lifting from his scaly scalp, before he lifted a hand to smooth them flat.

"Ssarah," he responded, drawing out the "s."

She pointed to herself. "Just Sarah. You don't need the extra s."

He cocked his head in clear confusion, so she repeated her name without drawing out the first letter a couple of times.

"Sarah," he dutifully repeated after she'd fallen silent, proving that he could say it without the hiss. Proving that they might even learn to communicate effectively with patience.

"Jotaha."

He watched her expectantly, no doubt wondering what the purpose of her repeating his name was. She fumbled for something else to say. She'd already rambled on and on for quite some time, and he hadn't seemed to pick up any meaning from her words, but at least saying them had felt strangely therapeutic for her. At some point, she knew she would face more emotional fallout from what had happened in that mine, and Beth's abandonment, assuming she lived long enough.

For now, she just wanted answers. Craved them so much

that even the drug didn't dull the strong desire for explanations. It wasn't merely her survival concerns that had her wishing they could understand each other. She was face to face with a literal alien, a "monster" the likes of which belonged only in sci fi, fantasy, and horror fiction. She'd played enough video games to have seen so many variants of lizard-men that facing one now shouldn't have been so bizarre, but in all her escapism into fiction, she'd never really believed she'd actually meet a living, breathing alien.

He wasn't wearing clothes at the moment, but he'd been dressed in some kind of armor when she'd first encountered him, though her terror had been so great that she might have only imagined him dressed like some kind of barbarian lizard warrior.

He certainly wasn't sporting anything that appeared high tech or space-aged. His pack appeared to be made of animal skin, and the weapon he'd felled her with hadn't been a death ray, but rather a dart gun. The mug he'd given her had been made of fired and glazed clay from the looks of it. The only difficult to explain items were the "coals" in the firepit.

She'd stared at them long enough now to notice that they were more like river stones than charcoal, and they put out a surprising amount of heat and light. Some alien kind of technology, or a natural phenomenon found in this underground cave system? Unfortunately, Jotaha couldn't answer in a way she could understand.

The seam she'd crossed over had been very odd too, and could be another example of advanced alien technology. Some kind of cloaking device or some other tech to keep humans out —or trap them in, which seemed to be the more likely purpose, given the death pit. Whatever caused that seam, she had a distinct suspicion that she would not have been captured by Jotaha if she hadn't stepped over the line.

Of course, she would have probably starved to death in that

mine if she hadn't, since there was no way she was getting back up the shaft. There was also the whole issue of the freaking bat-cat furry monster that she'd accidentally killed. It likely wasn't the only one in those caves, and its intention to rip her to shreds had not been questionable. She might actually be safer with Jotaha, who looked like he could handle a bat-cat with ease if another one followed her trail down the mine shaft.

"Sarah," Jotaha suddenly said, breaking the long silence that had fallen as she'd debated what her next step needed to be.

She shifted her attention from the river coals back to Jotaha, realizing that she'd been staring into their strange, pulsing glow like she was in a trance. A side effect of the drug, or perhaps something caused by the stones themselves, she couldn't be certain.

Once he had her full attention, Jotaha pointed to her with his injured hand. He glanced at the bitemark that had scabbed over with a slight narrowing of his eyes, then returned his gaze to her. "Sarah, drahi arxi Jotaha."

"Draw he?" She knew she'd heard that before from him. "Ar-chee?" She wasn't able to add the strange hiss on the second set of sounds that he had, but she hoped he understood her attempt anyway.

Perhaps encouraged by her repetition of the words, Jotaha spoke in a rapid-fire way, interspersing that odd hiss into some of his speech that she suspected was part of their language. The sounds all ran together in his apparent excitement that they were communicating. When he fell silent, she almost felt sorry for him when she had to shake her head and shrug at his expectant look.

She might not understand his words, but his body language was closer to human than one would expect from such an alien creature. At her head shake, he seemed to deflate, leaning forward in his cross-legged sitting position to rest his elbows on his legs, his broad shoulders rounding with defeat as he stared into the pulsing river coals. He muttered something beneath his breath, occasionally making a soft hissing sound.

His frustration was clear, but the drug he'd given her kept her from feeling the same defeat. An unusual optimism still kept her as warm and cozy as the feeling in her belly. "Jotaha, Sarah draw he?"

He jerked his head up at her second attempt to repeat the word he'd said to her multiple times. "Drahi."

"Draw he?"

He made a huffing sound, turning his head as his nostrils flared and his mouth curved upwards. His head spines quivered slightly. She had the sneaking suspicion he was laughing at her. Probably at her pronunciation of the alien word which never quite matched the way he said it.

She shrugged. "Okay, so I can't say 'draw he' with that weird inflection you add to it. I wish I knew what it meant." She studied him as he returned his gaze to her. "I wish you could answer all my questions! I have so many of them."

His head spines twitched as he studied her in silence. Like her, he probably wondered what he could possibly say to bridge the communication gap. Maybe he was as curious about her people as she was about him.

A quick glance at the trophy necklace reminded her that this wasn't his first encounter with a human. He probably knew a hell of lot more about her people than she thought, though he clearly hadn't taken the time to have conversations with them.

Given the likely reaction of a human soldier to a creature like Jotaha bearing down on them, it wasn't really surprising that a language lesson never took place in his previous encounters. She honestly couldn't blame the soldiers for firing first and asking questions later, and even had a difficult time blaming

Jotaha, since he was probably defending his territory from armed intruders.

Still, he didn't have to take such grisly mementos.

"A-yee Weesh? Hako-os a-yee weesh?"

"A-yee weesh?" He'd managed to confuse her again. The uprising tone at the end of his words suggested that his kind asked questions much like humans did, but she had no idea what he was asking.

"A-yay We-ish? Hako-os a-yay we-ish? Sarah shiru a-yay we-ish."

She repeated his words under her breath, suddenly noting the familiarity of the sounds. "You mean 'I wish'?" She realized as she considered what she'd said earlier that she'd repeated those words multiple times. Perhaps, like her, he was looking for patterns in her language. Words that he could recognize from multiple use and repeat.

His shoulders squared as he sat up straight. "Dree," he said, his tone suggesting excitement. "Eye we-ish."

"Dree?" She wondered if that meant "yes" or was it more like "hurray, this alien doof finally got what I was trying to say!"

He dipped his chin to his chest, once. "Dree."

Sarah rubbed her palms together, finally feeling the same sense of excitement that he must be feeling, given the change in his body language. "I wish Jotaha understood me." She pointed at herself. "I, Sarah."

His spines, which had lifted slightly from his head in his apparent excitement, flattened again. "Aye-Sarah?"

She sighed, realizing it wasn't going to be that easy. "I am Sarah."

"Aye yam Sarah." He still seemed confused about what she was trying to say, and she had the sinking feeling that he thought she was telling him more of her name. Perhaps her hopes were too ambitious.

She pointed at him. "You are Jotaha."

When he merely blinked at her, his spines now completely flat as his shoulders slumped again, she sighed, cursing the complexity of the English language. She shook her head, realizing that this was hopeless. Drug-fueled optimism be damned. She wasn't cut out to teach an alien the English language. Especially when she didn't know his. She had no idea how they were going to manage, and suddenly, she wasn't feeling so pleasant.

Her stomach loudly growled as the warmth filling it faded. Jotaha tensed, his gaze shifting from her face to the source of the sound. His spiny brows drew together, shadowing his eyes.

Sarah sighed as another growl from her demanding stomach caused him to rise into a half-crouch, staring at her stomach like he thought an alien was going to burst out of it. His spines now fully erect like a crown on his head, his body began to glow the blue color that contrasted nicely with the glowing orange tattoo on his dark green scales.

"Sarah hungry," she said, rubbing her hand over her belly. When he still looked concerned, backing away from the river coal pit a few steps as his hard stare never left her stomach, she motioned to her mouth like she was eating something. "Hungry." She patted her stomach again as it gave another impatient rumble.

"Hon-gree?"

She nodded, pointing to her mouth, then her stomach. "Hungry, yes! Dree!"

She sure hoped she'd understood that word correctly. Now that the warmth was leaving her belly, it was reminding her that it had been a long time since she'd eaten. She wished she knew how long exactly, but that was a concern for another time. Right now, she just needed to feed the beast grumbling in her belly before Jotaha decided to cut it out of her.

8

Jotaha rose to his feet, staring at his drahi's stomach with concern. Within him, the chanu zayul—little spirits—pulsed, sharing their glow when they sensed the rise of his aggression in response to a perceived threat. He could repress the glow through calming mantras, but saw no reason for stealth in this situation.

Though he had slain many nixirs, he had never bothered to study their corpses closely before throwing them into the zayul pit to feed the brood. He had no idea if nixirs carried another life form within them that benefited from them, as it gave them advantages. If his drahi had some form of barruk zayul—inner spirits—then it would explain the strange growling coming from her stomach.

The hunger of zayul could be a terrible, agonizing thing. Though Sarah appeared to be comfortable, she patted her belly as if to soothe her zayul, and made a motion that they must be fed. In Jotaha, the chanu zayul lived within his spine, enhancing his strength, senses, and reflexes as well as adding their glow to his blood and scales so that he could better serve as Guardian of the Dark Paths. If they were starving because he had failed to feed his own body, he suffered, his muscles seizing and his nerves screaming in pain until he ate enough to replenish his nutrients. He'd learned his lesson well after only one protracted hunt where he'd failed to eat for many cycles. He never let himself get to that point again.

He had already intended to feed her, once she was calmed enough by the yanhiss, but he had waited until her speaking slowed. It had been clear to him, despite not understanding her, that she took comfort from the mere act of talking. Maybe to him, or to some nixir deity, though she must know he didn't understand her words any more than she understood his.

He had not planned on finding a mate with her own zayul. Only the Jotaha endured the combined blessing and curse of the chanu zayul. No female had ever been chosen as Jotaha. The very idea was unthinkable. Nixir warriors who posed a serious threat to a fully-fledged Jotaha would decimate a female, with or without the chanu zayul lending their gifts to her.

The hon-gree growled again from her stomach, and she made a face as she once again motioned to her mouth with one hand, repeating the name of her zayul.

Jotaha wasted no more time, uncertain what price the zayul would demand from her for allowing them to grow angry enough to growl. The chanu zayul within him never did such a thing, but the nixir were an alien and strange species. Who knew what oddities their bodies contained? He would have much to learn about his nixir before their first mating ceremony.

He rushed to his laden pack, brushing aside his armor and sheathed daggers to extract his packet of kirev cakes. The kirev cake was laden with nutrients that would feed a body and its zayul well.

He withdrew one of the cakes and returned to the stone ring, cautiously approaching Sarah this time, mindful of her skittishness. It was clear the yanhiss was wearing off as her agitation began to show. Perhaps her zayul had sped the dissipation of the drug within her blood. His darts had always felled the nixirs quickly when his aim was true, and he'd never hesitated to dispatch them immediately in the past, so he had no idea how long it took for their bodies to flush drugs or poisons.

He crouched down when he noted that the inferno stones cast his shadow upon Sarah as he neared. The disparity in their size was yet another thing to which he would have to grow accustomed. Farona was only a couple of handspans shorter than him—being taller than most female yan-kanat—though much smaller and more delicate than him. He towered over his nixir drahi—who was smaller than most female yan-kanat. He would need to be mindful of the difference in their size, especially during the first mating. He had hoped to avoid that issue, since his size had always been a problem for him and having a taller lover had been a relief.

Again, he questioned the wisdom of Seta Zul in choosing a tiny nixir for his mate. Though the bitterness had faded some as he'd dealt with her, realizing that she was not like the others —despite her occasional violent ferocity—he still resented having his own choice taken from him. He and Farona had grown up together, were perfectly suited to each other, and had always planned to be mated. It was difficult to accept the abrupt and dramatic change in the path of his life.

He handed the cake to Sarah, noting that she bared her teeth in what he suspected was a positive expression for the nixir. Then her gaze fell upon the cake, and her lips drooped, her brows coming together in a frown as she took it from his hand.

She slowly drew it towards her face, her nostrils flaring as she cautiously sniffed it. The nixirs lacked the forked tongue of the yan-kanat that could detect the faintest of odors, instead apparently relying entirely on their breathing orifices to smell things.

His tongue flicked out as if reminded of its purpose, and her gaze immediately shot to him. She shivered at the sight of it and scooted backwards, putting more space between them. He kept his tongue in his mouth after that, though he watched her sniff the dense kirev cake again, her expression crumpling up as her lips peeled back from flat but somehow still painfully sharp teeth.

"Ew, it stinks like raw meat," she muttered.

Then her rounded, obscenely fat tongue poked out to touch the kirev cake. She drew it back in, smacked her lips, and shook her head, her face once again crumpling with pulled back lips. Her eyelids clenched shut as she shuddered. "Gross."

She pulled the cake away from her face, her gaze returning to him as her tongue darted out—fleshy and pink and slick with saliva—to lick her lips.

He contained his own shudder. This was his drahi, and he would learn to appreciate the strangeness of her body. He glanced down at the glowing seal he'd exposed to her, vulnerable in his nudity. He really had no choice in the matter. Then he watched her shrug her shoulders as she sighed heavily, bringing the kirev cake back to her mouth.

He would not take his resentment out on his drahi. She had no more chosen him than he had her. Seta Zul had decided their fates and guided her path to intersect his for some unfathomable reason of her own. The will of the Ajda was not always clear. He would not punish Sarah for that. He would make the most of this mating, and try to find something to love about his vicious nixir mate, even though she was incapable of loving him in return.

She took a cautious bite of the kirev cake. He would have worried about her flat teeth breaking on the hard cake, but he'd felt too much of their bite to assume she couldn't crush the cake into manageable chunks. Some of the cake broke off with a loud snapping sound. She chewed it, though the expression on her face suggested it was not a pleasant experience.

He wondered what nixirs regularly ate, wondered what food their zayul demanded and if it differed from their own tastes at all. The kirev cake was a popular treat for many yan-kanat, but it also served well to nourish the chanu zayul. Most yan-kanat loved anything made with kirev, and there were many dishes that were. Farona had been an anomaly in that, far preferring anything *ane*—sweet—to anything savory like kirev dishes.

Again she smacked her lips after swallowing her bite. "I suppose it's not so bad. A little salty. Very irony." She narrowed her eyes, studying the cake closely. "This is made of blood, isn't it?" She pulled another face that he was now coming to associate with disgust, given the tone of her voice and body language.

Despite her apparent distaste, she sighed and took another bite, then another. "It's an acquired taste, I guess. I tried blood pudding on a dare once. It tasted a lot like this. As in, really gross."

Since her hon-gree remained silent as she consumed the rest of the cake, he assumed it was appropriate food. If the hon-gree lived in her stomach, then they probably tasted the food directly, as opposed to the chanu zayul, which only benefitted from the nutrients after they entered his blood.

He wondered if the hon-gree caused her any strange feelings, stirring in her stomach the way the chanu zayul sometimes stirred in their position latched onto his spine. He always felt the flutter of their movements in the base of his skull, or as brief shooting pains through his arms and legs before their tendrils again settled.

"When in Rome," she said after swallowing the last bite of the cake. She glanced at the mug as if she was thirsty.

He hoped she did not want another crock of yanhiss. Too much could be dangerous and turn the belly fire into poison. It might even kill her hon-gree, perhaps leaving her vulnerable in some way he could not comprehend.

He figured he would try to give her vandiz instead. He'd found containers on the nixirs he'd killed that were filled with vandiz. He believed it was for the nixirs to drink, and figured that they required it like the yan-kanat did. In some ways, they weren't all that different. The containers themselves had smelled strange and felt too smooth and unnatural in his hands, so he had discarded them and the vandiz they contained along with the nixirs' bodies.

He picked up the crock and rinsed it clean with some of the vandiz from his skin, before filling it with more. Then he handed it to her, again crouching so he didn't overwhelm her. She was calmer than she had been before drinking the yanhiss, but the tension in her body was rising with every movement he made as she watched him warily. He didn't want to frighten her again and see her shying away from him.

She took the crock, glanced at the liquid inside, then raised it to her mouth, her nostrils flaring again as she scented it in the inefficient, nixir way. A cautious sip seemed to please her, and she took a large swallow from the crock. She made a long, drawn out sound as her eyes closed that he wasn't certain was a nixir word at all. Then she raised the crock to her lips and gulped the rest of the liquid down.

When she held the empty crock out to him, licking her lips with her thick tongue again, he went to take it from her. Instead, she pulled it away as she sensed his intent, and jerked her head towards his vandiz skin.

"More?" She licked her lips again. "Please?"

"Mo-err?"

She gestured to the skin with her empty hand. "More water please."

He picked up the skin and held it up. "Mo-err?" At her nod, he poured some liquid into the crock.

So, they referred to vandiz as "mo-err". He could remember that.

She finished off the second serving, then set the crock down. "Thanks. I actually feel better now that the nasty taste of that blood-protein bar thingy is washed down."

He lifted his vandiz skin. "Mo-err."

At her negative head shake, he was confused. "Mo-err?"

She blinked at him, her mouth opening as if she would speak, then her eyes narrowed. She shook her head slowly again. "No more water, thank you."

He set down the skin, reining in his irritation, reminding himself again that it wasn't her fault. He would simply have to try harder to understand her, and to make her understand him.

9

The blood bar hadn't been that disgusting, thanks to her hunger. She'd scarfed it down, trying to ignore the little, gristly bits that suggested it wasn't only the blood that came from an animal. A part of her wondered if it had come from a human, but she quickly pushed that thought away. The human bodies in the pit had been too old and rotten to have provided food at this point. At least, that was what she told herself.

The problem with eating and drinking was that it seemed to turn on functions of the body that had been in a state of dormancy while lacking those things. Now, her bladder and bowels were adamantly reminding her that they were still there and her grace period had ended. She watched Jotaha pace back and forth on the other side of the stone ring, seeming lost in his own thoughts. She had no idea how she would communicate her more delicate needs to him. They'd managed to muddle through when it came to her hunger and thirst, though she suspected something had gotten lost in the translation there. Miming hunger though had been fairly simple compared to miming something like urinating or, well, the other.

She wasn't even sure if he did those kinds of things. As far as she knew, all animals did it, and even insects, in order to eliminate waste from the body, but how a lizard man did things was never covered in her biology class. That lesson might have made her pay more attention. In fact, she wasn't even sure how a simple *lizard* did things in that department.

She held it for as long as she could while she studied the cave, hoping desperately for a convenient toilet, or outhouse, or, heck, even a hole in the ground to appear. Jotaha had stopped pacing and was now crouching by his pack, digging around in it while muttering under his breath. He'd withdrawn several cloth and leather wrapped bundles, a couple of what appeared to be tins, and a little glass bottle tied to a leather bundle. He set those all aside.

He avoided looking her way, though the tension in his body and the way his tail whipped back and forth like he was agitated told her it wouldn't be a good idea to make another escape attempt. Especially not in this dress that fit her like a mummy costume. Even the split seams didn't return full motion to her. In her cross-legged position, the dress had hiked up her thighs, exposing a lot of bare flesh, but the lizard man didn't seem overly interested in her naked skin.

She wasn't above trying the old seduction routine to escape, if it came to that, but it didn't seem to be an option. Also, she wasn't sure it would be a good idea. He was huge, muscular, and covered in scales that appeared to provide a natural armor. Though she had broken his flesh by biting him, she'd caught him off guard. She suspected if she did manage to get him on the hook, she would be the one reeled in, not the other way around.

She was almost disappointed to reject that idea. For a creature covered in scales, he didn't look all that bad. Perhaps it was because she'd seen so many different versions of lizard men in video games and movies—from monstrous to weirdly sexy—

that she wasn't as put off by his scales as another woman might have been. His musculature was very male, all bulging biceps and pulsing pecs, with a nice set of washboard abs that few human men could ever achieve without a dedication to gym time that was probably not healthy.

His face was not traditionally handsome as human men went, though he had a strong jawline. His lips were thin, instead of full and sensuous. His nose was flatter to his face than a human nose, and he had hard, pointed ridges over his eyes instead of eyebrows. The lack of visible ears was also a bit startling, though not as off-putting as she would have thought. She'd spotted a hole on each side of his head, neatly tucked behind his prominent cheekbones.

Overall, now that some of her initial panic and horror had faded, and she felt more wary and cautious than outright terrified, she didn't see him as such a monster. Ghoulish trophy necklace aside. Since he'd ripped it off his neck and tossed it to the ground at her feet, he hadn't looked at it again.

She still felt a bit like she was handling a ticking timebomb. There was certainly an air of tension that suggested danger from him. The inability to communicate was even more frustrating because he seemed more than willing to try. That in itself gave her hope that his intentions towards her weren't hostile. If he just wanted to kill her and maybe even eat her, why would he bother trying to converse with her first?

Of course, she could be making a huge mistake by viewing his body language and actions through a human lens. For all she knew, chatting with their victims might be par for the course for lizard men. It didn't seem likely that he did that though, since he appeared to speak not a word of English and those soldier's uniforms had looked like they came from the U.S. military, despite the lack of markings. The location also implied that the humans he'd previously encountered had spoken English.

All that probably meant that his attempt to communicate with her was the exception and not the rule. Maybe she was in a different category than those other humans as far as he was concerned. She just wished she knew why. If it was because she was a female, then she wasn't sure which outcome she could reasonably hope for.

If his goal was to make lizard babies by using her as a breeder, he'd made no move to do so, thus far, and again, his attempts to talk to her seemed unusual for an alien monster just looking to breed.

Or maybe she just watched *way* too many monster movies and played far too many video games. His intention could be something so far outside the human experience that she could never guess it, and all this time she'd spent trying to figure it out was a waste when she could be considering and escape plan instead.

Although, perhaps it was actually helping to keep her mind *off* waste—the kind her body was looking to shed.

All these thoughts distracted her from the more primal fear that still huddled in the back of her mind, waiting for any sign from the lizard man that it needed to take over. When he rose from his crouch, holding a cloth wrapped packet and turned his focus back to her, that fear stirred, pushing to make its way to the front of the line of her thoughts.

It hadn't been Jotaha who had ripped a man's throat out right in front of her, but it very well could have been. He had claws, he had sharp teeth. And, somewhere, he even had a dart gun, though it must be hidden on the other side of his pack— out of her reach. Not that she could hit the broad side of a barn with a blow gun. The one shot she'd wounded him with from the M16 had been sheer luck, and from the looks of his arm, she'd only grazed his scales.

As much as she wanted to run or fight, she had enough sense to recognize the futility of either of those actions. Now that she could think a little more clearly, she saw the wisdom in attempting to communicate further, in the hopes that she could get him to lower his guard enough for her to escape.

Or even better, that he could provide her an escort back up to the surface. She wasn't looking forward to facing more creatures in the caves or the mine, and she also had no idea how to scale that vertical shaft, but he might know how. Or he might know another way out of the cave system.

She quashed her primal panic when he approached her, trying to remain calm and avoid flinching. He moved towards her slowly, as if aware of her anxiety. He didn't seem to want to scare her. That in itself was telling of his intent.

He held out the packet with one hand as soon as he moved within her reach, again crouching low as if he didn't want to tower over her.

After she hesitantly took it from him, he backed away, moving again to the other side of the fire ring. It was like an unspoken boundary between them, that ring of glowing, heated river stones.

Since he sat down, mirroring her cross-legged pose, then watched her in silence, she figured he wanted her to investigate his newest gift.

She hoped it wasn't another ill-fitting clothing item. As beautiful as the dress she wore was, it seemed wildly impractical in the caves. It also seemed like his kind spent most of their time naked.

She unwrapped the cloth that seemed to bind the items inside. The contents spread as she opened the wrapper. She noted that they were a bundle of large, soft petals. A pleasant floral scent filled the air as she lifted one of the petals, studying it with interest.

It was very large for a flower petal, if that was even what it was, each one the size of her palm. The silky surface of the petal gleamed like velvet in the light warming the cave. It released a sweet, somewhat fruity scent when she accidentally pressed her fingers together too hard while holding it.

The petal wasn't as delicate as a rose petal, despite squishing between her fingers. It had some durability to it.

It was a lovely gift, though again, impractical in a cave setting. The perfume alone seemed to soothe her senses.

She smiled at Jotaha and held up the petal. "Thank you. It's very nice."

His spines twitched as she spoke, though he waited for her to fall quiet before attempting to repeat her words. "Tank ew. Ess ver ni-cee." He pointed at the petal in her hand. "Ver-os voneill gemant."

"Ver-ohs von-I gemont." She dutifully repeated the words, but then followed it up with a shrug. She set the petal back in the pile and began to fold the fabric back up around it.

To her surprise, Jotaha rose to his feet, making a sound that she didn't think was a word. It was more like a grunt, probably of frustration. Maybe she hadn't shown enough appreciation for the gift.

Maybe it was another food item. She picked the crushed petal out of the pile and lifted it to her lips, the strong perfume making her eyes water. Figuring it couldn't taste any worse than the blood bar, she took a tentative nibble of the petal's edge.

She was wrong. It tasted worse. Like spraying perfume into her mouth. She pulled a face, instinctively turning her head as if to get it further away from her mouth as she rubbed her tongue on her palate to wipe away the gnarly ear-wax taste.

A snorting sound came from Jotaha and he lifted his hand to rub his brow ridges. Then he turned his back on her, his spines quivering on top of his head. More snorting issued from him, though it was muffled, as if he was covering it up with his hand.

She glared at his back, suspecting he was laughing at her.

He got himself under control and turned back around to

face her, his spines still quivering as if he struggled to conceal amusement. He saw her narrowed glare and his spines settled flat against his head. Then he held out a hand.

When she glanced at the petals, then back at him, he gestured with his hand that she come to him.

This was a pivotal moment. Sarah could feel it. He could just stride over to her and haul her up by her arm with ease. Instead, he was letting her choose, though she suspected the option to refuse was only an illusion.

Since she had no reason to, she rose to her feet, smoothing the dress fabric down her legs as she stood. When she looked up from the shell-clad skirt of the dress, she caught him staring at her legs.

He stood very still, his head spines half lifted, his tail unmoving. Only his tongue moved as it flicked out from the small space between his lips.

Since he hadn't shown that reptilian tongue much before, she could only guess at why it made an appearance now. Clearly, he was using it like a serpent, but she couldn't be sure what had caught his interest enough for it to flick out now. She had her suspicions, based on his fixed gaze, but again she wondered if that was only because she was viewing him through a human lens.

Snakes went still before striking. She couldn't assume anything.

As she straightened to her full height, which felt insignificant compared to his, he seemed to shake himself out of whatever trance held him. Then he motioned again for her to come to him. When she made to move towards him, he gestured with his other hand towards the bundle of petals.

Guessing his meaning, she bent awkwardly in her dress to collect the bundle, wincing as she heard the seams tearing further. Then she turned her attention back to him, feeling the draft of air from somewhere in the cave brush against the skin of her sides that was exposed by the torn seams. As she slowly stepped towards him, he backed up, keeping his eyes on her but moving with purpose.

He wanted her to follow him. That much was clear. He led her out of the large cave through a tunnel low enough that he had to duck down, curving his shoulders as the thick ridged scales of his back scraped against the stone overhead. As they left the light of the main cave behind, his body begun to glow with bioluminescence, lighting their way.

She still had plenty of headroom and followed easily in his wake. She caught a scent hanging in the air the further she followed him down the tunnel. There was more of that floral petal scent like what she held in her hand, but also a stronger, earthier odor, with an undertone of stink, like the whiff of an outhouse.

She had a clue as to where he was taking her now, and her bowels were cheering in relief.

They entered a cave that was much smaller than the other one. Several of the glowing river stones gave it light and warmth. His bioluminescence faded, leaving her eyes to adjust to the dimmer light in the pungent cave. It was definitely a bathroom of sorts. The scent was unmistakable now, as was the small hole in a flat rock that was tall enough that she would have to climb up on it, but not so tall that she couldn't do so fairly easily.

If she wasn't wearing the strait jacket of a dress.

Jotaha gestured to the petals, mimed wiping under his tail, then tossing them into the hole.

The lizard man had made toilet paper out of flower petals. She could have kissed him for his brilliance but her guts were demanding her surrender. She'd been fighting against them for too long, and even the embarrassment of having to hike her skirt up to her waist to make the climb onto the rock was not enough to slow her down.

Jotaha turned his back on her and made his way to the entrance of the cave, lowering his head and shoulders to make his way back into the tunnel, much to her relief. Apparently, lizard people understood privacy. Or, they just didn't want to be in the cave when the kraken was unleashed.

Her relief was so overwhelming as she let go that she sighed loud enough for Jotaha to call her name, maybe in concern.

"I'm fine, Jotaha" she said, her voice echoing slightly. She tried to put as much calm in her tone as she could.

A strange chittering sound beneath her had the hair on the back of her neck lifting. Quickly making use of a couple of the petals, she shifted to one side of the hole, glancing down into the darkness.

Only it wasn't completely dark down in that fetid hole. Instead, a mass of glowing beetles clambered all over the feces pile.

Sarah shrieked and jerked backwards, toppling off the rock ledge. Her dress tore further as she jerked her limbs wildly, the sound of scale-shaped shells raining down on the stone floor barely heard over her scream.

Jotaha appeared in the entrance of the cave, glowing so brightly that she was nearly blinded by it.

"Oh my god, they could have crawled up my butt!" She barely felt the pain of an already bruised body impacting with stone. She was too freaked out by the thought of carnivorous beetles worming their way up her anus to eat her alive from the inside.

She shot to her feet as Jotaha repeated her name in a demanding tone, clearly upset, since he was glowing and his head spines stood fully erect. He noted her frantically swiping her naked buttocks to brush away phantom beetles.

"Did they get me?" She craned to look over her shoulder, turning around like a cat chasing its tail as if—after a lifetime of not being able to—she could suddenly see her own ass without a mirror. "I feel like one is on me!" Her voice rose in panic, even though her desperate swipes didn't brush anything but her own naked skin.

Her agitated tone was only making Jotaha more agitated. His grip was hard as he drew her out of the cave and into the tunnel, glowing like a beacon.

Sarah didn't resist him. In fact, she was pushing against his chest, struggling to make him move faster away from the poop beetles. Despite having to stand hunched over, he still moved rapidly, drawing her back into the main tunnel as she struggled to calm herself, reminding herself that the brush against her naked buttocks was only a draft in the cave and not some beetle ready to make its home in her intestines.

By the time he settled her down in front of the river stone ring, she had regained some coherence, sucking in deep breaths and then slowly releasing them to slow her pounding heart.

Jotaha had said many things to her in his language, but he had spoken so rapid-fire in his own agitation that she hadn't even been able to detect any patterns in the sounds. It was only when she was seated and holding her knees close to her chest that his glow faded and his spines settled flat against his head again.

Now that she had calmed, he was calmer. No doubt recognizing the futility of asking what had happened, he simply said her name, his tone rising in question at the end of it.

She released a huge sigh and lifted a hand to smooth the tangled rat's nest that her hair had become since falling into this hell. "I'm okay." She held out both hands in front of her in a stopping motion, more for herself and her panic than as a visual signal to him. "I'm okay."

"O-kay?" His gaze never left her face as he slowly sank into a crouch on his side of the ring.

Sarah nodded. "I'm," she pointed to herself, "o-kay."

Jotaha grunted, his teeth bared for the briefest of moments before he rose to his feet again and began pacing on the other side of the cave, as far from her as possible.

Sarah watched him for a moment, then turned her gaze back to the glowing river stones. It looked like her foolish panic had once again frustrated him. She didn't know how many times that could happen before he just gave up on trying to communicate with her at all.

10

Jotaha needed to think, to plan his next move. If his drahi had turned out to be Farona, she would have understood the urvaka—cave maze—that protected their city from the denizens behind the veil. She would have greeted the urvak zayul with respect if she ever encountered them, rather than being frightened of them. She would have understood their nature, and honored their role in the survival of the yan-kanat.

His drahi was nixir, a species that was no friend of the urvak zayul. Though she was his, and they must understand that by now, he wasn't entirely certain they would guide her if she grew lost, and was less certain she would follow such guides. The nixirs found the pheromones and projected ghostly forms cast by the bioluminescence of the urvak zayul both alluring and terrifying, based on the state of their minds when they saw them. That was how the urvak zayul lured them or chased them into the dead ends of the urvaka so they could not escape Jotaha's relentless hunt.

He had intended to earn his drahi's trust before leading her through the tunnels. Given how skittish she was, and how afraid of him she was, he worried that she would try to escape by breaking away from him. Near this cave, there were no dead falls, but the urvaka had many of them, as well as other dangers one unfamiliar with the cave system would not spot in time to avoid them. He needed her to follow him obediently, and he still wasn't certain she would, though she had calmed enough in his presence that she had turned *to* him in her fear, as if looking for him to protect her.

That was as it should be for a drahi. If she had faced a true threat, he would not have hesitated to destroy it. Unfortunately, once he realized what had frightened her, he understood that the urvaka itself was only contributing to her fear, and possibly even slowing down any progress he could make in gaining her trust.

He prayed at least one of the elders spoke her language. Elder Arokiv had learned to communicate with the nixirs in several different languages, for the nixirs had many. He, along with elders from other regions, and an unknown number of infiltrators, maintained contact with their enemy to renegotiate the treaty every time it expired. The elder *should* know Sarah's language, but it wasn't a guarantee, since the fractious species could not even get along with each other long enough to standardize their language, even when living in the same regions of their world.

Of course, when Jotaha needed to communicate with her the most, when her life might actually be in danger if she didn't follow him obediently, he had to rely on gestures and repeating words he wasn't even certain had the meaning he thought they did. His language seemed to be a struggle for her. She could not hiss as the yan-kanat did for some of the words, but at least he could guess what she was trying to say. He hoped she understood when he tried to repeat her words.

Even if she did, their progress was slow, and they seemed to keep encountering setbacks. If Sarah could not even relieve herself without fear after eating, then she would only grow more uncomfortable and miserable in the urvaka.

He'd had a home built for his drahi, knowing that this generation of the chanu zayul within him would mature soon and leave him. Then he could fully retire, allowing a new Jotaha to step into his role. He was more than ready to end his many lonely passings spent in darkness so he could finally start his family. He'd had so much hope when Seta Zul's seal was painted upon his body.

He hoped Sarah would like his home on an out-terrace of the skilev, though he had no idea what dwellings the nixirs occupied. He did know that they didn't live underground, and they were not made for darkness. He just needed to lead his drahi back home and show her what he had to offer, since she seemed not to understand the significance of the harzek—treasure—he had given her and, even now, wore it with clear discomfort.

It was unfair to expect her to make her way through the urvaka in a sitak that didn't fit her properly. Though he found her clothing unflattering and it was still filthy, stained with blood, and riddled with holes and ragged tears, he had kept it, in case she felt too vulnerable being naked and rejected the harzek altogether.

She had not rejected his mating gift, but it had suffered much damage. Nothing he couldn't have repaired, eventually, but for now, she needed clothing that she could move around in. After her reaction to the urvak zayul merely cleaning away her waste, he knew he needed to get her out of the urvaka so she could feel safe.

There was another advantage to returning the hideous nixir clothing to her. The way the sitak fit her so poorly revealed far too much of her body. Though he'd initially considered its softness off-putting and alien, his body seemed far more drawn to it than his mind. The blood of Seta Zul, goddess of fertility, that sealed his arousal had identified a drahi that appealed to him on a primal level, even if he resented it. His response to her pheromones was unmistakable, even if he resented that too. He wanted her. Wanted to perform the first mating ceremony with her. His body was eager for it. It was ready to pass the brand of the seal to her, even as it seared his own scales.

His mind might reject the idea, might find the fullness and roundness of her body too alien, too outside his experience—too reminiscent of his enemy—but his body had made up its mind.

Her original clothing would conceal most of her flesh, which he wanted to stroke and taste to explore her alien form. That curiosity and desire felt wrong to him after all these passings of viewing the nixirs as prey.

Sarah remained still and silent by the stone ring, sitting again with her knees pulled to her chest and held there by her arms. She stared into the pulsing light of the stones, though he felt her glances fall upon him as he paced. She obviously sensed his agitation. He wished he could explain the reason for it, and reassure her that it was not because of her.

Even if it was.

He was not above manipulating the truth. From what he knew about the nixirs, they were masters of falsehood. Lying was so second nature to them that they did it from the moment they learned to speak. Would Sarah truly judge him for omitting some of the truth, when her people had invented the lie?

That question didn't matter yet. Sarah couldn't really understand what he said anyway. Gestures were sufficient for the basics, and she knew how to ask for food and vandiz, or mo-err, as her people called it. If she grew hungry or thirsty, he could meet those needs. He'd packed enough food and drink to cover four cycles in the urvaka, just in case the invaders the urvak zayul had sensed approaching proved too cunning to be quickly dispatched. It turned out that Sarah was the one to cross the boundary, alone, so the extra supplies proved unnecessary. He could leave the urvaka in less than a cycle, since he knew its secrets, but taking her along meant slowing his pace considerably.

The other nixirs had carried strange things in their packs, and he'd claimed some of their weapons, abandoning the ones that smelled like nixir alchemy to the pit with their bodies. He would never bring such terrible things back to the skilev as trophies—though not all Jotahas held the same view on that. The daggers, though, while not beautiful, were strong and serviceable. Most of their possessions he left to the urvak zayul to destroy or spirit away to some unknown hiding place for their own, unfathomable reasons.

His drahi had not carried a nixir weapon with her, though she had found one in the pit, making him realize the folly of not destroying its functionality before leaving it behind. A nixir with more training could have done more damage to him with that weapon before he took them down. If he hadn't been so distraught by the activation of his seal at the sight of a nixir female, he would have approached her with more caution. Jotahas in the past had made the foolish mistake of forgetting how dangerous the nixirs were, growing over-confident after previous hunting successes.

He cast a glance at his drahi, noting that her eyes kept closing. When that happened, her body would sag. Just as it looked like she would fall over, she'd jerk them open again, suddenly tensing.

She was probably exhausted. Whatever had left those marks on her body had no doubt worn at her spirit too. Traveling through the nixir tunnels had been harrowing for her. That much was obvious.

After the third time of her eyes closing, he realized he couldn't wait for her to ask to return to the furs he'd laid out for her. For whatever reason, she fought her exhaustion and would not move to sleep on her own. If he was going to take her through the urvaka soon, then he needed her to be well rested and alert.

He turned to her, and she immediately tensed as he approached, regarding him with wide, wary eyes. He paused far enough away from her that she wasn't in his shadow. Certain that he had her full attention, he gestured to the furs.

"Sarah, akonrir."

"A cone rear," she said slowly, in what was obviously an attempt to repeat him. She looked from the furs to him, then back to the furs. "I sure hope that means sleep and not 'time to make alien babies'."

He remained silent, and she sighed and pushed herself to her feet. It was clearly an effort for her and the sound of her pained groan had him rushing towards her to help her. He froze in place when she violently flinched away from him.

As he slowly backed away, she sighed and shook her head. "Sorry, big guy. You still kinda scare the shit out of me when you move like that." She regarded him with a steady gaze, squaring her shoulders as if she had bolstered her courage. "Inhumanly fast and all that. Like a snake striking."

Then she stretched her arms towards the stone ceiling, groaning again, though it sounded less pained than when she was climbing to her feet. He'd been so concerned about her pain that he'd failed to notice her seam was bared to him until she shoved the fabric of her shift down with both hands, as if only just realizing it herself.

He turned away, feeling the seal on his groin pulse as his salavik responded to the sight. She had a seam, like the one all yan-kanat had—male or female—only hers had a patch of curly fibers partially concealing it. He knew that nixir males were different than yan-kanat males. He had seen images of their anatomy. He had also come across some males who were lost in the urvaka relieving themselves, dropping their guard just long enough for him to dispatch them. They were obscene with their exposed salaviks, and he still wondered how it could possibly be safe always dangling outside their body. It was also disgusting that they passed their fluid waste through the same organ that they used to mate, instead of from their clavek with their solid waste, as the yan-kanat did.

Her seam appeared to trail from low on her pelvis down between her legs, whereas a female yan-kanat's sat on the front of her pelvis, like his did. He had no idea how her vessel was shaped but knew that it would be compatible enough to bear him nestlings. If she couldn't produce a family for him, it wouldn't be because of her body being mismatched with his.

He had not satisfied his curiosity when he was treating her wounds. It would be unacceptable to explore her body with desire while she was unconscious. Not to mention unwise, given the need to wait until the sata-drahi'at before his salavik could even leave his seam in arousal without experiencing painful burns.

That didn't mean the sight of it lacked an effect on him. He tried to calm his agitation, keeping his spines lowered with effort. High emotions caused them to stand erect, and sometimes it was a battle to flatten them to avoid giving away his internal turmoil.

At least his desire didn't affect the chanu zayul, causing them to share their glow with him. She didn't seem all that impressed with his glowing scales anyway. Any yan-kanat would feel respect and admiration for the sight of them, understanding what they meant, and what his role was. A female yan-kanat would see him as a desirable guardian, capable of defending her in even the most dangerous of situations, because he was Jotaha.

He did not have even that to impress his nixir drahi. If and when she understood his role, she might end up even less inclined to accept his claim and bear his mark.

He heard her movement and turned back around to find her sitak covering her again, though the sides still gaped open with broken seams as did the tail opening in the back. Some of the shells had fallen off. He would have the garment repaired after their seclusion. She wouldn't need clothing during that time anyway, since he intended to keep her beneath him unless they were sleeping or eating.

She'd made her way to the furs, her motions jerky and accompanied by winces of pain. He wanted to help her, support her as she took careful steps as though she didn't want to jar her body. He also realized he might cause more harm than good. She was still too wary of him to trust him so close to her, and might pull away, hurting herself even more in the process.

However, she appeared to understand what he wanted as she sank down onto the furs with another of the drawn-out groans. Once she was sitting, she looked up at him, seeming pleased that he had retreated to give her the feeling he was too far away to harm her. The mistaken belief that she was out of his reach worked as her shoulders slumped, her tension easing.

He would never harm her. Not even if she came at him and chomped on him again, though he certainly wouldn't enjoy it. A stray thought of her burying her teeth in his shoulder or biting at his neck in passion made him reconsider that idea.

"I'm just sleeping, right?" She shook her head at his silence as he waited vainly for a clue to what she was saying.

Then she pressed her palms together and laid her head on them, closed her eyes, and mimed breathing in and out in a heavy, steady pattern. Her voice whistled in a reedy way as she made an ah-choo, ah-choo sound. After a short time of this baffling behavior, her eyelids popped open again.

"Sleep." She pointed to herself. "Sarah, sleep." Then she gestured to the furs, and slowly lowered herself into a supine position. "Sleep."

Her repetition of the sounds was deliberate, and he understood that she was trying to tell him her meaning. "Sleeeeep," he repeated, priding himself on forming the long, drawn-out sounds she had made.

Her eyes rolled alarmingly, bouncing from one side of her sockets to the other to show far too much of the white that surrounded them. "Sure. Sleeeep. Whatever works."

Then her mouth stretched wide open, her hand lifting to cover it. Her eyes closed, and didn't open again, though she muttered something under her breath in a voice too soft to differentiate sounds before trailing off into silence.

Within moments, her breathing steadied, telling him his drahi had finally found her rest.

11

"Did anyone catch the truck that hit me," Sarah groaned as her eyes opened, the aches and pains in her body dragging her out of a deep sleep that hadn't felt long enough.

A cave ceiling swathed in shadows stretched above her.

She turned her head, spotting Jotaha seated by the glowing stones. His visible scales glimmered when he shifted, the light passing over them as he turned to meet her eyes. This time, he was wearing the armor she'd recalled from their first unfortunate meeting. It was fancier than she remembered, but then again, she had been in mortal danger at the time so details had eluded her. She hadn't had the chance to notice that the armor looked to be formed of layered, apparently lacquered, strips that had a pearlescent shimmer to them. What she took to be leather had been worked with an elaborate design on one pauldron that had been dyed to make it stand out on the light brown of the hide. That single decorated strip was stained with blood and scored by the bullet Jotaha had taken to his arm.

So her lizard man was real. Apparently, it hadn't all been a bad dream. She turned her head to the other side, looking away from him as she processed this. At least he wasn't cradling her against his chest this time, although, in a way, that was disappointing. Initially, there had been some comfort in the strong embrace. Until her awareness grew sharp enough to recognize the threat.

He didn't appear to be threatening now, and much to her excitement, she spotted her jeans and shirt folded up beside her, right where she couldn't miss seeing them. Her socks sat on top of her shirt, and her hiking boots sat beside the small pile.

The clothes looked as though they had been cleaned, smelled faintly of a light, fruity scent, and still had the appearance of being slightly damp.

If the return of her own clothes wasn't a sign of progress, then she didn't know what was. Apparently, he'd even taken the time to wash them. If she wasn't mistaken, she could swear that one of the tears caused by her fall had been mended. It was so well done that she could barely see the seam of the repair. It wouldn't have been noticeable if the clothing wasn't right by her head.

She sat up slowly, noting that he had drawn a fur over her at some point, though she still wore the dress and the cave wasn't overly chilly this close to the glow stones. Still, it revealed a level of care that someone about to kill her probably wouldn't show for her comfort. As she sat up, she cast a quick glance his way, noting that he remained quiet, staring into the pulsing glow of the stones. A large mug sat on one of the stones, steam rising from the top of it, carrying a scent of herbs and a hint of something spicy.

Her stomach growled, apparently ready for breakfast. Despite the sound being muffled by the furs, Jotaha's head still turned towards her, his gaze dropping to her concealed belly. "Sarah zayul, hon-gree?"

She nodded, relieved that he had picked up that one

English word, then gestured to her mouth to reinforce her agreement with that statement.

He rose gracefully to his feet, clearly comfortable moving in the armor. The way it shifted with his body, the banded layers giving him more freedom of motion than solid pieces of armor would, told her it had been designed for easy movement.

His tail remained uncovered, lashing back and forth from a hole in the back of his armor as he strode towards his pack, presumably to fetch another one of those disgusting blood bars. Sarah wasn't thrilled about eating another one, but she was hungry. She also wasn't about to be demanding towards an alien creature that seemed to mean her no harm, but could kill her in a flash if she angered him. Best to cooperate fully and graciously, and use his generosity to build her strength for a potential escape.

When he crouched down, his attention focused on digging in his pack, she used the opportunity to toss the fur covering aside and begin working the remains of the beautiful dress off over her head. The condition it was in was a true shame, as the shells were so beautiful and the silken fabric so soft and shiny. Even if it had fit properly, it wouldn't have been the kind of thing she'd wear casually. This was red carpet fashion as far as she was concerned, and she was not a red carpet kind of girl.

She hadn't even gone to her high school proms, so had never had the opportunity to wear a fancy ball gown type dress, though she'd dreamed of someday having a wedding with a dress that would please a princess. Given her inability to trust men to stick around after they got what they wanted, her chances for marriage were getting slimmer by the year as she turned to fictional characters and other anonymous players in video games for her primary socializing.

This dress reminded her of those princess dreams. She winced as she finally pulled the dress off, some of the shells getting caught in her matted, tangled hair. She winced again when some of the shells rained down onto the fur beneath her. They lay there gleaming like bright stars against the dark brown fur that had probably belonged to some breed of bear, given the size, coarseness, and coloring.

After carefully folding the dress and setting it aside, far too aware of her nudity—though Jotaha had already had plenty of chances to look his fill—she set aside her socks and picked up her mended shirt.

A pleased sound escaped her as she saw her bra and panties folded neatly beneath her shirt. They had also been cleaned. It made her blush to realize Jotaha had put his claws all over her underthings, but it was hardly something to get embarrassed over now.

Again, he had shown that he wasn't hostile or threatening to her, caring for her clothing and then returning it to her. He'd also done something to treat all the splinters and cuts that she'd had when he'd captured her, because they weren't painful anymore. Even the largest of the cuts had scabbed over, without any sign of infection. The only real pain came from her bruised and battered body, and she suspected that was something Jotaha had not been able to heal with the paste that she had flaked off the largest of her cuts, the others having shed their paste coating without her notice.

She dressed quickly and awkwardly, her back towards Jotaha, though she sensed his eyes on her. Without rising, she pulled on her panties, then wrestled into her bra, grateful to have some support again. Not that the dress she'd been wearing hadn't been very tight in the chest region. It had actually felt as binding as a really tight sports bra, and her breasts had ached at first when she'd removed it.

Marks dented her skin where some of the shells had dug in while she'd slept. It figured that the one time she wore a dress like that, the only thing she got to do in it was sleep. She wondered where Jotaha had gotten the dress, and why he had it in his pack while living in a cave. Sadly, she might never learn the answers to those questions, or so many others she had that she wanted to ask this alien stranger.

She was finally forced to stand up to pull on her pants, but once armored with more comfortable, human clothing, she felt a bit more confident as she turned back to face Jotaha. He'd unfolded the wrapping on a bundle, revealing what looked like a baked bun, about the size of a six-inch sub.

He watched her pull on her socks and boots in silence. She noted that despite being armored, his clawed feet remained uncovered, making her wonder if his people even wore shoes. The scaled soles of his feet looked more than capable of handling rough terrain.

When she finished tying her second boot, she rose again to her feet and made her way to the stone ring. The scent of something sweet drew her like a lodestone, her gaze lowering from his face to the bun thing he had set on a warming stone by the time she joined him.

Yeasty and sweet, the scent of the bun made her mouth water. Jotaha poured some liquid from the larger mug into the smaller mug, then held it out to her as she made to sit down on the opposite side of the warming stones from him.

It would be difficult for him to hand her things from that side of the stone ring, as the heat the glowing stones put out was as strong as a campfire. After a slight hesitation, she settled into a cross-legged position a little closer to Jotaha, accepting the mug from him once she was fully seated.

His gaze grew more intent when she shifted closer to him, and she hoped he didn't get the wrong idea. His appearance was growing on her—in that she no longer found him so alien and terrifying. Still, that was a long way from wanting to cuddle up close to him and have those big, strong, muscular arms close around her to cradle her against his firm chest, while he rubbed his chiseled jaw gently against her hair, whispering sweet alien words to her.

Right. She totally didn't want any of that from him.

Over the scent of sugar and yeast, and the hint of lacquered leather, she caught an earthier scent of some exotic musk. It could have been coming from the warming bun, but she suspected it came from him, because she remembered smelling it before.

The drink in the mug also gave off a pleasant scent, the steam fragrant, like a black tea flavored with something reminiscent of cinnamon, but lacking that distinctive and powerful scent. She blew on it, and then took a cautious sip. Jotaha seemed to be waiting expectantly, and at her pleased sigh, his shoulders relaxed like he was relieved she found the tea palatable.

She wouldn't have turned it down anyway. Living out of her van for a couple of years while she finished high school meant she wasn't one to turn away free food or beverages, even if they weren't flavors that she would normally prefer. She'd eaten what she could get and drunk whatever was potable. Now, that was even more critical when she had no idea if Jotaha would take offense at her rejecting his food and drink offerings.

She'd come a long way since those dark days, and with the help of an excellent guidance counselor who had the courtesy not to ask too many probing questions about her personal life, she was able to get financial aid to attend college. She'd worked her ass off to finish her bachelor's degree in computer science, while everyone around her partied their youth away. Even then, she'd been near to starving, living only on Ramen noodles and peanut butter and jelly sandwiches.

Those "freshman fifteen" pounds didn't come until after she graduated and got a good job, a townhome of her very own, and access to a bank account that wasn't in the negative. Her grocery shopping trip after she received her first paycheck had been like a shopping spree. Every food and drink she'd ever loved or craved went into the basket. Her new indulgences ended up pushing those pounds beyond the original fifteen.

All her hard work to create a life for herself seemed like it would amount to nothing now that she was trapped underground, the captive of an alien lizard man.

Yet, as he cut the bun in half with a wicked looking dagger that was clearly very sharp, she couldn't look at such a remarkable creature and completely regret discovering his existence, even if it had been in the worst way possible. There were actually aliens—intelligent life that wasn't human—living right there beneath the human world, unknown and undetected by the population above. Though the price for that knowledge had been everything she had and everyone she'd ever known—including the one person she'd hoped would someday seek her out.

That dream would probably never happen now, because she couldn't imagine how the daughter she'd given up for adoption would be able to find her down here in the darkness, once she was old enough to start searching for her biological mother. Assuming she would ever do that. Shayla's adoptive parents had promised they would give her the letter Sarah had written. The one that reassured her that her mother had loved her very much. So much that she had chosen to let her go so that she could have a good life and grow up with every possible opportunity.

Jotaha seemed to understand her pensive mood, and kept his silence as he folded one half of the bun to hand it to her, keeping the steaming contents trapped inside.

She set down her mug beside her and took the offering. She was used to him watching her now, and didn't blame him. Her body language was probably the only way he could understand her.

The bun tasted delicious, though not as sweet as it had

smelled. There was a hint of honey, or perhaps some other syrupy substance in the bean-like paste inside the bun, but it had a stronger savory rather than sweet taste. Though it didn't taste like sweet cornbread, the combination of sweet and savory reminded her of that food.

She scarfed down the bun, a little embarrassed to have Jotaha watching her pig out, but too hungry to care at the moment, and too delighted with the food to slow down. As she was licking the last little bit of filling off her fingers that had escaped the casing, he offered her the second half of the bun.

"No," she said, with regret. "That's your half. I won't gobble up all your food. You've been pretty generous already."

"Hon-gree?" He gestured to her stomach.

She was still a bit hungry, but felt bad about acknowledging it. He couldn't have carried that much food in his pack to feed them both for any length of time, and she had lost her own pack, not that there had been much food in it other than a couple granola bars.

He seemed to read her indecision and pressed the last of the bean-bun on her, insistent as he handed it to her.

Sarah took it without attempting to argue. If he wanted her to have it, she wasn't going to complain. After he handed it off and she settled in to eat it, Jotaha suddenly rose to his feet, his head spines standing erect. For a moment, his visible scales blazed with light, which quickly faded.

His head turned towards the entrance of the tunnel, rather than the exit that led towards the poop beetle cave. His tail lashed back and forth, and his hands clenched into fists.

Sarah slowly pushed away from him, feeling dwarfed by his massive size and the threatening body language. Though he wasn't looking down at her, his demeanor was terrifying. This was the hunter that had taken her down with a dart while she was armed with an assault rifle.

He suddenly started pacing one way, then another,

muttering in a way that suggested he was deeply upset, though it was low enough that even if she could understand his language, she wouldn't have caught his words.

Then he stopped and turned to regard her, causing her to tense, concerned with the intensity in his stare. His gaze shifted to the tunnel entrance, back to her, then back to the tunnel entrance. His lips pulled back in an intimidating snarl as he stared into the darkness beyond the warm bubble of light from the stones. His spines remained erect, and bioluminescence darted across his cheeks and over his head in flashes, lighting up the spines, then quickly fading.

Finally he growled as he turned and stalked to his pack. He bent and picked up a tube-like thing that she suspected was his dart gun. It was as long as her forearm and looked like it was made of carved ivory or bone. He attached it to the belt that circled the waist of his armor, then tucked a handful of darts into a pouch beside the blow gun. A sheathed dagger joined the weapons on his belt, along with another sheath that looked like it held a combat knife that could have come straight out of the movie Rambo. It seemed out of place with the rest of his armor, and served as yet another reminder that she wasn't the first human the lizard man had met.

She was probably just the first to survive the encounter.

He strapped a third sheath onto the outside of his forearm, then strode back to the river stone ring and bent to retrieve his dagger. He wiped the blade on the fabric that had held the bun, before sheathing it.

Then he turned his attention back to her, and Sarah shivered at the intensity of his fixed, reptilian gaze. "Sarah, fanak." He gestured with a flattened palm towards the ground in front of her.

Confused, she slowly pushed herself to her feet, stopping mid-crouch as his hand fell upon her shoulder. He pushed her back into a sitting position with just enough pressure that she couldn't resist.

"Fanak." He pointed again at the ground. "Fanak auje."

His words and intent might confuse her, but his frustration was obvious as he rubbed his other hand over his spines. They popped back up immediately after his hand passed over them, still sparking with bioluminescence.

"Fanak," he growled as if repeating the word enough would be all it took for her to understand.

"Do you... mean 'stay'?" She couldn't imagine what else he could be saying.

It looked like he was arming himself to go somewhere, and she was obviously no warrior. Perhaps that was why he was so agitated about getting her to understand him.

He growled again, and she took that to be more frustration, since he didn't seem to be forming any words. After a moment where he seemed to be considering, he tapped his chest with his open hand, then pointed to the exit of the cave. "Jotaha golex." He pointed to her and repeated, "Sarah fanak," pointing again at the ground.

She nodded, hoping she understood his intent now, though the thought of him leaving her alone in this cave gave her a strange urge to beg the giant lizard man to keep her with him. After all, wasn't she supposed to be planning an escape? With her own clothes on now, and him leaving her alone in the cave, she had the perfect opportunity.

"Sarah, uh... fan-ack. Uh... o-gee. Jotaha golesh." She tried to hiss like he did, but it wasn't happening with that sh sound. It came off more like a lisp from her, when Jotaha made it sound natural and fluid.

He studied her with obvious suspicion, and she had to admire his instincts.

She patted the ground in front of her. "Sarah will fan-ack o-gee right here. Sarah is not an idiot to go chasing after you or go running into the dark tunnels without a light."

The crazy thing was, she meant it. She had rejected the idea of taking this opportunity to escape him almost immediately after it occurred to her.

Mostly because she *wasn't* an idiot. She had no idea where she was, how big the cave system was, how she could possibly find her way back to the surface, and most importantly, just exactly why he was arming up for bear. It was dark out there, and she didn't see her head lamp anywhere. She supposed she could try to take one of the glowing stones with her, but they were hot and she had no idea how to carry them without burning herself. If Jotaha felt the need to leave this cave armed, then she sure as hell didn't want to head out into the darkness with nothing but a hot stone to light the way.

There was another reason she didn't want to run away from him. He'd been kind to her, feeding her, repairing her clothes, taking care of her wounds. After some of the worst moments of her life, he'd comforted her. Granted, he'd used a drug to do it, but she had to admit, it had been effective, and he'd been a perfect gentleman while she was under the influence and in a relaxed state.

Jotaha was watching her with narrowed eyes, his brow lowered as if he could guess the thoughts running through her mind.

He slowly crouched in front of her, still towering over her seated form even in a crouch. "Sarah." He reached towards her as if to touch her face, pausing with his clawed hand between them, before lowering it to settle upon her shoulder. "Fanak. Vaelin gurez."

She nodded again. "Sarah fan-ack. I promise."

12

The chanu zayul were insistent as they transmitted the message from the hive. The elder zayul, the urvak zayul, had detected more nixirs crossing the boundary into yan-kanat territory. More nixirs breaking the treaty.

Before his drahi, the last nixir he'd been tasked to hunt had come a season ago. A large team of them, with their alchemy weapons and armor made of strange materials that looked nothing like hide or bone or metal or wood. They'd had lights like his drahi had worn, attached to head coverings far stronger than hers had been.

They'd been dangerous alone, even more so together. Unlike the solitary hunters of the yan-kanat, the nixirs preferred to fight in groups. Despite being generally smaller in size, with rare exceptions, they were clever and inventive and could prove quite deadly in numbers. The role of guardian was not an easy one, and other Jotahas had been lost to nixir groups in the past.

With the help of the zayul, the nixirs were usually separated, lured off in different directions by the urvak zayul's projected phantasms and pheromones until they grew lost in the urvaka. Then Jotaha hunted them down and dispatched them before their cunning minds figured out a way out of the maze.

The last team had been more focused, and possessed tactics and combat movements that were impressive enough that Jotaha had taken note of them for future training of jotahs. Their use of teamwork was also something he wanted to discuss with the elders, because it was time for the Jotahas to consider working together like the nixirs did, even if yan-kanat usually preferred solitary hunting. If the backstabbing nixirs could manage to unite for a singular cause, then the yan-kanat should be able to overcome their territorial instinct to protect their hunting grounds from encroachment by others of their kind.

If the urvak zayul had not driven those last nixirs half mad with their disorienting phantasms and alluring pheromone trails, he might have struggled to take them down alone. Given the increased number of incursions into the urvaka by nixir warriors lately, it was time the yan-kanat started learning from their enemy—before the nixirs managed to overrun them and defeat the urvaka and its guardians in numbers large enough to pose a real threat to the yan-kanat people.

If he had not been close to the boundary when his own drahi had crossed it, she also might have been led astray by the urvak zayul phantoms. The realization of how vulnerable she was in this place only made him more determined to get her back to the skilev, where she would be safe.

He hadn't wanted to leave Sarah alone, but it would take time for another Jotaha to make their way to this side of the urvaka, since this was his territory. No matter what, the nixirs must be stopped. It was possible the urvak zayul could lead them to dead falls, or into traps Jotaha had set up, but the most recent batch of nixirs had been far too cunning to blunder into those easy kills.

Strays from elite warrior teams like that had managed to escape the urvaka in the past, though never under his watch. They had either found their way back through the boundary to their own tunnels, or made it to the barrens above—the last territory that protected the skilev from discovery by the ruthless invaders.

Sentils hunted the rare nixirs that made it aboveground, but in daylight, the alien creatures held more of an advantage with their strange weapons. The sentils of the barrens were more accustomed to hunting animals, not sentient killers with ranged weapons that killed from a distance so vast that an average yan-kanat hunter could not even see them when their projectile struck. Too many sentils had to fall before a single nixir escapee was dispatched in open lands.

He had been close to defying his duty, determined to get Sarah out of the urvaka to safety, when it occurred to him that the nixirs might be here for her. Why else would they arrive so close on her heels? It only made sense that they were tracking her down. His initial belief had probably been accurate. She was a shataz, cherished by the nixir males, and they would not allow the yan-kanat to keep their skillful breeder without a fight.

That realization filled him with an even stronger urge to kill these invaders. They had come here to steal back what was rightfully his. Seta Zul had decreed it. Sarah belonged to him, and he would destroy anyone who tried to take her from him.

He relayed his concern to the hive through the chanu zayul, demanding they repay his vigilance by keeping his drahi contained within his cave. Given her fear of the urvak zayul, she would probably avoid either exit if she spotted them blocking her way, but he wanted that to be a last resort. He didn't want to terrify her, unless he had no choice, but he also couldn't have her wandering around the urvaka. Not with all the dangers she could stumble into.

She had appeared to understand his warning, and he tried to take solace in that belief. There was sincerity in her body language, but he knew the nixirs were masters of deception. Their body language couldn't always be trusted. Not even with his drahi.

It was because of this lingering distrust of her motives that he left the cave with more fear than he'd ever felt when hunting nixirs. Not fear for himself, but for his drahi. He wasn't worried the nixirs would find her and hurt her. Even for such a brutal, vicious species, historical documents claimed that it was rare for the nixirs to kill their own females. Rare, but not unheard of. Still, the shataz were prized, and the nixirs would not seek her out only to harm her. They would try to reclaim her, but he would find them before they escaped with her.

No, he was afraid she would find her way out of the safe area surrounding the cave, perhaps overcoming her fear of the urvak zayul, only to disappear into some dead fall, or fall upon a pike trap, or topple into a lava well. His mind could not stop cataloguing all the potential dangers the urvaka held for the unwary.

For now, he had to focus. As he made his way through the tunnels towards the boundary, his concern only grew. The nixirs were not responding to the urvak zayul's attempts to lead them astray, heading in a fairly direct line along the path Jotaha had carried his drahi earlier.

Heading towards his cave.

He heard them before he entered a grand cavern not far enough from the cave where he'd left Sarah. They made sounds he had never heard the nixirs make, and those sounds came from all around him. They echoed even far above him, in the shadows of the ceiling between the stalactites.

They were short, shrieking sounds, not loud, but with a

high enough volume to echo in the empty space. The sounds did not appear to be the nixirs' usual language—though he was told they had many, and those languages changed over the generations of nixirs.

He kept his glow suppressed as he crept into the cavern, his tongue flicking out to taste the air. The scent of the nixirs lay thick on the damp, heavy air, but it was slightly different from what he'd tasted before. They smelled wrong. It wasn't just that they appeared to have traded their odd clothing and weapons for fur.

He closed his inner lids and allowed his thermal vision to guide him. He spotted three heat signatures, and his concern grew as he noticed that two crouched along the walls and one had climbed to the ceiling, where it clung upside down with apparent ease.

If the urvak zayul weren't so convinced that these were nixir invaders, he would have suspected that both he and they had made a mistake in identifying them as anything more than some new animal that had left the nixir world and found its way into the urvaka. The way these new nixirs moved seemed very animalistic. They crawled along the walls and ceiling like beasts instead of walking upright like both yan-kanat and nixir.

Their soft shrieks continued as they made their way from one end of the cavern to the other, approaching Jotaha, who was concealed in darkness as he slowly withdrew his blowgun and loaded a poisoned dart.

He raised the blowgun, aiming at the first heat signature that clung to the wall closest to him. Its shrieking grew louder. Then its head suddenly turned so that it appeared to be staring right in his direction, even as he blew a gust of air to release the dart.

There was no way a nixir could spot him in pitch darkness. Even with their strange eye coverings, they could not detect him by heat, as his body temperature took on the temperature of the surrounding cavern.

Yet, as he watched the body of the strange nixir topple to the ground, he knew it had detected him somehow.

It's shrieks seemed to set the other two off. They raced along the walls and ceiling, making louder and louder calls, either to each other or for some other purpose. He'd never seen nixirs move so fast. He stalked on silent feet to the fallen nixir, withdrawing his favorite dagger with barely a whisper, before crouching to slit its throat.

His hand encountered fur, warm beneath his palm, as if it was part of the nixir's body, rather than layered over top of it like clothing. He quickly dispatched it, rising to his feet as blood spurted from the slit in its throat, glowing brightly in his thermal vision even as the extremities of the creature began to fade.

The echo of the nixirs' sounds grew cacophonous, disorienting Jotaha. He spun to find the next one, his blowgun in hand, when the third one suddenly dropped from the ceiling. The heavy weight of it struck his back with the momentum of its fall.

Jotaha's body lit up with the chanu zayul glow. The sudden light gleamed on his blowgun that slipped out of his grasp as he was driven to the ground by the force of the nixir's body. He heard it rolling away, but was preoccupied with the maddened nixir slashing away at his armor with unnaturally long claws he'd never seen on a nixir before.

He flipped over, throwing the heavy nixir off his back. As he did, he drew his dagger from his arm sheath.

The nixir shot to its feet, remaining in a slight crouch, as if it was only moments away from dropping to all fours. In the light of his glow, it looked nothing like the others he'd seen. Nothing like his Sarah. Yet it still tasted of nixir as his tongue flicked out.

It also still seemed intelligent. Instead of charging and slashing at him again, it turned and raced towards his fallen dart gun. He realized its intent and rushed after it. Even his superior speed wasn't enough to stop it from kicking the blowgun farther away with a triumphant shriek.

An answering shriek sounded as Jotaha tackled the creature with one arm wrapping around its body to pull it towards him. He brought his dagger around to stab it in the gut. His glow caught the silhouette of the other nixir creature scrambling down the wall to snatch up his blowgun. It scurried away with the weapon as the one he'd caught shrieked in pain when he impaled it.

He wrestled with the struggling nixir. His dagger jerked out of his hands as it twisted its body to break free of his grasp. Despite his superior strength and size, he could not match its ferocity. It seemed to recognize the difference between his armor and his scales, and aimed its rapid slashes at his glowing, exposed scales. It's eyes gleamed as they caught the light of his bioluminescence. The wound in its gut slowed it down, but wasn't enough to bring it to its knees.

Other lights than his own darted around the cavern as nixir-shaped phantasms suddenly danced along the walls. As the urvak zayul had warned, these new nixirs appeared to ignore the ghostly forms cast by the zayul. They seemed to know who and what their target was, and their focus remained completely on Jotaha. Even the pheromones the urvak zayul released failed to sway them away from their intent.

The other nixir scuttled down the wall as quickly and easily as any zayul to join its partner in attacking him.

The nixirs shrieked to each other, but were no longer constantly making sounds other than their struggling grunts. He moved to keep them from flanking him, but they tracked him quickly. When he cornered them at a wall, the uninjured one easily climbed up it. Normally, pinning them so they couldn't spread out was the best tactic to deal with multiple attackers in the urvaka, but these creatures used their ability to scale walls and ceilings to gain higher ground.

They recognized that he was faster and stronger. They also recognized that they had an advantage of numbers, and used it to split his focus.

He had to move quickly to take one out to eliminate their primary advantage. Even when their number was down to one, he would still have to deal with the one ability they had that he could not match. He had never needed to climb to the ceiling before to kill a nixir. If he could chase it into a low tunnel, it would lose that advantage.

He charged the wounded nixir and ducked its slash at his head to slam the dagger deeper into its stomach. His fingers curled around the weapon and dragged it upwards as the nixir shrieked. He used his other arm to block its desperate attacks as he gutted it.

The second nixir leapt at him from the wall, but Jotaha managed to pull the dagger from the gut of the first and slash at the creature. His blade connected with the side of its face, parting the fur of its cheek. It backed away but only for a moment, seeming to change its mind as its companion slid to the floor, leaving a trail of blood on the stone wall.

Enraged by the sight, it threw itself at him, one hand grabbing for his dagger arm as the other slashed at his face.

They wrestled as it grabbed hold of both his wrists, strengthened by rage. Jotaha kicked the creature's legs out, only to give it another advantage he hadn't counted on as it fell onto its back. Like its hands, its feet were tipped by vicious claws, and it brought its strong legs up to its belly and began to rapidly kick at him.

The claws shredded the lacquered surface of the armor covering his stomach as he was dragged down atop the kicking legs. He broke his empty hand free and drew his inferno dagger, which blazed with heat and light when he shifted the crystal band on the hilt.

He managed to slash the creature again, but it jerked away before he could strike its throat. The scent of scorched fur filled the air between them. It barely shrieked, as if it hardly felt the pain, and managed to catch ahold of his wrist again. Its back claws continued to slash with force, digging deeper and deeper into his armor, shredding the leather apart. Soon it would bare his stomach to those lethal claws.

Suddenly, a weight fell on his back. The wounded nixir—the one that should be dead by now—had managed to crawl up the wall enough to leap onto him. It bit down on his neck with the last of its strength, sharp teeth that were unnatural for nixirs piercing his scales and flesh. He felt the agony of some of his chanu zayul as the creature crushed them between its teeth. He jerked his body upwards, knocking the dying creature off. Even if it somehow managed to survive the gutting, that bite doomed it to death.

The weight of it disappeared from his back as it toppled off him. Jotaha returned his full attention to the nixir whose back claws finally broke through his armor and slashed his belly scales. He drove his weight down on the nixir, pinning its legs to its chest with great effort given their strength. With a roar of rage, he ripped his arm free of its death grip on his wrist, his grip firm around the inferno dagger.

Despite his weight crushing its chest, the nixir managed to capture his hand again before the dagger tip impaled its eye. It squealed in pain as the heat from the blade burned its retina, but held on. The nixir was stronger than any other he had ever fought. It clamped onto his wrist with its clawed fingers. The strength of its grip might have even crushed his wrist if he wasn't armored. The nixir's lips peeled back from its teeth, revealing the pointed edges of them. Its eyes were as dark as the urvaka itself, and yet glowed whenever they caught the light.

The pain from the wounded chanu zayul pounded in his head, and the chittering sound of urvak zayul rising from the hive en masse filled the air. They rarely left the rock in such numbers, and only something like this could spur such a reaction. So many of them would die at the hands of the nixirs, even if they eventually swarmed the creatures. That was why they needed a Jotaha to guard their hive.

The sound of the swarm on the move nearly deafened him to the shrieks of the nixir beneath him. The dagger's tip shifted closer to the creature's eye, scorching the fur around it.

Then something punctured the back of his armor, stealing his breath as it slammed through his scales and pierced the flesh beneath. Sharp shards of lacquered bone impaled muscle, causing agonizing pain as he jerked upwards to face the other attacker—the one who should already be dead from the chanu zayul's toxic ichor if not from its opened belly where guts had begun to slip free.

He couldn't believe it had managed to find his blowgun and break it, then have enough strength to force the weapon through his armor. He had no idea what still animated the creature, but its endurance was unthinkable before this moment. No other nixir could have survived even this long after such a wounding, much less find the strength to impale him with his own weapon.

That act seemed to use the last of whatever reserve it had left. It barely managed to stand, swaying on its feet as it clutched its stomach to keep most of its entrails inside. Glowing chanu zayul ichor stained its teeth and the fur around its mouth, which dripped with bloody foam.

Jotaha roared, his glow blazing even more as adrenaline and chemicals from the chanu zayul filled him, allowing him to ignore the agony of the blowgun still piercing his back. The nixir beneath him took advantage of that brief distraction of his impalement to shove him off of it with a mighty heave of its powerful legs. It flipped to its stomach and skittered away as he was pushed backwards, towards the other nixir.

The mortally wounded creature chuckled like a maddened thing, sounding very much like the other nixirs that he'd fought in the past, though it didn't look at all like them. It staggered towards him again, clearly intent on shoving the blowgun deeper, just as he had slammed the dagger home in its gut.

The nixir spat glowing ichor darkened with its own blood and foam as the toxin shredded its mouth and throat. Jotaha jumped to his feet and turned to face it. With a final shriek of defiance, it threw itself at him, claws raised as if to slash him. Its arms sagged from its weakness and entrails poured from its gaping stomach wound.

He brought the inferno dagger up to stab it through the throat as the force of its body struck him. The reek of burnt meat filled the air as it finally collapsed in his arms. He rapidly stabbed the corpse several more times in kill zones before finally whipping the blade free one last time. He pushed it away from him, watching it fall to a heap on the stone. He wondered if he should dismember it before turning his back on it again. Given what he'd already seen, he couldn't be certain it wouldn't pop back up again.

Once he was sure it remained unmoving, he turned back to the other nixir, only to find that it had used his momentary distraction to escape.

13

When Jotaha had told Sarah to stay, or fan-ack, or whatever he'd been saying, she figured he didn't mean she had to remain sitting right in front of the stone ring where he'd left her, and she hadn't meant that she would with her promise.

She finished her sweet and savory bun, wondering at what the filling could be made of, since it was like a slightly gritty paste that she had initially assumed to be made of some kind of bean. Yet it was thicker than the beans she was familiar with, and much stickier. It was baked into the thin, pastry shell that looked like unleavened bread, and flaked when she bit into it. Despite that biscuit-like flakiness, the shell tasted more of a sweet base like corn, rather than of flour.

She polished off her breakfast and the rest of her tea, then had nothing to do but sit there and worry about whether Jotaha would return for her at all—and what her future held if he did.

Or didn't.

He'd left his pack, the glowing stones, and the majority of his possessions in the cave, so it didn't look like he was abandoning it, or her, altogether. Clearly, he'd simply left for some purpose of his own. Perhaps he had an appointment to keep.

The kind that involved poisoned darts and daggers.

She tried to push that aside, worried about any kind of threat that someone like Jotaha needed so many weapons to face. Instead, she focused on the cave, trying to distract herself by examining her surroundings really well for the first time, now that she wasn't wholly focused on the alien in the room.

She also had to distract herself from a body relaying its needs. For the moment, those needs could be denied. She wasn't about to head out either exit from the cave in search of the poop beetle cave, even if she could bring herself to sit on that rock ledge over the hole again, knowing that there were creepy beetles down there, waiting for her to drop a load. She shuddered at the thought.

Her first turn around the cave proved that it was larger than she'd initially thought, about the size of her living room and kitchen combined. The stone ring was closer to one side of the cave, near the tunnel opening where Jotaha had disappeared. He'd stowed his pack on the other side. She made her way towards his pack, discovering rolled up furs that propped it up, revealing that the pack itself wasn't as big as she'd thought. It wasn't much different than a human pack, though it was made of leather with a gathered top tied off by coarse, narrow rope. It was as neatly sewn as a sewing machine might make it, and had one soft leather strap that probably wrapped across the chest.

After glancing back at the tunnel Jotaha had gone through to make sure he didn't suddenly appear in the doorway to catch her riffling through his things like a thief, she crouched down and pulled open the pack.

The inside smelled of a combination of herbs, other foods, and some acrid scents she couldn't identify. She took out a bundle wrapped in cloth and sniffed it. It smelled like the bun she'd just eaten for breakfast. Setting it aside on the ground next to her, she selected another item. This was a metal hammered square tin the size of her palm. The flip lid had a catch on the side and she opened it to discover a pale green powder that smelled like herbs of some sort—or maybe just weeds. She'd never been good at identifying the differences in plant odors.

Another tin had a soft pink colored powder, and some of the other bundles revealed more food. More of the gross blood bars mostly, though she did find some dried roots in a bundle. She also found several leather pouches. Opening the first released the earthy mushroom scent of the relaxing tea drug that Jotaha had given her. She quickly pulled the string on that pouch to close it again, then shoved it back into the pack where she'd found it. It was way too tempting. Given the fact that there didn't seem to be much left in the pouch, she wondered if Jotaha also indulged in that particular drug. Why else would he have it in his pack?

The other pouches held different teas, she suspected, though she only recognized the one she'd drunk that morning.

The final bundle had a small glass bottle tied to the top of it. The bundle was wrapped with a thick square of suede. When she untied it after setting the bottle next to her she saw why. Sharp pointed darts were neatly lined up inside the suede. A thin, suede strap kept them in place. Each was as long as her middle finger, with small feathers on their ends in colors that might have come off the most exotic of parrots, but could also have been dyed.

The darts looked to be carved of bone, given the slightly yellowish cream color of their shafts, but the tips were most definitely metal, with unpleasant barbed edges. She had no idea how Jotaha had taken the dart out of her without leaving a wound that was no bigger than her other cuts and scrapes. Those tips looked nasty.

Given the darts, she could figure out the contents of the

bottle that had been attached to them. Still, she set the darts aside and picked up the small, glass bottle. It had a thin neck, slightly shorter than the dart shaft and just wide enough to fit the tip of the dart along with the shaft. Below the neck was a bulb of glass. When she gently shook it, she heard the liquid sloshing inside. The glass was colored dark red, like a garnet, so the liquid inside probably couldn't be exposed long term to light.

The bottle was corked by something firm, perhaps wood, coated in wax to give a tight seal.

Recalling the necklace of teeth and finger bones that had disappeared from the cave after she fell asleep, she pondered the small bottle of poison and the darts.

One dart had dropped her like a stone. She had no idea how long she'd been out, but it must have been a significant amount of time, given the fact that she'd awakened in this cave with no memory of the trip here from wherever Jotaha had captured her.

He'd been kind to her so far, and more than generous to an alien stranger, of a species he clearly wasn't in the habit of welcoming. She couldn't say if any human encountering him would show the same restraint or generosity if they somehow gained the upper hand on him.

She withdrew a dart from the suede bundle and balanced it on her leg as she turned her attention back to the cork in the bottle. It popped from the bottle with only a slight sound, and Sarah was careful to keep her nose away from whatever fumes might rise from the opening.

Holding the bottle in one shaking hand, she used the other to dip the dart into it. A few turns of the tip in the liquid filling the bulb should coat it thoroughly. She hoped it wouldn't be a lethal dose. Just enough to slow someone down.

Someone like her seemingly benevolent captor, if he grew hostile and completely changed his behavior towards her. This weapon, one of his own, was the only one she had that might be able to give her a chance at fighting back against him if he were to suddenly attack her—or lead her to her imminent death.

She actually liked Jotaha, or at least the person he was presenting to her. He seemed like a nice guy—lizard guy. Even if he didn't always treat humans so gently. Given the uniforms and weapons she'd found in that pit with those bodies, she had no doubt it hadn't been a peaceful envoy attempting to make first contact with underground aliens that he'd killed. The military was great to have around when the bad guys threatened, but she often wondered if the government even knew who the real bad guys were—or even if they'd become them. She respected the soldiers but didn't trust the people giving the orders.

Thus far, Jotaha hadn't been a bad guy to her, but he was still an alien, with unknown motives and a wholly unfamiliar culture. She had no idea if he was planning to make lizard mutant babies with her, or fatten her up to eat her, or take her back to his village as a sacrifice to some unknown alien god. She'd consumed way too much horror and science fiction in her life to just trust Jotaha on his actions alone, and sadly, she couldn't understand his words. Being able to ask a slew of questions might clarify his intentions, or it might just mean he lied through his forked tongue.

She recorked the bottle carefully, pressing the wax stopper down to be certain it sealed properly. She wrapped the newly coated dart in a folded length of cloth she'd found at the bottom of his pack, after making certain the blue, viscous liquid on the tip had dried and hardened before surrounding it in a thick barrier of the coarsely woven fabric. Crumbs of blood bar suggested the wrap had once held the food item, and had no doubt been folded and stored for future use.

Jotaha might notice it was missing, and might suspect she'd

taken it, but she was hoping he wouldn't, given that there were several other used cloths in there with it. A human probably wouldn't keep count of how many discarded food wrappers they had at the bottom of their pack.

As for the missing dart, she hoped he wouldn't count them, and made certain the dart she'd taken had been from the end of the neat line of them, where other darts were missing. If he wasn't paying super close attention, he might just assume it was one of the ones he'd already used.

She was careful to put everything back in the pack exactly the way she'd found it, hoping Jotaha didn't have the alien version of OCD to the point that he would notice slight variations in the positions of the items. The whole time since she'd made the decision to steal a poisoned dart, she'd feared that he would return. Her heart thudded in her chest as she packed everything back up, her hands shaky as she pulled the strings on the opening of the pack tight, then settled it against his fur bundle.

If he discovered this theft, she could create the very problem she feared. She could anger him to the point that he hurt or killed her, even if that had not been his original intention. The problem was that she didn't like to have anyone else in control of her fate, especially if their motives were uncertain. She'd learned the hard way that she couldn't trust anyone but herself.

The risk of stealing the dart was high, but not higher than leaving her life completely in the hands of an alien stranger. She tucked the bundled dart under her bra strap, pointing the tip away from her skin, even though it hopefully wouldn't pierce the thick fabric sheath she'd wrapped around it. The feathers tickled her collar bone, but were successfully hidden beneath her shirt. The heavy flannel fabric pressed them flat enough that they didn't betray the presence of the dart.

She was sweating with nerves by the time she returned to

the stone ring and sat down. She groaned as the movement put pressure on a bladder filling up from the tea she'd had that morning. It was still not at critical volume, but she hoped now that Jotaha returned soon, or she would have to find a solution to that problem, even if she could hold off the other for a bit longer.

The dart seemed to weigh on her chest as she watched the tunnel opening, awaiting Jotaha's return.

14

The chanu zayul could not heal him fast enough, several of them damaged beyond survival. He could feel them releasing their hold on his spine, withdrawing their tendrils, crawling towards the bite mark at the base of his skull. Their agony was almost paralyzing as they made the final effort to leave his body before their death became toxic to him. If some did die inside him, he hoped enough of them would survive to consume the bodies of the dead so they did not fester and kill him.

His steps were slowing, the pain in his back negligible in comparison to the pain from the neck wound. The nixir could not have chosen a better place to bite him, as long as it was prepared to die in order to defeat him. Given that it should have already been dead, he didn't feel a sense of victory that the loss of the chanu zayul had taken its life in return.

He left the broken dart gun in his back, right beside his shoulder, because the chanu zayul were too weak to slow his bleeding. He would have to wait until he could use his healing powder to staunch the wound. He suspected the nixir had been hoping to strike his heart, perhaps believing it to be in the same place as the nixir's own. He was fortunate that it wasn't. This new type of nixir had used strength and force he'd never encountered before.

They were growing stronger. Deadlier. As if they weren't already deadly enough to pose a significant threat. This was something the elders must be told. A single Jotaha per boundary might not be enough anymore.

First, he had to stop the escaped nixir from recapturing his drahi. He was also no longer certain it would not harm her. Fear for her life kept him moving, long after his legs wanted to fail beneath him and send him collapsing to the ground.

The nixir was also moving slower. The zayul surged up from their usual tunnels in the rock, crawling ahead of him and behind him, lighting his path. Their collective minds mourned the loss of the chanu zayul that had been killed, and they wanted to stop this nixir at all costs. It was they who told him the nixir had slowed, no doubt because of the wounds to its face. The inferno blade had scorched off most of its fur before it managed to break away from him and had probably also damaged its sense of smell, making it harder for it to track Sarah.

The urvak zayul were attempting to swarm the nixir, and had succeeded in slowing it down even further, but even en masse, they were having difficulty stopping it. The creature was simply too strong and agile. It crawled along the ceiling, flinging the zayul off its hide with vicious force, or crushing them against the stone as it crawled through their numbers. Its furred hide seemed impervious to their pincers, proving far stronger than the normal nixir flesh they usual fed upon.

Every zayul death rippled through the hivemind, causing the pain in Jotaha's spine to increase from the distress of the chanu zayul inside him. The cost of their aid in slowing the nixir was staggering.

Even with the need to fight off the swarm, and the damage

to it, the nixir increased the distance between it and Jotaha. There was no doubt in his mind that it was heading straight for Sarah. Based on the information he received from the hive-mind, his suspicion was confirmed as it approached his campsite, with him too far behind to stop it.

He could only pray to the Ajda that it had come to take Sarah home, not to punish her for leaving.

15

Sarah jumped with nervousness at every sound, from the slightest shift of Jotaha's pack to the faint sound of a small stone pattering to the ground somewhere out of sight, perhaps in the bathroom tunnel. She felt so skittish as she waited for Jotaha's return, and so guiltily aware of the hidden dart, that she at first though the low hum she began hearing as she paced the cave was her own imagination. Kind of like the heart in that Edgar Allen Poe story—a sound pounding in her brain because of her own feeling of guilt.

Then she heard a hair-raising chittering sound, like a mass of video game giant spiders were suddenly on the move in the tunnels. She shuddered as she rushed towards the river stone ring, hoping the light and heat would keep any creepy bugs away.

She'd seen the glowing beetles, and they hadn't been giant bugs—though they'd been large enough to rival some of the biggest dung beetles she'd ever seen in person. She knew there were much larger insects in places like the Amazon.

When the stone wall around the tunnel exit through which Jotaha had left started moving, Sarah thought she was hallucinating. Maybe it was an optical illusion from the heat of the stone ring causing a wavering in the air. Then she realized that the moving wall was a mass of camouflaged beetles—the same color and even apparent texture of the stones.

A huge mass of them moved along the wall, their chitinous limbs making the sounds she'd been hearing. Like the glowing poop beetles, the individual insects were not huge, but there was a whole shit load of them, and her shock was enough that she could chuckle at the pun. Until reason returned.

"Oh hell no," she muttered, looking around desperately for something to smash any ambitious beetles that came her way. "This is so much cooler in a video game! In real life, it sucks!"

Fortunately, they seemed more intent on moving out of the tunnel entrance, not surrounding her to swarm over her like the glowing beetles had over her poop.

Some of the beetles lit up with the same kind of blue bioluminescence that Jotaha and the poop beetles had, and she suspected these belonged to the same species of beetle. They looked like flashing LED lights along the moving stone wall as they surged out of the tunnel.

Then they all lit up at once as she stared at them, trying to determine the level of threat they posed to her. She was hoping they were scared of the heat and light of the stone ring.

Like a blanket of light, they covered the stone walls around the tunnel entrance, illuminating the horrific shadowy creature that crawled through the opening, clinging to the ceiling like with the ease of a gecko.

"No," Sarah whispered, backing away from the stone ring. "Not *again!*"

The bat-cat creature turned its head so that it was looking down at her from its perch on the ceiling, seemingly undeterred by the beetles that swarmed its fur. It would swat them off with one clawed hand, sending the insects flying. If they were biting it, they weren't having much effect.

It clambered along the ceiling as quickly as the beetles, heading rapidly towards her. Sarah screamed and turned to run towards the poop tunnel. Her hand desperately groped at the dart, and it was sheer luck that her panicked movements didn't end up piercing her with its tip.

She pulled it free as she raced towards the other tunnel, the fabric wrapper unraveling from the tip.

She wasn't fast enough to reach the tunnel before the creature beat her to her escape. It crawled as fast as a giant spider along the ceiling. The furry monster scuttled down in front of her, causing her to scream again as she staggered backwards, away from it.

It charged her, and then clawed hands closed around her throat. The grip on her throat tightened as it lifted her off her feet. Sarah choked, her empty hand scraping at the impossibly strong, furry hand as it slowly crushed her airway. Her strength rapidly failing as her oxygen was cut off, she used one last surge of adrenaline to swing her other hand, slamming the poisoned dart home in the eye of the bat-cat creature.

It shrieked, dropping her as it instinctively covered its face. One clawed hand shook as it encountered the shaft of the dart sticking out of its eye. Sarah collapsed in a heap when it dropped her, gasping for air, clutching her bruised throat.

She expected the creature to pass out from the poison, but it roared in rage instead, lowering its hand and turning to face her. Its lips peeled back in a snarl as its one remaining eye glared with hatred that she swore held intelligence. Half of the fur on its face was burned around the eye that she'd thrust the dart into.

This was no wild animal, acting on an instinct for survival. An injured animal might run away after being wounded like that. This creature was there to kill her, and it knew exactly what it was doing.

She rolled as the creature leapt for her, barely escaping its slashing claws. Her roll gave her the momentum to jump quickly to her feet. She saw the stone ring through eyes still blurry from watering while she was being choked. Sucking in pained gasps of breath, she raced towards the stone ring, wrapping the fabric still clutched in her hand around it to cover her palm.

The creature was much faster than her, even wounded and poisoned. It slammed into her from behind, throwing her to the floor. Her breath rushed out of her lungs as its weight fell upon her. She screamed as it slashed her back, ripping her shirt and slicing the flesh beneath it. She tried to roll over to throw it from her back, but the weight of it proved too much for her to dislodge it.

The ring was just beyond her reach. She felt a shift of the weight on her back as the creature lowered its head towards hers, perhaps to bite her. Slapping her bare hand backwards, she struck the shaft of the dart, pushing it deeper in the creature's eye.

The weight of the creature lightened as it reared backwards, shrieking in pain again. That was enough for Sarah to crawl a few inches forward. As soon as the stone ring was in reach, she grabbed one of the larger glowing stones with her wrapped hand, feeling the radiating heat even through the layers of fabric.

The creature slashed blindly at her as she put all her effort into rolling onto her back. Her arm swung around with the burning stone in hand to slam into the side of the creature's head.

The sound of sizzling meat joined the creature's agonized screams as the impact of the stone rocked its head to one side, burning more of the fur off its cheek.

Sarah's own hand was now growing too hot to hold the stone, the fabric not providing enough protection, but she slammed it against the creature's head a second time before she was forced to drop it.

A normal animal would have tried to escape the source of the pain, but this thing wanted her dead. Even wounding it horribly only seemed to piss it off more. Sarah lost hope when she saw its single eye turn back to her as she pushed herself backwards on her propped up elbows.

Movement in the entry tunnel caused her eyes to shift in that direction, and the creature seemed to notice the motion. It turned just as Jotaha rushed towards it. A combat knife impaled the skull of the creature, burying deep into its brain.

This time, it slumped over, finally dead.

Jotaha released the handle of the knife, catching hold of the creature with his other hand to haul it off of Sarah. Once she was free of it, he pulled the dagger from its head to stab it multiple times in different places like the heart and throat, as if he wasn't quite certain it was dead. Then he dragged it towards the exit to drop it in a heap by the tunnel opening, leaving a messy blood trail. After that, he turned his attention to her.

He returned to her and knelt on one knee in front of her, his gaze traveling over her, from her face down her body to her feet, then back again. "Sarah, olar-iv zula?"

"Jotaha, am I *glad* to see you! Suddenly, you have the most beautiful face I've ever seen," Sarah said with a weak laugh, her body trembling as reaction finally set in. Then she winced as the movement caused the slashes on her back to sting in earnest, reminding her of their presence.

Jotaha's eyes widened at her pained expressions. "Iv-olar zula!"

He rose to his feet, and it was only then that she noticed it appeared to be an effort for him. Then he turned towards his pack and she saw his blowgun sticking out of his back, piercing even the lacquered layer of his armor as if a great force had slammed it home. His neck was also torn, just above the highest layer of his armor.

"Jotaha! You're hurt!" He glanced her way and she pointed to her shoulder. "You've got a little something, right about there."

Her trembling turned to a full-blown shudder as she realized how injured Jotaha was. Something had done that to a seven-foot tall lizard man in full armor. If he'd been killed, she wouldn't be breathing right now. It was frightening to realize that sometimes, no matter how hard you fought, you couldn't always win the battle alone. She'd had to rely on someone else to keep her alive, and that was a difficult thing for her to do. It meant being beholden to someone, and Beth had taken advantage of that before, making Sarah feel guilty about being a burden—until Beth had abandoned her to save her own skin.

A glance at the bat-cat corpse caused her to shudder again. Jotaha cast his own glance at his wounded shoulder without much apparent concern in his eyes, though he moved slowly towards his pack, limping as if he had to drag one leg. She saw that the front of his armor, right over his stomach, had been shredded, and his blood seeped from deep scratches that scored his belly scales.

He knelt on one knee beside his pack, his groan barely audible to her. Guilt filled her as she recalled her recent pilfering. Of course, the dart had given her a chance at surviving. If she hadn't had that to injure the bat-cat creature, she would have been choked to death before Jotaha could come to her rescue.

Jotaha withdrew both of the tins from his pack, then picked up his waterskin. With all three items he returned to the stone ring. After retrieving the mug, he poured water into it, then glanced her way as he set the mug on a heat stone.

"Sarah? Draho komin?"

She figured he was asking her to join him, so pushed

herself to her feet, biting off her own groan of pain. His injuries looked far worse than hers, and he remained stoic. She could keep her complaints to herself. He wouldn't understand them anyway.

"Mito olar-iv zula?" His gaze roved her body, but not in a sexual way. She realized he probably wanted to know where she was injured.

She turned her back towards him, hearing a sharp gasp from him that made her grateful she couldn't see the damage to her back.

"Vauteg!" he said in a vicious tone as Sarah turned back around.

She caught him shooting a narrow-eyed glare at the corpse, and automatically glanced in the same direction, then instantly regretted it.

As bad as the bat-cat corpse was, it was made a hundred times worse when she saw the carpet of glow beetles crawling over it, blinking in and out like macabre Christmas lights as they stripped its flesh. The mass of insects had also dragged it through the tunnel entrance, and she suspected it would be gone from the cave in mere hours.

Jotaha seemed unconcerned with the bugs, just as he had been with the poop beetles, so she got the impression they were not a threat to him or—hopefully—her. Though that didn't make her relax in their unnerving presence, she could appreciate the service they were doing. Perhaps they had been helping her all along, though they hadn't been very effective against the bat-cat creature when it was moving.

When she returned her attention to Jotaha, scooting closer to him and further away from the corpse, she noticed that he was tapping powder from a tin into the boiling water filling the mug. After dumping a fair amount into the water, he closed that tin and picked up the second. He added a far smaller amount of the pale green powder to the mug before capping that tin to set it aside.

He stirred the mixture with one of his daggers that looked like it was made of stone, though it was not worked like a prehistoric weapon, but had been finished and polished to a high shine. The granite blade sparkled as it moved, glittering with tiny crystals.

To her surprise, he shifted a finger on the hand holding the hilt, causing a small band of crystal beneath it to rotate. The crystals in the blade started glowing with a light like the hot river stones as he stirred the mixture. By the time she'd settled down beside him, she could see that it had turned into a thick paste.

He saw her staring at the dagger blade and lifted it out of the paste so she could see it better. "Yan sutaz." He gestured with his free hand to the glowing river stones, one of which had probably helped to save her life.

"Yawn suit oz."

He huffed, his head spines quivering, and she had the impression he was amused at her attempt to repeat him. Yet he dipped his head once. "Natna. Yaw-n sue toz." Another brief snort widened his nostrils and he turned his head away from her, but she couldn't miss the quivering head spines.

Sarah made to cross her arms, but the movement caused a spike of renewed pain in her back. Her hiss of pain immediately sobered Jotaha as his gaze shifted back to her, his spines now half-erect.

He gestured to the paste as he set down the dagger. "Trilneva." He then pointed to her, then touched his back. "Ja neva'at Sarah."

When he lifted the dagger out of the paste, he flicked his finger again to spin the crystal hilt, and the glowing in the crystals of the blade faded.

He removed the mug from the heat and set it between

them. Then he reached back and grasped the dart gun still sticking out of his back. He yanked it out with one hard pull. His expression barely twitched, though every muscle in his body tensed.

Blood spilled from the wound, staining the leather where the lacquer had cracked from the impact of the makeshift weapon. He dropped the broken blowgun and unlaced his armor, shucking off one pauldron with a shift of his shoulder, while dragging the other off with his opposing hand.

"Do you want help?" She lifted her hands, showing them to him before pointing to his bleeding wound.

His gaze fell on her scorched palm, his brow ridges coming together. "Iv-olar zula."

Ignoring her offer, or perhaps not understanding it, he unlaced his armor breastplate, then shucked off the damaged pieces as easily as she might drop a button-up shirt off her shoulders.

The hard, ridged scales of his back had been penetrated despite their apparent durability, and his blood poured rapidly now from his wound, as red as her own. His movements only made the bleeding worse. She wanted to offer to help again, but figured it would be wasting time and might draw his attention away from tending to his own wounds while he tried to understand her.

Instead, she watched with interest and concern as he opened a pouch he'd taken from a cleverly concealed pocket in his armor, hidden beneath one of the layered strips on his greaves. He pulled a large pinch of dried moss from it, then dipped it in the cooling paste, coating the moss. Then he reached back and stuffed the moss into the wound, contorting his body in a way that would be painful for a human spine.

As she stared at the stuffed wound, where the blood immediately began to clot, she noticed movement by the bite in his neck. Glowing ichor mixed with his blood at the holes in his neck, and at first she didn't see the fat, grublike worm that crawled out from beneath his skin, because it still glowed weakly, blending into the ichor. It was small—a little larger than the tip of her pinkie—and it moved sluggishly, dragging a trail of blood and ichor as it crawled down his neck to the heavy scales of his back.

Sarah yelped and jerked away, instinctively horrified and disgusted.

Jotaha noticed her reaction, his head spines fully erecting as he reached back and gently plucked the glow worm off his upper back. He cradled it between his fingers as he brought it around to his front, looking down at it with sagging shoulders. His head spines also dipped along with his upper body, and his body language spoke of sadness.

"Vaelin rin itov Zigaro Yan, chanu zayul." He carefully placed the worm, which had stopped moving, onto a glowing stone. It sizzled briefly, before crisping up, then disintegrating.

Though his words were incomprehensible, his tone sounded solemn, rather than horrified with fear that he was being eaten from the inside out by glowing maggots.

Sarah shook her head, reining in her disgust to stop her shudder as she avoided looking again at the vicious bite. Sometimes, she almost forgot she was dealing with an alien. Then something like this happened to remind her exactly how different she was from Jotaha.

16

After stuffing some of the healing moss into the holes in his neck, now reassured that the last of the mortally wounded chanu zayul had left his body, Jotaha managed to communicate to Sarah that he wanted to treat her wounds.

The ones he could treat. There was little he could do for the marks around her neck that were already darkening into ugly purplish stains on her soft flesh. He was certain they had to bring her pain, because her breathing seemed more labored and she would wince from time to time as she spoke. Her hand would also rise to touch her throat as if she was unaware of the movement.

The healers might know a treatment for the marking of the skin, but Jotaha was no healer. He only carried with him treatments for staunching blood that also helped speed healing, and a pain inhibitor. The yan-kanat did not experience such visible damage to their flesh.

The marks also served as another reminder of how close she had come to death, and that would haunt him for the rest of his life. To find his drahi, only to lose her because of his failure to reach her in time would have destroyed him. He owed her survival to her own ferocity. The nixir that had attacked her had suffered for it, with one of his darts buried in its eye and a face further burned by one of the yan sutaz—inferno stones. Her fierce self-defense had slowed the creature down enough for Jotaha to reach her.

He studied her as she turned her back to him, taking a seat on the ground right in front of him. She removed her shirt and the strange garment beneath it that strapped around her mounds with a pained sound that filled him with a sense of guilt and failure. The fact that she bit off the sound only made him feel worse. She was ashamed of her pain and sought to hide it. A female yan-kanat would be far more vocal if she was so wounded, knowing her mate would seek to attend to every one of her needs without her having to move a muscle in a way that might cause more pain.

He wondered at her stoicism. It was the kind a warrior would have, a Jotaha like himself who trained for many years to battle the nixir invaders. Did the nixirs demand silence from their females when they were in pain? His opinion of them sank even lower, when he hadn't believed there was a level beneath where it already was. Only Sarah herself impressed him, but then again, he had never encountered a nixir female before.

He was strangely proud of his nixir female, though he never would have thought he would appreciate such traits in his drahi. It was his role as her mate to fight for her and protect her. She was to be his delicate gem, his harzek, kept comfortable and safe. A drahi should never have to fight, especially not in a battle so deadly that it had left the terrible slashes across her back, or the marks on her neck where the nixir had attempted to squeeze her life from her.

She flinched and made a small hissing sound when he first touched the healing paste to one of the angry slashes that scored her soft skin. He pulled his hand back, debating whether to give her some of the yanhiss to help distract her from the pain until the pain inhibitor kicked in, but it could be dangerous for her to consume too much of it in such a short time. He would prefer to avoid that. After he treated her wounds, he would give her some xirak to comfort her instead.

She straightened her spine, reaching up to pull her long, tangled head fringe to one side, exposing all of her bared back. It was a sign that she wanted him to continue. She was visibly bracing herself for the pain.

Like a warrior.

He was as careful as he could be in spreading the paste on her wounds. She remained silent, though he could feel the tension in her muscles through the brush of his fingers against her delightfully warm skin. He could also see the ripple of tightened muscle in her shoulders and back. She trembled slightly, but did not break down as she had when he'd first met her. She was handling the aftereffects of her near death far better than he would have expected.

There was nothing he could say that she would comprehend to even soothe her, or reassure her that despite the terrible appearance of the slashes, they did not cut deep enough to do more than surface damage to her flesh. With the paste laid thick over them, all bleeding had stopped and the pain inhibitor would soon numb the area, bringing her more comfort.

When he finished treating her back wounds, he was tempted to stroke some of the soft, temptingly warm skin that she had exposed to him. Now was not the time, even if she could understand his intent. Moving in that direction before they could have the sata-drahi'at would only be torture for him, as his salavik would ache with the need to fulfill his desire to join with her.

Besides, he wanted to speak to his drahi and understand her words before they completed the sealing and he marked her as his forever. For now, all he could do was dream about the feeling of her warm skin pressed against his scales, the heat of her alien body seeping into him, filling him with some of her warmth. He would never have to keep an inferno stone close in the cold again with her beside him.

He thought guiltily of Farona, and how quickly he'd pushed her from his mind after a lifetime of loving her. He wondered if this, too, was Seta Zul's influence—or if it was some magic of the nixir female.

The thought of his childhood love filled him with a sense of sadness and regret. Telling Farona about Sarah would not be easy, but she revered Seta Zul as much as any yan-kanat. She knew that only the drahi chosen for him had any chance of bearing his nestlings. She also knew how much he wanted nestlings of his own, and how worried he was about not being able to produce them, even with his drahi and Seta Zul's blessing.

Despite his feelings for Farona, he could not regret now that Seta Zul had decreed this nixir to be his drahi. She had more than proven herself, even though he hadn't expected to claim such a fierce drahi. He had never imagined being in an unthinkable situation where his mate had to defend herself, without him there to protect her. He never wanted her to be in that position again. Even his duty to his people would not draw him from her side again until he had her safe in the skilev.

As he motioned for Sarah to give him her hand so that he might coat her singed palm with the paste, he accepted that he might have eventually grown too complacent with a partner like Farona. He had seen even the most compatible couplings turn sour many passings after a sealing, as if they had let Seta

Zul's fire die from neglect when they fell into a cyclic pattern that led to dullness and discontent. Too much familiarity seemed to breed in them a sense of boredom.

The kind of female who would try to crush an attacker's skull with a scorching inferno stone, or bury a stolen dart into its eye to save herself, was the kind of female who would never grow boring. She would always keep him on alert, even after he became Jotahan—a retired guardian. Her deviousness would challenge him. Her ferocity would heat his blood as much as her body would warm his scales.

For now, her eyes were lowered as he tended the burned skin of her palm. Her free hand clutched the fabric of her torn tunic to her bare chest, concealing her full mounds from him. They were for feeding nixir young, he'd been told, like the teats of a snow stalker fed its kits. Except that the nixir females were always swollen, even when they weren't producing for young. It was yet another intriguing, alien thing about his drahi that he wanted to explore.

From what he knew about crossbreeding with nixirs, the yan-kanat traits were almost always dominant because of the Ajda blood—except in very rare cases where some nixir traits were passed on through multiple generations—meaning any nestlings born to her would likely be able to eat the same foods an adult yan-kanat could eat at birth and would not require her milk to thrive.

By the time he was finished with the paste, he realized that the lowered gaze and tight skin around Sarah's mouth, coupled with her trembling muscles, was a sign that her stoicism was cracking. When her gaze lifted to meet his for only a brief moment before it lowered again, returning to studying the inferno stones, he saw that her eyes looked wide and slightly wild. He realized that she was barely holding it together, and suspected that she did so thus far because he was there.

He would have been flattered by that, if he didn't also

suspect her tight grip on herself had more to do with a distrust of him than a desire to impress him. The nixirs kept their guard up at all times, always prepared for an attack. It must be exhausting to live among their kind, always watching one's back, always waiting for your own people to turn against you and try to kill you at the first sign of weakness. Without the yan-kanat to slaughter, nixirs turned on their own kind, as if they could not end their violence even when their enemy left the battlefield.

It was strange that the nixir that had attacked his Sarah had not looked like her. It had looked more beastly. More like the vurruk that provided the heat-resistant furs that the yan-kanat used to keep the warmth of inferno stones close to them when the heart of Theia grew cold.

It had still smelled like a nixir. It was a pity that the nixirs were creatures with such darkness in their hearts that they would seek to destroy the yan-kanat, and even had the arrogance to go after the Ajda themselves. This new breed of nixir, which the urvak zayul had dragged from the cave by the time he finished tending Sarah's wounds and rinsed out his crock, looked even more vicious. More twisted by the darkness that plagued their spirits.

Sarah had pulled her tunic back on with far more ease than she'd taken it off, now that the pain inhibitor had dulled the area. She still stared at the pulsing light of the stones, seemingly unwilling to meet his eyes again. He wondered if he had the strength to banish the darkness that lived inside her, as it lived within all nixirs, born from the betrayal of the titans. He had to trust that Seta Zul would not have chosen her for his drahi if he was not strong enough to save her from her own nature.

For some reason, the goddess had chosen her to be his drahi, and it was unwise to question the wisdom of the Ajda. He would teach his nixir that she could lower her guard among the yan-kanat, and trust that his people would not attack her at every turn. She would know that she could be safe, and find happiness among them. Perhaps then, she would avoid the fate of turning into something as monstrous as those beastly nixirs. He would ensure that his love would be enough to save her from herself.

17

Sarah accepted the mug of tea from Jotaha, but met his intent gaze only briefly before returning her contemplative stare to the hot river stones. Her shoulders tensed every time he moved to his pack, and the anxiety about him discovering her theft and finally understanding why the bat-cat thing had a dart in its eye was enough to pull her out of the darkness of her thoughts.

She wondered what he would do when he realized that she'd stolen from him. He would also have to realize that she was planning to use the weapon on him. There was no way she could explain to him that it was only a contingency plan, in the event that he posed a threat to her. Now, she didn't have a plan, and because of her actions, he might very well retaliate.

Though, if she was being entirely honest, she didn't truly believe he would hurt her. Not now. Not after he went through so much to come to her rescue. He had been severely wounded. So much so that worms were coming out of his neck. That was something she couldn't unsee, but his reaction to the freaky event proved that those things were a part of him, and the one leaving his neck was a sign of a bad thing happening to him. Yet, he had still made his way back here from wherever he'd been wounded by the monster, in order to protect her.

No, she was more worried that he would simply leave her. Just pack up his stuff and walk out of the cave, leaving her to find her own way home in the darkness because of her ingratitude. Leaving her alone again.

They couldn't even talk to each other, not really, but she found comfort in his presence, even with her anxiety about his possible anger. Especially now, as the reaction to her close call with death was finally setting in. She was a bit calmer this time than her last confrontation with a bat-cat. At least this time, she hadn't taken a heart-stopping plunge first. Nor had she seen someone get brutally slaughtered in front of her, just moments before she had to run for her own life, feeling completely alone and abandoned. With the bruises and aches of that fall still plaguing her, she now had a new set of wounds. If things kept going at this rate, she'd be nothing but walking pain when she left this cave.

Jotaha hadn't abandoned her. He'd come back for her, and now he'd shown true concern over her, treating her wounds with something that even numbed her pain, making her far more physically comfortable. Her mind remained uneasy, roiling in turmoil, reeling to find its footing again after a shocking series of traumatic events. She almost felt bad for all the video game avatars she'd put through so much danger. There was no glory in this. No excitement in the aftermath of defeating a foe. Just exhaustion, pain, and fear that another enemy hid right around the next corner.

Jotaha remained silent as she sipped the tea he'd given her, and she worried that he had already figured out about the dart and was mad at her. Logically, she knew that him talking would be mostly pointless. She doubted either of them had the energy to put any effort into a language lesson. She was fortunate that they'd been able to muddle through their system of charades enough to end up at this point.

It was likely that he realized the same thing and that was why he chose not to speak, but doubt ate at her, making her want to talk just to break the heavy silence that fell between them. She resisted the urge, growing increasingly more tired as all the adrenaline seeped from her system and her pain no longer kept her alert.

Her stomach chose to break the silence for her, growling in a reminder that the sweet bun she'd eaten earlier had done little to fill it and the tea wasn't cutting it.

Jotaha climbed to his feet more slowly than he usually did, letting her know that he was still in some pain himself, despite the paste he'd put on his wounds. Still, he went to his pack, and she knew he was about to dig through it to fetch some of the food stored in there. He planned to feed her, simply because he knew she was hungry. She'd offered him nothing in return for his generosity but her mistrust.

She couldn't bring herself to look in his direction as he dug into his pack, keeping her gaze firmly fixed on the pulsing stones. They should have been hypnotic, but she was too aware of Jotaha's movements to be lulled into a trance, even considering how tired she was.

She heard no sound of outrage at the discovery of the missing dart, or at items being in the wrong places in his pack. Instead, he returned to the stone ring with a wrapped blood bar that he handed to her. He pointed to his stomach, where she could just barely see the edge of the glowing tattoo that covered his groin, just below the gashes in his belly scales that he'd coated with paste. His greaves still covered most of the circular design.

"Hon-gree."

She nodded and took the blood bar, though she had no enthusiasm for the unpalatable food. It would be the height of rudeness to reject his offer at this point, given all he'd done for her. Besides, he was right. She was hungry, though she had no appetite. Her stomach had demands that she would do well to fill, especially with the need to recover after her ordeal.

Jotaha stood beside her for a moment longer, after she'd taken the food. His tall form towered over her, but she didn't feel intimidated by it in that moment. It was more like he wanted to communicate with her, but couldn't figure out what he could say that she would understand. She knew the feeling, and the frustration.

Instead of speaking, he finally returned to his seat, closer to her than he'd been before, but still giving her some space. The sounds of her dutifully chewing the hard, minerally tasting bar, while trying to ignore the gag reflex the gristly bits caused her, filled the silence. She wished wholeheartedly for a loudly crackling flame, instead of the silent glow stones.

When she finally finished the tea and the bar, she was grateful she didn't feel the immediate need to relieve herself. She wasn't ready to face the poop beetles again, though she felt a strange sense of kinship with them. They'd been right there with her, joining in the battle against the bat-cat. They'd tried to stop it before it attacked her. It was likely they'd been doing that solely for their own unfathomable insect reasons, but they'd never once attacked her or Jotaha like that, so she shouldn't fear them. It was only her lingering distaste for bugs that made her hesitant to return to this cave home's version of an outhouse.

Instead of a need to visit the toilet, she felt exhaustion pulling her lids closed, forcing her shoulders to relax and curl inwards. She slumped forward, and strong hands caught her before she fell into the glow stones. She was barely conscious when Jotaha gently lifted her onto her feet and drew her over to the furs he'd laid out for her. She let him support some of her weight as she sank onto her knees, then laid on her side, favoring her back.

It was only when she awakened later that she felt the weight of another fur lying over her and realized he'd added that after she'd drifted off to sleep. The first thing she noticed when she opened her eyes was that she felt like hell warmed over. On the plus side, her back was only a small inferno, but her throat was another story entirely. She could barely swallow.

With a groan, she pushed herself up into a sitting position, propping on one hand, while rubbing her eyes with the other. She picked up sounds of Jotaha moving around the cave, though they were very soft. If it wasn't so quiet, she would not have heard the slight shifting of his scaled feet against the stone, or the faint creak of his leather armor.

She turned to look in the direction of the sound and saw that he had brought his pack to the stone ring and had settled on the rock beside it. He had dressed fully in his damaged armor again, though he must still be as aching and wounded as she was. His expression looked pensive, or would if he was human. His brow ridges were drawn together, his mouth nearly flat, with the slightest downturn at the edges. His head spines were partially lifted off his skull.

He glanced her way as she struggled to get to her feet. When he saw her difficulty, he jumped to his own and rushed to help her stand up.

She was embarrassed by her own weakness when he seemed to be so strong and unaffected by the wounds he'd suffered. She shrugged off his hold on her arm as soon as she stood on her feet. It was only then that she realized they were bare, as she felt the surprisingly soft fur beneath her soles. At some point, Jotaha had removed her shoes and socks, although he'd left her dressed in all her other clothes, save the bra she herself had not put back on after removing it.

When she swayed on her feet, he took her arm again, and

this time her attempt to break away from him failed. With a firm, but gentle, grip, he drew her towards the stone ring, lending support as she limped along. The bruising in her body seemed even worse today—whatever day it might be—than it had been before she went to sleep. She had probably taken some new impact damage when the bat-cat creature had knocked her down and jumped on her.

He didn't release her until he had her seated by the stone ring. It was only a brief time after that before she had more blood bar in her hand and a steaming mug of tea sitting on the ground beside her. She stared at her breakfast feeling almost dumbfounded, still a bit groggy from not getting enough rest, though she suspected she had slept for longer than it felt to her body.

Jotaha watched her eat, and she looked up several times to catch him studying her face with an inscrutable expression. Maybe there was something in his body language that might tell her what he was thinking, but she knew very little about lizardman social cues, so she could only guess. Given the fact that he had his pack sitting beside him, he'd probably taken inventory, realized her theft, and now didn't trust her. He was keeping his belongings close so she couldn't steal anything more from him.

As humiliating as that thought was, it filled her with a sense of relief. He was still there. He hadn't abandoned her when he realized the truth. He still shared his food and drink with her. He didn't seem to hate her. Or even to be particularly angry with her.

She held up the last of the blood bar. "Thank you. For this."

She glanced around the cave, her gaze pausing on the place where the bat-cat's body had been. The blood stain that streaked the stone had been covered up while she slept with some of the sand that piled in the corners of the cave.

She relaxed, only realizing she'd been tensing to face that

stain and the memory it recalled when she saw that he'd concealed it. "And thank you, for that."

Her gaze returned to him, noting that he was paying her his full attention, his shoulders lifted, his head slightly cocked to one side, his head spines flexing enough that she could see their spiky tips roughing up the smooth outline of his skull. He was listening to her words, trying to find some meaning to them. She could tell.

Fresh guilt filled her as her gaze shifted to his pack. "I'm sorry." She pointed to his pack. "About stealing from you. I swear I only meant to use it as a last resort." He couldn't possibly understand her confession, but it felt a little better to put it out there.

He was silent for a long moment, and she wasn't sure if he was thinking about what she might mean, or if he was waiting to see if she would continue speaking.

Finally, his head straightened, his spines smoothing flat again. "Rir draho zigun ita tizan arxi anzha skilev."

She blinked at the complexity of the sounds he'd just made, though he'd pronounced the alien words slowly. Despite that pace, she didn't think he expected her to understand them, any more than she expected him to understand her monologue. Maybe he was saying something he just needed to get off his chest as well. She couldn't imagine what that would be.

He'd treated her as well as she could expect. Most humans probably wouldn't treat Jotaha half as nicely if he bumbled into their home. She was pretty convinced that half the horror movie monsters and aliens were just poor suckers who'd gotten lost and had the misfortune to end up among humans.

They both fell silent as she finished her breakfast. She returned her gaze to the stone ring. He kept his on her. She feared his intent watchfulness was because he didn't trust her. That would only be her fault at this point. She'd given him a reason not to. He probably wondered what other weapons she might conceal to use against him later.

It figured that the more she liked Jotaha and appreciated his company, the more reason she'd given him to dislike her.

When she'd completed her food and drained the mug, he collected the empty cloth wrapper and the mug, rinsing out the latter, before tucking both into his pack. Then he rose to his feet and strode to the furs she'd slept on, crouching to roll them into a neat bundle that he carried back to his pack. With practiced movements, he strapped the bundle to his other rolled fur, then hooked it all to his pack. After that, he drew the combat knife that was again sheathed on his thigh, and began to push the stones in the ring apart. As they were separated, their glow faded.

The cave darkened a little more with each dying stone. When the shadows grew too thick for her to see as he separated the last stones in the pile, he seemed to realize her difficulty, because his scales began to glow, returning some of the light.

Once finished pushing all the stones with his dagger tip until they were all a short distance away from each other, he sheathed it and stood to his full height, glowing softly.

Like the beetles glowed.

He shouldered his pack on the side that hadn't been impaled by the blowgun. If he winced in pain, she didn't catch it, since his face was distorted by strange shadows because of the way his head and body were glowing.

He motioned to her to follow him, and led her to where her shoes and socks sat neatly on a stone.

Sarah sat to pull on her socks and shoes, feeling as if his gaze was curious this time as he watched her perform the practiced actions. When she finished, he made a gesture that very clearly implied he wanted her to follow him.

"Kavaric oma, Sarah, iri drahi." He waved her towards him again. "Kavaric."

She followed Jotaha out of the cave, through the entrance he'd gone through before, where the bat-cat had come from. Her heart thudded with fear, but she felt better that she would be with him this time. As crazy as it seemed, given his appearance and the initial threat he'd posed, she now felt safe with him. Far safer than she had when she'd walked through the darkness alone, aware that the bat-cat creatures might still be out there.

The tunnel system was complex, with so many branching paths that she would have easily gotten lost if she wasn't with Jotaha. Some of the beetles glowed along the path they took, lighting their way, then fading as they passed. Jotaha seemed to know exactly where he was going without the help of the beetles, so she got an impression they lit up for her sake. Was it too arrogant to assume these insects wanted to make her feel more comfortable and safer by adding more light to her path?

Maybe she had forged some strange bond with the insects after fighting their enemy. She certainly felt far more sanguine about their presence now. So much so that she did not balk when Jotaha led her to another cave with a similar set-up to the previous toilet cave.

He asked her something in his questioning tone as he withdrew the bundle of petals she'd left in the previous toilet cave from the pouch at his waist. Handing it over to her, he used his free hand to gesture to the stone ledge and the hole within the slab of rock. Since they had been walking for some time by this point, she did have to use the bathroom. She suspected he was concerned she would freak out like an idiot again about the beetles far down at the bottom of the hole.

She had grown since then. She had a new respect for the insects. Without comment, she took the packet, grateful he'd retrieved it, and set it on the ledge. Then she unzipped her pants and started to pull them down before freezing in place because he was still watching her. She made a spinning gesture with one hand.

"Could you please give me some privacy?"

Though he couldn't know what she'd said, he seemed to get the gist of her gesture. After a long moment of consideration, he did turn his back and retreat to the opening of the cave. His pack was still slung from one shoulder because of the hole in the other, visible due to the damaged armor. There was still moss tucked into the holes at the back of his neck, but his shoulders were squared and he stood as tall as he could in the tunnel beyond the cave opening, demonstrating an endurance that seemed as inhuman as he was.

The least she could do was take her poop in peace, without scaring the crap out of him with her freaking out over nothing.

If he heard or smelled anything, he was polite enough not to show it in his body language, and Sarah finished her business as quickly as possible. The petals left a much more pleasant scent in their wake after she wiped and discarded them, and she hoped the slightly medicinal-scented moisture they released when they were pinched or crushed had antiseptic qualities. She hadn't seen any bars of soap in Jotaha's pack when she'd rifled through it.

He made no comment when she left the cave. She didn't have to hunch over like he did, since the ceiling gave her head plenty of space at her full height. Poor Jotaha did not look like he was made for these smaller tunnels. She wondered why his species was so tall if they lived in this vast cave system. It seemed like they would have evolved to be shorter, or to crawl like those creatures in that cave horror movie she'd recently watched.

She hadn't seen any more of his kind in all the walking they'd done, but there were plenty of places others like him could be hiding in all the many forks they'd passed.

She had plenty of time to ponder these questions, as Jotaha

remained mostly silent during their long, seemingly endless journey through tunnel after tunnel. The mysteries could only keep her distracted for so long. Eventually, her strength flagged and she started stumbling, every muscle in her body aching from a lack of rest, damage, and walking forever in the wake of Jotaha, who seemed to possess endless stamina.

Probably noting her fatigue, he led her to another cave with a higher ceiling that he could stand tall in. This cave contained more of the glow stones, a fact she discovered when he used his combat knife to push them together into a ring that started glowing as soon as one stone came near another. Within minutes, he had a warm, light ring glowing, and had dropped his pack to withdraw his mug and waterskin.

After seeing that she was fed and hydrated, Jotaha unwrapped the two furs she'd used and rolled them out near the stone ring. The cave wasn't spacious enough for him to place his fur anywhere else but right beside her two.

She would have to lay right next to this alien stranger. The idea should have made her nervous at the very least. He would be very close to her while she slept. She'd be easily within reach of his hands—his body. Instead of horrifying her, the thought intrigued her, and made her feel warmth in a place she'd tried for so long to pretend was dead.

There was no way she was perving on her lizardman alien protector. That would be a step too far, wouldn't it? Her life had changed so much in a time frame she couldn't even pinpoint because she hadn't seen the sun for so long. But had she changed so much that she could consider being with an alien without a macabre undertone of horror to the idea? Had she changed so much that she could consider such things and experience an actual tingling between her legs, and a flutter of anticipation in her stomach, instead of a sense of fear and dread?

Her unwelcome and unexpected feelings of attraction to

Jotaha turned out to be irrelevant, as he didn't touch her at all while lying beside her. She would know, because she couldn't sleep and ended up just lying there listening to his soft, steady breathing, wondering if he would make a move on her. His deliciously masculine scent surrounded her, reminding her that for all his inhuman traits, there was still much about him that resembled a desirable human male.

She had the unnerving realization that her feelings towards Jotaha had experienced a radical shift the moment he buried his blade in the bat-cat monster trying to kill her. He'd come to her rescue. A knight in shining armor—literally—was a tough thing for a girl to resist. Even when she wanted to.

18

His drahi's scent was driving him crazy with need. The only thing keeping him from reaching for her when her body heat was so close to him as they lay beside each other was the grim reminder of the cost of his salavik everting while the seal remained active. If he ever wanted to mate successfully with his drahi, he could not afford to risk his mating spine in such a reckless way.

The seal was a lifetime commitment for a male yan-kanat. If he followed through the sata-drahi'at with his drahi, then he would never be able to evert for another female. Even on the rare chance that a yan-kanat male stopped loving his mate, he would always cherish her and be gentle with her, because she would be the only mate he'd ever have after the sealing.

There were rare occasions where a drahi refused to be marked by the male Seta Zul chose for her. She could not be forced. The seal would not brand her if she rejected it and turned away from her male. For a male who could not convince his drahi to accept his seal, all yan-kanat would know he was a failure. In that event, the blood of Seta Zul could be removed safely by Seta Zul's priests, allowing the male to seek solace in the arms of another lover, but neither the male nor the female who rejected her role as drahi would ever produce nestlings after that. Seta Zul did not appreciate her will being denied.

When he'd requested the seal so that he could start working on a family, he'd had no fear that Farona would reject his claim and his mark. She would have been right there with him, gladly entering into the sata-drahi'at with the same meditative chants and serene calm with which she approached all their lovemaking. It hadn't even occurred to him that he might have to win the affection of his drahi before claiming her.

Now, he faced a difficult challenge. He had been so frustrated and angry about the fact that he had been sent a nixir drahi that he hadn't thought about whether she would even accept him as her mate until he started them on the path home. Though concern over her safety remained at the forefront of his mind, he could not keep it from straying to thoughts of what would happen once her safety was assured in the skilev.

Sarah, thus far, had shown no interest in his naked form. He couldn't be certain if it was even a nixir custom for a female to study the lines of her future mate's body to ensure that he would be a good partner for her and provide strong nestlings that she would not have to fear losing before they had even left the nest.

Jotaha was at the peak of his strength and vigor. He had trained for his role for the majority of his life, ever since he was taken out of the nest to become a jotah—guardian in training. He was far stronger than any of his peers, and even most males of the yan-kanat, barring the other Jotaha who shared his training and bond with the chanu zayul.

Yet she had not shown much interest in his body, hardened by muscle and honed by his physical prowess. He knew his shape was not significantly different from the males of her species, though his size exceeded theirs, and he was much stronger than they were.

His height had been an issue that had almost altered his path when he'd suddenly hit a growth spurt during training, and he'd nearly been switched to a sentil path. If he hadn't learned to fight in a crouch or crawl almost as rapidly as he ran, he would not have been allowed to enter the initiation room at all. Even then, if the chanu zayul had rejected him, he would be hunting snow stalkers and visloga and other deadly predators in the mountains or in the deserts of the barrens, instead of the far deadlier nixirs in the urvaka.

Despite growing to the height of a sentil hunter rather than remaining the shorter height of the typical Jotaha, he didn't think his size alone would be enough to distress his drahi. It was more likely that it was their differences that kept her from seeing him as a male. When he could speak to her and truly explain things, and understand her words in return, perhaps he could make her see that they were more compatible than she might believe.

Until then, he had to rein in his growing desire for his soft, warm drahi. He tried to dredge up his initial resentment about her being chosen by his seal, just to cool his ardor. The problem was that the more time he spent with her and saw how courageous and determined she was to survive the challenges that were thrown at her, the more he respected her. As he learned to respect her, he saw her as more than simply a nixir, a female of the species that had been so arrogant as to slay even one of the Ajda in their never-ending quest for power.

As his respect for Sarah grew, so did his attachment to her. He was not certain he would ever love her as he did Farona, but he knew that he could learn to care about her, and he had no problem even now with desiring her. His concern for her safety told him that his feelings for her had already shifted, growing stronger with each moment he spent in her company. He needed her to be safe, and thus he pushed them both harder than they should be pushing to get her out of the urvaka and back to the skilev.

They were wounded and tired, and Jotaha's chanu zayul were weakened by the loss of some of their number, so they weren't able to heal him as quickly as they normally did. The fact that they would soon be approaching maturity meant they were stronger than when he'd first accepted them into his body, but it also meant they were slowly withdrawing their tendrils from his nervous system in preparation to leave him, though there was still time before that happened.

He could handle the pain he currently felt, and had trained with sentils who were not blessed by chanu zayul to soothe and heal their wounds, so had taken the same punishment to his body as they did to harden him. It was Sarah's suffering that concerned him the most, even while he pushed to get them home. He knew they couldn't survive another attack from the twisted nixirs while he was in a diminished state. Though the urvak zayul had not sent word of any more creatures approaching the boundary, the nixirs had proven they could move with a purpose through the urvaka now, sniffing out the trail Jotaha and Sarah left behind, in order to find their own way through.

This was a complication he must tell the elders as soon as possible. He could not delay in bringing this news back to the temple, even if he was willing to risk Sarah's health and safety. Though he suspected the zayul residing within the temple priest who spoke for the urvaka would give him some knowledge of what had taken place here, that priest would need Jotaha's combat perspective to truly understand the message the zayul sent.

The fact that nixirs only rarely found their way through the urvaka and were able to be led astray by the zayul was a huge boon for the yan-kanat. If these new nixirs were capable of defeating those weaknesses of theirs, then more than one

Jotaha might need to patrol each hunting ground to safely defeat them. This could spread the chanu zayul too thin. He'd lost four of them already, though eight more remained within him. Lower numbers meant they were weaker and provided less advantages. It also made it more difficult for him to "hear" the hivemind speaking to him through their chanu zayul.

This new development could change the way they had dealt with the nixir invaders since they first came to Theia, escaping their persecution on Gaia. The urvaka had been Theia's ribs, protecting her heart—their home—for thousands upon thousands of passings. The Ajda had either left this world, or allowed their physical bodies to go dormant like Seta Zul. They would not serve as the guardians they had in the past. Theia's body and their own bodies were their final gift to the yan-kanat before most of them left to seek a new home for themselves to escape the wrath of Theia's brethren.

It was up to the yan-kanat to defend themselves now, and they had been given enough gifts to do so. They had simply grown too complacent, secure in the knowledge that the nixirs would never figure out how to successfully navigate the urvaka. Even their clever machinery could not function for long after crossing the boundary, which forced them to send their warriors instead.

Nixirs had failed all their invasion attempts, even as elders like Arokiv infiltrated their societies and began to manipulate their leaders. This repeated failure was why they'd finally agreed to a treaty, and promised never to cross the boundary. It was a promise the nixirs, unsurprisingly, broke far too often, though their leaders always swore the trespassers were rogue elements that were unsanctioned by their governments.

Jotaha led his drahi through the tunnels of the urvaka, growing more concerned as her exhaustion was apparent in her long silences, broken only by her labored breathing. He considered that the enmity between nixirs and yan-kanat would soon come to a head. If the nixirs attempted to claim Theia, as they had Gaia, then every last yan-kanat would die to defend it.

There were also some yan-kanat who wanted to return the favor and invade Gaia to take back what was rightfully theirs. The elders tried to quash such rumblings, knowing that the danger the nixirs posed with their clever, twisted minds had only grown over the generations. Their tools and weapons had become more advanced, even as Gaia lost what magic the Ajda had given the ancient body after they abandoned it, condemning the nixirs to a world bound by physical laws they were unable to alter on their own.

The nixirs had, unfortunately, only risen to the challenges posed by those new boundaries. They managed to create things of such wonder—without the use of the magic of the Ajda—that most yan-kanat didn't believe in the stories when those who traveled to the nixir world returned with tales of them.

Jotaha believed. As much as he despised most nixirs, he did not dare to underestimate them, and the new twisted nixirs were proof that he couldn't. None of them could. If there was an obstacle in their way, the nixirs always seemed to find a way around it—or through it—given enough time.

He need only look at what Sarah had gone through and survived, armed with nothing but her own wits, to see how determined the nixir mind was. It never gave up fighting, even when the battle seemed lost. That relentlessness had been so effective that it had chased a physically more imposing species from Gaia, leaving the yan-kanat relying on the generosity of the Ajda to save them.

There was much the yan-kanat could learn from the nixirs, and Jotaha realized that his people might have made a mistake in treating the rare nixir females allowed on Theia to become drahi like pampered pets, instead of as teachers and guides. Perhaps Seta Zul had chosen a nixir for his mate because the yan-kanat needed more ruthlessness in their bloodlines and more nixir knowledge in their heads. It was possible they should be interbreeding more often with their enemy to increase the cunning and deviousness of their own people, not avoiding the nixirs as much as possible. If that was Seta Zul's ultimate plan, then he could not argue with the logic of it.

Whatever Seta Zul's reasons for choosing Sarah for him might be, he could no longer resent them. With too much time to think about the situation while he led her safely out of the urvaka, he came to realizations that made him uncomfortable. He had to admit that the nixirs ultimately had an advantage, and that only a matter of time separated them from a confrontation that could prove deadly—or beneficial.

Sarah would become his new cipher, his window into the alien mind of the nixirs, who were never content to leave the world the way they found it. He would learn from her what made the nixirs the way they were, and why they were so determined to gain the power of the titans that had spawned their creators. If he could only understand how his enemies thought, then perhaps he could be the one to lead his people back to Gaia, either in peace—or armed with the same weapons the nixirs possessed.

He would bend himself to the task of earning Sarah's affection so she would willingly accept his seal. If they were blessed with nestlings, then he wanted her to be loyal to him and his people, because her nestlings and their nestlings would probably end up going to war with the nixirs if things didn't change. He didn't want to end up torn between his duty to his mate and his duty to his people, so he had a challenging task ahead of him.

Considering that, it was odd that he felt so much anticipation.

19

Sarah followed Jotaha without knowing where he was leading her, mostly because she had no other options. Of course, even if new options presented themselves, nothing short of a teleportation device that would deposit her back in her living room could convince her to leave Jotaha at the moment. She couldn't bring herself to face the darkness alone again. Not even if the glow beetles lit her way through the seemingly endless maze of caves and tunnels.

In fact, even if she could return to her townhome, she wasn't certain she would take that opportunity. She couldn't imagine what she would do after that. With Beth's abandonment, she'd lost the last person in the world she trusted and counted on. It didn't take much reflection to realize that Beth had taken advantage of her isolation and introversion. Sarah had no other close friends, and her co-workers were mostly introverts like herself.

She certainly couldn't turn to her parents. They had tried to re-establish contact with her after she'd given Shayla up for adoption, but she'd told them in less-than-polite terms that she never wanted to speak to them again. Even the traumatic things she'd been through wouldn't change that.

That meant that she'd end up sitting alone in her newly purchased townhome, in a newly built development, surrounded by strangers living lives completely ignorant of what lay beneath their comfortable and civilized world. She couldn't tell anyone what she had seen. No one would believe her, except for those who already knew that her stories were real. Those people probably wouldn't let her live long enough to convince anyone else.

As much as she wanted to deny it, she couldn't return to the life she'd left behind when she'd made the fateful decision to follow Beth on this venture. She knew too much, and couldn't bury that knowledge and slip back into blissful ignorance.

She looked up from the ground beneath her feet to see Jotaha's back a few feet in front of her, leading the way through the tunnels, his body glowing softly beneath his armor.

There was no way she could walk away from the mystery he presented, not without answers to so many questions she couldn't ask him yet. Questions she may never be able to ask him.

She'd remained mostly silent on their journey through the tunnels, even when they stopped for a rest in the larger caves that had heat stones in them, like little campsites. Her throat still hurt, though the tea Jotaha gave her helped to soothe it. Eating was still difficult, but the blood bars mashed into a disgusting paste that was easier to swallow than a granola bar.

He pulled other food from his pouches and pockets to feed them as well. Mostly the blood bars, though he did offer her a strip of meat that could have been jerky. It was clear his kind were primarily carnivorous, though the sweet bun he'd given her had been made of something that tasted more like beans than meat, so they did round out their diet with plant matter to some extent.

She had to turn everything down that wouldn't be easy to swallow, which left her eating the blood bars and wishing for a nice, cold ice cream instead to soothe her throat.

For his part, Jotaha seemed to prefer the blood bars with their squishy, chewy, gristly bits to the sweeter stuff.

They rested three times, sleeping for short stints that didn't feel nearly long enough to Sarah, but probably were significant, since her body ached a little less each time, despite the pace he had them moving through the tunnels. She had no idea how long they had been traveling since they'd left the first campsite, but Jotaha had filled his waterskin a half dozen times at various water sources within the caves, the last being a small river that rushed through a cave. The water that came from that was icy, and as clean and fresh as bottled water, lacking the heavy mineral flavor of the other fast drips and natural wall fountains where Jotaha had filled the skin.

Following that river led them through a sloping tunnel, the water rushing past them down into the depths they'd just left. The temperature steadily grew colder as they moved closer to some surface that Sarah didn't think was the desert she'd left behind when she'd entered the wildcat mine. When she began to see actual daylight spilling downwards from an exit ahead of them, her steps sped up, until she was so close to Jotaha that she was practically walking on his heels.

He increased his speed at her eagerness, perhaps eager to stand up straight himself, since much of their journey had seen him forced to hunch somewhat due to his height. He'd still moved much faster than her, despite his burdens and his wounds, though he'd never let her fall too far behind him.

That first step out of the cave system and into a bright, sunny day was glorious—and blinding. As Jotaha's body stopped blocking the exit, Sarah followed him out. Her boots crunched on a snowy ground, her eyes squinted against the sunlight. She held one hand up in front of her to shade her eyes until they adjusted.

It was a pity she'd lost her sunglasses in the mines. She could have used them now, though there had been a time when she'd worried she would never see the light of day again. While she was blinking, her eyes watering and blurry, she felt the weight of a heavy fur settle on her shoulders. Jotaha had unwrapped one of the furs and put it on her to keep her warm. It was the one he must have slept on, because his scent still clung to the soft fur that surrounded her. She clutched the edges of the fur at her neck with one hand, finally lowering the other as she glanced his way.

"Thank you," she said, hoping her tone and body language was enough to let him know she was grateful he'd thought of the temperature change and had considered her comfort.

She watched in surprise as he made his stone dagger glow, then wrapped it in a small length of fur and tucked it into his armor. She wondered how it put out heat to keep him warm without somehow burning the fur. She would have loved to ask him how the glow stones worked, but realized the futility of such attempts at complex communication. It would be too frustrating for them both. At least for now.

Jotaha took her arm to guide her forward. It was clear that he didn't want to linger in this area long. She could understand why, since the cold breeze chafed her cheeks and slipped under the fur like a knife.

Her eyes soon adjusted to the sunlight, and she saw that Jotaha led her down a narrow foot path paved with flat stone steps, his hold on her arm keeping her from slipping.

The breeze remained chilly, though the air grew drier as they descended the slope of a mountain. He didn't give her the time to stop and look around, and she wasn't sure if it was because she had started shivering even with the fur or if it had to do with him being cold. If he was, he didn't show any sign of discomfort. Then again, he almost always seemed stoic.

Her prolonged silence had not made him more talkative, either. If anything, the less she said, the less he tried to speak to her, communicating with her only through gestures as they'd traveled. She'd learned to read some of his body language, but even that changed as they moved through the tunnels in near complete silence. She feared that he had changed his mind about trying to communicate with her unless he had to. His head spines remained flat, his tail steady, his expression almost always inscrutable and unchanging. There was very little change in his demeanor to allow her to gauge his mood.

It figured that she would be growing more interested in her alien companion, and he was growing less interested in talking to her, seeming to distance himself from her.

The stone path led down to a desert valley, and it was only there that the chilly air warmed enough so that it no longer nipped at her cheeks. It was still cooler than the usual Arizona desert during the day, but not to the point where she was shivering.

The desert, though, did not look like the one she had left behind when she entered the mines. Jotaha gave her little time to study the landscape, determined to lead her somewhere without a tourist stop. Instead of resisting his grip, she let him set the pace, which was steady but seemed to take into account her shorter legs and lower stamina.

The path disappeared as they entered the valley, which was more like a dried mud basin. Cracks crazed the ground as far as the eye could see as the sun blazed down on them from a sky so washed out it was nearly gray. Giant, roughly spherical stones littered the valley like barnacle encrusted cannonballs. Occasionally, they passed a cluster of these spheres, and Jotaha seemed to be using them as landmarks, since there were no recognizable paths that he could be following.

After what felt like hours of walking, and probably was, based on the sun's movement across the leaden sky, they rounded another cluster of stone spheres and came upon one that had a door sized chunk cut off of one side of it, revealing a geode the size of a small cabin.

Just as she was realizing that all the massive round stones were probably impossibly giant geodes, a lizard man stepped out of the hole in the open one.

He was as tall and wide as Jotaha, and looked just as scary, especially with his head spines fully erect and his lips pulled back to reveal his sharp teeth. His green eyes had the same slit pupils as Jotaha's, and they were narrowed in a glare, fixed directly on her. His hand tightened around the long spear he held as his snarl deepened. The setting sunlight sparked off gold and silver rings on his head spines, and revealed a slight iridescence to his green scales that Jotaha's didn't seem to have.

He wore lighter armor than Jotaha. His leathers were not lacquered or layered, but studded and supple. She spotted no less than three daggers strapped to his huge body.

He fired off rapid speech to Jotaha, who responded in the same rapid-fire manner. The only words she recognized where "draw-he" and "niche-ear" but whatever Jotaha's answer was to the other lizardman's question, it caused a noticeable reaction.

The stranger's expression softened with a moment of what had to be shock, his head spines dipping, then it hardened again as he gestured to Sarah, snarling as he spoke in a low, angry growl to Jotaha.

Jotaha tugged her behind him, then released her arm. She saw his hand drop so that his fingers hovered just above the combat knife sheathed on his thigh. His shoulders squared and his head spines rose to stand fully erect. His tail whipped in short, sharp jerks as he faced off against the other lizardman, the end of it coming just short of slapping her calves as she stood uncertainly behind him.

She wasn't completely clueless, despite her inability to understand their speech. Introductions were clearly not going well. The other lizardman did not like her, and was not happy about Jotaha bringing her around.

She had no idea what she'd done to offend. Maybe it was the tangled and filthy mat of hair on her head or her dirty face, but she highly doubted it was her disheveled appearance that bothered the scaled alien. He probably had no concept of how a civilized human was supposed to look.

This wasn't Earth. She had to admit that now, even if the gigantic geode-strewn landscape had not been enough to convince her. Somehow, she hadn't just met an alien living underground on Earth. She'd instead entered some kind of parallel dimension, which explained the strange seam in the ground that had completely disappeared and turned into an impassable wall after she crossed over it.

The low, growling tones of the two aliens—or was she the alien—increased in volume as their tension rose. Then Jotaha's scales started to glow, and the other alien fell silent. After a long, unnerving moment of silence, the other alien slowly backed away from Jotaha, heading towards his geode house.

The tension between the two males—if they were even male—slowly dissipated as Jotaha turned to draw her back to his side. His spines remained erect and his body still glowed, but the other alien had flattened his spines and lowered his spear. His broad shoulders curved inward as if submitting to Jotaha as he tilted his head slightly, almost like he was exposing his neck. His tail hung motionless and pulled close to his body when he turned to the side and gestured for Jotaha to enter the geode.

Sarah really didn't want to go into that crystal-laden place, despite how beautiful it looked. The last thing she wanted was to be trapped inside a tight space with an alien who still shot hostile glares her way when Jotaha passed him, tugging Sarah behind him, his strong grip circled around her wrist.

The inside of the geode was exactly what she would have expected, though the floor beneath her feet had been cleared of crystal clusters, leaving a highly shined crystalline floor behind. Actual wax candles brightened the cave-like interior, the light reflecting off the myriad of crystals surrounding them. They lent a soft herbal scent to the air as their flames flickered when she and Jotaha passed.

Pouches and bundles and stone or clay jars and glass containers packed shelves that had been cleverly built into the clusters of sparkling crystal. Short swords and a selection of spears, their shafts bound by leather grips stained black with blood, hung on the walls, integrated among the crystal clusters. The geode looked like it had been cleared with as much restraint as possible. In one corner of the geode cave, the clusters formed an alcove, where she spotted the edge of a wooden frame, topped by what might be a mattress, based on the furs and woven blankets that spilled over the edge. Large jugs that came to her mid-thigh sat on the ground near the storage shelves. The lid of one sat propped against it, instead of atop it, revealing what appeared to be clean water inside the jug.

The strange lizardman had followed them into the geode, and now stood at the door. He'd crossed his arms over his chest and his shoulders were squared again, as if he didn't like to be in a submissive stance. He'd propped his spear against a cluster of the clear crystals at the entrance, so at least he wasn't armed, but he still looked more than threatening as he said something to Jotaha.

To her surprise, Jotaha responded by dropping his pack off his shoulder, then he unhooked the clip that held his belt on. She shifted her attention from the stranger to Jotaha, and saw him lower the belt with all its pouches to the floor. He then began to work on the laces that held his greaves on.

Alarm filled her as Jotaha stripped off his lower armor under the watchful gaze of the stranger alien. She didn't even want to know what was going on here—or about to go on. Was she to be witness to, or worse, participate in, an alien orgy?

Jotaha's greaves came off, exposing the glowing orange tattoo that covered his pelvic area. His blue glow had faded when he'd started stripping, so the orange light seemed even brighter against his dark green scales.

Sarah had avoided looking closely at his tattoo out of a desire to not get caught staring at an alien's private parts, but the stranger alien was not so deterred, apparently. He took several steps closer to Jotaha, making Sarah wonder if she should be stepping out to give them some privacy.

She also wondered why that made her feel jealous, and far more disappointed than she should be at the thought that maybe Jotaha already had a partner. Maybe Jotaha wasn't male at all, and this was her mate, and Sarah had been attracted to a female for the first time in her life. The thought didn't do anything to change her strange attraction to Jotaha.

"Vauteg!" the stranger said. "Ver-os troka!" Since he spoke slowly, though forcefully, she could distinguish word patterns in the sounds, but still had no idea what he was saying.

"Os troka," Jotaha answered, one hand gesturing to his groin and the remarkable glowing tattoo.

It had a really nice design, with thick lines that curved around and around inside the outer circle in a maze pattern. Wherever their starting and end points were, the lines all terminated in tapered tips.

The stranger spoke rapidly again, and again, the only patterns she could make out from his speech was draw-he and niche-ear, and one other pattern that was repeated multiple times as Jotaha responded and they fell into a conversation. Set-ah Zool.

To her relief, the stranger suddenly stopped speaking and

left the geode altogether, after waving his hand towards the shelves with a final burst of his language towards Jotaha. He didn't sound happy, but he didn't look her way again, almost like he was now ignoring her presence. Jotaha bent to collect his greaves and started lacing them back on again as Sarah glanced his way. He looked up from his task and met her eyes. His fingers stopped working the laces and he slowly pulled his greaves off again, once again exposing the tattoo. His gaze never left her face.

She couldn't stop herself, human curiosity as strong as any cat's. Her gaze dipped to his groin, and she saw the tattoo shift with the scales beneath it. A slit appeared in the scales as the tattoo glowed brighter. Jotaha hissed as if in pain, but Sarah was too distracted by the bulging beneath that slit. If he was human, that would unmistakably be the ridge of an impressive erection she spotted twitching beneath his scales. It pressed on the slit, causing it to become slightly visible, even under the increasing glow of the tattoo.

She quickly turned her back, gasping at the realization of what she was seeing. Of course, she'd already considered the idea that he had internal genitalia, which was why she suspected he could still be a male, despite not having any visible penis. It was just unnerving to have it confirmed, even though she had to admit that it was what she had hoped, now that she could admit that she did find him attractive.

She had been gawking at him like an idiot, and she hoped he didn't take offense. He'd hissed, and though it had sounded like pain, it might have been anger at her staring so openly.

That didn't mean the other alien wasn't still his partner. She might be in the way of them reuniting, which was why his erection was showing beneath his scales now, when it hadn't before. He was probably eager to be with his mate, and she was hanging around like a third wheel. She should have left as soon as she saw him stripping, even if it would have meant squeezing past the other alien who clearly didn't like her.

Maybe that other alien was jealous of her being with their mate. Well, now that the other alien wasn't blocking the exit, she could leave the geode and give Jotaha and his partner privacy. She rushed towards the exit, freezing at the opening when he called her name, his tone harsh, gravelly. Maybe he was angry, but she couldn't tell if that was what put such hardness and roughness in his voice.

Then he said "vauteg" like it was a curse. She'd heard both aliens say it now, and started to think it was.

20

Nothing had gone as Jotaha had hoped it would. Sentil Kevos' initial reaction to the sight of Sarah was understandable. As the last line of defense, the sentils who patrolled the barrens had been given the same training as the jotah when it came to the nixir enemy. Though Kevos had never seen a live nixir, he knew enough about their appearance to instantly recognize what Sarah was.

Yet, Jotaha had foolishly believed Kevos would change his demeanor when he understood that Sarah was Jotaha's drahi. Instead, Kevos' hostility towards Sarah had not faded. It had expanded to include Jotaha, despite their previous friendship. Kevos' menacing behavior had come as a big surprise. No sentil would dream of confronting a Jotaha with aggression. He was the highest ranking of all yan-kanat guardians, and the chanu zayul gave him a distinct advantage over the sentil, even as wounded and depleted as they were in Jotaha.

Kevos had backed off when Jotaha reminded him of his place, and had allowed them into the outpost to refill his supplies for the last leg of the journey to the skilev, but he had still been insistent upon seeing the seal for himself. As if Jotaha was somehow lying in order to smuggle a nixir back to the skilev. To what end, Kevos wouldn't speculate, but he hadn't hesitated to remind Jotaha about the duplicity and cunning of nixirs. Historical tales told of the enemy using their own females and nestlings to sneak into yan-kanat strongholds and poison their water supplies or sabotage their food stores during a siege, because the yan-kanat had been hesitant about harming females and nestlings, even nixir ones. All yan-kanat knew that a nixir could offer peace in one hand, while concealing a dagger in the other.

The way Kevos still glared at Sarah made Jotaha eager to leave this outpost as soon as possible. He didn't think Kevos would dare to harm her, but it was clear that the enmity remained strong. Knowing that Seta Zul herself had chosen Sarah for Jotaha didn't seem to be enough to wipe away Kevos' hostility. Although he had left them alone after verifying the seal.

Then Sarah had shown an interest in his seal, her gaze lowering to study it, causing an instant and painful response from his salavik. With her scent constantly surrounding him for four sun cycles now, he felt as if it had become a part of him, and his body was awakening and eager to claim his mate.

Sarah, though, had dismissed him, turning her back upon him. Then she'd rushed to leave the outpost, only stopping at the exit when he called her name, desperate to keep her from storming outside where she would have to face Kevos.

He wasn't angry at her. Stung by her rejection, maybe, but she had every right to be insulted by his open display of lust. He had not even formally asked her to perform the sata-drahi'at with him. Giving her his mating gift didn't count, since she hadn't understood its purpose.

He was angry at himself. First, for not realizing that the sentils could still hold onto lingering hostility, even when they knew Sarah's role, and then, for allowing Sarah to see his loss of control. It had not sent a comforting message to her. Seta Zul's seal was to protect females from overeager males who showed no patience in claiming their mates. It was also to keep them from discarding those females when they were no longer new and exciting to the males. The goddess's name, Heart Wound, spoke of her own legendary pain, and explained why she had created the seal to bind her mortal subjects to their mates so they would never experience the same pain.

Though he had no intention of losing his honor in claiming Sarah, he could understand now how it would be difficult to control himself if he was not sealed.

Sarah had paused at the exit, babbling in her language, her tone distressed as she refused to turn around to face him. By the time he had his greaves fully in place again, he had calmed his salavik, and it no longer pressed against his sealed slit, causing the heat of the seal to rise to a painful level.

He wished he understood even a fraction of what she was saying, and wished even more that he could respond in a way that would reassure her that he would not press himself upon her without her agreement.

He also wished he could completely trust Kevos enough to allow Sarah to rest at the outpost, before setting out for the last leg of their journey to the skilev. He now suspected introducing Sarah to the people of his skilev would be far more exhausting than he'd planned. They should not hold the same degree of enmity towards the nixirs, since they were not tasked with guarding against the invaders, but Kevos' unexpected reaction to Sarah had shown that Jotaha could take nothing for granted.

She only turned around to look at him when he approached her. Her cheeks were a bright red color beneath the dirt that smudged her soft skin.

"I'm sorry. I shouldn't have been so nosy. I swear I'm not a perv."

She was still babbling incomprehensibly, but her eyes were

not filled with the hard gleam of outrage at his dishonorable behavior. Though she would not directly meet his eyes, her gaze shifting to the side as her cheeks grew ever brighter with the strange reddish tone, her relaxed body revealed that she did not see him as a direct threat. That, at least, gave him some relief. He hadn't scared her away. She still seemed to trust him.

He gestured towards his pack, then towards the shelves, not bothering to explain his intent in words. Her gaze followed the direction of his movements. Though her eyes were still clouded with confusion, it was enough to stop her from talking in her rapid, nervous way. Instead, her efforts to understand his intention appeared to focus her mind. She tapped one finger on her bottom lip in a way that he had seen her do several times before as she'd tried to understand his words and gestures.

It was an affectation he found increasingly appealing. A small, nixir gesture that he had never seen a yan-kanat make while in thought.

Seeing that he had her attention on something more important than his previous, overeager behavior, he left her side to collect his pack and belt, then carried them to the shelves, eyeing the items stored there. As he selected a bundle of kirev cakes, wrapped in coarse woven fabric, he heard a drawn out sound from Sarah.

"Ooooh." She followed it with, "Duh! We need to restock. This is probably some kind of general store type place. The proprietor isn't really big on customer service, is he?"

He'd paused to hear her words, but finally had to accept that nothing she said made any kind of sense to him. Still, she had apparently figured out his intent, because she joined him at the shelves after setting aside the fur she'd worn around her shoulders since he'd placed it there. She'd hung it on one of the crystal spears with a nonchalance that would make most yan-kanat wince. Legend had it that the crystal spheres were formed from drops of Theia's blood that were shed when Bal

Goro slayed her to create this world for the yan-kanat. The crystals within each drop were treated with reverence, and even in creating these outposts, builders were careful not to disturb too many of them.

Still, he could not expect a nixir to understand this world, as the yan-kanat did not allow their kind to visit it freely. If nixirs made it this far into the barrens, they would be hunted and killed without hesitation or remorse.

Sarah took the bundle he handed her and bent to put it in his pack. He was pleased to see that she understood what they were doing even without words. He selected a full pouch of xirak to refill their depleted supply of it. When he handed it to her, he saw her lift it to her nose, take a cautious whiff, then bare her teeth in an expression he'd come to associate with her appreciation. After that, she added it to his pack.

He did not want to take much, as they only had one more night cycle to walk before they reached the edge of land that surrounded the skilev. It was a pity the sentils rarely used mounts, because they drew the attention of large predators to the hunter's outposts. A pair of rituks would get them to the skilev much faster.

At least once there, they would have transportation to the temple, which was the first stop he would need to make with his new drahi.

He added one more bundle to the pack, and Sarah had shown interest when she'd sniffed the pouch of dried berries from the anetaak plant. Along with ane sap taken from certain trees, the berries were used to give sweetness to the flavor of things. Eaten alone, they were too sweet for Jotaha's taste, but Sarah had seemed to relish the sweet pastry he'd given her, so he thought she might also enjoy the treat of the berries themselves.

He'd been pleased that he'd kept Sarah's zayul, the hongree, well sated. They had not growled in anger since he'd led her from his campsite and began the dangerous journey out of the urvaka. He intended to keep her hon-gree content as long as it took for them to reach maturity and leave her. He hoped she would not need to acquire more at that point, but figured Seta Zul would not have chosen a drahi for him who needed something in order to survive or thrive that could not be found on this world.

After filling his vandiz skin, they were as supplied as they needed to be for one more night in the barrens. There was a campsite within a few sandfalls' trek from this outpost. They would rest there for only four sandfalls, before moving on. He was eager to get home, and even more eager to get Sarah to the elder priests so one of the healers among them could see to her health and comfort. She had been through an ordeal, and the marks on her body were turning more appalling colors with each cycle that passed. At least they had faded somewhat, no longer as dark as they had been, but they were still turning colors of sickly green and yellow that did not look natural for a nixir. In contrast, the rest of her skin had only grown paler with each passing cycle, and he didn't think that was natural either.

He hated to push her so hard, and suspected she needed more rest than he was letting her take, but he hadn't felt that she was safe in the urvaka when he was still recovering and could not protect her as readily if more of the twisted nixir crossed the boundary. Now, he feared she might not be as safe in the barrens as he'd hoped. Even if Kevos would never harm her directly, there was no guarantee he or any other sentil would come to her aid if a barren stalker attacked their camp and managed to overwhelm Jotaha.

Jotaha had never felt this kind of distrust for his fellow yankanat before, and he wondered if this was the way nixirs lived every cycle of their lives, always hesitant to turn their backs on the ones they should be able to trust the most.

Sarah rose to her feet as he finished refilling the vandiz. He slung the skin from his belt, then reached for the pack. She shook her head and shouldered it herself, grunting a bit as the weight of it settled on her back.

"No, your shoulder is still hurting you. I can tell by how you've been favoring that side. I can carry this."

He wanted to demand she give him the pack, knowing that her back was still healing from the slashes of the twisted nixir. At the same time, he could now better understand her mistrust of him. Though he would never have allowed a female yankanat to shoulder such a burden, he could tell that Sarah needed to have control of the supplies to make herself feel safer. Perhaps the pack itself covering her back even gave her a feeling of protection, in addition to knowing she had control of the food to continue her journey.

She also knew he kept his extra darts and poison in there, and no doubt wanted that additional protection. It pained him that she still didn't trust him, but his experience with Kevos made him realize what it must be like to be uncertain of your own allies all the time. For the first time in his life, he pitied the nixirs for their back-stabbing natures.

Strangely enough, he didn't mistrust Sarah. He didn't think she would attack him or betray him. Part of that was because Seta Zul would not have chosen her for him if she were capable of betraying him so readily. But another part of him had come to admire Sarah. Her tenacity did not come from a life lived by taking advantage of the unwary. She did not complain when driven at a hard pace, she fought back only when feeling threatened, and she cooperated when she felt safe. She might be nixir, but she was not a monster. He understood that now.

The revelation that not all nixirs were the same as the violent and aggressive enemies he'd fought in the urvaka was an uncomfortable one, though he was grateful Sarah was different. Things would be much harder if she was like all the others.

Or perhaps they were not all the same, and some of the lives he'd taken had belonged to nixirs like Sarah.

He pushed aside that thought. It did no good now to reflect upon the nature of his enemies. The others had come to the urvaka with evil intent, breaking a treaty their own leaders had agreed to, fully understanding the consequences. He had simply acted as the hand of yan-kanat justice, to show the nixirs what their perfidy would gain them.

He would not allow himself to dwell on the question of why Sarah herself had broken the treaty. He told himself it was only because Seta Zul had willed it.

21

Sarah still felt the burn of her embarrassment as she helped Jotaha fill his pack, and distracted herself from the awkward encounter by sniffing the food items. She recognized two of them, but was pleasantly surprised by the last pouch. It smelled delightfully sweet with a hint of fruitiness. She couldn't tell what kind of fruit, but there was something fructose-scented in that pouch. Her mouth watered at the thought of it, even as her stomach had protested at the iron scent of another bundle of blood bars. She didn't think she'd ever truly acquire a taste for them, but Jotaha seemed to love them.

If he was hoping for a sexy reunion with the other alien, he made no effort towards that end. He'd put his greaves back on and had remained in the geode with her, instead of heading out to seek the other alien. It left Sarah confused about what his intent had been. Had it been arousal that had caused that alien erection, or had it even been an erection? Maybe it had something to do with how he relieved himself. Maybe he just had to drain the little lizard.

Despite their travel in close proximity for what felt like

days, she'd never actually seen him go to the bathroom at all. He must have been relieving himself when she slept, because he was always awake before her. Perhaps that was why he understood her desire for privacy and always turned his back and gave her space when she needed to use the bathroom. Maybe he also liked to keep those things private.

They hadn't stopped for a potty break since they left the caves, though it had probably been an entire day of walking before they reached this geode. She had snacked as she walked, and she and Jotaha had both drunk from his water skin as they walked. Fortunately for her, her body appeared to be using the water she drank rather than needing to get rid of it. In fact, she was constipated as all hell, so there wasn't as much need for bathroom breaks in her case.

Jotaha also hadn't needed a bathroom break, but that had to change eventually. That was probably what she had seen then, and she shoved away the feeling of relief that he wasn't necessarily involved in a romantic relationship with the other alien.

It shouldn't matter to her, but she was finding that it did. She felt oddly possessive of Jotaha. He was *her* hero, dammit. She should get to keep him. How often did a girl get rescued by a handsome warrior? It was true that he was a little bit on the scaly side and had claws and a tail, but those attributes were ones she was growing accustomed to, and if she really was in an alien world, she had better get used to seeing lots of tails and scales. It wasn't likely there were a whole lot of humans around.

The teeth and fingerbone necklace probably meant humans weren't all as welcomed as she had been by Jotaha. So too did the reaction of the other alien when he'd caught sight of her.

Jotaha led her out of the geode after scooping up her fur and tying it onto the pack on her back. It was clear he wanted to take the pack away from her, and there was even a long pause after he tied it to the pack where she swore he was debating doing just that. Then he let it go, and she was relieved they didn't have to fight about it. The pack chafed against her scabs a bit, but they were surface cuts. Jotaha had been impaled in his shoulder. He shouldn't have to carry the pack in that condition.

He had already done so much for her, and she felt guilty accepting all his help without giving him anything in return but a burden. A burden that didn't make him popular with his fellow alien, as she found out when they left the geode to encounter the meanie again.

The other alien said something to Jotaha in a low, dark tone, and Jotaha responded in kind, his scales beginning to glow. This seemed enough to back the other guy off, but he didn't look kindly at either of them. With a final hostile glare in her direction, he turned on one heel and strode back to the geode, turning his back on them in what was so clearly an insult that she figured that kind of stuff was universal.

"Prick," she muttered, glad that the other alien wasn't Jotaha's mate. Her hero deserved better than that.

She was going to make Jotaha's life miserable by her very presence. She just knew it.

He'd turned to glance at her when she spoke, but apparently realized she was talking to herself and returned his attention to the path ahead. It wasn't actually a path, or any visible sign of a trail through the cracked desert, but he seemed to know exactly where he wanted to go, moving confidently in one direction towards a flat, distant horizon.

The sun was setting, and the leaden sky lit up with purple and orange colors, much like an Arizona sunset. Though it was far more colorful and beautiful than the washed out grayish color of daylight, it was also a reminder that they'd soon be walking in darkness. She felt the weight of exhaustion pulling at her, wishing she could collapse and sleep for a month straight, but continued in Jotaha's wake without complaint. He had somewhere he wanted to go, and she wasn't about to be left behind because she couldn't keep up. At least Jotaha could light the way with his glowing scales.

Their walk in relative silence gave her a lot of time to think about her situation. She'd taken a peek at the mountain they'd left, and it still rose like the imposing spine of a sleeping giant at their back, despite the distance they'd walked from the cave exit. The labyrinth of caves and tunnels it held would be impassable without a guide, and she didn't think Jotaha would take her back through it to the seam even if she could ask him.

Even if he did agree to guide her back to that place, she had no way of getting out of the mines the way she had entered them. She would need Jotaha's help and a whole lot of ropes, and pitons, and all the other climbing gear she knew nothing about just to scale the horizontal shaft. Assuming it hadn't collapsed completely.

Then there were the creepy bat-cat creatures they might encounter again. She couldn't handle another life-threatening battle with one of those. Two close calls with evisceration were two too many.

Then she would have to find a way out of the Arizona desert and back to the road. Her phone was long gone, probably lost in the fall. She couldn't call Beth, even if she wanted to talk to her former friend again. There were coyotes and mountain lions in that desert, not to mention rattlesnakes and scorpions and really big centipedes that came out at night. It was no friendlier to traverse without food or water than this barren desert they were walking through now.

But ultimately, the biggest barrier to her returning home was what she would do once she made it safe and sound to her townhome. She would have to face a future where she knew things—wondrous, impossible things—about the world, and no one would ever believe her if she tried to tell them about it. She would be isolated and alone—even more so than she had been before—because of that knowledge. That meant there was really no future on Earth that promised as much as the unknown one that faced her if she kept following Jotaha to his destination.

Part of that possible future could be Jotaha himself.

As she walked, she pondered all their interactions, wondering if she could trust her instincts about his body language given that he was an alien. Some things he had done made her think that the kind of things she'd been daydreaming about might not be out of her reach.

A different perspective than the two she'd already considered could be placed on the incident inside the geode, where Jotaha had taken off his greaves. He hadn't stopped to go to the bathroom yet, so if he'd had to do so at that time, then he was still holding it, which didn't seem sensible. He clearly wasn't all that friendly with the other alien, so she doubted now that they had ever been romantically involved.

No, he had been looking directly at her when his unusual alien groin bulged. Considering the possible meaning of that made her flush with a different emotion than embarrassment. It had been so long since she'd thought about having a sexual relationship with an actual person instead of a battery operated appliance. James had ruined her in that regard, just as he'd ruined her innocence, using her until she became pregnant, then casting her aside in anger when she refused to abort the baby.

She had tried a couple more times in college to have a relationship, but they had both been abject failures, mostly because of her hang ups. She feared they would throw her away her like James did—like her parents did—so she never let them get close enough to her emotionally that it would hurt her if they did. College-aged men weren't known for being patient and mature about relationships. They'd been happy for the sex, but had moved on fairly easily when they realized that it would take effort to gain anything more from the relationship.

Now, she thought about sex again, but knew it wouldn't be so simple if that was what Jotaha was interested in. This wouldn't be some fling with a frat boy, just as human as she was and perhaps even from a similar background. She couldn't even understand what Jotaha was saying, much less comprehend what kind of culture he came from. That wasn't even taking into account all the physical differences between them.

His size alone was intimidating. It was very rare that any human grew so tall, and the breadth of his shoulders and size of his muscles was proportionate for his height. That bulge of his certainly had been as well. She wasn't sure he would even fit her body in a way that was comfortable. He was huge, and the claws that tipped his fingers and the sharp teeth he had also concerned her. Would he end up hurting her by accident in a moment of passion? Or did his species bite and scratch each other as a matter of course during mating?

Since she couldn't ask these questions of him, she had no way of knowing just how dangerous a sexual relationship with Jotaha would be. That should have had her pushing the thought away, along with the fantasies that thought inspired. Instead, she found herself stealing glances at Jotaha's broad back, her gaze roving guiltily down the v-shape of his torso to take in his waist, heavy with muscle rather than fat, then down to the ridged line of his tail, swaying back and forth with each step he took.

Her fingers itched to touch his scales. She wanted to know if they were as sleek and smooth as they looked on the front, or as rough and ridged as they looked on his back and tail.

She pondered the mobile spines on his head that seemed to speak of his mood far more than his expression did. At times, those spines would lay tight against his well-formed skull. At other times, they would bristle just a bit, making him look more relaxed and at ease. She knew he was angry and filled with aggression when they stood fully erect, but still had trouble with interpreting his body language when they sat at other positions on his head.

He appealed to her, and she couldn't deny that anymore, at least not to herself. Whether she appealed to him in the same way was up in the air, and she couldn't imagine why she would. She looked terrible—filthy, hair matted, desperately in need of a hot bath and a toothbrush—yet there were hints that maybe —just maybe—he might be interested in her too.

The uncertainty gave her hope, and anxiety. Her stomach fluttered with nerves whenever she thought about just how she could eliminate that uncertainty. She didn't think she had enough courage to make an unmistakable move on him to see how he would react. The fear of rejection was too great.

22

Jotaha watched Sarah sleep on the furs he'd laid down as soon as they stopped at the campsite, which was little more than a lean-to built between two of Theia's blood drops. He bit into the fibers of his mouth cleaning brush, grinding them together in an almost unconscious sign of his anxiety. The glow of the chanu zayul still recovering inside him sparked along his scales with his concern.

Sarah did not seem to be doing well. She'd been clearly tired from the time they left the cave, but this last stretch to the campsite had seen her stumbling with exhaustion. He cursed himself for allowing her to bear the burden of the pack, even though he understood her need for that bit of security. He would not allow it again. Instead, he would furnish her with one of his belts and some pouches filled with food as well as the nixir dagger for a weapon so she would feel more prepared. It would be a far lighter burden, while still keeping her supplied to her satisfaction.

After his drahi had fallen into a deep sleep, her skin

sheened with moisture and disturbingly pale beneath the dirt that smudged her face, he'd settled on his fur beside her. He'd watched her face as it relaxed in sleep, the lines of strain and discomfort fading from her alien features as the light from the inferno stones highlighted her jutting nose, full lips, and fibrous brows, casting deep shadows on her eyes that made her face look far too similar to the nixir skulls that were on display in the temple.

After rinsing and then returning his mouth brush to its pouch in his belt, he picked through the items in his pack, withdrawing the harzek, the sitak that had a fortune in kivan—seashell currency—sewn onto it. Some of the shells he'd had specially carved for the robe had been lost in the urvaka when the garment was torn, but it hadn't mattered to him, and he understood why now. It had been made with Farona in mind. The expensive beauty of it would please her, which was why he had chosen such a treasure to present to her.

The robe was no longer an appropriate gift for his drahi. It belonged to a future that was not to be, and he couldn't even dredge up any more resentment for that fact. In his worry over Sarah's health and the way it seemed to be suddenly failing, he realized that he already thought of her as his, though he had yet to bind her to him with the seal. Sometime in the cycles since he'd found her in the urvaka, his feelings towards her had drastically changed. Now he knew he couldn't let her go, nor could he again present her with a gift intended for another.

He would have a new harzek made up, one designed specifically for his nixir mate. Something unique and special that no yan-kanat could appreciate. He studied the matted fibers atop Sarah's head, suspecting that they were not intended to be so tangled. Perhaps she would like a tool to straighten them, so that they lay sleek and flat atop her head. The shataz that had been taken from nixir lands in the past had been fond of jeweled implements they called "combs" made of precious metals that were prized by both nixirs and yan-kanat, like gold and silver. Even the Ajda coveted gold and silver, and had originally been drawn to Gaia because of her bountiful supply of it.

So it would be a gold, jeweled comb for his drahi, which would take time to have made, but then again, he needed time to learn to communicate with her. He needed her to understand what the first mating ceremony entailed so that she would come to him with full knowledge and willingness. He wanted her to choose to be his forever.

He stuffed the expensive garment back into his pack, knowing that he would be trading all the kivan for the materials to have the comb made. He would also need to add even more kivan to have it crafted by the most talented jewelry smith in his skilev. His sacrifice as Jotaha had been well rewarded, with some of the tithes paid to the temple being diverted to the guardians of Theia. Still, the harzek he planned for his Sarah would be exceedingly expensive, even for him. He could not help but think she was more than worth it and was eager to see her use his gift.

As he sat there watching her, he considered other ways to make her more comfortable. She had not demanded much in the way of hygiene products, though perhaps she had and he simply hadn't understood her, but nixirs in the past had not been known for hygiene. Granted, the other ones he had encountered in the urvaka had seemed far cleaner, despite their exertions, than he'd been told to expect when learning about nixirs and their history.

Though Sarah had been dirty when he'd found her, he'd gained the impression that it was recent dirt, as her flesh beneath the dirt had looked clean, without grime layered into the porous skin. That was yet another reason he'd believed her to be shataz, who were unusual in their hygienic practices among the normally filthy nixirs.

He had intended to teach her about proper hygiene, once they returned to the skilev, and imagined that one of the elders who communicated with the nixirs would know ways that the nixirs could clean themselves better than any other yan-kanat would. Until he could communicate with her, he had not considered it an issue, but now he was growing concerned as the moisture her body produced slicked her skin, creating streaks in the dirt that encrusted her face. Her scent was strong in that moisture. It was pleasant to him when it was fresh, but when it grew stale, he scented what he took to be sickness. It could simply be the scent of dirty nixir, but he'd never smelled the like in the others that he'd hunted.

Her breath had also changed, growing sour and pungent with each struggling gasp she'd taken in this last stretch. He'd expected her to be pleased with the anetaak berries to sweeten her mouth, but she had only eaten two of them before she'd rubbed her stomach, shaking her head as she pushed the pouch aside with her other hand. Her eyes had been pinched in the corners, her normally puffy lips thinned out and tight and surrounded by skin paler than the rest of her face.

She had refused any other food, shaking her head at his offers. She had also seemed to gag when she'd tried to drink a crock of xirak, which she had never had an issue with before. She had eventually set the crock aside, unable to continue drinking it. The most concerning thing was that she had only been able to eliminate liquid from her body for many cycles now without any solid waste, despite eating solid food. He didn't think this was normal, even for the nixirs.

It was these worries that kept his mind occupied even as the chanu zayul tried to lull him into his usual trance-like rest that allowed him to remain aware of his surroundings while he traveled.

His awareness sharpened when he heard the shift of movement on hard-packed dirt beyond the circle of light and heat cast by the inferno stones. He looked towards the direction where he'd heard the sound.

A barren stalker would be warm-blooded, like his drahi, making it easy to spot in the darkness once his inner lids were closed over his eyes. Since he only saw the shifting of shadows in the darkness, nearly the same temperature as the night air, he knew that it was not a barren stalker creeping up on this campsite.

Rage filled him as he drew his bone dagger from the sheath on his forearm, rising gracefully to his feet in near silence. Not that it mattered. The ring of warming stones lit him up like a beacon. The multiple shadows moving towards them stealthily could easily see him. They could also easily see the threat he posed.

He had fought many sentils during his training. They sparred against each other during their trials of passage, the best warriors being selected to become jotahs, and the best of those being chosen by the chanu zayul to become Jotaha. He was a better fighter than the sentils surrounding the camp, even without the help of his diminished chanu zayul. If it wasn't for Sarah's vulnerability, he would relish the thought of taking them all on at once in a vicious battle to punish them for daring to offend him like this.

They had not come here for him, and he had no doubt that they would not consider the sacrifice of a few of their number to his claws in order to keep him busy a small price to pay to dispatch the nixir invader. He could not even hate them entirely, though his rage sparked through him unchecked, adding a fierce glow to the light of the warming stones.

If he was the one on the other side of this situation, he might not be deterred by his reverence for the will of Seta Zul either. Hatred for the nixirs was strong in so many of the yan-kanat—and had been in himself, before he met Sarah. He had been naïve to think an activated seal alone would be enough to wipe away generations of anger towards the creatures that had chased the yan-kanat from Gaia and slayed an Ajda.

He was prepared for the battle when Kevos left the shadows, stepping far enough into the light that Jotaha could see him clearly.

"Just take a walk into the darkness for a single sandfall, honored Jotaha. You deserve better than this creature as a drahi. In this, Seta Zul has erred, but we will make it right and free you from such a terrible obligation."

Jotaha snarled, his head spines fully erect. "And what makes you think I want to be free of this 'obligation?'" He squared his shoulders, dropping them back as he took a fighting stance, positioning himself between Kevos and Sarah, who still slept soundly. "My drahi has already claimed my heart."

Kevos hissed, his lips peeled back from his sharp teeth. "You are blinded by the fire of Seta Zul's blood. The seal can be removed. You know this. You do not need to sacrifice in this, as you have in taking the role of Guardian of the Dark Paths." He jerked his chin towards Sarah. "This creature will sabotage our skilev and murder our people, as so many like her have done to our kind in the past."

Jotaha flexed his claws around the hilt of his dagger. His awareness spread with the aid of the preternatural senses of the chanu zayul within him. There was a half dozen other sentils surrounding them. The fact that the normally solitary hunters had come together like this showed how serious their intentions were.

"You do not know her, Sentil Kevos. She is not the nixir you have been trained to hate." He returned his focus to the foe in front of him—the leader of this blasphemy. "It is you and yours who should walk away now. You will never escape justice if you harm one fiber on the head of my drahi."

Kevos raised his chin, his head spines fully erect as his jaw tightened, muscles beneath the scales lining it twitching. He was still empty handed, failing to draw his dagger as Jotaha had, but Jotaha knew that there were others who were already armed and prepared to slit Sarah's throat while he battled Kevos and whoever else was ready to die with the sentil.

"We are prepared to make this sacrifice, as you were prepared to accept a life in the darkness of the urvaka. To protect our world and our people from the evil nixirs, we will gladly shed our own blood."

Jotaha knew that trying to convince Kevos that Sarah was not evil would be a waste of breath. There was no time for him to explain. He had to appeal to the twisted honor of the sentil. "You were not given the right of judgement, Kevos. I am taking my drahi to the temple to meet with the elders. If they decide that Seta Zul has made a mistake, then I will bow to the wisdom of *their* judgement."

He would not, but that was not something Kevos needed to know. If the elders decided Sarah would not be accepted, then he would leave and take her with him. He would go as far away as he needed to, to keep her safe. Even if that meant taking her back over the boundary to her own world.

This argument seemed to hold more sway with Kevos. For the first time since he'd stepped into the light, he looked uncertain, his head spines dipping slightly as his lips fell into a frown.

Jotaha knew he would need to push the point home, or Kevos might decide that even the elders themselves were somehow corrupted in their judgement. "They stand atop the mighty skull of the Wise One, and you would place your own will above them?" He shook his head. "This is not coming from a place of honor and sacrifice, Kevos. It is coming from a place of pride and ignorance. Your hubris will not find you a home among the Ajda in the Inferno."

"Ha'tah!" Kevos' expression shifted from determination and

hatred towards the helpless female Jotaha would do anything to protect to one of frustration.

"Do not use that name," Jotaha snarled, angry that Kevos would try to use his nest-name to call upon the friendship they had once shared. Their past closeness would not serve to change his mind, and given Kevos' hostility, recalling a name Jotaha had given up for his title was a sign of disrespect, whether intentional or not.

Kevos flinched at the censure in his tone, his shoulders rolling forward and his spines flattening in submission. He had gone too far in disrespecting Jotaha, though threatening his drahi should have been far enough. In the sentil's mind, it would not be because she was a nixir, but losing all honor by disrespecting the Guardian of the Dark Paths was enough to cut through his hatred.

Jotaha didn't bother to say anything in parting as Kevos melted back into the shadows, keeping his gaze away from Sarah. Even though he felt Kevos' departure and the retreat of the others who had followed him here, he did not relax until he heard the distant call of the horn, calling off the hunt.

Sarah would be safe, for now. He didn't think Kevos would try again, and the other sentils would scatter, leaving his territory now that he had dismissed the hunt. Still, his unexpected enmity towards Sarah, and the fact that he had been able to rally other sentils to perpetuate this blasphemous murder attempt, meant Jotaha had vastly misjudged the reaction other yan-kanat would have to Sarah. It had been a long time since a shataz had lived among his people. Several generations, in fact, but the records were there. Not one of those records had spoken of open hostility between the yan-kanat and the nixir females claimed as mates.

Had the situation grown so strained that even a soft, seemingly harmless nixir female would no longer be tolerated?

He would speak to the elders about Kevos' behavior, but

suspected the sentil would not suffer much punishment, given his motivations. The guardians and the sentinels were trained to hunt all threats to the safety and security of the yan-kanat, and the nixirs had always been the biggest of those threats. They all knew the nixirs continued to build their world of weapons and nightmarish machines beyond the boundary, and they also knew the nixirs would relish claiming Theia and the magic of the Ajda as their own. Only the urvaka kept their unstoppable armies from invading in force.

He settled back onto his fur, his gaze returning to Sarah, who had slept through the whole confrontation, much to his relief. Her silence and apparent helplessness would challenge the murderous intent of even the most hardened of the sentils. However, if she had woken up in the middle of their stand off and had behaved in a manner the sentils found threatening, they might have made a rash move against her.

As the sandfalls passed, his relief at her slumber changed to concern. He finally awakened her after several more sandfalls passed than he had intended to rest, and she was groggy and out of sorts. Her eyes looked unfocused, and given the way she clutched her stomach with a cry, he feared it was because of pain.

She curled up on her side with her knees pulled to her chest, whimpering as her hands gripped her stomach. When his panicked attempts to communicate with her failed, he tried to pick her up in his arms, determined to run the entire way back to the skilev and the healers if he had to. One of them would have to know how to help her. He feared something had happened to her hon-gree. Perhaps they were dying inside her. Maybe the lack of their growling sounds hadn't meant they were sated, but that they were weakened.

She struggled, fighting against his hold, punching with weak fists against his head and chest. It wasn't her physical attacks that made him release her, but her own panicked shouts. As soon as his hands left her, she turned onto her hands and knees and crawled a short distance away to vomit nothing but fluid onto the hard-packed dirt.

Some of that fluid was red, like blood.

23

Sarah was being carried, cradled in the inhumanly strong arms of a sexy, barbarian alien male. The only problem was that she couldn't really enjoy the experience, because she felt like she was dying. Her stomach ached like she had the worst kind of stomach flu. She wanted to vomit as each step Jotaha took jostled her unavoidably. She felt like her belly was bloated like a balloon.

She had no idea how long he carried her, but his body was glowing the entire time. His tone had shifted from panicked to soothing as he carried her rapidly towards some destination. She hoped it was a pharmacy with a really good selection of dietary fiber. Perhaps she should have been a bit more concerned about her constipation.

Despite his attempts to keep his voice soft and rhythmic in a calming manner, he was practically running while he carried her. If she felt better, she would have been impressed by his stamina and endurance. A human man could barely even pick her up, much less carry her for what felt like miles upon miles at a jogging pace. She just hoped she didn't repay him for the ride by vomiting all over his pretty armor.

His pace finally slowed after what seemed like hours, though her perception of time was all off, given that she had dozed off several times, only to be jostled awake again when he passed over a particularly uneven patch of ground. She knew a significant amount of time had passed because night had given way to daylight, and the alien sun in its leaden cradle moved across the sky even as they moved over the ground.

She jerked awake the final time when Jotaha's steps sped up into a full run, opening her eyes to a sight that stole her breath. They had apparently arrived at their destination, and Jotaha was heading towards a sky lift-type vehicle that looked like it would carry them up strong cables to a structure at the top of a massive hill. Much of the hill looked like it was covered in bones. Not small animal bones, but gigantic, monstrous bones, some so large that she could see even from the bottom of the hill that they had been hollowed out to form dwellings.

The most striking aspect of the hill was near the top, where two huge structures cast long shadows that stretched down even to the base of the hill of bones. These structures were made of bones arranged in the form of outspread wings. They had been braced by something that looked a bit like scaffolding all along their height and breadth, and more buildings or dwellings had been built along those scaffolds like suspended apartments.

Jotaha's arrival at the sky lift station with Sarah in his arms caused a symphony of startled shouts in an alien language followed by shocked gasps. Sarah saw only a blur of different lizard alien faces passing her at a rapid speed as Jotaha was clearly in a hurry. Given the tone of his voice when he snapped responses to the other aliens, he wasn't in the mood to answer questions about his burden.

She felt like a burden too, as he bundled her into the sky lift. Other aliens that had apparently been in the lift abandoned it as soon as they saw the glowing behemoth bearing down on it with a human in his arms. They cast wide-eyed stares her way as they rushed away from Jotaha, shying back from what she suspected was his growing anger, based on the tension in the arms that cradled her against his chest.

This was not the way she wanted to meet his people. She also hadn't expected the place, which looked to be the size of a large town or small city, to be made of giant bones, thinking she might see more geodes like the one where they'd met the other alien.

Jotaha settled her onto a padded seat next to him as the sky lift lurched into motion. Sarah slapped a hand over her mouth, begging whatever god might be listening that she wouldn't humiliate herself by vomiting all over the fancy wooden and bone sky lift. At least it was only her and Jotaha in the vehicle, but it appeared to be a public transport. She didn't want to taint it with human vomit, especially given the beauty of the crafted and carved seats and paneling. There were even mother of pearl accents around the folding door into the transport.

The journey seemed interminable, but Jotaha remained close to her, his strong body supporting her so she could remain sitting upright. She even dared the occasional peek out the window despite her nausea. His arm rested on the back of the seat, his hand on her shoulder to keep her pressed against him so she didn't fall when the transport swayed with a strong breeze.

The city of bones had terraces surrounding it like the round petals of a flower, built into the hill over which the bones lay scattered. The terraces created many levels, with a central stone paved stairway rising all the way to the top, deep into the shadows cast by the outspread wings.

The city was so amazing—so otherworldly—that she wasn't even surprised to see the massive dragon skull perched at the top of the city, though it was certainly awe-inspiring.

It looked like Jotaha's people had made buildings even out

of that, but these were even fancier, with walls from the same glowing stone as made up the river stones Jotaha used as campfires. Atop the huge skull stood another building, centered between two horns that had to be ten stories tall. The building had a sharp steeple like some gothic cathedral, built out of granite and glow stones. The top of the skull appeared to be paved with golden tiles leading up to the stairway that led to massive double doors.

There was no way a dragon that size could ever fly. It would be physically impossible, even with the gigantic wingspan. Yet, she couldn't deny what she was seeing laid out before her. Jotaha's people had built a city out of a dragon's skeleton. In fact, she could now see that they'd made it a beautiful city that seemed to work with the sinuous form of the massive dragon curled up upon the hill. It was likely that the dragon had once been the size of the hill, and the dirt and stone perhaps filled in the skeleton after it died.

She could have studied the incredible view for hours if she was feeling better, but as it was, she was only able to catch quick peeks at it as the sky lift made its way to the top of the dragon skull, towards the gothic building in the center of the horns. Finally, the sky lift stopped and Jotaha gathered her up, despite her verbal protests. She was too weak to resist him, and a part of her didn't want to. She was shaking, not only from the way her body felt ill and exhausted, but also from fear and awe.

She had no idea what awaited her in that beautiful and forbidding building. She'd pictured a village of huts, or hide dwellings, or natural cavities like the giant geodes when she'd thought of Jotaha's home, not a wondrous city built of dragon bones, boasting buildings of such impressive architecture.

So much for the "barbarian" part of her alien male fantasy. She had no idea why Jotaha used only daggers and a blow gun. Surely, he could be using crossbows, at the very least, considering the technology that could create such beautiful buildings.

He carried her out of the sky lift. She had to bite her lip now, just to keep her mouth tightly closed as bile burned her throat. Soon, she would not be able to resist the demands of her rebelling stomach, which felt like it was on fire and had knives cutting into it.

The worst part was that her bowels were also shifting. Suddenly, she didn't feel so constipated anymore. She was probably about to be carried to the king or some other leader of Jotaha's people, and she felt like she was going to crap herself any minute now, and there was no way to get Jotaha to understand her need verbally.

She struggled against his hold but it had no effect. He was so strong that he could probably crush her with a mild squeeze of his arms. He seemed not to even be fatigued by his jogging trip with her as a burden. Realizing the futility of fighting his hold, she sagged in his arms, focusing all her effort on keeping her butt puckered and her lips sealed shut. If she wasn't so sick to her stomach, she would probably be blushing with shame that her body had betrayed her, but right now, her skin was pale as a ghost. It also felt slick and clammy with sweat.

Finally, they entered a building. She'd been clenching her eyelids shut to focus on controlling her body, so she hadn't seen what door they went into, but the scent of fragrant incense filled the air as more alien voices speaking rapidly surrounded her.

Jotaha laid her down on a soft, silky surface that gave like a mattress. She wanted to tell him that expensive fabric was the last thing she wanted to be near in that moment, but didn't dare to open her mouth even to try.

As soon as he released her, she opened her eyes, seeing him standing beside two other aliens in long, elaborate robes that also looked to be made of embroidery covered silk. He was speaking quickly to them, and they kept casting glances her way. They had faded green scales, and were missing most of the spines on their heads, but their eyes still looked sharp and reptilian as they met her gaze.

If she felt better, she would have been unnerved by the aliens. Instead, she desperately searched the room, oblivious to the opulence surrounding her. When her gaze alit upon a low vase sitting on the stone floor beside a short table, she crawled off the bed, making her way towards it, her entire body trembling. As soon as she reached it, she yanked out the plant that filled it, dumping the soil on the tiled floor along with it.

All sound ceased except for her painful vomiting as she evacuated her stomach into the pot. Tears blinded her as she sat up, swiping at her mouth. Her desperate fingers clawed at the fly of her jeans, shivering as waves of pain surged through her bowels. There was no waiting now. She'd gotten away from the fine fabrics, but she couldn't stop what was coming. All she could do was try to aim for a container that could be washed out.

She felt them all staring at her, doubtless shocked by her behavior, but she wasn't going to look at them. This was a hell of a way to make a first impression, but her body didn't give a damn. It was ready to go, and there was a point where she just couldn't deny it anymore. Her legs trembled as she squatted over the pot. She screamed as the block of days' worth of stool tore her anus, coming out of her in a massive, reeking ball. The blockage was followed by the explosive diarrhea she'd feared. It felt like long, thick, mucus strings came out with the foul, liquid waste.

But it didn't all come out. She felt something against her torn and bleeding sphincter. Something squirming. Something big enough to cause serious discomfort. She collapsed off the toilet, vomit dribbling out of her lips as she tried to keep them closed, her mouth filling with more bile. She turned towards the stinking pot. She looked down into it as she prepared to spit the bile from her mouth into it.

She saw them then—the worms. Thick as slugs, writhing in her feces. There were so many of them that it seemed like the entire pot was filled with them.

She screamed and screamed, scratching at her stomach as if she could tear the parasites out of her body.

Then a scaled hand fell upon her neck and the hard grip tightened at her throat. She fell blissfully unconscious, the darkness claiming her.

24

His drahi was dying and Jotaha felt more helpless than he ever had in his life. The elders had been unable to offer useful advice, and the healers were baffled by her illness, unfamiliar with nixir anatomy. The one elder who truly understood the nixirs, who communicated with them as part of the treaty, was currently gone. The other elders could not say when he would return. They explained that Elder Arokiv was in the nixir world, negotiating with the nixir leaders for new treaty terms. He could travel back and forth between worlds via a means unknown to all but his secret society of infiltrators. The other elders said they could scry him, but there was no telling when he would respond, since scrying was difficult on Gaia and nixir communication devices did not work well on Theia.

Elder Arokiv might speak Sarah's language. He knew the most about the nixirs, even moving among their people disguised as one. He might understand what was happening to Sarah—and how to cure it.

Sarah's face grew paler as blood left her body though her clavek, along with the hon-gree that he feared were abandoning her because they'd grown weak or unsatisfied with the food he'd provided her. What he did know was that their abandonment was killing her, and there was no way to communicate with them to convince them to return. The hon-gree they had fished out of the vase appeared to be hostile, immediately latching onto his gloved hand with a ringed mouth filled with sharp teeth. No doubt it was angry to have been forced out of its host. It did not appear to have reached maturity.

Every time the healers managed to staunch the blood from her clavek, another hon-gree would push past the barrier of bandages, causing more blood loss. Jotaha had no idea how many of the hon-gree lived inside her, but her stomach was distended now, bloated from their anger.

"You have my sympathies, Honored Jotaha," Elder Kireva said, his remaining head spines tight against his skull as he approached Sarah's bedside, where Jotaha had sat for so many sandfalls that he'd lost track of the time. He could only mark it by each breath Sarah took. When her labored breathing stopped, he felt like his life would end too.

"To finally find your drahi, only for her to end up in such a state, is a cruel fate to endure."

"Her hon-gree have left her. I feel like I failed her. I should have known how to—"

Kireva's hand fell upon his shoulder, silencing him. "A nixir drahi has always been a difficult choice for the yan-kanat. She would not be the first of their kind to pass on because this world was not kind to her."

Jotaha jerked his shoulder away from Kireva's hand, his lips peeling back in a snarl, though he didn't turn his attention away from Sarah's increasingly haggard face. "I don't care about the challenges. I want Sarah to be mine. I would do anything to save her."

He glanced up at Kireva, who stood beside him, his own gaze fixed on Sarah. "She already claimed my heart. She is courageous, and fierce, and tenacious. She never gives up, and she won't give up now. She will keep fighting to live, even without her hon-gree. I just need to figure out how to help her win that fight!"

"Like all the nixirs," Kireva muttered. "Fighting is in their blood. It burns through them until it consumes them and their world."

"Honored Kireva, tell me that you have not taken Kevos' path and doubt Seta Zul's wisdom." Jotaha didn't want to look at the male whose endless wisdom he'd trusted from the moment he left the nest to begin his training. He feared he would see the same hatred for his drahi that had twisted Kevos from an honorable sentinel to an attempted murderer.

"No, Jotaha. I believe in Seta Zul's choices. Your seal has led you down a challenging path, but you are more than prepared for this battle. Elder Arokiv has said that things among the nixirs are changing. We may need more of them on our side if the nixirs storm the urvaka in force. Your drahi can help us to understand them in a way even Arokiv has not been able to."

"I have seen those changes. Like the twisted nixirs we fought in the urvaka. They will be a significant challenge if they invade in large numbers."

"Since you told us about them, we have summoned Jotahas from the other skilevs to search the urvaka in our region for more of them."

Jotaha slowly shook his head, reaching to brush a tangled hank of fibers off Sarah's damp cheek. "The urvak zayul have not sensed the nixirs since I killed the last of the twisted ones."

"But they may return, and they move faster and are not deterred by the zayul as the other nixirs are. They are more focused. This is a true concern."

Jotaha barely heard Kireva's words, his mind shifting from the subject of the possible nixir invasion to his chanu zayul. A crazy, wild—perhaps even blasphemous—thought had suddenly occurred to him when he mentioned the zayul.

"Her hon-gree have abandoned her."

"Not all of them. Some still move within her, according to the examinations by her healers."

Jotaha rose to his feet, both excited and fearful that his new hope was about to be dashed by the voice of reason. "She needs her hon-gree to survive, but what if the chanu zayul could heal her and take their place inside her."

As he'd expected, Kireva seemed stunned by the suggestion and immediately negated it. "If she requires the hon-gree, then the symbiotic relationship is mandatory. The chanu zayul inside her will eventually reach maturity and leave her body as well. You would only be delaying her death, and causing more heartache for yourself, Jotaha."

He had considered that. "She could accept a new generation, just as I would have, if I had not chosen to retire."

Kireva's sparse spines bristled. "The chanu zayul honor the Jotahas. It would be blasphemous to use their gifts simply to maintain the life of a single…civilian."

He left the word "nixir" unspoken, but it was there in his tone, and made Jotaha bristle as well as he turned to face Kireva, towering over the shorter yan-kanat.

"Is that not a choice the chanu zayul must make? Do we believe we have the right to choose for them? After all, they were gifted to us by the Ajda themselves to guard the urvaka. They have the wisdom of their creators within them."

Kireva's spines flattened, and his hard expression softened. "Ha'tah…."

He saw Jotaha's spines fully extend, his lips peeling back in anger, and shifted his tone to one that was more respectful and placating. "Honored Jotaha, this path will only bring you heartache. The chanu zayul honor the Jotaha because you protect their home. You are hoping they will choose your drahi as a host, but she will return nothing to them for that honor. They will reject your request, and you will be left hopeless again. What will you feel about the chanu zayul when they allow your drahi to die? You must keep them within you until they have fully matured, but you will be angry at them. It could create a conflict that ends up causing you physical pain as they sense your resentment."

As always, there was wisdom in Kireva's words. It was likely the chanu zayul would not help Sarah. It was also likely that he would resent them for failing to help her. They could sense his thoughts and emotions, and would probably feel his anger. Such anger could corrupt their connection to him, and affect their maturation and adult form.

Yet, at the moment, they remained silent within him. They had to suspect he would make such a request. Why had they not immediately accepted or rejected it, even before he spoke it aloud?

Ultimately, it didn't matter. One glance down at Sarah's diminished form, dying in a slow and agonizing way, her body ravaged by the anger and abandonment of her hon-gree, was all it took to convince him to beg the chanu zayul if he had to.

He knelt beside her bed, gently taking hold of her shoulders. She barely stirred at the feeling of his cool hands against her burning body. Her temperature was so hot that he wondered if the Ajda had not given the nixirs some of their inferno. There were rumors that the Ajda had mixed their blood with the yan-kanat's enemies from time to time for their own amusement, but there had never been any confirmed cases of nixirs hybridized with the divine blood.

"Do not do this, Jotaha!" Kireva clapped a hand on his shoulder again, squeezing firmly enough to catch just the briefest moment of attention from Jotaha. "You will regret this path, even if the chanu zayul agree to your plan. You have no idea what their effect on the nixir body will be!" Kireva was not deterred when Jotaha shoved his hand off his shoulder. "You trained for many passings to accept the chanu zayul into your body. Your drahi has not had any training—"

"She has hosted the hon-gree, and they are creatures of violence and hostility. If she could keep them within her without her mind and body being destroyed, then the chanu zayul will be like a balm to her both physically and mentally." It didn't surprise him that the hon-gree were drawn to a nixir body. The nixirs' ferocious natures seemed suited to host such creatures.

He could not imagine what it had been like to subdue the angry hon-gree for so long inside her. The creatures were so hostile that they had to be trapped within a stone jar to keep them from escaping to bite at the feet of the elders.

He gently turned her onto her stomach. The fact that this jostling did not make her stir again and her skin seemed to scorch his palms only increased his determination to convince the chanu zayul to aid her. Pushing aside her matted head fibers, he exposed the skin at the base of her skull, then took a deep breath.

He felt Kireva watching from behind him now. Perhaps he was even halfway to the door of Sarah's sick room, ready to call the guards to stop Jotaha, but it would be too late. Either the chanu zayul would reject his request, or some of them would migrate to Sarah's body to save her by the time the guards arrived in enough force to pull a Jotaha away from his drahi.

He rested his head on the fabric pillow beside her, feeling the softness of the feathers beneath his cheek as he bumped his neck against her head. His thoughts were clear, and the chanu zayul could not help but pick up his intent.

There was no movement inside him, and his heart began to break, knowing that Kireva had been correct. The chanu zayul had no reason to save Sarah.

Just as he was about to lift his head in defeat, he felt the tickle of movement in his spine.

Kireva did call the guards, but the three chanu zayul who had chosen to leave through the almost completely healed bite in the back of his neck were already crawling over Sarah's matted head fibers to the base of her skull by the time a squad of guards rushed into the room.

It was too late. The elders and guards wouldn't dare to intervene now. The decision was no longer theirs to make.

Gratitude towards the chanu zayul filled him as he watched the first one to reach the base of her skull eject its pincers and tear into her soft flesh, cutting a path to the base of her skull. Insertion would take a little time, but soon enough, the chanu zayul would spread their tendrils through her spine and brain, and they would release chemicals that would soothe the hongree still in her stomach and begin to heal her.

Sarah would be saved, and she would also be honored by the chanu zayul. He knew that would not go over well with people like Kevos, but that was a concern for another time. For now, he was simply grateful that she would live.

25

Sarah heard voices speaking nearby, though they were slightly muffled, as if they came from behind a door.

"I could not wait any longer, my beloved. The elders refused to let me see you. They said our separation was for the best."

She didn't recognize the high-pitched, feminine voice that was speaking, but the responding voice she did recognize, though it shocked her that he spoke English quite clearly.

"Farona, I tried to come to you after visiting Seta Zul's priest to get the seal, but my first duty had to be to the urvaka." Jotaha's tone sounded sad, regretful, and Sarah felt the bite of her own sadness.

The female voice had called Jotaha her beloved, which meant that he was already taken.

Unless this was all a dream. There was certainly a strange dreamlike quality to the whole experience, and she still struggled to open her eyes. Her lids felt so heavy, as did her limbs, like she wanted to melt into the soft mattress beneath her.

"I missed you," the female said. "Your duty has kept you away from me for so long, and I had hoped that it would be over soon. I watched the lifts endlessly, praying to the Ajda that I would see you alighting from one of them as each cycle passed. I always fear that you will not return from the dark paths, especially when the elder spirits have sensed danger."

Had Jotaha been lying to her the whole time? Had he understood every word she'd said, and only pretended not to be able to communicate. Her sadness morphed into outrage at being fooled for some alien purpose. Maybe so he could laugh later with his woman about the stupid human doing charades. The burst of anger seemed to fill her with energy, pumping into her leaden limbs and sagging eyelids, so that her eyes shot open and she lurched unsteadily into a sitting position, then swung her legs off the bed.

There was a door nearby, and the voices were coming from behind it. She was in a room that should have been dark because there was no light source in front of her, but one seemed to glow from some light source at her back. Oddly, when she turned her head to see where that blue glow came from, the light source followed her, always ending up at her back.

The strangeness of this only added to the surreal quality of her surroundings. As she rose to her feet, she felt energized, like she'd just taken a double shot of pure caffeine. She strode towards the door, only vaguely aware of the shifting of a soft tunic that covered her nudity down to her mid-thigh.

The voices had fallen in volume to a low hiss, making it difficult for her to hear them, but she was moving so fast to the door that they wouldn't have been able to say much before she jerked it open.

A slender, feminine lizard person clung to Jotaha like a leech, her arms hanging off his neck as her stunning, delicately sculpted face stared up into his adoringly. If she wasn't covered in scales, she would look like a super model, blessed with high, shapely cheekbones, a sharp jawline, and wide, beautiful eyes that turned towards Sarah in shock when the door flung open on their embrace. The female's lips were thin, like Jotaha's and the other lizard people Sarah had seen, but other than that, her features screamed cover girl for some fashion magazine, including her tall, slender body that still had her standing at least a foot shorter than Jotaha.

Jotaha had his hands on the female's shoulders as he too turned, his eyes widening when he caught sight of Sarah standing in the doorway.

Her anger sparked into a full-blown fury that was more than a little from pure jealousy and possessiveness over an alien that had never belonged to her in the first place. It was still shocking and painful to see him clasped in the embrace of another woman. One who made her feel short, ugly, and fat. Sarah had started to think of Jotaha as hers, and now she knew he never had been.

The glow at her back seemed to brighten the room they stood in, which appeared to be some kind of sitting room. It was filled with furniture and décor that would have interested Sarah if she wasn't so focused on the surprised couple.

"So, you understood me all along, Jotaha? Was I a big joke to you this whole time?" She waved her arms wildly. "Making all kinds of stupid gestures like a big, dumb, naked ape just so you would understand me!"

Jotaha's jaw dropped, his sharp teeth gleaming in the rising blue glow filling the room as he stared at her. "Sarah!"

She crossed her arms, never breaking eye contact with him. She wanted him to experience the full force of her anger and hurt. "I don't know what game you've been playing this entire time, but you could have been honest with me from the start."

"You didn't tell me she spoke Inferno-blessed," the female said in a shaking voice, finally slipping her arms from Jotaha's neck to sidle behind him, putting him between her and Sarah as if she were afraid Sarah would lunge at her and rip her face off.

To be fair, Sarah thought about it, but only in a hypothetical sense. Sort of.

Jotaha took a step closer to Sarah, reaching one hand out towards her as if to touch her like he wanted to reassure himself she was real. "Sarah, I understand you!"

She closed the distance between them and shoved his hand away, before propping her hands on her hips as she glared up at his face. She had to crane her neck this close to him, but she didn't care. She was too outraged to feel the discomfort of the awkward position. "I know you do, *now*, you asshole! You knew English all along, and you pretended you couldn't figure out what I was trying to say."

"What is een-lish?"

She growled low in her throat, causing the female behind Jotaha to yelp and back towards the door, somehow making even a frightened retreat look graceful and feminine. "You played me, Jotaha! And now I know all about it. Don't bother keeping up the game with me now. Your little prank is over."

"The little spirits!" Jotaha said in a shocked voice. "They have made you understand Inferno-blessed. They have taught you how to speak it!"

"I don't know what the hell you're talking about, but I'm speaking English."

He tried to touch her shoulder but she smacked his hand away from her. "No, Sarah, you are speaking Inferno-blessed!"

Sarah crossed her arms in front of her, scoffing at his words. "I have no idea why you keep saying Yan-kanat, but you...."

Her brows came together as her own words struck her. She heard Inferno-blessed, but when she said it, it came out as 'Yan-kanat'. She shook her head as if she could dislodge a brain block. "Ir-olan shir'at English!"

Her eyes widened as she paid attention to the sounds

coming out of her mouth. They were definitely not her own language.

"Vauteg!" She'd meant to say 'oh fuck' but that had come out of her mouth instead.

"Sarah," Jotaha said in a soft voice, holding a hand out in front of him as if he was facing down a wild animal.

Given the female alien's cowering form by the door, she suspected that was what she probably looked like to them.

Way to make a good impression for humanity.

"You are glowing. That means you are emotional, and probably angry. If you thought I tricked you, then I can understand why you would be, but I swear, I have never understood your language."

This brought more confusion from Sarah as she narrowed her eyes on him. "Glowing? I'm not—vauteg!" She shook her hands out in front of her as if she could fling off the glowing bioluminescence that traced beneath her skin along her veins. "Why the vauteg am I glowing?"

She slapped at her body as if she could smack away the light that was beaming from it. "Make it stop!"

"You must remain calm, Sarah," Jotaha said, grabbing her by both wrists and pulling her close to him. He wore a tunic that looked like it was made of fine linen, over a kilt-like garment, and had laced sandals on his feet. His body was cool against her skin, which felt like it was heating up as adrenaline pumped through her blood.

Her skin only glowed brighter the more anxious she got.

He brushed a hand over her hair, pushing it off her sweating brow. "The little spirits were not able to save your hon-gree. When the last remaining ones left your body, they were lifeless, but the little spirits said that you would recover, and they were right."

"Hon-gree?" Those words didn't make sense in her language or his. She pulled out of his embrace, suddenly feeling self-conscious, remembering that his girlfriend, or wife, or whatever she meant to him was in the room.

Only she wasn't. She'd left them alone, apparently not concerned that Sarah would hurt her man.

Or steal him.

"Your spirits," he said, his expression mirroring her confusion. "The growling ones within your belly."

"My...." She patted her stomach. "You mean '*hungry*'?" She'd used that word often to tell him when she needed to eat. "That's...." She chuckled and shook her head. "You thought I had...." Then the memory returned. The memory of her stomach infested by disgusting alien parasites.

She clutched her stomach. "Oh my god! The worms!"

Jotaha pulled her to him again, holding her in his iron-strong embrace until she grew calm, panting against his chest, her panic all burned out of her by the fruitless struggle against his superior strength. He was making soothing sounds to her as he stroked her hair with one hand.

"I am sorry, Sarah. We could not save them all. We have contained the ones that survived in a clay jar, but they are very hostile, and we needed you to tell us what they must eat to complete their maturation."

"Jotaha," she said, her voice muffled against his shirt. It smelled good. Like him.

"Yes, Sarah."

She patted his chest. "I'm calm now. Super chill. I'm a block of ice. You can let me go."

He slowly released her, as if reluctant to do so. Pity he was taken by the lizard version of a beauty queen. Now that she could understand him, she would be all over him, given half the chance.

Once they cleared up some of the confusion between them.

"You still have those nasty parasites?"

"Parasites?" His brow ridges came together as he repeated the word, which was actually "nixeran."

She bobbed her head in a sharp nod. "Yep. Those are not spirits. They're parasites that were probably killing me." She glanced down at her hand, which was still glowing, though only faintly now. "Jotaha... when you said 'chanu zayul' you didn't... uh... mean those worm thingies that came out of your neck, did you?"

"The chanu zayul have honored you. They have chosen your body to host them while they mature. In doing so, they must have purged the parasites from your system."

She lifted a hand to rub the back of her neck. There was no sign of a scab or scar there. "Did you put glow worms inside me?"

He still seemed confused as she slowly backed away from him, breathing deeply to avoid hyperventilating. "They will protect you and heal you, and they have somehow made it possible for me to understand you. This is a great blessing."

"Blessing," she whispered, her throat dry as she thought of the wriggling worm that had crawled out of Jotaha's wounded neck. "I still have a parasite inside me!"

"No!" Jotaha said and his tone sounded offended as he tried to reach for her. His spines rose to half-mast when she dodged him and stepped backwards. "The little spirits are not parasites. They give much and take very little in return. For you, they demand even less. You are not Jotaha. To have them choose you anyway is an honor that was unthinkable before I brought you here. You were dying, Sarah. They saved your life."

As if to reiterate his point, she suddenly felt a rush of endorphins, like she'd just finished a heavy cardio workout and was pumped with energy and positive feelings. "Oh, my god, they're manipulating my hormones, aren't they?" Despite her words, she still felt pretty good, all things considered.

Glow worms in her brain that sent her happy hormones—

or vicious parasites in her belly, eating her alive from the inside? It wasn't really a tough choice, but it was a nightmarish one.

"What, exactly, did you mean about the, uh, chanu zayul maturing?"

"You have seen their adult form in the urvaka. They came to your aid when you fought the twisted human."

"The beetles!" her voice rose as she started to feel panic again, despite the flood of endorphins. "How the *hell* do they get out of my neck if they're vauteg beetles the size of vauteg walnuts?"

He managed to catch hold of her as she started to panic pace, and he pulled her close again. "They will numb your body so you feel no pain when they leave it. You will not be harmed as the parasites harmed you. I swear this to you, Sarah. I would never have asked them to choose you if I thought they would hurt you."

She tried to pull away from him but he held her firmly against him. Despite the bioluminescence of her body increasing in intensity, she eventually had to sag in defeat against his chest. She felt stronger than she ever had before, but it was nothing compared to Jotaha's immovable strength.

"You did this to me?" she asked through numb lips. "Why?"

His hand rubbed her back, close to her neck where she just knew those little worm thingies were latched onto her brainstem. "I had to do whatever it took to save your life. We did not know the hon-gree were parasites. I thought you needed them to survive. I believed replacing your spirits with the chanu zayul would be enough to save you."

She couldn't help it. She chuckled, her cheek mashed against his firm chest, the linen slightly rough against her skin. "Hun-gry, Jotaha. It means 'atya.' My stomach makes that growling noise when it is empty. Humans don't have worms inside us. Well... let's just say we don't have *beneficial* worms inside us."

Feeling her submission to his superior strength, Jotaha relaxed his arms, allowing her to shift against him until she could rest her chin on his chest, craning her neck to look up at his face.

"Nixirs are strange creatures," he said.

"Nixir...." She shoved at his chest. "Hey! I just realized that you use the same root word for 'parasite' as you do for 'human'!" She glared up at him, wriggling in his hold. "That's not very flattering, you know. I mean, first you put worms in my head, then you call *my* people parasites!"

He released her, allowing her to step back, though she didn't bother to move far away from him. He could always grab her again. She wasn't fast enough to avoid him.

"What would you call a people that invaded your world and took your land, destroying your civilization and chasing your people underground?"

Sarah tapped her chin. "Some humans can be assholes. I'm not gonna pretend otherwise. But I swear we're not all conquering, genocidal dickheads." She cocked her head. "You have words for 'claveklin' and 'salavidu.'"

He seemed distracted, his gaze fixed on her chest, his head spines at half-mast, his tail lashing back and forth behind him. He made no comment on her discovery that his species had names for asshole and dickhead—well, the latter was more like dickless, but it was certainly intended as an insult.

"Yoo hoo, Jotaha," she waved a hand in front of her, catching his gaze. His eyes lifted to meet hers. She smirked. "Human parasite eyes are up here, on our face. I can see how you'd get confused."

Despite her poor attempt at humor, Jotaha still seemed serious as he stared at her. "Sarah, now that we can understand each other, we must speak of important things."

"Oh, right. Because bugs in my head isn't really an important topic." She put her hands together in prayer position. "Please, *please* tell me you aren't about to sacrifice me to some ancient dragon god that lives in a volcano and loves to feast on human flesh."

His spines flattened to his skull as he seemed to be taking her words seriously, which only made her fear she should be too. There weren't enough endorphins in the world to make her feel good now.

"Seta Zul would not send you to me, only to demand your flesh as an offering. She is sometimes known for capriciousness, but never for such cruelty."

"Soooo, there *is* a dragon god living in a volcano?" Her voice ended on a squeak as her stupid glow worms decided now was the time to light her up like a firework.

Jotaha also looked a bit disturbed. When he spoke, his tone sounded like he was trying to reassure himself as well as her. "No, she would not do such a thing. It would be unheard of. She would not choose you as my mate and then demand your life in sacrifice."

"Choose me as your *what* now?" Her body flickered as contradicting emotions warred inside her. This bioluminescent stuff was going to make playing poker a challenge. "Did you just say I was your 'drahi?' Vauteg! *That's* what that word means! That's what you were saying the whole time!"

It was difficult for her to think straight after such a revelation. It was perhaps even a confirmation of some suspicions she'd had during their journey. At first, she felt a rush of excitement at his explanation, but that was quickly dashed as she recalled the embrace she'd walked in on.

Jotaha was watching her silently, as if waiting to see what her reaction to such shocking news would be. She wondered if he had any idea that she was already attracted to him. Then the old self-esteem issues rushed to the forefront, making her wonder if he was even attracted to *her*.

"If I'm your mate, why were you hugging that other woman who called you her beloved?"

The fact that Jotaha didn't immediately respond with a quick explanation that she was actually a sister or a cousin or some other non-sexual relationship to him made Sarah's stomach twist—and this time, she was fairly certain it wasn't with parasitic worms.

He swiped a hand over his head spines, then down to the back of his neck as his gaze shifted away from her. He looked to the side of her like there was something deeply interesting in a stone vase with dragons carved into it.

It was pretty enough, but she didn't think that was why he wouldn't meet her eyes. She crossed her arms over her chest, mostly to appear like she was totally in control of the situation, despite her glow worms flickering with what she suspected was a reflection of her internal anxiety at what his answer would be. "You said we needed to talk, so here I am. I'm ready to talk."

That wasn't entirely true. She felt good physically, but she also still felt dirty, and her hair was still a tangled, matted mess, and the tunic she was wearing didn't fit her and looked like a grain sack covering her body. She needed a long soak in a bath, a really good comb, and a toothbrush. Then maybe she would feel better prepared for this conversation. Like she could ever be on equal footing with the lizard woman beauty that had scurried out of the room the moment Sarah started behaving like a savage.

"Farona is... *was* my tagez drahan. We grew up together. I can't remember a time when we weren't together, before my duty as Jotaha had me spending most of my time in the urvaka."

Tagez drahan meant "touch friend" literally, according to the glow worm provided translation in her head, but that was the Yan-kanat equivalent of "fuck buddy," according to the innate understanding of the language that the bugs in her head also seemed to provide. Only there was perhaps more emotion involved between the yan-kanat in that kind of relationship, because that female, Farona, was definitely in love with Jotaha, and he hadn't exactly shoved her away from him, even when Sarah walked in on them.

"Why isn't *she* your mate, if the two of you are so close?" It hurt. She couldn't deny that. Jotaha might have saved her life and brought her to his home, but his heart seemed to belong to another woman.

He still wouldn't meet her eyes. Only this time, he turned to pace the room, side to side, in front of her. "We had planned to be mated, but Seta Zul had other plans. I was sent to the urvaka right after I was sealed, before I could meet with Farona. That was where I met you and my seal activated to let me know you are my drahi."

The words kept hurting, and she wondered why she kept asking more questions when she was afraid to hear the answers. But she had to know. She wouldn't shy away from the truth. "So, you love her, and you wanted *her* to be your mate, but this dragon goddess chose me for you instead."

Jotaha paused in mid-pace, his tail flicking back and forth in jerky movements, his head spines completely flat against his skull. His jaw was tight beneath the small scales that covered it. "All of that is past. You are my destiny. My seal activated for you, not Farona."

His head bowed, his gaze fixing on the polished stone tiles beneath his feet. He still wouldn't look at her.

Sarah's arms shook and her stomach sank, feeling like it dropped to her feet. She was grateful she was braced with her arms crossing her chest so he couldn't see how much his words shook her. She would get over it. She had faced far worse emotional trauma. She had walked away from the child she loved more than life itself, knowing that it was for the best. Knowing that someone else could offer her daughter a better future. Her heart had broken then. It was only severely bruised now. After all, she barely knew Jotaha. Even if he *had* taken on a hero status in her mind. She could get over this.

"I don't know what this 'seal' is, but your goddess didn't bother to ask my permission before 'choosing' me, and I don't follow her orders, so I free you to be with the woman you actually want to be with. I just need a nice hot bath, a good brush, and a change of clothes, and then you can have someone point me in the direction to find my way back home." She bit her lower lip, shoving her sadness deep inside her, as she'd had to do before. The heart healed. Maybe it even got stronger, like when a broken bone healed.

Jotaha's head shot up at her words. He turned to face her, his eyes narrowed on her. He moved to grab her by her upper arms. He held her in place when she would have instinctively backed away from the seven foot tall giant looming over her. He suddenly looked menacing, his teeth bared as a sharp hiss escaped him. "You're mine. I will never let you go, Sarah. Never."

She tried to push off his hold with both hands, and failed, as she always did, to move him when he didn't want to be moved. "I'm not your prisoner, Jotaha. You can't keep me here when you don't even want me."

His grip tightened until it was almost painful as he lowered his head until his face hovered above hers. His forked tongue flicked out, touching her cheek as she turned her head. "No, Sarah. You are not my prisoner. We don't take nixir prisoners. We learned that lesson long ago. If you were not my drahi, I would have left your corpse in the urvaka with the others of your kind."

She struggled in his grip, shooting him a furious glare. "You know, I liked you a lot better when I couldn't understand a word you were saying."

"I can relate to that, nixir," he snarled, suddenly releasing her arms with a sharp motion that made her stagger a few steps back.

"Well, I'm sorry your goddess decided to saddle you with an enemy for your mate. You should really take that up with her, instead of taking it out on me, you salavidu claveklin!"

Jotaha startled her by suddenly huffing loudly with what she realized was the yan-kanat version of laughter as his head spines quivered. "I am not salavidu, Sarah. Our mating spine does not hang outside our bodies at all times in an obscene manner, like your nixir males, but I most definitely possess one."

She propped her hands on her hips, her skin sparking with bioluminescence in veiny patterns. "One minute you're threatening me, and the next you're laughing at me!"

His amusement evaporated, but he didn't get angry and snarly again. Instead, he looked serious, finally meeting her eyes with a steady gaze. "Forgive me, drahi. I have not done enough to comfort you. You were ill for five cycles, and even with the help of the chanu zayul, we weren't sure you would survive. I have not slept much in that time. Farona's unexpected arrival, along with your sudden awakening, has caused me to behave like a nix—like an untamed beast."

He lowered his gaze, his shoulders curving slightly inward, his spines tight against his skull. "I should not have frightened you, but I can't stand the thought of losing you."

"You have Farona," Sarah said, because she was apparently a masochist who couldn't let that last statement of Jotaha's settle in and soothe her battered heart.

Best to get it all laid out from the start, because she didn't want to fool herself into believing he could possibly care about her, only to be disillusioned later, when it would be the most devastating.

"I told you, Sarah. That time is past."

She held up a hand to stop him from stepping closer to her. He paused, much to her relief, because she couldn't hold him off otherwise.

"Sure, you told me that. But you haven't told me you don't love *her* anymore." She lowered her hand and crossed her arms over her chest. Bracing herself again.

Which was a good thing, because Jotaha had no answer for that, unable to meet her eyes as a long silence fell between them.

It was Sarah who broke that silence. "That's all I needed to know, I guess."

Then she turned on her heel and retreated to the bedroom, slamming the door behind her loud enough that he shouldn't be able to hear the sob she bit off.

26

Sarah was alive, and that should have been all that mattered to Jotaha, but now that they could understand each other, he felt conflicted about their future together. Farona couldn't have chosen a worse moment to bribe the guard watching over Sarah's sickroom so that she could sneak in and visit him. Seeing her delicate beauty and grace again reminded him of what they had once had together—and of the future they had planned. Even the home he'd had built for his future drahi had been designed with Farona in mind.

Farona was always soft-spoken, kind, gentle, and submissive. She would never have been as combative as Sarah, facing off against him with her alien eyes glaring, her full lips tight in a frown, her arms crossed in front of her like a warrior. He couldn't help but make a comparison between the two females. Though he found Sarah's ferocity strangely glorious, especially with her body glowing so beautifully from the chanu zayul that had honored her, he realized that his future would probably always be like this. Strife, verbal combat, misunderstandings. Doors slammed in his face when he had not given her permission to leave the conversation.

Sarah would always struggle against his control. It wasn't the nixir way to submit. She would not glide elegantly among his people like Farona. She would likely charge through them like a nixir siege weapon. Her voice was commanding, her tone sarcastic, and her words sometimes sharp and crude. He couldn't picture her sitting among the yan-kanat females, sipping xirak and politely exchanging stories of their days crafting and shopping and doing whatever other arcane activities the females did.

He could also picture her turning their mating room into a battleground. For some reason, that thought excited him instead of worried him. The thought of her clawing at him, her skin scorching against his cool scales as her flat teeth clamped on his shoulder or arm while he thrust inside her made his salavik shift beneath the seal, eager for the first mating ceremony—very eager to make Sarah his forever.

A part of him—a small part he didn't want to acknowledge —enjoyed antagonizing her, watching her light up with anger and outrage, her eyes flashing as her body glowed with her fury. He could acknowledge that she was magnificent when she was at her fiercest, and he would never forget seeing her smash a burning inferno stone into the skull of the twisted nixir, giving him just enough time to slay it. He realized now that he had fallen for her hard in that moment, the way his heart suddenly seemed to burn for her catching him by surprise.

His drahi wanted him to disavow his feelings for Farona— and rightly so. Any honorable yan-kanat would always put his drahi first, dismissing all his previous lovers from his mind— and also openly to those lovers, if necessary. Farona should not have visited him. She should not have seen him in person until after he had sealed himself to his drahi. The elders were right to insist upon separation. Anything else caused confusion and doubt, especially when he had such a long history with Farona.

She was comforting and familiar. She was the symbol of the

life they'd planned together. As much as he *should* do it, he found it difficult to completely deny that some feelings remained for her, even if they were as soft and gentle as she was, versus the inferno inside him that burned for Sarah.

No matter what his misgivings were about his future with his alien drahi, the panic he felt when he thought of her leaving him was enough to make him a little crazy. If he wasn't bound by his honor, he would have pinned her against the wall behind her when she dared to suggest returning to her own world instead of staying with him. He would have shown her that he still held all the power, despite the chanu zayul that had undoubtedly made her stronger.

He would have tasted her the way he had wanted to since she first stumbled into his hunting grounds and scored a hit on him with a nixir weapon. Even then, she had fascinated him, intrigued him, made him hungry for the delights the nixir shataz were rumored to deliver to their partners.

Instead, he had released her when her words dripped with nixir scorn. She didn't like him. Not now that she could understand him. She'd barely reawakened, and he'd already lost her affection—if he'd ever had it. She was slipping away from him before he even had a chance to make his case to her.

Seta Zul had been wise to create the seal so that the drahi had to voluntarily submit to being marked. It would be too easy for him to use his superior strength against her to claim her as his forever. In his panic at the thought of losing her, he might have even lost his honor to keep her.

She changed him in ways he didn't like. Ways that made him worry that her nixir nature could rub off onto others, like a contagion. With Farona, he was civilized and honorable. With Sarah, he was on the verge of becoming a savage.

The door between them faced him like a daunting barrier. He wanted to knock it down, march into her room, and claim her right then and there. Instead, he managed to do the right thing and turn away. He left the anteroom, speaking sharply to the guard who had let Farona enter. He didn't like the pity in the guard's eyes. They thought he was being punished in some way by having a nixir drahi.

He found a servant and asked her to send hygiene items to his drahi's room. Sarah had made it clear that she wanted to bathe. Though the hygiene practices of a nixir female had long ago been forgotten by the residents of Draku Rin skilev, they probably still had some items in the museum that might be useful to his drahi.

After seeing to it that Sarah would receive supplies to hopefully please her, and also that she would be offered a variety of foods to fill a belly that should be healed now, he made his way to the training grounds, eager to burn off excess energy caused by his confrontation with Sarah.

He was angry at himself, not her. He should have immediately told her he didn't love Farona. He knew that beginning their mating with a lie wasn't the best idea, but it would have smoothed things over for him, making it easier to claim Sarah. Eventually, he knew he would put Farona out of his mind. Eventually, it would be the truth. He didn't think the feelings he had for his lifelong friend and former lover would survive the conflagration Sarah caused inside him.

The jotahs training in the arena were quick to greet him with bowed heads when he arrived, and equally quick to accept his challenge. Normally they sparred alone, but he was too strong for that to be a decent fight, so six of them surrounded him at his request, then charged him at once, attempting to tackle him to the ground.

Jotahs were usually shorter in size, though generally very stocky. The lesser height made navigating the smaller tunnels in the urvaka easier, though Jotaha had grown accustomed to moving and fighting in a crouch, and now could do so rapidly.

He tossed one jotah to the ground as the others punched

him, clawed at him, or tried to grapple him. Two others went down fairly quickly, as the last three threw their full weight against him, causing him to stagger and take a knee. It wasn't enough to put him off balance. He hooked an arm around the neck of a jotah clinging to his flank and squeezed until the younger yan-kanat sagged in unconsciousness.

Jotaha rose to his feet, dragging the remaining two jotahs up until their legs dangled as they hung onto his neck and back. The one on his back grunted as Jotaha crashed into a stone column, slamming his attacker into it again and again. At the same time, he punched the other jotah in his face.

Both sets of arms loosened around his neck, as both jotahs recognized the futility of trying to choke him. The chanu zayul had strengthened the scales around his throat, making crushing attempts extremely difficult for those with unenhanced strength.

This power was what every jotah hoped for. All so they could one day face down the nixirs in the urvaka.

Many even dreamed of crossing the boundary into nixir land and confronting them on their own turf. Jotaha knew this would be a suicide mission. The nixirs' machines actually worked in their own world, even though the urvaka rendered the metal constructs inoperable. The most highly trained and blessed Jotaha would struggle in a fight against a nixir machine that felt no pain, exhaustion, or hunger. There were also tales of nixir weapons so destructive that they had the power to destroy Gaia herself.

Then there was the twisted nixirs. Jotaha had no idea how many of those roamed the nixir lands. They were stronger, faster, and more agile than the other nixirs, and could climb walls and ceilings as easily as they walked along the ground. They were also not confounded by the absolute darkness of the urvaka, as the other nixirs were.

Jotaha freed himself from the final pair of jotahs with relative ease, casting them aside without a single labored breath.

"So Jotaha needs to practice on nestlings?" Kevos' mocking voice came from behind Jotaha, and he turned to see the other yan-kanat walking towards him, a spear in each hand. "Is that so you have the strength to defeat your new nixir mate when she eventually turns on you and buries a dagger in your back?"

Jotaha caught the spear Kevos tossed to him with ease, feeling his eagerness for battle rise along with his glow. This fight was long overdue.

"I see the elders let you out of confinement," he snarled at the sentil with contempt. "You should have taken the opportunity to remove your sorry hide from Draku Rin. Return to your barrens, Kevos. There's no place on this hallowed ground for those without honor."

Kevos hissed mockingly as they circled each other. "I have honor, Jotaha. I also still have respect for you, which is why I tried to free you from your burden. You know this as well as I do. As well as the elders do. They set me free because they know I am right. The nixir female will bring ruin to you." He spread his arms, raising the spear high as he gestured to the audience forming in the arena. "She will bring ruin to *all* of us!"

A handful of voices in the crowd rose in agreement, falling quickly silent when Jotaha turned his head to seek out their sources.

With the watchers properly cowed, he returned his attention to Kevos. "Sarah is not like the others. She brings no ill will with her to this land."

"You cannot even understand her, Jotaha!" Kevos growled, swinging his spear down until the tip pointed towards Jotaha. "How would you even know her intent?"

"I understand her now. The chanu zayul have given her knowledge of our language and she can now speak it."

Kevos' spear tip dropped to the dirt as he straightened from his fighting stance. His mouth gaped open in shock. "The chanu zayul? What do they have to do with this?"

Jotaha realized that Kevos had not heard about the chanu zayul choosing Sarah as a host. No doubt the elders wanted to keep this information concealed until Sarah was officially introduced to the residents of the skilev.

Kevos had a sharp mind, which made him a dangerous hunter. It took only a few grainfalls for him to understand. "She has been honored by the chanu zayul? A *nixir*!" He bared his teeth and took up his fighting stance again. "I don't believe that. This is some trick you and the elder priest of Seta Zul are playing to convince us to accept your unwanted drahi."

With head spines high, the sentil charged Jotaha. The crash of spear shafts meeting filled the suddenly still air as the audience watched the confrontation in silence.

Kevos was a good fighter—the best when it came to spears. If Jotaha had not been blessed by the chanu zayul so that he was stronger and faster, Kevos might have defeated him with skill alone. Instead, Jotaha was able to break Kevos' spear after they sparred for nearly a full sandfall, sending the steel tip flying as he closed the distance and grabbed Kevos by the throat.

He lifted the other male up by his neck, reminding him and the watching audience that Jotaha was the strongest among them, as his glow increased with his anger. Kevos still glared down at him, though he struggled to breathe as Jotaha's fingers tightened around his throat.

Then Kevos used the last of his flagging strength to slash at Jotaha's face with his bared claws. Jotaha released the other male, his own teeth showing in anticipation. He stepped back, giving Kevos enough room to rise to his feet, one hand at his throat as he coughed.

Jotaha tossed his spear aside, turning to face Kevos again,

squaring up as the other male did. They were both hissing now, tongues flicking out to detect the aggression filling the air.

"Now it gets primal," Kevos snarled, lifting a hand to lick Jotaha's blood off the tip of one claw.

"That's just how I like it," Jotaha said in a low growl.

The audience cheered as the two fighters came together in a brutal clash.

27

The servants came to her door not long after she heard the anteroom door close. She assumed Jotaha had left, without making any effort to convince her that he actually wanted her as his mate.

It turned out her assumption was correct. He'd just left, and sent some terrified servants in his place. She didn't think they were afraid of him. They were clearly afraid of Sarah. The skittish female yan-kanat wouldn't meet her eyes, even as they showed her to the room hidden behind a screen in her bedroom that held a large tub made of hammered metal.

They brought her folded-up fabric which she assumed was clothing, probably like the simple dresses they wore that enhanced their slender forms, making them look feminine and graceful, despite their lack of breasts and their very subtle curves at waist and hip. They also brought her a scented cube of wax, which she couldn't divine a purpose for, a pot of some light, perfumed oil, an actual sea sponge, a small, narrow brush that appeared to be carved from stone and tipped with coarse tan hairs, and a grainy, herby paste in a clay jar that reminded her of an exfoliating scrub.

One of the females slid aside a small stone tile in the wall above the tub, then cranked a handle that had been cleverly concealed in the greenery that seemed to fill the entire room. Plants were everywhere—in pots and planters sitting on the floors or on shelves, or hanging from the ceiling. They were every shade of green, brown, red, and even orange, with leaves of many different sizes—some as large as her hand. The majority of the ceiling center consisted of a pyramidal skylight that looked like it was made of quartz crystal rather than glass, allowing sunlight to spill into the chamber in a prismatic rainbow.

After a handful of cranks on the handle, water poured out of the wall in a rapid gush. The servant kept cranking the handle until water filled the tub.

The other servant knelt to push at some stones that were set beneath the metal tub. Sarah realized they were the same kind of warming river stones that Jotaha had used for campfires as they lit up beneath the tub to heat the water.

Not long after the two servants deposited the items, filled and heated the tub, then bowed out of the room—never meeting her eyes or saying more than two words to her—one of them returned with an armload of folded linen squares that Sarah assumed were meant to be her towels. Sitting atop the towels was a silver hairbrush that looked straight out of the Victorian era, along with a matching hand mirror and a decorative comb that were probably from the same era.

The servant presented these items to her like offerings, holding them out at arm's length, her head down and eyes fixed on the floor. As soon as Sarah had taken them, the servant backed away, head remaining down, slender body trembling as if she feared Sarah would beat her if she dared to look up.

Once Sarah was alone, she finally had a chance to think, though her surroundings provided an interesting distraction. She'd stared at the greenery-cloaked stone walls for long enough. She'd already spotted the seat with the hole in it that she took to be a toilet. It had another crank beside it, and yet another crank beside a basin sitting atop a stone shelf on the wall that would put it at waist level.

She was in a bathroom, and apparently, the yan-kanat liked their bathrooms to look like jungles, for some unfathomable reason. It was good to be in a bath tub, though she would kill for some soap, and definitely shampoo and conditioner. She figured she was just lucky they gave her an exfoliator scrub to remove what felt like layers of dirt and filth.

Despite her focus on hygiene, her thoughts remained fixed on Jotaha while she scrubbed her skin, then wet her mass of tangled hair, adding some of the exfoliator to scrub at her scalp.

He was in love with someone else, but told Sarah she was his mate. This wasn't how the fated mate thing was supposed to go. Sarah loved paranormal shifter romances that always had the fated mate trope. She'd preferred that type of romance, because it meant the guy wouldn't leave if his mate suddenly fell inconveniently pregnant. In fact, in the romance novels, the obviously gorgeous and usually rich hero would be thrilled about the news that a baby was on the way.

Jotaha wasn't a shifter—she didn't think—but he wasn't human either, and apparently these aliens also had a "fated mate" thing going. It figured that she would get the alien who didn't want his mate. A mate chosen for him by a volcano dwelling she-dragon goddess, instead of some innate recognition of the other half of his soul.

That explained all the dragon art everywhere. Paintings and statues and tapestries and vases and sculptures, all covered with dragons in every possible sinuous pose. Obviously, they worshipped the mythical beasts—that were also obviously not so mythical in this place, given her memory of the city built on the bones of a giant dragon.

She shivered at the thought that there were real dragons,

but then again, the existence of lizard men had also been shocking to her at first.

Before she'd walked across that seam, she'd lost all belief in anything magical after her parents told her that if she didn't go with her mother to that fateful appointment, she might as well pack her bags and move out. Sure, they'd claimed later that they didn't expect her to actually leave, but they'd also made few attempts to reconcile with her during the pregnancy, only coming around after the baby was safely in the care of her adoptive parents to tell Sarah she could move home again. As if she could ever forget that their love and approval had a price.

Instead, she'd remained at Beth's house, then eventually had to move out of there, living out of an old van she'd managed to purchase with money saved from her job and some cash from Beth. Never, in those rough years, had she entertained the idea that such wondrous things as magic heat stones, or mythical dragons, or sexy lizard men could possibly exist in the same universe as internet challenges and Instagram selfies and Black Friday mobs where people fought each other to save a few bucks on coffee makers or televisions.

She seemed to be safe, for the moment, and that meant she had time to truly evaluate her situation. She barely knew Jotaha. Not really. Despite their time together, she'd never actually understood him, and he'd never understood her. Was it any wonder he wasn't ready to toss aside a lifelong love for a virtual stranger—an alien to him at that? Was she even being fair to be so hurt and angry by what felt like his rejection?

He would have chosen someone else for his mate, if he'd been given the choice. That was a hard truth to acknowledge, but it gave her a starting point. She had to decide where she went from there. It was clear the yan-kanat didn't like humans. The servants were terrified of her, and she doubted it was because she cut an imposing figure. Slender as those delicate females had been, she didn't think she could take them down in a fight. Not with their sharp teeth and claws.

Returning home would probably be the choice that would leave her heart most intact, assuming she could find a way to get back to her own world, because she was sure now that this wasn't Earth. Not with giant, city-sized dragon bones just lying around in the open for any satellite to spot. The caves were the key, she suspected, that would lead her back to her old, boring, dragon-less, and Jotaha-free world.

The bugs in her head could probably guide her back to the seam, though she wasn't sure how to communicate with them, if she even could. They were clearly able to give her knowledge of the yan-kanat language, so they must be able to interface with her mind in some way, but they didn't come with an instruction manual, and she had no idea where to even begin when it came to communicating with them. That, and the idea that they were inside her body at all still creeped her out. If she hadn't been so grateful to them for killing the parasites in her stomach, she probably wouldn't be taking their presence as calmly as she was.

Then there was her other option. She could remain in this world, and maybe—someday—she could figure out a way to make Jotaha love her, and not have the other yan-kanat scurrying away from her like she was the boogie man. Maybe she could prove herself to them all. Prove that she wasn't like the worst of her kind, and somehow teach them that humans had a good side to them too.

She could speak their language, and apparently, having the bugs inside her was a good thing as far as the yan-kanat were concerned. Jotaha had them inside him too. She got the idea that he was respected because of his glowing scales, which she now understood came from the bugs. That unpleasant yan-kanat that lived in the geode had stood down when Jotaha glowed, like he was chastened by the sight of that bioluminescence.

Farona was the sticking point though. Sarah had never been very confident of herself when it came to being lovable. She was introverted and socially awkward, and there was nothing remarkable about her physical appearance that would make her more appealing despite those obstacles. Even the things that a human man might like about her—like her long, thick, wavy hair—wouldn't appeal to the hairless yan-kanat.

She was already at a disadvantage with Jotaha. Farona was his childhood sweetheart. That was an impossible situation for Sarah.

Wasn't it?

He'd brought her here. He seemed like he intended to keep her as his mate, even though he was still in love with Farona. She wasn't sure she could commit to someone who loved another woman, but he had grown angry when she'd suggested leaving.

That should have sent up a red flag, but instead, she'd taken it as a good sign that he didn't want her to leave, even if he wasn't in love with her. She couldn't help that little part of herself that wanted him to be possessive of her, unwilling to let her go, even though she knew that wasn't healthy in most relationships—human ones, at least. She had no idea what constituted a healthy relationship for the yan-kanat.

Everyone else she'd ever cared about had left her, or let her walk away without stopping her. Jotaha was the first person who told her he would never let her go. Healthy or not, that kind of possessiveness made her feel wanted.

The outfit the servants had brought her was a shift-like dress, and it skimmed her full hips and clung tightly to her breasts, but she could tell that it had been made with her build in mind, rather than the delicate female yan-kanat.

Either there were other females with bodies similar to hers, or this dress had been made for her. Jotaha had said she'd been sick for five cycles, which the bugs in her head translated to the Theian equivalent of days. That would have been enough time for Jotaha to have clothes made up for her. Further proof was the fact that the dress didn't have a slit in the back for a tail.

At least he'd thought of her need for clothes, and probably for this bath. After dressing, she used the narrow brush to scrub at her teeth, wishing she had some toothpaste. Combing her hair was a great deal more difficult, and she had to begin the process with the wide teeth of the decorative comb. Eventually, she tried adding some of the scented wax to the comb out of sheer desperation, which allowed it to pass more smoothly through her hair.

Combing out her hair took what seemed like hours, though her hair was still wet when she finished. She ended up with a ball of shed hair the size of a guinea pig, and couldn't find a trash can anywhere in the bathroom jungle to dump it.

Although she suspected she was half bald after the ordeal, she still felt a million times better than she had before her bath. After a stop at the toilet bench, a wipe with some scented petals, and a flush with the hand crank, she could add another million to that score.

Now, she was hungry as a bear, so she practically cheered when she saw the food set up on a small wooden table with carved dragon legs that had been set next to her bed, which also had carved dragons all over the headboard. They really stuck with a motif once they picked it.

To her relief, there was only one blood bar among the small feast of food that filled the entire table top. She shoved it to the very edge of the table as she considered her other options. She was starving but she didn't think she'd ever eat those things again. Something had given her parasites, and it might have been the water, but it could also have been some of the food she'd eaten in the cave. She wasn't taking any chances.

The variety of different dishes was extensive. Some smelled sweet, some savory, and she even spotted the bun that she knew was both, sitting among the offerings. There was only a small sampling of each type of food, and most of them were beautifully presented, like she might get at some gourmet restaurant. There were little colorful squares, garnished with herbs, stripes of fragrant sauces, and even the odd flower or two. There were also hockey puck-sized circles, and small spheres, some of which burst open to spill out fragrant contents when she touched them with the flattened end of a stick that she suspected was an eating utensil, even though it looked more like a small spatula.

Some foods tasted amazing, others had an organ-y flavor, like liver and onions. Still others were a toss-up, with the textures being off-putting but the taste being quite good. Her hunger drove her to try everything but the food she'd eaten in the caves, and she found many delights that she truly enjoyed. She completed her meal by clearing most of the stone or wood or glazed clay plates and shallow bowls. She also drank all the different beverages provided, including the familiar tea in the delicate two-handled mug with dragons beautifully painted and outlined in gold on the dark blue background of it.

There were five different drinks, including water that tasted as clean as any bottled variety, as well as something fermented and probably made of grain. The others were apparently juices, including one that had a nutty flavor and milky consistency.

If the variety of foods was intended to determine her likes and dislikes, the yan-kanat would definitely be confused by the fact that she ate and drank almost everything. Or perhaps they would be happy their foods appealed to the parasite-boogie man-human-monster. Maybe they were afraid she'd start killing and eating them like a horror movie alien if they didn't keep her belly full.

The idea of herself being the scary one, when everyone

around her had sharp teeth and claws and scales, made her chuckle. Even that small bit of amusement gave her a mood boost, probably helped along by the full stomach and slight buzz she was experiencing. It was also possible her brain bugs were pumping more happy hormones through her blood.

She would take it. Eventually, she would have to face the music, and make a decision about Jotaha, and how she wanted to proceed. Huge, life-altering choices shouldn't be made when you were feeling overly optimistic and a little drunk.

28

Jotaha had subdued Kevos, and the arena battle should have been the end of Kevos' open protest and hostility towards Sarah. Major disputes had always been firmly settled in the arena in the past, allowing the yan-kanat to free themselves of the negative and violent energy that arose during such cases. This kept fights from spilling into civilian areas, where the innocent could be hurt. It also decreased the chance that anger and hatred would fester until it burst out of a person and resulted in crimes of passion.

Such crimes as murder were very rare in Draku Rin, and were usually the result of foolish males pursuing drahis that had already been claimed. Even then, they were typically exiled or sent on a pilgrimage to beg Seta Zul's forgiveness before the situation got that out of hand.

Kevos was no coward, and had faced him fairly in the arena. The problem was that the sentil still didn't see Sarah as one of them. He didn't even see his plan to kill Sarah as an attempted murder, viewing it more like an extermination, or the hunt of a deadly animal. In Kevos' eyes, Sarah was a monster, like all nixirs. The fact that his confinement had been so short and the elders had given no additional punishments for his threat told Jotaha that Kevos wasn't the only one who thought this way, and some of the others who did held sway with the elders.

Kevos wouldn't even be sent on a pilgrimage to one of the shrines, perhaps even to Seta Zul's shrine to pay for his disrespect of her will. Instead, he would be allowed to remain in Draku Rin, free to roam among its people.

Perhaps free to try to harm Sarah again. Or worse, to spread his poison through words to the other citizens.

Jotaha sat beneath the peaked pavilion of his favorite drinking den, suspended among the lattices on the left wing. The fabric of the pavilion snapped in a sharp breeze rolling in from the ocean, where waves crashed against the rocky base of Draku Rin's perch. His gaze fixed upon the temple atop Draku Rin's skull, and his feet wanted to carry him back there, but the turmoil in his mind kept him rooted to his bench.

He had no idea what to say to Sarah, now that she could understand his words. They literally came from two different worlds, and her people had spent their entire existence trying to wipe out the yan-kanat and erase all memory of the Ajda from Gaia. Where did one even begin to talk, much less form a lasting bond, when that kind of history existed between them?

Sarah made him feel desire that was more powerful than anything he'd ever felt before. He wanted her so badly that his salavik ached whenever he saw her, pushing against the seal until it was scorched by the heat of Seta Zul's blood. His drahi's scent was now so engrained in his memory that he no longer had to flick his tongue to fill his senses with it. He could probably track her all across Theia by her teasing scent alone.

He didn't know if this unnatural desire was a result of Seta Zul's will, or of the divine blood that formed the seal over his salavik—or if it truly was inspired solely by the alien pheromones of his drahi. He did know that it wasn't enough to erase all the obstacles that stood between them. There had to be more for their mating to be successful. More than the promise of passion that only existed between a drahi and her mate.

When a flick of his tongue caught the flavor of Farona's light, familiar scent, his tension eased. He turned to see her approaching the pavilion along the walkway. Her tail swayed behind her with her happiness as she sped her graceful steps to reach him faster, never quite breaking into a run that would disrupt the others walking along the suspended path of the lattice, yet still moving quick enough that she was joining him within a handful of breaths.

She sank onto the bench beside him, her eyes bright as she looked up into his face. "I heard about your battle with Kevos. You put on quite a show that pleased the crowd."

Jotaha shrugged one shoulder. "He will be out of the healing pavilion by the end of the cycle." He lifted his crock to take a long swig of his jetaak, made of fermented beach-grass seeds.

Farona snorted delicately in amusement. "I'm sure he regretted disrespecting you. Ane-ata was beside herself with upset at the condition you left him in."

"Ane-ata is often beside herself with upset. It is one reason Kevos finds her so tiresome." He smirked, his head spines vibrating as he met Farona's eyes. "I hope she is visiting him now, and driving him mad with her endless fussing."

"I did suggest to her that he would appreciate her company during his recovery." Farona's eyes gleamed as they met his.

He huffed with amusement. "You are wicked."

Her head spines lifted. "Kevos offended you. He should have to pay a higher price than a defeat in the arena."

Jotaha huffed again. "He *is* paying a higher price. I'm sure Ane-ata took your suggestion to heart."

Farona's expression lightened again, her gaze fixed on his

face. "So, how is your nixir? I am surprised you have not returned to check on her."

"Her *name* is Sarah," Jotaha said flatly.

Farona looked away, her head bowing in apology. "I meant no offense, my beloved. I will refer to her by her name from now on."

Jotaha sighed, his shoulders curving towards the table as if heavy weights had suddenly been added to his back. "Farona... you cannot call me that anymore."

A long silence fell between them. He felt her gaze studying his face, though he kept his eyes on his now-empty crock.

"You don't have to mate her, Ha-tah," she said in a soft voice. "Seta Zul's priest will remove her seal if you cannot bear the thought of taking this nixir as your drahi."

He had considered it. The chasm between his world and Sarah's was far greater than the size of the urvaka. While they were isolated in the caves, he could pretend everything would be okay, and that she could integrate easily into his society and become like another yan-kanat—albeit a strange-looking one. His first doubts had come when he encountered Kevos in the barrens and realized that not all of his people would be so eager to have Sarah living amongst them.

Almost losing her to the parasites that had infested her stomach made him realize how important she already was to him. The thought of sending her away—likely to a larger skilev like Bal Goro, because the elders would never let her return to Gaia to spread news of their lands to the other nixirs—made him more anxious than he had ever been before any dangerous battle. There were some nixirs in Bal Goro—a small enclave of them—but they were not from the same region of Gaia as Sarah. She might not feel any more at home among them than she did among the citizens of Draku Rin. Nixir cultures and languages were vastly varied, which was probably why they warred among their own kind so often.

Yes, he had considered having the seal removed, despite the consequences, but had to reject that idea. He couldn't let Sarah go. He knew he would only end up following her, seal or no seal.

Farona sat silently, watching him as if she could read his thoughts in his expression. She knew him better than anyone in Draku Rin. If he was revealing his inner turmoil, she would understand it.

"I would be dishonored. Unable to sire nestlings. I would have to plead to Seta Zul to forgive me, and make a sacrifice to her simply to earn back any of her favor. That pilgrimage alone would take many cycles." He shook his head, his head spines flattening. "I would return broken, impoverished, and forever infertile."

Farona gripped his arm, her slender, long fingers settling on his bicep. "I would still love you! You will always have me, Hatah!" Her hold tightened as she pulled herself closer to him on the bench. "I don't care if I can never have nestlings with you. You belong to me."

Jotaha gently dislodged her hand, setting it on the table and settling his own over it for the briefest of moments. Her hand was cool beneath his palm. As cool as his own. Her scales were smooth, small, shiny—and familiar. Her scent reminded him of many warm seasons spent walking along the beach, searching for kivan shells together as they planned their future home.

None of that was enough to chase away the memories of hot, soft nixir skin warming his scales, or that teasing, otherworldly scent filling his head, or the flash of alien eyes brightened by the dangerous fire that seemed to burn inside all nixirs.

He pulled his hand away from Farona's, wrapping it back around his crock to lift it up in a signal to the brewer to refill his drink. "I regret the outcome of my sealing, Farona. I regret that it is hurting you." He fell silent as the brewer arrived at their table with a warm clay jug to pour another round for him.

Farona rejected his offer of a drink, her gaze never leaving his face, her eyes shadowed with her pain as she sensed his rejection.

When the brewer left, he kept his gaze fixed on the pale green liquid in his crock. "Seta Zul chose Sarah to be my drahi for a reason. One that is incomprehensible to us mortals, but she is a goddess and can see far beyond our narrow view." He glanced her way only briefly, then looked away again, unable to face the growing pain he saw on her face. "I want to be with Sarah, Farona. I cannot think of being with anyone other than her, now that I have been marked."

He heard her choked gasp. Knew it meant she was biting back tears. He wanted to be anywhere else in that moment, but knew that standing up to leave would only hurt her feelings more. He took a heavy swig of his drink without looking her way, giving her time to compose herself.

She drew her hand from the table, lower it to grasp her other hand in her lap to twist them together. "I only want you to be happy, Ha-tah. If this is your decision, then I will honor it. It will hurt. I cannot lie to you, my... old friend, but I will welcome your... Sarah to Draku Rin as a friend. She will need them among us, I suspect. You know that Kevos is not the only one who will defy Seta Zul's will because of hatred for the nixirs."

His shoulders slumped as all the tension left his body, gratitude for Farona's understanding and kindness filling him with relief. Her commitment meant that other females would also accept Sarah more readily into their circle. That would help with integrating her into yan-kanat society.

Now he just had to figure out what to say to his drahi, because he still had no idea how to explain what she meant to him.

Farona had risen to leave, promising that she would call upon Sarah after the first turn of the following cycle, when a temple acolyte running along the lattice caused sharp rebukes from other pedestrians. The commotion drew both his and Farona's attention, since it was unusual to see such rude behavior.

They both turned to see the acolyte rushing towards them. Jotaha jumped to his feet, his heart thudding as he recognized the panic in the young yan-kanat's eyes.

The acolyte skidded to a halt in front of their table, his hands waving with his anxiousness. "The nixir! She has left her room and is wandering around the temple. No one knows what to do about it, and the elders said to find you so that you could contain her."

"She is not a wild animal!" Jotaha snarled, exasperated by the behavior of elders who should know better. He wished Arokiv was around to calm their nerves. That elder seemed to be quite comfortable around nixirs.

"You should go quickly, Ha-tah," Farona said, her expression sympathetic. "She might be distressed to find herself in such a foreign environment alone. She will need you, not a doddering elder, to comfort her."

Farona was correct, as always. Her wisdom was as expansive as her kindness. He had been wrong to wait so long before returning to Sarah. Even if he couldn't find the right words to speak to her, he could not simply ignore her until inspiration struck him. Sarah was not the kind of female to sit quietly in her quarters until her mate came knocking to escort her.

29

Sarah could feel eyes upon her as she made her way through the building where she was being kept. At least one of those pairs of eyes had to belong to the guard that had been stationed outside the rooms where she'd recovered. He'd seemed startled when she'd suddenly opened the door, and had backed away several feet when she'd walked out of it. He'd also stuttered when she'd asked him where Jotaha was, seeming not to have an answer.

She'd told him she would go exploring on her own then, growing truly irritated with Jotaha leaving her to her own devices for so long. Granted, the servants had brought her generous offerings, but if he thought he could just ignore her indefinitely while sending gifts and comforts her way, he had another think coming.

The building she was in filled her with awe as she roamed its wide corridors, beneath vaulted ceilings that stretched far overhead. She had seen the steeple from the sky lift, and had noted the similarity to gothic architecture even with as sick as she'd been then. The horns of the dragon skull had formed towers surrounded by the flying buttresses that supported the primary cathedral.

The rooms she passed were accessible through peaked archways, with sun-bleached wooden doors that towered above her head. Heavily carved stone columns supported the bases of the vaulted ceilings, and many of them glowed with light and warmth, clearly made of the same inferno stones Jotaha used in place of campfires.

Instead of gargoyle grotesques, dragons clung to every surface, carved from stone—glowing or simple granite— and crystals of ever color, or wood of many different shades, from the darkest ebony to the palest birch.

Gorgeous and intricate woven rugs, softly gleaming with silken threads, warmed the stone floors as light spilled through tall, multipaned windows. That sunlight seemed to nourish the multitude of potted plants tucked against every column and surrounding every stone bench. There were even trees planted within the corridors, their blossom-laden branches stretching towards the vaulted ceilings.

She could explore this place forever. It was so beautiful it was almost breathtaking. Elaborate architecture was rare in Arizona, limited primarily to a few city locations, and she'd seen nothing like this in her admittedly sparse travel experience.

Her surroundings reminded her unequivocally that she was in another world, and after seeing this place, she couldn't imagine ever returning to her dull and sand colored world, with the boxy, flat-roofed buildings and metal pop-ups that were painfully utilitarian and obviously designed to be cheap rather than beautiful. Even expensive modern architecture lacked this kind of style and beauty, aiming for a futuristic design that seemed to defy the classical understanding of aesthetics.

This place spoke to her on some primal level that made her

pause so often to soak in her surroundings that she could hear the frantic whispering of the small entourage of yan-kanat following at a safe distance. They would dart behind columns or plants or statues when she turned to look in their direction, but she knew they were there. It would be funny, if it wasn't a stark reminder of how alone and isolated she felt. They were too afraid to approach her, and she didn't think it was because of her veins faintly glowing beneath her skin.

She entered a massive room that had to be some kind of library. It was filled with shelves and cubbies groaning under the weight of thousands upon thousands of bound books and scrolls. Carved bas-relief images covered one entire wall, some of which glowed with inferno stones. She was drawn to that wall, despite the many distracting shelves and pedestals with carvings and intriguing objects upon them.

In the bas-relief, a beautiful woman writhed as though in pain, her hair floating around her head as if she were moving in water. The artist had managed to capture the motion of her body in the static stone with such brilliance that Sarah could almost see her struggles unfold. She might be floating like she was submerged, but a halo of flames surrounded her, glowing with the light and warmth of inlaid inferno stones, that could have been the cause of her pain.

Or it could have been the dragon that was rendered so small as to be the size of a brooch on the woman—though instead of clinging to the filmy fabric that barely concealed her naked body, it hung onto her throat, and close inspection showed that its teeth were embedded in her flesh.

Given the number of dragons that filled this building, it was strange to see one carved so tiny in comparison to a beautiful human woman, even though the little dragon appeared to be winning whatever battle they were locked in.

"That carving depicts the battle of Bal Goro and the titaness Theia," Jotaha said from behind her.

She yelped and spun around to face him, realizing she'd been so entranced by the carving that she hadn't even been aware of him approaching her. "You're here! Finally."

He stepped closer to her and the carving. "I'm sorry for leaving you alone so long. I had to take care of something that couldn't wait."

Before she could respond with the many questions she had, he gestured to the carving as if he wanted to distract her. "After the children of the titans—the cursed Olympians—created the nixirs who immediately decided to conquer Gaia, the elder god Bal Goro knew that his children—the yan-kanat—needed a refuge of their own to escape the massacre. He challenged the titaness, Theia, to a duel."

Jotaha slowly shook his head as he stared at the carving. "She agreed, believing there was no way he could win. She vastly underestimated him. After he slayed her, he made her heart into our world, her ribs into the urvaka that protects it from the nixirs, and her flesh into the veil that binds us to Gaia through the urvaka."

She couldn't resist the distraction, even though that was what she knew it to be. Jotaha clearly wasn't ready to talk about the whole "mate" thing yet. "So, the titans really existed, huh? Just like dragons. On Earth, we just assume they were all myths invented to explain natural phenomenon." She cocked her head, studying Theia's image with even more interest. "She looks like a human woman. A beautiful one."

Jotaha huffed. "She is a titan. She can choose to look however she wishes to look. They are not usually bound by any corporeal form, nor by time or space. They can be as big as worlds, or as small as the chanu zayul. They take on an endless variety of forms, based on whatever suits their unknowable desires. They live between many different realities in ways mortals cannot comprehend. Only the Ajda are their equals."

"The dragons—the Ajda—live between realities too?"

Jotaha now stood beside her, his eyes remaining on the mural. She had to crane her neck to look up at him as he studied the carving so intently that she suspected he was using it to avoid looking in her direction.

"The Ajda do not stride through multiple realities. They were born from the stars in this dimension. They are powerful and immortal, but even they cannot follow the titans to other dimensions."

"This whole city, it's a dragon skeleton, isn't it?"

He glanced down at her and she bit her lip, hoping she wasn't asking anything offensive. He already looked so remote, his expression closed off as if he was talking to a stranger.

Was that what they were now? Could they ever go back to their comradery in the final days they spent in the urvaka, working together to survive without the need for many words between them?

He turned his focus back to the carving. "Despite the fact that the duel was fairly accepted, the other titans were angry that their sister would be forever bound to this form. They demanded the Ajda surrender to them and become their slaves in return. A war was inevitable, but the Wise One, upon whose head we now stand, advised that the Ajda make a compromise and shed their mighty forms to adorn Theia's body for all time. This sacrifice was not made for the Ajda, for they are children of the stars and would survive even the wrath of the titans."

He tapped the middle of his chest with a quick glance at her. "It was made for *us*, so that the titans would not destroy our world to keep us from living upon it." He waved a hand as if to indicate their general surroundings. "We live upon their bones to honor their sacrifice and make something beautiful out of their remains."

"So they all died for your people." She sighed. "You're lucky you have gods that cared about you. Seems like any gods that humans might have had abandoned us long ago, without giving a single damn what happened to us."

She felt his gaze fall upon her again, but when she turned her head to meet his eyes, he quickly shifted it back to the bas-relief. "The nixirs rejected their creators and eventually turned upon them. They wanted to decide their own path and set themselves above all others to become gods in their own right. This is what the legends say about your people."

Sarah's nod was automatic. "I can't actually disagree with that. I think that is the end goal for a lot of humans—to become gods ourselves. That's why interest in transhumanism is growing so fast right now in my world."

This managed to gain a curious glance that lasted long enough for Sarah to meet his eyes. "What is this word? It is in your een-lix, is it not?" He hissed the "sh" sound when he attempted to say "English." She found it rather adorable, even if it was an inhuman accent.

"Transhumanism. It means some people want to evolve our species into godlike superbeings by blending our bodies with machines to get rid of any human limitations."

"Nixir machines are virtually useless in this world. Most of them die immediately in the urvaka, and none of them last long enough to use once taken away from the boundary."

"That's probably a good thing," Sarah said, imagining what it would be like if the military could manage to send unmanned probes through the vast maze of caves and tunnels and discover this beautiful world hiding behind that barrier.

Jotaha shrugged as if the thought of a war against human-made machines wasn't an issue for him.

He gestured to the dragon on the neck of the titaness. "Our Ajda did not die. Most of them left Theia once they shed their skins. We do not know where they have gone, but we know their infernos continue to burn. As long as that is the case, they will eventually regrow bodies as powerful as the ones they left behind." He broke eye contact, his jaw tight as if he bit back words better kept silent between them. "I believe the Ajda would return to protect us if the humans found a way to send their machines against us."

Silence fell between them as Sarah pondered that. If the dragons still lived on in some form, she wondered if they would eventually decide to return to Earth to take up their place there among the apex predators. Although Earth might be too much of a challenge now, even against massive dragons. After all, fighter jets and stealth bombers might not make it through the urvaka, but they had no problem navigating Earth's skies.

"Do you miss them?" Her voice sounded loud as it broke the tense silence.

Jotaha took a long moment to respond. "Seta Zul remains. She chose not to follow Bal Goro's ruling because of the enmity between them. Yet, she did agree to remain upon Theia, and so the titans accepted the compromise. Now, she is the one who dictates our destiny. She decides if we are to have a family and continue our line—and whose bloodline will share it."

"And she chose me to be your mate." She nodded slowly. "I can see why you probably think you would be better off without your gods around, mucking up your own plans."

"Sarah...." Jotaha turned towards her, but she kept her eyes on the carving, her gaze trailing across the mural to take in other images of battles depicted in what could be chronological order.

"Is that another titan?" she asked, noting a dragon lying on its side, its head turned to look upwards in an almost pleading fashion. A human-looking male stood over it with a spear buried in its chest. This time, the titan and the dragon were depicted as much closer in size.

Jotaha must have picked up on the fact that it was her turn to avoid the subject that still hung between them, unresolved. He turned back to the mural, taking several steps towards the carving in question. "That is a nixir. The only one who ever successfully slayed an Ajda. The betrayer." His voice hardened, his head spines twitching upwards as if they wanted to fully extend.

"Oh...." The image looked somewhat familiar, now that she knew the man depicted was human. Almost like she'd seen something like it before. "I'm surprised an immortal dragon could be killed. Especially by a single human."

He shot her an unreadable glance. "Even the stars themselves will die when they have no more desire to burn."

"That's... sad. And poetic."

Another long silence fell as they stood there staring at the mural. Sarah was the one to break it, again. "When are we going to stop doing this?"

His expression was startled as turned to face her. "Doing what?"

She sighed, crossing her arms over her chest as she rubbed her upper arms, even though the warmth of the inferno stones kept the temperature in the vast room comfortable. "When are we going to stop dancing around the subject of you having a mate you don't want?"

He closed the distance between them so fast that she barely had a chance to blink before he caught her in his arms and pulled her against his chest. The tunic he wore was thin enough that she could feel the bulge of hard muscles twitching against her trapped arms.

"I *do* want you, Sarah," he ground out in a harsh voice. "More than I've ever wanted anything. I don't know what our future will be like, and that worries me, but I can't seem to care enough about that to give you up."

She tried to push away from him, feeling suddenly vulnerable trapped in his arms, even as she also wanted to sag against him and let his strength support her. The conflicting emotions caused her voice to waver, as hope warred with caution gained from far too much hard life experience. "You want Farona. She's the mate you hoped for."

He released her enough to set her a few steps away from him, yet still well within reach of his hands. They shifted from her back to cradle her face, his claws tentatively trailing through her now smooth hair. He looked down at her face as if he was studying her features, perhaps trying to learn to read her expressions as she struggled to read his.

"Ever since we were born, Farona and I spent almost every moment of our lives together. It was simply understood that we would end up being mated. I never even considered it turning out otherwise."

At the flinch Sarah wasn't able to hold back, his hand tightened in her hair, tugging her closer to him, so when he lowered his head, his breath sighed over her brow, cool against her hot skin. "I had my entire life figured out, Sarah. Until you entered it and destroyed all my neatly laid plans. You've changed everything. Even the way I look at my own world."

His lips stroked over her brow, his nose pressed against her hair. She felt his tongue flick out to stroke along her temple, as if the warmth of skin throbbing with her rapid pulse drew him to taste her.

"I resisted that at first," he said, his voice deep and gravelly, as if he drew his words from some dark well inside him. "I didn't want to change. I clung to the idea of being in love with Farona, because loving you scares me. I am afraid you cannot love me back, because I am yan-kanat and you are nixir. The nixir that slayed the Ajda claimed to love her, until she bared her inferno to him, and he struck her through it with his spear. If a nixir cannot even learn to love an elder goddess, then how could one ever learn to love a simple yan-kanat."

Sarah tilted her head upwards, capturing his mouth with her lips. She shivered as he hungrily claimed her mouth, his tongue flicking along her lips as his parted. Her own tongue darted out, brushing against his in invitation. One he accepted, his tongue slipping past her lips as he groaned.

The stroke of his lips against hers was masterful, telling her that the yan-kanat—despite their differences from humans—had certainly discovered the pleasure of kissing in their culture.

When he broke the kiss, she moaned in protest, realizing that she was clinging to him with both hands clutching his waist and one leg lifted. Her inner thigh pressed against the kilt-like garment that covered his lower body as if she was planning to climb him like a tree. To get closer to the source of that kiss, to have him drive his tongue deeper as he claimed her mouth, she just might.

He lifted his head, one hand stroking over her hair, smoothing it in a way that reminded her he had knocked the decorative comb from her hair as his claws dug through it during their passionate kiss. She'd only vaguely heard the soft tinkle as it struck the ground behind her, freeing the heavy mass of her hair to swing loose at her back.

"You did not say you could learn to love me, Sarah," he said in a soft voice, nearly a whisper.

A wicked grin stretched her lips, still sensitive from his kiss. "I think you might be able to convince me. If you do more of that."

He huffed with amusement. "Is that all it takes to please a fierce nixir female?"

Her gaze shifted from his face, trailing down his body. "I think I can think of other things that might also please this... human girl."

"I knew you were a shataz, beautiful Sarah. You possess the kind of passion a yan-kanat dreams of in his drahi."

She pulled away from him, her brows drawing together. "Did you just call me a prostitute?"

Hurt and confusion caused a glow to spark along her veins as she crossed her arms in front of her, as if she could defend against the implication of his words. Perhaps drahi for the yan-kanat was not what she'd assumed.

He looked confused as well when she withdrew. "Is that not the correct word for a nixir female with great skill and passion in the mating chamber? The shatazurans are highly prized nixir females that your males send armies to reclaim from those yan-kanat daring enough to steal them away."

Sarah held up a hand. "Hold on. I think we're suffering a translation error here. Human males treat prostitutes like they're nothing but trash. In fact, 'polite' human society reviles sex workers where I come from. It's even illegal, and yet somehow, it's always the sex worker and not the client who seems to pay for the crime."

He shook his head, his head spines at half-mast in what she was coming to learn was a defensive, uncertain posture for them to take. "I'm sorry, Sarah. This is not what our legends have said about the shataz. Even the female whose comb you wore was one such woman, and several human males tried to follow to reclaim her when she crossed the boundary into the urvaka with the yan-kanat who captured her."

Sarah bent down to pick up the decorative comb, noting again that it looked like something made in the nineteenth century. She was no expert, but she would guess Victorian era. "I don't suppose you have more information about this shataz, do you?"

Jotaha nodded once. "It would be in our museum if we do. She did not live within Draku Rin when she was here. Her mate chose to take her to live in the baselands to avoid...."

Her eyes lifted from the comb to meet his when his voice trailed off. "To avoid the bigotry, right? She wasn't any more welcomed here than I am."

Jotaha turned his head, breaking eye contact. "She would have been allowed to live here. Seta Zul decreed she was his drahi. She had a right to live within the skilev. It is said that she felt more comfortable in the countryside, away from others. There were many who were envious of her mate because her skills were said to be legendary, and she possessed the grace and passion of a titaness."

Sarah quickly twisted her hair into a bun and tucked the comb into it to hold it in place. "I'm sorry to disappoint you, Jotaha, but I am not a shataz. I don't have much skill in the bedroom. I... I work on computers for a living. I design software, which probably means absolutely nothing here."

"You create nixir machines?" Jotaha's expression, his spines lifting even higher than half mast, told her maybe it would have been better if he hadn't understood her English words as much as he apparently did.

"You... know what 'software' is?"

He straightened, swaying away from her as if it was an automatic reaction to move away from her but his feet wouldn't budge. "The elder, Arokiv, is familiar with the nixir world. I have heard of 'software' and 'comp-u-doors' that make the nixir machines work better." He lowered his chin, his eyes narrowed. "As Jotaha, I have encountered the machines sent through the boundary by the nixirs. Though they do not live long in the urvaka, Arokiv believed that I should have some understanding of their danger."

"Does this mean you don't want me as your drahi anymore?"

Had she really been this close to finding a true love, someone who was destined to remain at her side—by a dragon goddess no less—only to have him turn her down because she engineered software? It seemed absurd, but she regretted ever mentioning her profession. She should have let him believe she was a shataz. Clearly, they had a much higher opinion of that profession in this world than in the human one.

He gripped her by the shoulders, his expression suddenly turning fierce, his brows meeting and lowering to shadow his eyes. "I don't care how many nixir machines you've created. You are my drahi, and I will never let you go." He pulled her against his chest, and she let him without resisting, sagging with relief at his words. "I will find a way to make you love me, Sarah. You will be loyal to *me*, not your people, and you will never create another machine again."

She knew she should protest such domineering statements, but she wasn't really all that loyal to humans, not that she'd ever had to consider that kind of thing before. She wouldn't participate in an alien invasion of Earth, and she would certainly stand with any army raised to defend her own world, but she sure as hell wouldn't help humanity invade some other world to conquer and dominate its people. She doubted there would ever be a situation where she would feel conflicted about her loyalties.

As for never creating a machine again, she did have to consider that for a moment longer. She wouldn't need video games for escapism anymore. Not if she was navigating a world as fascinating as any game she'd ever played. She'd also discovered that there were many modern-ish comforts in this world, so she didn't see a need to invent some more advanced options, not that she was that kind of engineer anyway. She'd chosen computer science because she knew it was a lucrative career and she had a knack for computer technology. She wasn't married to it, nor in love with it.

She had no problem picking an exciting, exotic, and intriguing lover like Jotaha over her career. "I think I can love you, Jotaha. I'm halfway there already."

More than halfway. She was pretty sure she was already in love with him, but they had only just begun to speak to each other in a way they could both comprehend. There was still so much to learn about him. She didn't want to find out that she had fallen in love with a dream, only to learn the hard way that the reality was a nightmare.

Jotaha suddenly lifted her off her feet, sweeping her into his arms as she yelped in surprise and clutched at his shoulders. "I'm taking you home, Sarah. I want you to see what I can give you. I want you to know that you will never want for anything, and you won't miss the world you left behind."

Carried like this in his arms, Sarah could see his face so clearly. She could finally touch him there, when he was usually out of her reach, being so much taller than her. She stroked hesitant fingers over his spines, which twitched against her palm. At her touch, he turned his head so his scales stroked over her palm, like a cat rubbing its head against a favorite person.

She was so fascinated with Jotaha that she almost missed her second view of the dragon bone city. She finally broke her gaze away from him when he carried her onto the sky lift. She caught sight of the relieved expressions on the faces of the guards that followed a respectful distance behind them as they left the temple.

The city was so big that it would probably take weeks to fully explore. She was fascinated by the odd buildings that spread out across the wingspan of the dragon skeleton. The scaffolding that linked the suspended pod-like buildings appeared far sturdier than she'd initially thought on her first, more distracted, journey to the temple.

Jotaha pointed out many sights along the way, and Sarah quickly grew overwhelmed, still seeing the shape of a massive dragon beneath the many structures that had been cleverly and artistically integrated into its bones.

"Draku Rin—Wise One," she whispered. "He must have been magnificent in all his glory!"

"There are many carvings and statues of him," Jotaha said, his eyes on her rather than the city that spread out below them. "You probably passed most of them in the temple."

"All of that was of him, huh?"

Jotaha huffed his version of a chuckle. "Not all. Bal Goro and the others are represented as well, but Draku Rin is our patron. He was the chief advisor to the Overlord of all Ajda, Bal Goro. He is the most often depicted in our skilev."

"Bal Goro—brutal teacher. Not two words you usually associate with each other."

Jotaha looked out at the skilev as they descended, leaving the outspread wings of the city behind them. "His lessons were often cruel and uncompromising. His advisor had far more patience and compassion, though the residents of Bal Goro's skilev do not appreciate being reminded of that."

"Yan-kanat history is fascinating!" Sarah gazed out over the city, noting that the bulk of the dragon's skeleton was now above them, with the hillside it adorned being laid out in huge terraced groves and farmlands, supported by massive rib bones.

"Nixir history also seems fascinating to my people. Your people are born from the children of titans."

Sarah scoffed. "Yeah, we didn't do much with that blood relationship, did we? Seems like we couldn't wait to destroy any myth or magic in our world. I'm not surprised we killed our own creators. It's something humans would do."

Jotaha slowly shook his head. "I cannot believe I am the one to say this, and to my nixir drahi, no less, but your people are impressive to us. We fear the nixirs, yes, but we also admire how powerful you have become, despite being so physically unimposing."

He waved a hand towards the city above them. "All of this was built with the aid of the elder gods, and much of it still benefits from their magic, which fills this world. Even Theia herself was a gift to us from our gods. Nixirs forged their own cities and created their own form of magic with their machines, bending Gaia to their will with their clever minds alone."

Sarah shifted on Jotaha's lap, grateful they were alone in this sky lift so she didn't feel self-conscious allowing him to continue holding her close. "Just... don't follow in our footsteps if you ever get tired of living in harmony with your elder gods and their gifts. We've made a lot of mistakes along the way, and I don't think we've become better people for it."

She laid her head on his strong shoulder, feeling the fine weave of his tunic beneath her cheek, the only softness to cushion hard scale and muscle. "I can think of the cities that cover Earth, the skyscrapers that pierce the clouds, the breathtaking cathedrals that glorify deities no one really seems to believe in anymore, and the Internet, that ties everyone in the world together, no matter how distant they are from each other. I can think of these wondrous things, and be proud of being human, but then I see what you have here, in this world, and I feel sorry for humanity. They will never know this kind of magic. I also don't think we have it in our hearts to stop pushing for more. I'm afraid that we will finally get exactly what we think we want, only for it to destroy us."

The sky lift came to a stop before Jotaha could respond to her, and she felt almost relieved by that. She was afraid that he would agree with her pessimistic assessment.

She tried to slide off his lap to step off the sky lift on her own two feet, but he wasn't having it. He gathered her back up into his arms and carried her off the lift.

She felt dainty, light as a feather, and unnervingly far off the ground in his arms. It was an unusual experience for her. Those thoughts fled when she caught sight of the home he was taking her to, as he traveled along a stone paved path through a small grove of trees towards a structure with multiple peaked roofs, shingled by what looked to be orange scales as long as skateboards and twice as wide.

The house itself was framed up by bones—a variety of animal bones, rather than the dragon bones that made up the city. To her relief, there were no human-looking bones among the mix, but it was still a startling sight. The bones appeared to be lacquered and carved, with some ubiquitous dragons on them, but also other fanciful-looking beasts that probably weren't all that fanciful in this world. Those horned, multi-tailed, ridge-backed, spike bearing monsters might even be the owners of the bones that now bore their carvings.

The walls were made of lacquered hide, stripped of any fur and appearing as solid as stone, though the stretch of leathery membrane was unmistakable.

The double doors were conventional wood, made of the same bleached white that some of the doors in the temple had been.

A garden of colorful flowers and plants surrounded the entire house, which was probably about the size of a small tract home, but definitely nowhere near as bland and sterile as one. Unlike the density of the buildings in the city, this one appeared to have some property surrounding it, which included the grove they'd passed through after leaving the sky lift station.

Jotaha carried her around to the back of the property to show her an incredible view of an ocean behind the house, along with a sweeping stone terrace that had a set of stairs leading down towards a beach below them.

He finally set her on her feet on the stone terrace so she could stand at the retaining wall to look down at the beach.

"This out-terrace is one of the most desirable in the skilev. I chose it to be a home for my drahi as soon as I saw it, and the final touches are almost complete for our mating. We will live in my old quarters in the left wing until the first mating ceremony. After we bond, we will begin our seclusion in this home."

She turned from the beach to study him, noting that he stood ramrod straight, tension clear in his squared shoulders, his spines shifting as he avoided her gaze.

She knew, before he mentioned that he'd picked this home

for his drahi, that he wasn't talking about her. This place had been chosen with Farona in mind. She would have to live with that, knowing that all those "final touches" probably were also meant to appeal to another woman. He undoubtedly figured this would occur to her, which was probably why he looked so tense.

"So, I have many questions, especially about this 'first mating ceremony' and 'seclusion'," she said, forcing a bright smile. "But they can all come after I finish the tour of our future home. What I'm already seeing is beautiful!"

She tried to focus on the beach view as she injected admiration into her tone, and ignore the bones and hide and oversized scales. The house did have a certain artistry to it, but it was alien in architecture and materials to what she was used to, and she didn't know if she could ever forget that it was built for someone else.

30

Everything seemed to be working out with his drahi. She appeared to be accepting of his claim, and it even seemed like she might care for him, and might someday be able to feel for him the way he felt for her. He should be relieved, and happy. Instead, Jotaha was tense and uncomfortable around her, though some of that was because his need for her only grew more difficult to ignore as her scent filled his head. They would need to have the first mating ceremony soon, or he would end up burning off his salavik because of his unquenchable desire for Sarah.

The idea to take her to their future home as a means to distract them both was a terrible one. There was so much within the home that he should have changed before bringing her here. Everywhere he looked as he led her into the house, he saw his plans for Farona. The furniture, the plants, the ornaments, the cooking room, the weaving room, the brewing chamber, even the mating room, had all been chosen for Farona.

He suspected that Sarah was aware of this. Her voice took on a falsely high-pitched tone as she dutifully complimented everything she saw, even though the drooping of her shoulders and the difficulty she had in holding onto her nixir grin told him a different story about how she felt about the house.

She didn't like this home, nor should he expect her to. She might not even like the location. He and Farona had daydreamed about living just above the beach where they spent so much time as nestlings, before he entered into jotah training. He had no idea if nixirs even liked the water, though Gaia was blessed with so much of it.

He also didn't know if Sarah even wanted a fruit grove of her own, or a full garden from which to harvest produce and herbs for her brewing and cooking. He wasn't even certain she did such things, though he was sure Farona would teach her if she asked.

When he and Farona were nestlings, they had dreamed big, though they both grew up on the bottom edge of the left wing, packed in like so many of the poorer yan-kanat. Jotaha had lost his father when he was just leaving the nest to enter training, and his mother had died not long after her mate, leaving Jotaha with no one but Farona and her family to turn to, since his parents had not had a fruitful mating and he had no nest-kin.

While Jotaha had focused on becoming a better hunter and fighter in the hopes the chanu zayul would someday choose him and elevate his status, Farona had built her wealth through learning many different skills. They were both successful now, but they both still lived on the wing, because they had planned to move to an out-terrace together.

He had no idea what Farona would decide to do now, and prayed that Seta Zul would find another mate for her soon so she would not suffer any more heartache, but he had to focus on Sarah, and find out what her dreams for her future were. He could not give her a life filled with the machines she apparently created, but he would promise her anything this world could provide for her.

Including a different home. One that wasn't built for someone else. One that Sarah herself could choose.

"What was your home like, on Gaia?"

Sarah turned from her examination of a silk-spider incubator in the weaving room. The confusion drawing her brows together eased as she focused on his question. "The townhome I lived in was about half this size. Just two nesting chambers, a living room, cooking chamber, and hygiene room. It still felt grand after living in my van."

"What is a 'van'?" It sounded as if she did not concern herself with space, if the home had been half the size of this one.

Sarah's tension returned, her lips flattening as she shrugged her shoulders. The movement caused the dress she wore to slide over her unbound chest mounds, causing the tips of them to harden. They were so alien, yet he could remember staring at similar mounds on the murals of the titaness Theia and wondering what they felt like. Whether they were as soft as some said, or as stiff as the stones beneath his feet. As deviant as it felt to him, he wanted to know, and his salavik was in complete agreement. He was so focused on that intriguing mystery that he nearly missed her answer to his question.

"....to explain. I guess it's like a carriage or cart, only it doesn't need any animals to pull it."

He pushed away the thoughts that made it difficult to stand so close to her without touching her, focusing instead on her words. That should distract him. As long as they didn't talk about mating chambers, or beds, or clothing and the removal of it. "So, it moves with the aid of nixir machines?"

She nodded. "It does. Some of our vehicles have become really advanced, and practically drive themselves."

"Carts are usually small, though some can be spacious. Your 'vans', are they often used as homes for nixirs?"

Sarah sighed, slowly shaking her head. "More often than

they should be, I suspect. There are too many people who don't have a home in my world, and I swear that number only seems to be growing as the years pass."

"Why didn't *you* have a home?"

Even the poorest of Draku Rin's citizens were housed and fed as they received skill training to apply to apprenticeships. Caring for the people was the responsibility of the temple, but the nixirs had probably killed their gods so they could take their place. They probably had no more temples to provide for their poor.

Sarah frowned. She didn't like that question. It made her upset or sad. He still wasn't sure which as she turned away from him, pretending to study a wood carving on a nearby stand.

"I grew up in an upper-class home. My parents were both professionals who made good money. They were career driven. Raising me was an afterthought. Then something happened that made them angry at me. When I didn't obey their orders, they told me to get out of their house, and I left. They never fought to get me back. They didn't care enough to make the effort."

Was this part of the nixir nature? To cast their nestlings into the street to live in a self-moving cart? Even the poorest of the yan-kanat would not throw their young out of their home, no matter how meager their provisions. They might turn to the temple for aid, but they wouldn't abandon their responsibilities. Yet, according to Sarah, if he was understanding correctly, her parents had more than enough resources to provide for her until her mate claimed her.

"If you ever left me, I would fight an army to get you back."

Her lips tilted upwards as she cast him a glance. "That should worry me, but I have no intention of leaving you, and I have to admit, it's nice to hear you care enough that you would go after me."

"You don't ever need to worry that I would hurt you, Sarah.

You are my drahi. When we are bound, I could not even raise an angry hand against you, even if that was in my nature." He shook his head, "and it is not. There is no honor in striking a female, for any reason."

She gestured like she was wiping her brow. "Whew! That's a relief."

Her nixir grin had returned, along with a lift of her shoulders. Her tone took on a lighter note, as if she wasn't seriously concerned that he might hurt her. "You know," she held out her arm, showing the faint glimmer of bioluminescence. "I feel really strong lately. It's like these bugs in my head are giving me super powers. I might even be able to kick your ass if you make me angry."

Her tone said she was teasing, but he had to make her understand, in case she seriously believed she was strong enough to fight any yan-kanat, much less him. "Even with the aid of the chanu zayul, who will make you stronger and healthier, you could not fight one of my kind effectively. The nixirs only succeeded in conquering our lands through superior numbers, underhanded tactics, and their clever weapons. Individually, your people don't have a chance against mine."

Sarah propped her hands on her hips, her full lower lip jutting out as she said, "Aw, and here I wanted to become a gladiator in your arena. Kicking ass and taking names."

He cocked his head, unsure whether she was teasing him or serious. Her choice of idioms was confusing. "Why would you take names?"

Sarah laughed, then shrugged. "You know, I have no idea. It's just a human saying."

"You don't *really* want to fight in the arena do you?"

If she did, he would have to find a way to discourage that foolish notion. Yan-kanat females did not fight. Not against each other, and certainly never against a male. They were graceful, elegant, and delicate. Fighting was only for the males, and no one in Draku Rin would look kindly upon Sarah trying her hand at such an activity. Least of all him.

She had a fighting spirit within her, and he admired her for that, but she would never win, she could get hurt, and she would end up reminding his people that the nixirs were filled with so much violence that even their females battled for fun.

Sarah waved her hand in front of her as if brushing aside his question. "I'm not a fan of pain, so I'll pass on that career option." Then her teasing expression shifted to a curious one. "Wait, you *do* have an arena, don't you? The chanu zayul keep giving me a word for it, so it must be something that exists for you guys."

"The arena is for males only, my drahi. You would not be permitted to go there, much less participate."

She tapped her lip with one clawless finger. "You know, I'm not sure how I feel about that."

Jotaha stepped closer to her to settle a hand on her shoulder, his fingers toying with her sleek head fibers since he couldn't resist the urge to touch them when he was this close. "It doesn't matter how you feel about such rules. They are the law of this land. Please, Sarah, don't break them. You will only make things more difficult for yourself."

She nodded, multiple times, as appeared to be the nixir way of agreement. "Fine, but I'm just curious. If I was a man, would I be allowed to participate?"

He stiffened at the question, wishing she wouldn't ask such things. Knowing she probably wouldn't like the answer. "No nixir male would be allowed to live long enough to see Draku Rin, much less fight in our arena."

She nodded again, this time more slowly, but she still met his eyes when he thought she would lower hers. "I figured as much. You say I'm safe with you, Jotaha, and I believe that. But what about threats from other yan-kanat?"

He cupped her face between his hands, lowering his head

to taste her lips, as if he could steal away the words, when it was already too late to stop her from speaking them. She responded to his distraction hungrily, as if she wanted him as badly as he craved her. Impatient with the uncomfortable position he had to take to kiss his tiny drahi, he caught her by the waist and lifted her off her feet, straightening without breaking their liplock as his tongue delved inside her hot mouth, past teeth he knew could be sharp and painful despite being mostly flat.

He trusted her not to bite him. He trusted her not to want to hurt him. He trusted her to be true to her word.

Before he'd brought her home, he'd also trusted his people to treat his drahi as one of their own, simply because Seta Zul decreed it. Now, he wasn't so sure he could give her a reassuring answer to her question.

The pain of his seal burning as his salavik parted his slit forced him to pull away from Sarah's hungry lips, though it was tempting to let it burn a little longer just to continue to taste her and forget all the problems they had yet to face. He held her against his body with one arm around her waist, the other stroking down her back to clutch at her round, tailless bottom, pressing the heat between her legs against his seal. She writhed against him, her hands moving over his scales, tugging on his tunic to expose more of them to her touch.

She moaned when he lifted his head, then her warm lips trailed over his jaw as her hands lifted to clasp behind his neck and her legs hooked on his hips, her ankles locking behind him. He could feel the brush of her naked flesh against the ridge of his tail through the sensory scales that tipped it.

He grunted in pain as the feeling of her lips working their way down his neck to his collarbone caused his salavik to evert enough that the fire of the seal scorched the sensitive flesh and muscle.

"We must stop, Sarah." He pulled her away from him, and his body immediately ached for the warmth of hers. Fortunately, the pain of the seal caused his salavik to retreat back into his slit, but it was still eager, just as he was, to find its place inside his drahi's body. "We cannot go any further until we are bound. My seal is burning with how much I want you right now."

She didn't have the strength to resist his withdrawal as he set her back on her feet, then steadied her and kept her in place as she swayed towards him again. Her eyes were glazed, her lips plump and reddened from his mouth and tongue. Her head fibers were wild around her shoulders, mussed by his embrace. He wanted to let her come closer, wanted to answer the need he saw in her eyes with his own.

Seta Zul's seal had never felt more like a curse than it did now. If it wasn't there, he would have taken Sarah to the floor in that moment, showing her everything he knew about mating, and learning everything he wanted to know about her body before entering her hot vessel to feel it burning around him. He would never need a warming stone with Sarah in his bed, wrapped around him, writhing beneath him as he thrust into her.

"When you are bound to me, Sarah, I will make love to you every single cycle of our seclusion."

Her gaze sharpened as she sucked in a deep breath, swiping one hand through her head fibers to smooth them. "I never did ask what seclusion was, or a seal, for that matter."

He huffed in amusement as her gaze lowered to regard his natuk—his lower garment. His seal burned so brightly from their recent activities that some of that glow showed through the thick weave of the fabric. "I know. You have so many questions."

Her eyes shot up to meet his. "Yes, I definitely do. Um, your crotch is glowing orange. That's from the tattoo I saw when I first met you, isn't it?"

He nodded, once. "That is Seta Zul's seal. I am bound by it

until the first mating ceremony, where you will take it upon you as well, and then my salavik will be free to enter you."

"So, I'm going to have a glowing orange crotch tattoo too?" Her brows drew together in obvious concern as she glanced down again.

He would have to approach this carefully. She had already told him she did not like pain. He wasn't sure how she would react to know that the seal would burn her flesh in a brand. He also knew that he had to tell her before the ceremony so she wouldn't hate him when it happened.

"It will not glow, once we are bound together. For either of us."

A yan-kanat female went into a first mating ceremony understanding the upcoming pain, and the euphoric pleasure that followed. Most looked forward to it, knowing that the first mating was the most intense, but the nixirs knew so little about magic, if they knew anything at all. He wasn't certain if Sarah would anticipate it—or fear it—if she knew all the details.

So instead, he focused on her other question. One that he hoped she would find more palatable. "The seclusion I spoke of happens after the first mating ceremony. We will be taken from the temple and returned to our home where we will be confined for fifteen cycles, which is the length of a yan-kanat female's fertile period once she has completed the mating ritual. No one will interrupt us when we are in seclusion, but food and supplies will be left on our doorstep so we will want for nothing during that time."

Sarah's expression was unreadable as he explained this, and he realized that certain things would not necessarily be the same for them. He knew that nixir and yan-kanat blood could mix, and there were those even among the Draku Rin citizens who had some nixir blood running through their veins, though it would not be evident from their appearance. Many were descended from the exodus to Theia, when nixir females were taken as captives to punish the nixir armies that hunted them to extinction—then kept and claimed as mates, in the time before Seta Zul decreed that all matings must have her blessing to be fertile.

Nixirs had different fertile periods, and some records said those periods of fertility happened continuously, without any rituals or aid from potions and elixirs. The idea that a nixir female could become pregnant at any time, without preparation, explained much about the fact that the nixirs had so many more people on their world, and had always held an advantage of numbers over the yan-kanat.

Sarah might not even need fifteen cycles. She might even become pregnant with his nestling during the first mating ceremony. The thought filled him with hope, though he would look forward to the fifteen cycles of uninterrupted mating with great anticipation. He could not wait to begin their family, though he had concerns, despite knowing that their offspring would take after him in appearance. It wouldn't be the physical appearance of his nestlings that would bring them judgement, but rather what inherent nixir darkness might twist their spirit.

"Sarah, our nestlings will inherit all that is good in you. I believe that. They will not become twisted like the nixirs we fought in the urvaka."

Sarah's eyes widened, her face suddenly going pale. "Nestlings?" She shook her head, one hand lifting to rub at her forehead. "I hadn't even considered that yet! Can we even have children together? We're so... different." Then her forehead creased and she spoke again before he could respond. "What do you mean, we fought 'nixirs' in the urvaka? Are you talking about the bat-cat monsters? Those weren't humans."

"You have never seen the twisted ones in your world before?" He studied her, realizing that she was not pretending her shock. "They were of nixir blood. Even the urvak zayul identified them as such."

She pointed to herself. "Look at me, Jotaha! Do I have fur? Fangs? Claws? Those things were not like me!"

He rushed to reassure her. "I know, my drahi. You are not twisted by darkness as they were. You are all that is good within the nixirs. I know that you aren't like so many of them."

Sarah rubbed her forehead so hard that her skin creased and folded from the pressure. "No, you don't understand. Humans don't just... *change* into monsters. That's not...." She shook her head hard. "We don't have magic, Jotaha. We can't just shapeshift. There's no scientific explana—oh, no! Please, *please*, tell me the government isn't experimenting with genetic engineering on humans!"

Her words confused him, especially since she seemed to be asking him a question to which he couldn't possibly have the answer.

She threw her hands out, her anger palpable, though it wasn't directed at him. That much he could tell. "*Damn* them! How could they be so stupid, and reckless, and unethical as hell? We don't even *understand* these technologies yet! Experimenting with human DNA is so... god! It's so incredibly idiotic! That's how half the goddamned horror movies freakin' start!"

She again cut him off before he could ask questions to hopefully clarify her words. She spun back to face him and stabbed her finger in the air, her eyes sparkling with her outrage. "One of those *things* killed a man, right in front of me. Just slashed his throat open the way I might slice open an envelope. Some mad scientist released a monster into those tunnels, and it started killing people. It *hunted* me. It almost killed me too. It would have succeeded, if it wasn't drawing out the experience, enjoying itself. I only escaped it because I accidentally impaled it on some broken wood."

The thought of the danger Sarah had faced made him glow with aggression and frustration that he couldn't have found her sooner and saved her from any threat she'd faced. It must have been Seta Zul's will that protected her long enough to reach the boundary. Yet the other nixirs had followed her. They had been hunting her too. Now, he knew that for a fact, though he had always suspected it. They had followed her trail across the boundary.

"Why was it coming after you, Sarah? Was it because of this... man? Was he your... partner?"

He had to bite off the bitter word as he thought of Sarah with some nixir male. He had not allowed himself to consider if she'd had a mate before crossing the boundary. It was not something he wanted to think about. That mate would never see her again, so it didn't matter. She belonged to him.

Sarah shook her head. "I think we were just in the wrong place at the wrong time. There's no other reason I can think of why the government would want to kill us. None of us was anyone special. We were all just normal people."

He took both her hands, tugging her closer to him. "You are very special to me, Sarah." He felt his head spines lift to fully extend as his glow increased, sparking an answering glow from her zayul. "If anyone else ever threatens you again, I swear that I will hunt them down and tear them to shreds."

She wrapped her arms around his waist, laying her head on chest as she embraced him. "I hope you never have to keep that promise, Jotaha. But I appreciate it. It feels good to know that someone will fight for me. I never wanted to fight all my battles alone. There was just never anyone else willing to stick around to face them with me."

31

Jotaha took her back to his bachelor home, though the yan-kanat called it "waiting quarters." Unlike some human men who seemed to revel in living single, most yan-kanat males apparently desired the chance to find their drahi and start their families.

Jotaha explained this to her on their sky lift journey to the "left wing." He also told her that he had grown up near the bottom of the wing, pointing the area out to her. The house pods looked like large, peaked tents formed of bones and hide and attached to a vast framework connected to the wing bones themselves. The "lattice" was actually a series of walkways that snaked back and forth and up and down the wing, connecting all the various levels. At the base of the wing, where Jotaha had grown up, the pods were densely packed and much smaller than the ones at the highest point, where each pod looked to be the size of many of the smaller pods sewn together.

Each wing district possessed its own suspended marketplace, complete with small buildings of bone and hide, as well as brightly colored fabric pavilions shading a variety of stalls packed with goods.

The whole city was fascinating, but this was the first time she got the opportunity to walk among the regular citizens. The bouncing walkways were both exciting and unnerving as Jotaha led her to his "pod" that sat at the halfway point between the top and bottom of the wing district. It was much smaller than the house he had taken her to earlier, but she liked the cozy pod far more than the large home filled with strange fixtures and items she suspected were things Farona wanted in her home.

This space was clearly Jotaha's only, and it was sparsely decorated. A wooden framed bed, a variety of unmatched seating around a large wooden table, shelves stocked with a selection of equally mismatched pottery, and a few scattered rugs. The nicest silken rug was laid out in front of what appeared to be a small shrine in one alcove framed by crystals. The shrine itself had a dragon statue on it that appeared to be carved of a reddish orange stone, wings outspread and jaws open as if caught mid-roar. The chest and throat of the statue glowed with the luminescence of the inferno stone that had been inlaid into the carving. Small gilded pots of sand sat on either side of the dragon statue, with half-burnt cones of incense smoking inside them.

"I know this dwelling is inadequate for you, Sarah. I have put in a request for temporary quarters for both of us until the ceremony." As she turned to him, he gestured to another alcove, formed by a curtain of sewn hides. Shelves laden with fabrics and furs nestled inside the tight space. "I will sleep on the floor until we move."

"You don't have to do that, Jotaha." She shot a glance at the bed, noting that it was spacious, probably because he was so large. "We can both fit on the bed."

His gaze was intent when she turned to meet his eyes. "I can't sleep in the same bed with you right now."

"Is it... are there rules against sharing the bed before the ceremony?"

He huffed, finally breaking his eyes away from her as he looked around the pod. "I want you so badly that I won't be able to contain myself if your warm body is curled against me, at least not until I end up doing permanent damage to my salavik."

Heat flushed through her body at his words until her core felt like it burned as hot as the seal that kept them from consummating their relationship before the first mating. "That's... it's probably a good thing, Jotaha. I want you too, and I don't think I'd be able to wait until the ceremony either."

He swept a hand over his head spines, flattening them from their bristled state as he turned to look around his quarters as if seeing them for the first time. "I'm sorry about this place. I didn't plan on bringing my drahi here to stay before the ceremony. Faro—I had believed that my mate would have a home of her own in Draku Rin already."

She pretended she didn't hear his slip up, because any other option stung, reminding her that she wasn't his first choice, and that another woman still held onto a part of him, no matter how much he wanted Sarah.

"I never spent much time here. As Jotaha, I live mostly within the urvaka, only coming here during rest periods before taking on a new generation of chanu zayul. It's not a beautiful place fit for my drahi."

She smiled at the embarrassed tone his voice took on. "I love it, actually. It's cozy, and all the different fabrics and pottery glazes make it colorful and bright."

His gaze returned to her, his pupils rounding from their usual slits as he studied her. "You say things to spare my feelings, even though I don't think you are always being honest. You did the same in the home I showed you. That is... kind."

Sarah chuckled. "Don't sound quite so surprised. Humans aren't *all* bad, you know. We've got some good qualities too."

He closed the distance between them and swept her into his arms, tucking her against his chest, where she felt like she fit perfectly, despite the differences in their sizes. "I'm learning that, Sarah. You make me reconsider everything I've ever known about nixirs."

She stroked her hand over the fine weave of his tunic, feeling the hard muscle beneath flex at her touch. Jotaha didn't put out heat like a human man. His body was the same temperature as the pod they were in. It was just another reminder of how different they were, and another concern about them having children together. How could a warm-blooded and cold-blooded couple successfully create viable offspring? If such a possibility was real, then magic really must exist in this world.

"You know, I wasn't just trying to spare your feelings about this pod. I really do like it."

She pulled away to take a step back, and Jotaha let her go, but she didn't move far. She liked being near him, having him tower over her, powerful and almost overwhelming in a way that excited her. He still looked terrifying, but also sexy as hell. She knew now that threat from him would always be aimed at her enemies and never herself.

"The only thing it's missing is a bathroom."

He cocked his head, clearly confused because she used the human word for it. Then he seemed to figure out her meaning based on the context alone, responding before she had the chance to correct herself.

"There is a hygiene chamber attached to this pod." He gestured to one wall near the bed. "That panel is a flap that opens onto the 'bathroom'."

Jotaha showed her that room, and patiently explained every item on the shelves next to the toilet bench and the tub basin. Both had drains that connected to pipes passing through the outer, lacquered hide wall, as did the smaller basin that served as a sink. All three had the same crank pumps, and the tub basin had the heating stones beneath it, which Jotaha showed her how to use.

The gritty paste with the herbal scent was for her teeth, and she chuckled at the realization that she'd walked all around the yan-kanat smelling like she'd scrubbed herself with their version of toothpaste. It was embarrassing but also funny.

They used moistened, herbal-infused fabric to wipe down their scales, and that had probably been the purpose of some of the "towels" the servants in the temple had brought her. The large basin itself was mostly used for soaking aching muscles, steaming sickened lungs, and warming their body temperature, like a hot tub. They finished off their bathing with oil for their body scales and wax on their head spines to make them shine and keep them from rasping against each other as they moved.

Jotaha said he would contact an alchemist to create the soaps and hair products she could use, and he had an order in already for a special comb, but planned on purchasing a brush from a craftsman that evening. He promised they would find something among the marketplace stalls that would work for her hair, even if it had to be one of their toothbrushes.

After her tour, he took her back out to the wing district. Sarah gasped at the beauty of the two moons shining bright and full, lighting up the night and dimming the mass of stars that filled the sky. Lanterns and inferno stones lit the walkways, and the city below them. The temple blazed with a beam of light shooting straight up from its steeple. Below that building, the eyes of the dragon skull glowed like beacons.

Jotaha pointed to the two moons, seeming to hang side by side in the dark blue sky. "Those are Theia's eyes, looking down upon the beauty that her heart has become now that it hosts the children of the Ajda."

"I like your creation story a lot better than all of ours."

He tucked her close to his side, his heavy arm resting on her shoulder, making her feel sheltered and protected as the other citizens enjoying the night cast them wary, or perhaps even hostile, glances. "Our stories are intertwined, nixir and yan-kanat. This world only exists because of the nixirs."

"It's just a pity all this beauty was born out of violence. If humans and yan-kanat hadn't always been at war, just imagine what Earth could be like right now."

The other pedestrians were definitely giving them a wide birth as they strolled along the walkways. She wasn't sure if it was because of Jotaha's softly glowing scales or because of the female beside him, but she felt the weight of their stares and it unnerved her. She snuggled in closer to him, and he responded by tightening his hold in a reassuring squeeze.

"Violence sometimes has its place," Jotaha said, seeming to ignore or not notice the other pedestrians, though the faint glow of his scales suggested he was more than aware of their glances. "The Overlord of the Ajda, Bal Goro, is a creature of destruction and creation. His violence was legendary, as was his brutality. If he wasn't tempered by the wisdom of the other Ajda, he might have bathed the universe in rivers of titan blood before they could rally to stop him. Yet the battle he'd fought against the titaness birthed our world, and it was necessary to our survival."

He gestured to a cluster of potted plants forming a little parklike sitting area on the latticeway as they passed it. "Our tree-keepers know that the forest must sometimes burn to be renewed. This is a lesson all yan-kanat learn at the knee of the elders. Violence can be tempered, but it is sometimes necessary for change and growth."

He paused on the edge of a walkway, and since they were at the peak of the wing district, standing among the multi-pod manors, they had an excellent view of the temple and skull of Draku Rin below them.

"The elder gods shed their skin knowing that it wasn't an ending to their journey. They knew that something new would grow in its place."

He turned to face her, capturing her hands in his as his gaze fixed intently on her. "I used to fear change, even knowing that it brought growth, because it also often brings loss. My destiny was clear, from the moment I left the nest. I would serve as a guardian and destroy any nixir that crossed my path. To find you, my drahi, and to know that I would be forced to change, forced to reconsider my beliefs and lose my certainty about the evil of the nixirs I killed without mercy—it freed me from chains I never noticed were binding me, even though I fought it, doubting the wisdom of Seta Zul."

He cupped her cheek, lowering his head until his lips hovered above hers. "I love you, Sarah. I'm so grateful to Seta Zul for tearing away the veil that blinded me by bringing you to me. You are a marvel, a wondrous creature of beauty and strength. I admire so much about you, and cannot wait to learn so much more."

Overwhelmed by the feeling of everything going right for once in her life, her world suddenly shifting into place as dreams she'd never dared to entertain finally came true, she was spared the need to find words to express herself in kind when Jotaha's lips claimed hers, drawing her deeper under his spell.

She was loved. Cherished. Desired. By someone who would fight to keep her, and who would chase her if she walked away. Someone she loved in return, opening her battered heart to the possibility of pain for the promise of fulfillment.

JOTAHA HAD to leave the following morning to make arrangements at the temple. There was also some meeting of the jotahans to discuss the latest developments, in regards to the mutated humans and their increased threat. Sarah wished she could be at that meeting, to tell her own story of her encounters with the creatures, but Jotaha told her that only jotahs, jotahas, and jotahans could attend.

She was sure he left her out of the meeting partly because she was human, given that they were all trained to stop humans from entering this world, and punish those who did with death. The fact that she was female could have also been an issue, since females did not serve as guardians. Ever.

The chanu zayul choosing to lodge within her spine was unprecedented, and Jotaha's tone when he spoke of the reaction other yan-kanat had to it carried a warning. Not all the citizens of Draku Rin would be impressed that she had been "honored."

Left to her own devices, she puttered around the pod, bored and out of sorts, until she heard a high-pitched voice calling her name from behind the entry door flap.

Surprised and intrigued, although also cautious, she pulled aside the flap to find Farona standing at the entry. She would recognize the female anywhere, scales or not. The beauty of the other female, and her slender delicacy, made Sarah feel heavy and unfeminine in comparison. The soft, tinkling voice of Jotaha's lifelong bestie and erstwhile lover didn't help diminish that feeling.

"Greetings, Sarah. I can see you are surprised by my visit. It appears Ha-tah failed to tell you I would call on you." She huffed, shaking her head. "Poor Ha-tah. He is clumsy with females. Focused too much on his duty and not enough on their tender feelings." Her lips tilted upwards at the corners. "It is so typical of males. Are your nixir men the same?"

Sarah pulled her gaping jaw closed, her mind spinning to find a response to this woman. She tucked away the name "Ha-tah" to ask Jotaha about later, not wanting to reveal to Farona that she was unfamiliar with it. It was probably an endearment of some sort, though her bug translators provided no translation of its meaning.

"I... Uh... yes, um... human men are often the same." She felt like she was babbling, standing at the door in one of Jotaha's tunics that she had slept in, which hung on her frame like a dress almost reaching her knees.

Farona was dressed in a toga-style length of fabric clearly made of some kind of silk and woven in colorful, stunning designs. She was elegant from her sandaled, dainty feet to the narrow, delicate head spines that adorned her head.

Farona huffed again in a way that Sarah now understood to be amusement for the yan-kanat. "It figures. We are not that different from the nixirs, despite what my fellow yan-kanat will tell you." Her slit-pupil gaze studied Sarah with open curiosity, and Sarah couldn't see any open hostility in her expression. "You know, I have always been fascinated by the nixirs. I always thought it was a pity this generation had no nixir drahis to learn from. I imagine your world and culture are very exciting!"

Her gaze shifted from Sarah's face to the pod interior behind Sarah. "Would you mind if I come in?" She glanced from side to side, then returned her gaze to Sarah. "I feel a bit exposed standing out here. There are some who would disapprove of my presence here."

Sarah stood aside, holding the flap open for Farona. Her alarm bells were going off, but not because of anything in Farona's demeanor. It was more that she wouldn't be so quick to trust a human female who just got dumped for her, not that it had ever happened to her before. "Sure. I'm sorry I'm not dressed for entertaining."

Farona's gaze circled the room, her lips twisting in obvious disdain. "Ha-tah," she sighed, shaking her head. "This place is unfit for his drahi. So dingy and ugly. I cannot believe he brought you here instead of requesting that the temple keep you housed until your ceremony."

"Uh... listen, uh, Farona. This is a bit... awkward, honestly. I'm not—"

Farona turned back to face Sarah, holding up one hand. "Please, I know you are concerned about my motives. I understand that nixirs often stab each other in the back, so it is not surprising that it is difficult for you to trust others. But you will learn that this is not the yan-kanat way. We all revere Seta Zul, and trust in her wisdom. If she has chosen another for Ha-tah, then I will honor that choice. I love him and only want him to be happy, and that means welcoming you into our city and introducing you to our circle."

She bowed her head briefly in what Sarah took to be a respectful posture as she lowered her hand. "There will be a time when Seta Zul chooses a mate for me, and I eagerly await that time, but for now, I can do my part in helping my oldest and dearest friend, by welcoming his mate."

She lifted her eyes to meet Sarah's. "Please, let me help you, Sarah. There is much that you will need to know, and Ha-tah is focused on male concerns and does not understand what females need to make them feel at home."

Her tone sounded sincere and her words were earnest. Sarah still had a hard time trusting her, but she knew that was, indeed, a human failing. Especially when it came to dealing with cast-aside lovers. Still, she could certainly admit that Jotaha had left her to her own devices with far too little information about the city and what she could do by herself until he returned.

"We must go shopping, immediately," Farona said as if she sensed Sarah wavering. She tsked as she studied the oversized tunic hanging on Sarah's frame. "There are clothing makers who can alter their dresses to fit your... *unique* build, or," she lifted her arm to show the swath of fabric that hung over it," you can choose a wrap like this, which will fit any form nicely."

"As much as I'd love a little shopping trip, I don't have any... well, whatever is used for money here."

Farona's dismissive snort somehow managed to sound feminine and elegant. "Jotaha has plenty of kivan in his coffers, given his sacrifice for Draku Rin, but for this cycle, I would like to purchase your wares, as a gift to my friend and his future drahi. It is customary for family and friends to provide gifts to the mating couple," she said quickly as Sarah opened her mouth to reject the offer.

Noting Sarah's hesitation, she continued, "I assure you, I also have plenty of kivan in *my* coffers, as well as a good relationship with most of the vendors in this city. I provide many of their wares through my craft-rooms. They will give me excellent deals. Far better than they would give Jotaha or you."

Farona might be slender, graceful, and delicate, but she had an aura of steely resolve to her that Sarah couldn't help but admire, even as she knew she was being subtly bullied into agreeing to let Jotaha's former lover pay for her stuff. It was possibly the most alien part of this culture she'd encountered yet. Not to mention the one that made her most uncomfortable.

SARAH'S UNEASE faded as Farona proved to be an enchanting companion, readily answering her many questions about the city as they strolled through the wing district. Strangely enough, the looks she got as she traveled with Farona were friendlier than those she'd received the previous evening with Jotaha. It was as if Farona's presence was an endorsement of Sarah's place among them.

She learned that Farona owned a series of "craft-rooms" which were the equivalent of workshops, filled with employees that labored to create many beautiful fabrics to supply the clothiers around the city, as well as many of the statues and carvings that filled the marketplace. She even employed brewers to supply some of the fermented beverages, treating Sarah to a delicious breakfast at a spotless food stall that featured one of her craft-room specialties—a light, carbonated fruity drink that tasted of the anetaak berries that lent their sweetness to much of the foods the yan-kanat ate.

She was a hard-nosed entrepreneur, bargaining with the ease and skill of someone accustomed to negotiating the best prices. She paid the vendors with mother of pearl shells, much like the ones that had adorned the dress Jotaha had given Sarah in the caves, what seemed like so long ago even though it had happened fairly recently.

It was just that so much had happened since then, and so much of her thinking had altered. Her worldview had shifted and changed so rapidly that she felt like a new person looking back at the old Sarah like she was a stranger. She could understand why Jotaha found the experience so unsettling, and even frightening. It was like shedding the old skin of her past, but without knowing what would grow in its place.

She was actually having fun with a woman who should be hostile to her, or at least not friendly. Instead, Farona was an engaging companion, filled with amusing and outright hilarious stories about everything, including Jotaha's youth. She also avidly questioned Sarah about Earth, and her previous life there. Sarah wished she could spin a tale as brilliantly as Farona did. Her past life sounded so boring and bland when she tried to relay it to the yan-kanat female.

Even so, Farona behaved as if the things Sarah told her were incredible and exciting. She wanted to know about airplanes and skyscrapers and smartphones and computers. She seemed fascinated with Sarah's description of video games, saying it was difficult to imagine traveling to other worlds without ever leaving the comfort of your own home.

Farona had their purchases delivered directly to Jotaha's housing pod, and she had bought several new shift-style dresses, and a chain-belted tunic dress with a plunging neckline that would have a much different look on Sarah than a yan-kanat female. Farona insisted that was a good thing, enhancing her alien beauty. She also added three wrap dresses, and had the vendor demonstrate on Sarah how to wear them.

Everyone they spoke to treated them with respect, and Farona's curiosity and fascination about Sarah seemed to rub off on the others. Soon, Sarah was fielding so many questions about humans and their world that she was running out of breath trying to keep up.

They drew a crowd as they made their way out of the wing district and down into the sternum district. Beneath the shadows cast by the looming skeleton city, they entered another marketplace. This one primarily consisted of what appeared to be clubs and bars and eateries, with a few boutiques, housed in stone buildings or fancy wood and bone structures.

They businesses were clearly fancier than the food stalls in the wing district. Even here, the proprietors and employees appeared to know Farona. Many stopped to greet her and Sarah when they saw her, their curious gazes sweeping over Sarah before Farona drew her onward.

They ended up entering an eatery where the dishes being served were as fancy as the ones she'd tried in the temple.

Farona led her to a table where five other females sat, all of them sipping from delicate china-style cups, rather than the heavier glazed mugs that the yan-kanat called "crocks."

All the other females greeted her, save one. The woman's scaled face was pulled in lines of tight disapproval, and Sarah's joy at being out and about with her sparkling companion dissolved as she recognized the hostility in the other woman's eyes.

Still, the other four were welcoming and waved for her and Farona to take their seats on fanciful chairs made of twisted vines on a light wooden frame.

The other women chattered away with obvious excitement, regarding Sarah with deep curiosity. Yet she felt the antagonism coming off the woman named Ane-ata, though that one remained silent, only sipping her tea, her glare shooting towards Sarah from time to time.

The servers brought drinks for Farona and Sarah, and Farona recommended several items for Sarah, since they didn't have menus.

"You are so interesting to talk to, Sarah!" a yan-kanat female named Rataka said, her high-pitched voice filled with enthusiasm. She was a lead sculptor who worked in one of Farona's craft-rooms, and also seemed to respect her employer and friend, leading Sarah to believe Farona treated her people well.

"She is probably lying about everything, since her mouth is moving," Ane-ata suddenly said, glaring at Rataka. She sneered as her eyes shifted to Sarah. "Isn't that what nixirs do so well. Lie whenever their mouths are open. That's when they aren't stabbing those who dare to trust them in the back."

"Ata!" Farona's voice snapped across the stunned silence of the others like a whip.

Ane-ata visibly flinched, though her burning glare only shifted briefly to the furious Farona before returning to Sarah.

"You will speak to our guest with respect or leave this table now," Farona said in a voice so chilly that Sarah felt like the temperature suddenly dropped below freezing.

The silence thickened as Ane-ata appeared to debate her choices. Her head bowed and her shoulders hunched inward when she shot an apologetic glance to Farona, yet she set her cup down and rose to her feet. "Kevos is right about her,

Farona. She will hurt Jotaha. She will hurt all of us. That's what the nixirs do."

She stabbed a finger at Sarah, who reeled back even though Ane-ata was not close enough to touch her. "You don't belong in our world!"

With that, she spun on her heel and stormed out of the restaurant, leaving a heavy pall on the conversation.

After that unpleasant encounter, Farona apologized profusely to Sarah, explaining that her friend was deeply in love with Kevos—who was apparently the big, mean bastard they'd encountered in the desert—and that he was trained, as Jotaha was, to view nixirs as the enemy. Clearly, his influence had rubbed off on Ane-ata. She was also probably angry that Jotaha had put Kevos in his place—and in a healer's chamber —after a fight in the arena.

That fight had been over Sarah's presence in Draku Rin, and that knowledge cast a cloud over the remainder of the meal for Sarah, despite the other females trying their best to keep a cheerful conversation going.

Finally, Farona settled with the proprietor and then joined them outside the eatery, where they parted ways with the other women, all of whom promised to call upon Sarah as soon as possible to show her around more of the city.

She and Farona ended their outing at the museum, where Farona had promised to take her to learn more about yan-kanat history. When they entered the building, she saw shelves upon shelves and table after table of artifacts. Farona explained each display as stone-faced guards looked on in silence.

They passed a table that was much different from the other —so much so that it served as a stark reminder to Sarah how out of place she was.

A cowboy hat sat on a stand beside a fancy belt buckle and a pair of boots with silver spurs. A heavy western duster hung on a body form beside the table. Other items included a .38

caliber pearl handled revolver and several cartridges sitting in a stone bowl next to it. A sheathed bowie knife lay beside the bowl.

There was an empty space beside the weapons, and the marks in the dust looked like a decorative comb and hairbrush had sat there. Beside those was a cameo, several silk ribbons, and a square of yellowed lace.

"Those items were taken from the last nixir female to mate with a resident from Draku Rin," Farona said, coming up beside Sarah as she stood staring down at the display. She indicated the weapons, "and from one of the nixir males who came after her, crossing the boundary to try to reclaim her."

There were other various items, like a small snuff tin and a flask, but she barely spared them a glance, zeroing in on the cameo, ribbons, and lace.

"Jotaha said she was a shataz. I wonder if she came from one of the brothel houses in the area near the mine."

She also wondered what had driven the gunslinger that had apparently followed the woman to risk so much to get her back. Clearly, he'd failed, and had lost his life in the process. She hoped he hadn't been a heartbroken lover of the woman and had instead been a villain, and the yan-kanat who took her had saved her from him. That made the idea of the woman being abducted easier for Sarah to accept.

The brush and comb had probably been heirlooms, maybe the last things of true value that the woman had owned. Sarah had left them behind in the temple the previous day, and hoped they would be returned to their place in the museum. The woman deserved to be remembered, even if the human world had long ago forgotten her existence.

"This display is a most interesting one," Farona said, pointing to the duster. "Look upon that garment! It has holes in it, and our experts believe they were caused by human weapons. Can you imagine? How does a human male survive in such a world?"

The duster did appear to have some bullet holes at the bottom of it, and the edges were ragged and torn. There were dark stains as well that suggested blood had been shed by someone near the coat.

"Well, it wasn't called the '*wild*' west for nothing."

Farona looked confused and Sarah realized that once again, she had switched to English when saying some words. "Wild West" didn't have a yan-kanat translation.

She turned to Farona, sweeping her hand out to indicate all the contents of the table. "It's not always violent everywhere on Earth. I've gone my whole life without ever being shot at, or struck by a weapon, or physically attacked. At least, not until I went into a dark and scary abandoned mine."

Although living in her van, stealth camping in parking lots or parks or campsites, had often been terrifying. She wasn't the only one living like that, and some of the other people out there in isolated areas—away from law enforcement who would have sent her back to her parents—had frightened her. The human world was not a safe one. Given her own knowledge of that, she could understand why the yan-kanat saw humans as unrelentingly violent and dangerous.

32

Jotaha's steps sped up with his eagerness to see Sarah again, after spending most of the cycle held up in meetings with the other guardians, as well as scrying with the guardians from other skilevs. Even after those meetings finished up, he had much to do in the temple, making arrangements for the sata-drahi'at. He wanted to have it as soon as possible, given that his need for Sarah was causing him physical pain whenever he was around her, and the further he moved away from her, the more the seal began to burn, leaving him uncomfortable even out of her presence.

He also wanted to bind her to him as soon as possible because he still worried that she would change her mind and demand he take her back to her home. Even if he wanted to do that, the elders would never allow it. If a mating didn't happen between them, she would be sent away to somewhere else on Theia. A place where those with nixir blood were less rare—and perhaps less resented.

Unless Arokiv could find a solution for her to return home that the other elders would accept, but he intended to have her bound to him before that elder returned from the nixir world.

He stopped at the communal cooking pod on his level to pick up food for both of them, selecting items he thought she might enjoy, given what she'd liked in the past. She was not a fan of anything made with blood, so he passed over all the kirev dishes.

Others who lived on his level tried to engage him in conversation, but he was too eager to return to Sarah to spend much time speaking to them. They were always curious when they saw him return to Draku Rin from the urvaka, and ever since he'd returned with Sarah in tow, his neighbors wanted to ask a thousand questions of him.

Finally, he escaped the evening crowd and headed towards his own pod. His mind returned to the conversation he'd had with a housing matchmaker that morning, and that recollection dimmed his excitement. He wanted Sarah to have a home that suited her and not another female. The other male had informed him that he had no properties available for Jotaha to consider in trade for the one he'd had built for him and Farona.

Jotaha knew the matchmaker was lying. There were many vacant homes available in Draku Rin, as the population had been declining over the past two generations, with higher nestling mortality rates and lower fertility, even with Seta Zul's blessings. There had been many choices when he'd selected the property he owned now, and the population had not grown since then.

Normally, stakeholders in any district would be eager to welcome a Jotahan into their neighborhoods, sometimes offering better trade deals on properties, as they had when he'd traded for his current home on the out-terrace.

The matchmaker probably knew he'd have a difficult time convincing the stakeholders in many of the districts to allow a nixir to live among them, even if she was mated to a Jotahan—even though she had the blessing of the chanu zayul herself. The enmity ran far deeper than Jotaha had expected, and that made things far more difficult. If he couldn't convince a neighborhood to accept Sarah among them, he would have to consider remodeling his existing home so that it was more to her taste.

Walking into his pod erased his sour mood, because the sight of Sarah waiting for him filled him with happiness. She sat beside the shrine of Draku Rin. When he entered the pod, her gaze instantly shifted from the statue to the door. Her lips spread in a nixir expression of pleasure when she saw him. She jumped to her feet, revealing that she wore an elegant wrap in colors that complemented her pale skin and dark head fibers and eyes. The design of the dress concealed some of her lush curves, but he could picture them beneath the swaths of silk fabric, and his salavik was already awakening as his tongue flicked out to taste her scent.

"I brought our evening meal," he said by way of greeting, carrying the fragrant wrapped bundles to the table.

She joined him there, and her arms wrapped around his waist as soon as he set his burdens down. He returned the embrace, pulling her close against him. Her head only came to the middle of his chest, but it didn't make her feel like anything less than a perfect fit for him.

He shivered in pleasure when her warm hands burrowed beneath his tunic to stroke the scales at his waist.

"I missed you," she said, turning her head to look up at him, her chin resting on his chest.

"And I you, drahi." He brushed her head fibers away from her face, allowing the silken strands to spill through his fingers before he released them.

Then, in a mercurial shift of mood, she slapped him on his abdomen as she pushed away from him. Her expression took on a fierce frown, but a slight up-tilt still lingered on her lips. "You didn't tell me you were sending Farona to visit me! That caught me by surprise."

There was a light tone to her voice that differed from the times he'd seen her truly angry, telling him she was mostly pretending outrage, but he didn't doubt that his failure to inform her about Farona visiting her probably did irritate her. He'd been distracted, mostly by her, and Farona's promise to call upon her had slipped his mind.

"I'm sorry. I should have let you know she'd made the offer to stop by."

Sarah crossed her arms. "Well... I suppose I can't be too mad. She did help me a lot today." She held out her arms, one hand waving at her dress. "She actually bought me this dress, and more clothes, and found me someone to make soap and shampoo and conditioner for me, and took me out to eat for breakfast and lunch. It was... sweet, but a bit overwhelming. I don't think there's a single woman on Earth who would do so much for the woman who took her man from her, even if that woman never intended to."

Jotaha shook his head at her words, saddened that she'd had to grow up around such a cruel and unforgiving people. "Farona is a good female, and she has a kind and generous spirit. I am not surprised at all that she has given you such gifts, though I should have made my coffers available to you, and I regret that oversight."

That was another lapse on his part. He wasn't accustomed to considering the needs of others, and a nixir in Draku Rin would have her hands completely tied without the help of a yan-kanat guide. He'd left her alone, without considering what she would do for the majority of the cycle without him. Someone like Farona would know her own way around the city without needing him to show her. He had to start considering Sarah's unique position, and stop treating her as he would Farona.

He was very grateful to his friend for stepping into the

breach he'd left to take Sarah around and even help her purchase the goods she'd need.

"Speaking of 'coffers,'" she said, pulling his attention back to their conversation to note that she'd unbound some of the food offerings and was setting them out on the table.

"Every kivan I have is at your disposal." He helped her lay out the final dishes from the bundle, then strode to his storage shelves for xirak leaves and a jug to heat vandiz for their drinks.

"I appreciate that, but I was wondering about how I can make my own... uh, kivan."

He spun around to face her, jug and leaf pouch in his hands. "Are you talking about employment?" He shook his head. "It's unheard of for a drahi to work if her mate can support her. If you took a job, it would imply that I did not provide for you properly. It would dishonor me."

She blinked wide eyes at him several times, before she huffed in a way that told him she was annoyed. "Well, that's very archaic."

She crossed her arms, tapping one sandal-clad foot. "I have to do something with my time, Jotaha. I'm used to working for a living. I don't want to spend all my days shopping and sitting around the house." She gestured to her surroundings with a sweep of one arm. "You don't even have cable or satellite TV in this world, much less video games. I need *something* to do."

He set the jug and pouch down on the table and took her by her upper arms, rubbing his hands down them as if to stroke her into submission, even knowing it wouldn't work on his independent nixir. "When our nestlings come, you will be very busy caring for them. Until then, I'm certain there are many hobbies a female can do for entertainment. Farona would be better suited to telling you about them."

"Oh, you caveman, you." Sarah chuckled in her nixir way, shaking her head. "I'm going to let that slide, because your culture isn't mine, and I love you enough to find a compromise that works for both of us, but—"

He silenced her with a kiss, hoping to distract her from her unreasonable demands to work. If she even inquired about taking employment, it would embarrass him. He hoped a nestling came along quickly, because he had no doubt his nixir's sharp mind would get her into mischief if she wasn't occupied.

The kiss backfired as she returned it hungrily, changing it from a quick distraction to a painful reminder that his seal remained active and he couldn't take the delightful activity to the conclusion he desired.

He had to pull away from her, grunting in pain as his salavik parted his slit and got burned in its eagerness to dive into her heat. Soon. He would speed up his arrangements with the temple to prepare the ceremony. He didn't know how much more of this he could take before he ended up permanently scarred. Seta Zul's will had a sadistic side.

She made a frustrated sound as he set her away from him, expressing a regret that matched his own. The fact that she clearly returned his desire only made things more difficult.

"I will fill the jug for our drinks." He snatched up the container and sped towards the hygiene room as if he could escape his need for her by putting distance between them.

He was cranking the pump when she appeared in the doorway and leaned her shoulder against the lacquered bone frame. "What does Ha-tah mean?"

He froze for a moment, startled to hear that name leave her lips. "Farona called me that, didn't she?" He straightened from the basin, shaking his head. "That was my nest name. She has never been able to stop using it, even when I abandoned it for my title."

Her expression appeared guarded, and he wondered why

she looked upset. "So, you let her use a special name for you, but you never told me about it?"

He set the half-filled jug in the basin and went to her, cupping her face. "Sarah, that name is no longer mine. I only tolerate Farona using it because we have known each other since birth. If you were to call me that, it would be considered disrespectful. Anyone who overheard it would see it as a denial of my position, only made worse by my drahi using it. I am Jotaha of Draku Rin. That is one of the most respected positions in the city—in fact, on all of Theia. I *earned* that title, and it is expected that everyone calls me by it."

"Jotaha, I do respect you, but if you let *her* call you that, why would I be any different? I want to be your *friend* too, not just the woman who bears your 'nestlings' and keeps your house clean."

He sighed, frustrated at this one quirk of Farona's that was causing problems with Sarah. "You are far more to me than a friend, and certainly more than just the mother of my nestlings or a housecleaner. You are the other half of my soul. You are the one that others will expect to hold the most respect for me. If they hear you calling me Ha-tah, then they will think you don't feel for me the way I do for you. They will see my nixir mate denying my status, and it will shame me in their eyes."

She placed a hand on his chest, her dark eyes troubled as she stared up at him. "I don't want to cause you any more trouble. I know that I'm already making things hard on you, just by being human. It's just that you have such a long and close relationship with another woman, and I... honestly, I feel a little threatened by that closeness."

When he opened his mouth to reassure her, she pushed on his chest as if to silence him. "Would you have let her keep calling you that if *she* was your drahi?"

"Never in public."

That answer didn't seem to appease her. "So, in private, she would still be able to use that name for you?"

"Why is this so important to you, Sarah?" He rubbed his hand over his head spines in frustration, turning back to the basin to return to filling the jug. "What difference does it make if Farona uses that name? She doesn't mean as much to me as you do! I don't care if *she* respects me enough to use my proper title." He froze with his hand on the crank, realizing his words only after saying them.

Why had it never bothered him that Farona called him by the same name his mother had, as if she was elder to him, rather than his peer? Why did it bother him so much to think of Sarah calling him an abandoned nestling name, even when they were in private?

And why *didn't* Farona use his title when speaking of him?

"Jotaha, I'm sorry. I'm not trying to upset you. I'm just confused, is all. I want to know everything about you, so I was taken aback when Farona called you by a different name. It hurt, a little, that the two of you have this secret language that even the chanu zayul can't translate."

Jotaha seized on that distraction, wanting to avoid any further introspection that disturbed him. "The name is in an ancient language that the yan-kanat spoke before coming to Theia. It means 'long awaited'."

This brought him a new kind of disturbance as he was forced to confess more to her than he had intended to so soon. The nixirs had so many nestlings that she might be upset that they could experience difficulty in that department.

He abandoned the jug to face her again. "My parents were mated in Seta Zul's eyes, but even then, they were not fertile. They tried for many passings to have nestlings, and had finally given up when they were approaching the end of my mother's fertile time. It was only near that end that she became pregnant with me."

He felt his head spines rising with his concern that Sarah would be upset at his next words. "They believed that Seta Zul had a purpose for making them wait so long, but the healers said that something in my mother's blood inhibited her fertility, and that it might have been passed on to me."

Her eyes had softened with sympathy and she embraced him in a way that spoke of comfort rather than desire. "I'm sorry, Jotaha. That has to be difficult news to hear."

"I may not be able to give you many nestlings, Sarah, even though you are my drahi. I know that nixirs have many offspring, and I worry that you will regret not having a large brood to raise."

She lifted her head from his chest, staring up at him. "I don't know what humans you're thinking of, Jotaha, but where I come from, having lots of children isn't that common anymore. My parents only had one, and they acted like I was a parasite, sucking the best years of their lives away. And I—"

Her eyes filled with moisture as she bit off her words and tried to pull away from him. He kept her close, trapping her arms against his waist as he sensed she would retreat. "You can tell me anything, especially if it is something that upsets you."

She sniffed, her lips quivering as she fought to conceal her distress. "I suppose there is something I should tell you, if we're being totally open and honest with each other."

She laid her cheek against his chest as he stroked a hand over her head fibers, soothing her, even as he enjoyed the guilty pleasure of touching the silken strands.

"I have a child, though I gave her up for adoption because I was too young to raise her myself and I was afraid that... that I would end up being as much a disaster as my own parents were."

She shook in his arms, releasing the pain she had clearly held onto. Her words surprised him, since the only fertile yan-kanat female was one already mated to a male for life. Yet, he also understood that nixirs were different.

"And the father of your nestling? What happened to him?"

"He told me to end the pregnancy. When I said I couldn't bring myself to do it, he told me he was too young to be a dad and that the baby would ruin his life, so he wanted nothing to do with her, or me after that."

"End the pregnancy? I don't understand?" Along with his confusion, he felt relief that she didn't appear even emotionally bound to the father of her nestling.

He felt the moisture of her tears through the cloth of his tunic. "Humans can end our pregnancies before they go to full term."

"Is this something a nixir body can do?" He was shocked now, unable to imagine having such bountiful fertility that a nestling would be flushed from the body at the mother's will rather than being born.

She pulled away. "I, honestly... I don't want to talk about things like that. I have a feeling it won't make our species look any better in your eyes, and I already have a tough road ahead to prove myself."

"You don't have to prove yourself to me, Sarah."

Her revelation made no difference in how he felt about her. The fact that she had a blood nestling in the human world saddened him, because it was clear she had not parted from her offspring without pain. The process of giving up a nestling when the parents were incapable of caring for it wasn't unheard of to the yan-kanat, though it was very rare, as nestlings were so highly prized and Seta Zul never blessed couples unless they could raise their young. It was only unexpected injuries, illness, or a mate's death that could leave a parent unable to continue to care for their own young.

The existence of her nestling meant that she still had a tie to her homeworld, and that did disturb him, though it seemed that she had fully committed to remaining here with him.

"I wish the other yan-kanat liked me as much as you do."

He huffed. "I would have to kill them all if they did. No one will touch my drahi but me."

That brightened her expression a bit. "You are such an adorable neanderthal."

"I am yan-kanat," he said, confused by the nixir word.

Her lips spread, baring her teeth in amusement. "I know." Her expression fell, her eyes growing shadowed. "I'm going to make your life miserable. When Ane-ata told me off, I realized how much your people dislike me."

He stiffened, his head spines rising. "What did Ane-ata say?"

She shrugged, but her lips turned further downwards. "She said nixirs can't be trusted. That all we do is lie." She gripped his wrist, her gaze intent on him. "I swear to you, Jotaha, I will always tell you the truth. I'm not a liar, just because I'm human."

Jotaha growled, rage building in him at this blatant disrespect towards his drahi. "Kevos has spread his poison to the females. He will be punished for hiding behind Ane-ata's skirt to spew his insults."

"Please! Don't punish anyone. Seriously, Jotaha. The bad blood between humans and yan-kanat won't disappear with more angry words or actions. Punishing Kevos or his girlfriend will only drive a deeper wedge. Give me a chance to prove that I'm not the monster they think I am. Let me show them that I can be trusted. I know there will always be people who resent my presence here, but if I could just convince those who aren't blinded by their hate, then their voices will drown out the few who are."

Her words held wisdom, but they did little to cool the anger that boiled within him. Ane-ata was a lovesick pawn of Kevos, so he did not hold the female responsible. It appeared that Kevos had taken a cowardly route to hurt his drahi, and Jotaha wouldn't stand for it. He would have to think on his next move to silence the other male before his venom spread further.

33

The days seemed to pass in a blur as Sarah waited for the ceremony that would make her truly Jotaha's mate. He had already made arrangements with the temple and the big day was approaching rapidly, which was a good thing, since they were both anxious for him to no longer be sealed.

They spent every evening together, strolling through the city, dining at one of the many stalls or eateries, and even visiting the yanhiss dens, though Jotaha said he did not regularly partake, since yanhiss dulled his combat skills, making him too passive with its calming warmth. She could tell he also didn't like to lose full control over himself because he also rarely drank alcohol. She was usually the only one who took advantage of the drug when they visited the dens. They both enjoyed the live entertainment of dancers and the short plays—most of them based on myths and historical tales—that took place in the dens.

She still felt guilty about imbibing afterwards, even though it was perfectly acceptable in this world. Too many anti-drug assemblies at all her schools left her with the unshakable message that "drugs are bad." Of course, those assemblies only talked about illegal substances, ignoring more beneficial medications. Yanhiss was treated as a therapeutic drink by the yan-kanat, like the soothing xirak tea, and would have been a boon for anyone suffering anxiety on Earth. The occasional taste of it helped her to cope with the endless stress of her new life.

Jotaha also spent most of every day with her, taking her around to all the shops to show her how to purchase goods and supplies, explaining what were good quality items and what were reasonable prices on most things she would be buying. They also visited the house on the terrace several times, since he wanted input from her on everything about the building and grounds, telling her that he wanted her to love her future home.

She would live in a cardboard box if it meant he would be right there beside her. The more time she spent with him, the more she fell in love with him. He was domineering, arrogant, and held views on gender roles that were right out of the Stone Age, but he was also attentive, generous, and supportive of most of her decisions, even when they went against his own archaic views. He even set her up with a "job" of sorts at the temple, assisting the lore-keeper by providing tales and knowledge about the world she'd left behind and the many wonders humans had developed since the exodus of the yan-kanat.

He still assumed she would quit working and focus entirely on their children if they were blessed by any, and Sarah wasn't certain where she stood on that. Her parents had ensured she had everything she needed when she was growing up, except for their attention and affection. They had been too distracted by their high-powered careers, and she had felt their absence, becoming more introverted and lonelier as she grew up feeling like a burden to them as one babysitter after another took over their roles.

She didn't want her children to ever doubt that they were her first priority, and if her job ever ended up detracting from her time with her children, then she would abandon it in a heartbeat. Still, that was a road she wasn't ready to cross at this point, because she knew that she and Jotaha might not end up fully agreeing on that issue. She didn't want to deal with it so early in their relationship when having children with him was still just a distant dream.

She ended up loving her new work, even if she had to be paid for it in a roundabout fashion that didn't make it look like Jotaha couldn't support them. The lore-keeper was a kindly, elderly yan-kanat who showed fascination for everything she could tell him about humans and Earth. They spent some of their time wandering through the museum, and she saw many more human artifacts that had been preserved, some from ancient times.

Her time at the temple mostly coincided with Jotaha's time spent preparing and initiating the warrior who would take his place in the urvaka, but as the time neared for the trial and choosing—that women weren't allowed to attend, of course—Jotaha had to spend more time away from her, leaving her with nothing to do during those many hours—or "sandfalls" as the yan-kanat measured it, based on the ancient and long abandoned use of hourglasses.

Farona and her circle of friends stepped into the breach, dragging Sarah off to craft-room meetings, "lectures" that turned into drinking and gossiping circles, and yanhiss den visits of their own. Not to mention lots and lots of shopping, where Sarah learned how to bargain and negotiate like Farona, who made Jotaha's bargaining seem like child's play.

The females were amused by Sarah's questions about equality and whether they thought they were being confined to rigid roles in their society. Farona explained that female yan-kanat had more freedom than males, who were bound by social rules and expectations that often made their decisions for them.

Expectations like Jotaha supporting his family completely, or being referred to by his title rather than his nest name. Males were also expected to be physically imposing and highly skilled at whatever career path was chosen for them by the elders. They were also the only ones who could work the dangerous jobs in the mines, or fishing on the stormy seas, or hunting the barrens, or serving as a guardian in the urvaka.

Females could choose their own career paths outside of those types of jobs, and kept all their own kivan until they were bound to a mate, which all the females Sarah spoke to seemed to think was their ultimate goal of life.

Farona gently mocked Sarah for her surprise at their desire to be "kept" by a male, during a den visit almost two weeks after they'd first met. "Are nixir males so incompetent that they can't provide a good home for their females? Is that why you say your females refuse to accept being bound to males?"

They were both mellow with yanhiss—as was Rataka, who often joined them on their outings—so Sarah didn't take any offense. "Human women just want to be free to choose the life we want to live."

Rataka huffed in a yan-kanat version of a laugh. "It doesn't sound like your females want *other* females to choose to be happily kept by their males. Why else would you speak so passionately to convince others to avoid that blissful state?" Her dilated gaze sharpened slightly. "Even when *you* are about to enter it."

Farona tapped her well-manicured claws on the tabletop beside her drink. The gemstones glued to her claws sparkled in the candlelight that flickered in the center of the table.

"Is it truly against your nature to accept the dominance of a male?" She studied Sarah with an expression of pity making a brief appearance on her serene features.

Sarah shrugged, still feeling relaxed, despite the conversation. "When you phrase it like that, it sounds bad to me. I don't want Jotaha controlling my life."

Farona and Rataka glanced at each other, then turned their attention back to Sarah. Farona leaned forward in her seat, her gaze steady on Sarah's face. "Jotaha is a yan-kanat male. He expects to be the ultimate authority in your home. If you lack the skill to work around him, while letting him believe he is in control, then this mating will make you miserable."

Rataka huffed again, then sank back in her chair, lifting her cup to take another sip of the green, earthy yanhiss. "You will learn, Sarah. Embrace the ways of the yan-kanat and put your nixir nature aside. You wouldn't be the first nixir female to *welcome* the dominance of a yan-kanat male. Our males do not beat their females, or neglect them, or leave them unprotected. There are horror stories told of the atrocities nixir males commit against their own females." Her inner and outer lids slowly blinked. "It is little wonder your females don't want such males to dominate them."

Sarah wished she could argue that point, and deny that sad truth. She wouldn't condemn every human male based on the actions of some, but from what she'd heard, there were no tales of yan-kanat males hurting their females. No overt domestic abuse, no rapes, and murder being extremely rare and shocking to the yan-kanat when it did happen. As impossible as it seemed in a city with tens of thousands of sentient beings, it was true. The idea was unthinkable in any human city that size. It sounded like a fairy tale or a kid's television show, where the world is portrayed the way people wished it was, instead of what it really is.

In fact, the skilev of Draku Rin was so peaceful that they didn't even have an official police force of any kind. Small incidents of altercations outside the arena or theft or other petty crimes were dealt with by the families of those involved, sometimes with a priest as a mediator, if necessary. The most major offenses—which were still minor by human standards—were presided over by the elders. The worst punishment possible being exile, which was used so rarely that it hadn't happened in Draku Rin in over a generation.

"Humans are...." She searched for some argument to justify the differences in their societies. "We...."

Farona patted her hand. "We understand that this is the nixir nature. The titans were betrayed by their children and that betrayal left a stain on the spirits of your people. It isn't something you can change, any more than the barren stalker can change its hunger for yan-kanat flesh."

She settled back in her chair and lifted her cup with both hands, her dilated gaze still fixed on Sarah. "You must accept that this will bring you in conflict with Jotaha throughout your lives together. He will expect you to become more like the yan-kanat, and you will expect him to tolerate when you are being nixir."

Sarah pondered those words, some of her mellow fading as the remains of her yanhiss cooled in its cup. "You really think it will cause problems?"

Farona finished her sip of yanhiss, then set the drink back down, her double eyelids closing for a moment as she sighed. "It will only be a problem if you can't bring yourself to submit fully to Jotaha, and become the mate he wishes you to be."

THEY LEFT the den after finishing their drinks, because Sarah knew that Jotaha would soon be home, and she liked to be there waiting for him because it always seemed to please him to see her. His apparent happiness at having her in his home was even more of a balm for her stress and anxiety than the yanhiss.

Its effects were mostly faded when he stepped through the pod door. He carried food from the communal kitchen, letting her know they would be spending at least part of their evening alone together.

If they spent much time in this space alone, without distractions, things got difficult. Every night, she wanted to leave her bed and crawl into the furs that Jotaha used to sleep on the floor. She wanted to stroke his scales, tease the sensitive ridges on the top of his tail, nip at his chest in a way that seemed to excite him.

She ached to touch him, to feel his hard, strong body pressed against hers, the alien rasp of his scales stimulating her naked skin.

Every night, she had to restrain herself, because even the mildest show of her desire for him would spark answering arousal from him. That left him snarling in pain as the seal burned his most sensitive organ.

Even kissing had become too much for him. Anything more than a quick peck had him groaning as his seam split. He confessed that having her scent fill this small housing pod drove him mad with lust, and anything that added to that only pushed him closer to losing control over his own body to the point that Seta Zul's will lashed back at him, reminding him that he had yet to bind himself to Sarah.

She had to admit that it was a heady experience. Jotaha's desire for her was so strong that it caused him physical pain. It made her feel more desirable than she ever had in her life. It also made her feel wanted and needed. No one had ever needed her before. Even her daughter had someone who could replace Sarah's role in her life.

For Jotaha, Sarah was his only drahi. The only woman for

him. He could never replace her, and it didn't seem like he wanted to, given how often he told her he loved her.

After he set the food bundles down, he greeted her with a quick kiss. He stepped away from her before she could wrap her arms around his waist, regarding her with a serious expression.

"You've been drinking yanhiss."

She felt an instant surge of guilt, though there was nothing forbidding the activity, and Jotaha had certainly never asked her not to. "Yeah. Me and Farona and Rataka dropped into the Drako Den for a quick drink before I came home."

He took her by the wrists to tug her closer. His hands fell upon her shoulders as she wrapped her arms around his waist, looking up at him. "Are you still so anxious, my drahi? Have you not yet found some peace in your new home?"

He lowered his head to rest his forehead against hers. "I worry that you will be unhappy here, and that nothing I can do for you will ever make this feel like your home. I don't want yanhiss to be the only way you can bear this life." He nuzzled her hair, then caught her lips with a hungry kiss when she opened her mouth to reassure him.

His hands tightened on her shoulders as he groaned in a mixture of pleasure and pain, his tongue flicking out to tease her lips for one delicious moment before the seal made him pull away.

"I'm fine, Jotaha. I'm happy here. I'm with you." Her heart pounded with her arousal, that single, brief kiss leaving her shell-shocked and aching for more. "I can't *wait* until we're mated." If the reality was anything like the dreams she had every night, then she would probably climax the moment he entered her.

He touched her cheek, stroking his claws gently over her skin, his gaze searching her face as if he sought a lie in her words. "A messenger from the temple approached me as I was leaving the training grounds. Seta Zul's elder priest has fallen ill and cannot perform the ceremony until he recovers."

She groaned in disappointment, pulling away from him. "Can't they find a back-up priest?"

She was so eager for Jotaha that she didn't think she'd make it another week without performing the first mating. Even the knowledge that his burning seal would brand her pelvis wasn't enough to scare her off. Seta Zul's priest had promised that they would give her a pain-inhibiting potion beforehand if she desired it. Although it would also dull the sensation of a powerful climax that came after the branding, which meant many drahis rejected the offer, willing to endure the pain for the promise of blissful pleasure.

Jotaha huffed in amusement. "I had much the same response, surprising the messenger, who expected me to first inquire about the health of the elder priest. It is clear he has not experienced the seal around his unbound drahi."

At her questioning look, he sighed, lifting a hand to flatten his head spines. "Sadly, they do not have a substitute fully qualified to perform the sata-drahi'at yet. Our ceremony was intended to be the last trial for the acolytes before they moved on to the final test for their robes."

She shook her head, finding it difficult to push away her frustration and disappointment. "Your people need to learn the concept of redundancy. It seems like you have a word for it, but the yan-kanat clearly aren't putting it into practice."

His head spines quivered as he huffed again. "And here I thought you would be more concerned about the acolytes attending our ceremony. Even for nixirs, mating is usually a private thing, is it not? Most yan-kanat females find the idea of having an audience for the first mating distressing."

She held up a hand. "Hold up. What's that about an *audience*?" Her voice rose on the last word.

He captured her wrist, then linked his fingers through hers, drawing her against him. "The branding doesn't frighten you off, but the watchers do?"

She nipped his hand, making him stiffen in reaction, bracing himself for his arousal. For some reason, it turned him on to feel her biting him. He was a freak ever since she'd bitten his hand, but she could totally dig that, as long as he didn't return the favor with his much sharper teeth.

"I never said I wouldn't do it in front of an audience. I'm just not thrilled about it. But it's only the one time, right? Only for the ceremony?"

His free hand fisted in her hair, gently tugging her head back so she couldn't bite him again. He lowered his head to graze his lips across her brow, then nuzzle her temple where he seemed fascinated by the warm, delicate skin he found there. "I want to kill every male who sees your naked body. Do you really think I would ever allow an audience after the first mating?"

The deep growl of his voice in her ear made her shiver at the promise in his words. Murders were exceedingly rare among the yan-kanat, but when they did happen, they almost always involved a male attacking another male for making a move on his mate. Most yan-kanat males weren't suicidal, and never even dreamed of doing something so stupid. Casual sex between unmated yan-kanat was perfectly fine, and males rarely grew jealous over their casual female lovers taking other males to their bed, but touching a mated drahi was inviting death.

"I'll be sure to keep my clothes on around all the guys, then," she teased.

His hand tightened in her hair as he lifted his head to meet her eyes. "There will be no other males around you without me there as well."

Her eyes narrowed as she released his hand. He held her in place when she tried to free her hair from his grip. "You know, human women can have platonic relationships with men right. Even when they have a mate."

He was silent for a long moment. When he spoke, his voice was gravelly with his anger. "Are you testing me, drahi? Is the thought of a life with me so unbearable to you that you want me to reject the seal, even if it means my dishonor and infertility?"

He sighed, slowly releasing his hold on her hair. Then he took several steps away from her, though his eyes never left her face, where her mouth gaped open in shock at his misinterpretation of her words.

"If you bind yourself to me, Sarah, you cannot live the life of a nixir female with no concern for how it would look to the yan-kanat around you." He tapped the center of his chest with one claw. "With no concern for how it would look to *me*. I love you, and I know that there are things about you that I can't change, any more than you can change my nature to better suit *your* view of the world."

His head spines fully extended and the glow of the chanu zayul sparked along his scales. "But you cannot accept my seal and then toy with my heart without consequences, even if that is in your nature."

She snapped her mouth shut and held up both hands in surrender. "I'm sorry, Jotaha. I was only teasing. I wouldn't hang out with other males by myself. I know that would be extremely disrespectful to you."

"You struggle to submit to me," he said, his glow fading as his spines drooped. "Even though it hurts me, I understand that you possess the nixir desire to fight, even against those who would protect you and love you, and give you everything you ever desired. A nixir would fight to the death to avoid submitting, even when it is in their own best interests."

He rubbed his head spines flat, his gaze shifting away from her. He stared at the shrine of Draku Rin with distant eyes, as if he was seeing something far beyond that. "I had hoped that you would come to trust me enough to give yourself to me. I've been told that other nixir females have done so in the past because they found life with a yan-kanat male preferable to one with their own cruel males. I believed that the fight was not as strong in your females as it is in your males. But you *are* a fighter, Sarah. I admire you for that, and respect it, but I do not know if you can bear to give in to my dominance because of that combative spirit."

She was suddenly afraid. Not of Jotaha, but of losing him. She was terrified that he would give up on her, give up on them, because she struggled to accept his culture and its demands on her. She knew he would never hurt her, so why did she fight so hard to retain an open and defiant independence, even when it might cause him shame and embarrassment among his people?

"I can submit!"

She rushed to him, every instinct going against her actions, telling her she was weak, and cowardly, and insisting that she didn't want to be controlled, even if it meant living life miserable and alone.

Her parents had raised her better than that. They'd taught her so well that she hadn't even surrendered to *their* will, despite the consequences. She didn't regret that choice, but she knew she would regret not surrendering to Jotaha.

She clutched his tunic like a desperate woman, emotional, so terrified of losing him that she was crying. "I surrender, Jotaha! I love you, and I want to be with you. I'll try to be a good yan-kanat mate. I'll let you make my decisions for me. I'll do *anything* you want, just please don't leave me!"

He gathered her in his arms, holding her close as she sobbed. He stroked her hair, the feeling soothing, letting her know he wasn't angry anymore.

"I don't want you to stop fighting me completely, my drahi. I don't want to destroy your nixir spirit. I'm willing to find compromises we can agree on so that we are both happy in our lives together."

She felt his lips brush over her hair. "I will never leave you, Sarah. Nor will I ever let you go."

34

The final trial of jotahs was a melee in tight conditions, after an extended hunt through the mining tunnels that snaked beneath the skilev. Jotaha and the Jotahans acted as the nixir prey, leading their hunters on a dangerous chase through the darkness.

They became even more dangerous for the jotahs when the tunnels brightened up occasionally from untapped veins of activated inferno stone that put out immense heat and light. It was there that the wrapped stones they carried to increase their body heat so they could be detected by the hunters like a nixir would become overwhelmed by an entire chamber of heat, blinding the jotahs' thermal vision, making them vulnerable to attack by the retired guardians and current guardian.

In the final melee, all four of the jotahs who had made it to the last trials would be facing off against Jotaha and five Jotahans in combat. The battle wasn't fair, but neither were the nixirs. The judges would use blowguns with untainted darts to simulate the far deadlier weapons of the nixirs. No one wanted to send a new Jotaha into the urvaka unprepared to fight against their deadliest enemy.

They weren't trying to kill the jotah competitors, but they would not avoid hurting them. The competitors were the best of the best the skilev had to offer, and Jotaha was proud and impressed by their skill. Stealth and darkness were the primary weapon of the Jotaha. The nixirs lacked the ability to see in the pitch black of the urvaka, requiring at least some light that often disoriented them as it cast deep shadows.

The key for any Jotaha was to avoid the chance that the nixirs could bring their deadly weapons into play. Jotaha himself had been wounded more than once by them, especially when he'd first begun his duty as guardian. Their weapons were incredibly destructive, and had their projectiles struck him in kill zones instead of winging his limbs or skimming his body, they could have killed him instantly. As long as he survived, the chanu zayul worked to rapidly heal his injuries.

Once a nixir was disarmed, they were at a severe disadvantage, even if they were the same size as the Jotaha. The chanu zayul made certain of that. The importance of silent weapons could not be overstated. The loud burst of nixir weapons brought the others of their group to their aid, but the whisper of a dart or the silent slash of a dagger dispatched them quickly and quietly, keeping the others unaware of the hunter's presence.

All of the jotahs did well, but one stood out among them. He nearly managed to get the drop on Jotaha himself, only failing because of Jotaha's enhanced senses and agility. Jotah Rin would be the first to approach the nest of the zayul in the hopes that the chanu zayul would choose him.

After the trial was called and the champion named, Jotaha and the others watched him make his way down the sacred tunnel to the nest. The other jotahs would be disappointed if Jotah Rin was chosen by the chanu zayul, but they understood that only one could go forward to take the title of Guardian of the Dark Paths. Most of the others would move on to become sentils.

For his sake, Jotaha was relieved to see the champion jotah returning from the sacred tunnel, his scales alit with the blessing of the chanu zayul as he knelt at Jotaha's feet and spoke his oath to guard the urvaka and protect the world from the nixir invaders—even if it meant sacrificing his own life. No longer bearing the nest name Kalanost, Jotah Rin became Jotaha, and Jotaha became Jotahan.

It was a powerful moment and life-altering for Jotahan. No longer would he be the Guardian of the Dark Paths. His role now would be to train the sentils and future jotahs for their duties. He would also be able to begin trying for nestlings as soon as he and Sarah completed the sata-drahi'at and entered their seclusion.

There was still so much to do, even as the new Jotaha packed his belongings and set out on his first journey to the urvaka, which relieved all of the Jotahans. Given the latest incursions of the twisted nixirs, they couldn't leave the urvaka unprotected for much longer.

His chanu zayul would be fully matured soon, though he wasn't sure exactly how long he had left before they withdrew their tendrils and began the process of leaving his body. He would know when it was time for him to travel back to the sacred nest here in the skilev, the one linked directly to the urvaka through passageways only the zayul themselves could travel.

Sarah's chanu zayul would also be leaving her soon, and she worried that she would lose the ability to understand his language when that happened. He didn't think that would be the case, and had reassured her that, usually, if the chanu zayul put knowledge in the mind of their host, that knowledge remained, even after they withdrew their tendrils.

Even if she couldn't understand him at first, he would not

let that stand in their way. He would find a way to communicate with her again. He would even learn her complicated nixir language if he had to. He would do whatever it took to make sure that his drahi felt like this was her home, and that she could be happy here.

Despite the celebratory atmosphere among the Jotahans after they saw the newest Jotaha off, he could not be as joyful as those around him. Seta Zul's priest was not recovering from whatever illness plagued him, and Jotahan was beginning to grow concerned about his health. As frustrated as he was that this meant another delay of their sata-drahi'at, he was now more worried about Priest Zan Cyall than about the change in his own plans.

It wasn't unusual for a yan-kanat adult to grow ill from time to time, and in most cases, they recovered after several cycles. It was rare for any illness to extend for a prolonged period of time once they passed the very vulnerable nestling stage of life. When it did, it was not a good sign. It usually meant the yan-kanat wasn't strong enough to survive.

Priest Zan Cyall had been hale and hearty when Jotahan and Sarah had met with him the last time for their final counseling. He was only in the middle of his life, and should not be weak enough to succumb to an illness that caused him nausea and vomiting and other complications that left him bound to his rooms and unable to entertain anyone but his healers.

The healers had done all they could for him. The usual treatment for such maladies was plenty of fluids and comforting teas to replace what he lost through his illness, and bedrest to give his body time to heal itself. There wasn't much else to do but wait.

Jotahan tried to set aside his concern for Zan Cyall and focus instead on breaking the news to Sarah that their bonding would be delayed yet again. He knew she would disappointed, but nowhere near as much as he was. Not only was it agony to be in her presence and not be able to make love to her, but he also wanted to bind her to him as quickly as possible and hopefully fill her womb with a nestling. Not only would he be overjoyed to have nestlings of his own—which had always been a lifelong goal for him—but he hoped bearing his offspring would further her loyalty and commitment to him.

She had sworn to submit to him, but she had done so out of the mistaken fear that he might leave her. He hadn't meant to scare her like that. He never wanted her to doubt his commitment to her again. He would be more careful about speaking out of anger and jealousy in the future. There were simply some things he must learn to tolerate from his nixir female. Her defiance of her expected role was one of them. He could be patient and guide her, and he could also compromise. They would make this work.

He knew it had not been easy for Sarah to let go of her nixir child, and she had only done so because she could not provide a good home for the nestling. He would give her nestlings the best home, and Sarah would never need to say goodbye to them and grieve for their loss.

Unless they passed on into the Inferno, as far too many nestlings did before they could grow strong enough to leave the safety of the nest.

He wouldn't think about that happening. He never wanted to think about that happening. It wouldn't happen to him and Sarah, because her nixir blood would make their nestlings resilient.

"Has passing on the title already stripped you of your hunting senses," a familiar voice said from right behind Jotahan.

He spun around to see Kevos standing close to him, watching him with a mocking tilt to his lips.

"I could have slid a knife between your ribs as you stood there cloud gazing, completely unaware of my approach."

He *had* been deep in thought. So much so that he'd barely noticed where his feet had carried him after leaving the training grounds. They were in the apothecary pavilion, next to the training grounds and arena, where he'd stopped at the waist high railing to stare out at the crashing waves of the ocean that bordered one side of the skilev.

"You are too honorable for such an attack, Kevos."

Kevos huffed in amusement, shaking his head. "At least *now* you believe that. I still think you are making a serious mistake you will forever regret, but I would never allow an empty-headed female—least of all Ane-ata—to speak my concerns for me."

"Ane-ata has been avoiding her usual circle since that incident. Farona has mentioned that she doesn't like the crowd your female has fallen into lately." The growing anti-nixir antagonism among a small group of younger yan-kanat had concerned Farona enough to speak of it to him.

Kevos pulled a face. "She's not *my* female. I have no idea why people keep insisting otherwise. I barely speak to her, and have been actively avoiding her since our last 'discussion' in the arena."

He joined Jotahan at the railing that bordered the marketplace plaza, sliding a sideways glance at him. "You still speak with Farona? I have heard that nixir females are jealous creatures, because even *mated* nixir males can stray to another bed and often do. Does she approve of your continuing friendship with your former lover?"

Jotahan glanced at Kevos with surprise. "I had not even thought of that. I couldn't imagine why she would concern herself. Now that I know she is my drahi, I would not," he gestured to indicate his covered groin, "*could* not betray her with another female."

He turned his focus back to the sea-tossed horizon. "Besides, Farona has taken Sarah into her fold and welcomed her to join her circle of females. They spend more time together than I spend speaking to Farona whenever she seeks me out."

Kevos shook his head again, bending to lean his forearms on the railing, his gaze fixing on the same horizon that Jotahan watched. "Farona is a beautiful female—the *perfect* yan-kanat female. You could have spent your whole life with her, without bringing Seta Zul's seal into it. She wants you so much that she would not have insisted you make things official. I never could understand why you chose to be painted with that mark. Did it not concern you that the goddess would choose someone else for you?"

Jotahan crossed his arms over his chest, shaking his head at Kevos' question. "I want nestlings. A large family, if possible. I want to pass my bloodline down to my offspring, because I am the only nestling my parents could have. I would not see our line completely die out simply because I was selfishly clinging to someone familiar and comfortable to me, on the chance that the goddess would not choose her for my drahi."

"I have two brothers, so I can understand why we would choose different futures." Kevos straightened and slapped Jotahan on one shoulder. "For your sake, I hope your nixir will not reflect the worst of her species, and will make a good drahi, in time."

Those words would be as close as Kevos would get to a positive response to Sarah's presence. Jotahan didn't dismiss them, or consider them an insult coming from the sentil. In fact, he considered them progress. Perhaps their time spent together in the arena had been enough to knock some of the hatred out of Kevos, or perhaps the fact that Sarah was willingly sharing so much nixir knowledge with the lore-keeper had something to do with Kevos being more willing to tolerate her presence in Draku Rin.

"We should set our grudges aside, Kevos." He nodded to the nearby food stall. "Let me buy you a drink."

Kevos sighed. "I wish I had the time to spend your kivan for you, Jotahan." He eyed the food stall with visible regret. "I need to prepare for a vislog hunt. I must leave at first turning to pick up the trail."

Jotahan regarded the sentil with curiosity. "A vislog has approached the skilev? I hadn't heard about this."

Kevos huffed, his head spines quivering, the rings decorating them sparkling in the sun, making Jotahan idly wonder if Sarah would like it if he wore more ornamentation. His glow had always been enough to impress, but it would soon be gone. Perhaps he should wear jewelry to replace it.

"You've been busy with many things, Jotahan. I imagine this is an important moment in your life. News of a vislog hunting the herds in the baselands wouldn't be much interest to you during these unusual times."

"This will be a dangerous hunt, Kevos." He clapped the other male on the shoulder. "May the Ajda protect you on your quest."

Kevos bowed his head briefly, then huffed. "If I get torn to pieces by the vislog instead of managing to drag my bleeding carcass back to the healer's tent, then at least I won't have to worry about Ane-ata constantly pestering me while I try to recover."

This earned an answering huff of amusement from Jotahan. "Somehow, I suspect you *volunteered* to hunt down the beast. Throwing yourself into the many-ringed maw of a vislog is a coward's way out, Kevos."

Kevos' expression sobered. "I will bring its hide back to the skilev to serve our people. No simpleminded vislog will feast on me." He regarded Jotahan with sympathy. "You have always hunted far more dangerous prey. I hope the nixir you captured doesn't become your doom."

Jotahan let Kevos walk away without further comment, despite the implied insult to Sarah. It would take time for her to prove herself to those who feared and hated the nixirs. He would consider any positive movement as progress. Besides, he didn't want to beat Kevos into a pulp right before a dangerous hunt.

Instead, Jotahan focused on a particular stall, one surrounded by the fragrance of many different herbs, with a hundred different uses. There was only one concoction he wanted in that moment. One that might make the next few cycles—or perhaps even longer depending on Priest Zan Cyall's health—bearable for him and Sarah both as they waited to be sealed as mates.

The herbalist listened to his request without expression, then nodded when he'd finished speaking. He turned to a shelf to pull down several containers of different sizes. He mixed a half dozen different herbs into a pouch, then handed it to Jotahan, accepting his kivan with a grateful bow.

"Do not drink too much," the herbalist reminded him as Jotahan turned to leave the stall. "Just two pinches to dull your arousal. Any more than that could do permanent damage."

Jotahan reassured the herbalist that he would follow the correct dosage, though he hoped two pinches would be enough for what he wanted to do.

He could not make love to Sarah yet, but he could explore her body, and learn what to do to bring her pleasure, as long as he did not grow aroused himself.

35

Lore-keeper Trazu Drakene was the one who told her that Zan Cyall's condition was only growing worse by the day. She'd been in the middle of cataloguing and updating the documentation of the gunslinger's artifacts when he informed her, his sparse head spines at half-mast with his concern.

She rose from her desk, going to him to put a comforting hand on his arm and offer her reassurances that she was certain Zan Cyall would recover completely, and that he just needed more rest. Her words seemed to help Trazu Drakene relax, and it was clear he needed to believe in her reassurance, but they did nothing to comfort her.

She was afraid for the kindly priest. Afraid that she had brought some human illness into this world that made him sick after he came into contact with her. Afraid that it would be something his immune system couldn't handle.

She'd been worrying about her potential hand in the yankanat's illness since she first heard that he'd fallen ill. At that time, it had only been a tiny thought that had popped into her mind, and had quickly been swamped by her disappointment at the delays to the ceremony. Now, it was a full-blown fear. She had no idea what to do if she'd brought something to this world that yan-kanat medicine and immunities couldn't cure.

If the elder named Arokiv was here, he might be able to help. He might have knowledge of human medical techniques that would allow them to test Zan Cyall's blood and identify the problem and hopefully determine a cure.

Unfortunately, they had tried scrying the elder many times since Sarah had arrived in Draku Rin, and they hadn't been able to reach him in the human world. This wasn't entirely unprecedented. Apparently, their "magic" did not work very well in the human world. The elders she'd spoken to said that all magic was dying on Gaia, and that soon, it wouldn't work at all there, forcing the elders who had infiltrated humanity to devise a new solution for their camouflage and communications back to Theia.

She still wasn't certain that what they used really was "magic." There was no denying the existence of dragons, and the inferno stones seemed to be an unlimited source of energy that appeared to be magical, but she suspected there were logical explanations for everything on the world of Theia that could be considered "magic." Humanity already understood that something that appeared to be "magic" was likely some kind of technology they just didn't understand yet. The yan-kanat accepted the wonders of their world as magic, and seemed to lack the human need to find a logical explanation for them.

She was afraid that "magic" wouldn't be enough to save poor Zan Cyall, but that didn't mean it wasn't worth trying. If nothing else, she thought it might be worth appealing to Seta Zul herself. The deity might not be a true goddess, but there was some kind of power in her worship that made her seals so effective. Power that Sarah could not even begin to explain.

She locked up the revolver and ammunition in the lockbox

on her desk along with her notes on how the weapon functioned. Then she stacked her other journals and loose sheafs of handmade papers neatly before bidding Trazu Drakene farewell for the day, knowing that neither of them would be able to focus when they were worried.

Instead of heading straight back to the wing district to wait for Jotaha to return from his work at the training grounds, she made her way through the temple to the small market that had been built in the grand lobby. There she could purchase items to offer the various Ajda that were worshipped in the temple, each within their own chapel attached to the massive building. The market was always busy, even in the evenings, when many yan-kanat came to worship and hadn't stopped in any of the shopping districts below to pick up offerings.

Though it was still midday, the place was packed, and she had to wait for some time before she could speak to the stall vendor and discover what offerings would most please Seta Zul. During her wait, she felt the eyes of the yan-kanat around her settle on her. Most of their attention was curious, and they would give her a friendly nod if she glanced in their direction and caught them staring. She suspected some weren't as welcoming, but none would dare to spread their negative energy in this place. Seta Zul herself wanted Sarah here, as far as the yan-kanat faith was concerned. Questioning her will wasn't a wise thing to do if one had come here to worship the Ajda.

The stall vendor knew her by now, as she often stopped on her way through the lobby to purchase small treats for herself and the lore-keeper from several of the vendors. The female was more than happy to provide suggestions for an offering to Seta Zul, and Sarah was pleased that none of them involved blood, though there were vials of various types of animal blood available at many of the stalls.

The fertility goddess liked flowers, perfumed oils and

waxes, scented candles, anetaak berries, and something that only a male could provide that caused Sarah to blush at the mention of it. She hoped she wouldn't walk into Seta Zul's chapel to discover a male yan-kanat preparing that kind of "offering." At her question about whether the chapel might already be "in use" the vendor seemed amused, as if she was aware of Sarah's concern, quickly assuring her that any "offerings" were always procured beforehand.

Sarah selected some flowers in a vibrant purple color. She was still learning the names of all the different plants and flowers, but there were so many. The yan-kanat seemed to love anything that grew from the soil and their ancient history implied that they'd originally evolved in a jungle environment, so they cultivated every plant and tree on Theia to some degree, leading to an overwhelming variety to learn. She couldn't name the flowers she'd chosen, but the vendor agreed that Seta Zul would appreciate them, as the goddess would approve of the oil she'd purchased.

Once she'd collected her offerings, she wended her way through the crowd in the vast lobby, walking through the light that beamed down from the crystal skylights in the ceiling and sparked off clusters of crystals that surrounded the many different dragon statues in the lobby. She passed beneath the massive and stunning central statue of Draku Rin and headed towards Seta Zul's chapel.

The lush antechamber of Seta Zul's chapel, filled with silken fabrics and elaborate sculptures and fragrant potted plants, was nothing compared to the beauty of the altar room, where a dais sat in front of a sinuous carving of the goddess herself, in all her draconic glory, her triangular head looking down upon the flat surface of the dais.

Sarah now understood the purpose of that dais, and also realized why there was so much room around it for an audience to sit upon the cushions that were now thankfully unoccupied.

When it was time for their first mating ceremony, a soft mattress made especially for them would cover the dais. She felt both excited and anxious when she thought about what would take place on that mattress—right in front of an audience of priests in training. If anyone had tried to tell her before she left Earth that this was how her wedding would turn out, she would have thought them insane—or perverted. Now, she could only feel frustrated that the very public event was being delayed, and deeply concerned that she was the reason for it, and that some human disease was killing a kind-hearted yankanat who only wished the best for her and Jotaha.

She made her way to the offering bowls that sat on the steps in front of the dais and poured the oil into one bowl. Then she set the flowers atop the fragrant oil that the vendor had chosen to complement the floral scent as well as the subtle incense that Seta Zul preferred. She lit the candles on either side of the bowl with one of the smoking incense sticks that always sat in a golden urn filled with sand at a side table. The highly flammable wicks burst into flame as soon as the heated tip of the incense touched them.

She knelt before the altar on a cushion intended for that purpose, bowing her head. Her hands moved automatically into prayer position, even though her parents had raised her to believe that all religions were pointless and an exercise in willful ignorance.

"Seta Zul, I bring you this offering to honor you, as I have come seeking your counsel."

If she'd expected an answer from the goddess, she would have been disappointed. She already knew that Seta Zul had not "spoken" to anyone—even her priests—for many generations, though her "blood"—if that was what it was—still worked to seal and then make fertile the males seeking their mates. Jotaha had said that Seta Zul was "dormant" but still so powerful even in that state that she could hear the words of her followers and would even sometimes grant those requests that moved her.

Into the heavy, scented silence of the chapel, Sarah spoke aloud, voicing her concerns about Zan Cyall, and her worry that his illness could prove incurable because it might have come from Earth.

Speaking to a "goddess" was strangely comforting to her, despite having never sought any type of spiritual solace before. She found herself pouring out her feelings with an openness she wouldn't have shown with a real person. Not even with Jotaha.

When she finished speaking, tears chilled her cheeks. She lifted a hand to touch her wet skin, surprised by their presence. She couldn't remember what she'd ended up saying, but it had felt like a confessional for her.

She still had a question and a purpose for this visit, even if she hadn't really thought it would make much of a difference. Maybe a part of her was hoping that all this "magic" stuff was actually real.

"Why do you allow your loyal and good-hearted priest to suffer from this illness, Seta Zul?" she asked, slightly cringing as if she believed she would be struck down by the dragon goddess for daring to question her motives.

A part of her kind of did.

She jumped when a feminine voice answered from behind her. "Seta Zul's will is rarely understood by the mortals who worship her, and because of that, it can often seem cruel."

Sarah climbed her feet and turned around, a smile of greeting on her face as she swiped her cheeks, hoping she'd wiped away all the dampness there. "Farona! I didn't hear you come in."

Farona returned her smile with a tilt of her lips that spoke of a friendly greeting. "I only just arrived, in time to hear you ask your question." She shook her head. "I apologize for intruding."

Sarah stepped aside and gestured to the altar. "No, it's okay. I was just leaving." Her gaze shifted to the offerings in Farona's hands. "I see I'm not the only one who seeks Seta Zul's advice."

Farona's dainty head spines quivered with her amusement. "I would not dream of expecting a response, but I revere Seta Zul." She held up the flowers, pouch of berries, and small glass vial that looked to be filled with a cloudy liquid rather than a transparent oil. "I came here in the hopes of petitioning Seta Zul for a mate."

Sarah had no idea what to say to that. Farona had never tried to make her feel bad for stealing Jotaha, always brushing off any apologies Sarah tried to make by insisting that she revered the goddess and therefore respected her choices.

It still seemed so bizarre for Sarah that Farona would forgive and forget so easily after openly stating that she'd loved Jotaha her entire life.

Instead, she tried for a hopeful, positive response. "I'm sure Seta Zul will reward you with a mate truly worthy of you, Farona. You deserve it!"

Farona's yan-kanat style smile stretched, sphinxlike, at the compliment. "Thank you, my friend." She lifted the vial. "I have taken a lover, and perhaps Seta Zul will choose him for my mate." Her close-lipped smile became a baring of teeth more like a human grin. "Once I convince him that he wishes to accept the seal, since he has already agreed to contributing to my offering."

Sarah felt a blush burn her cheeks at Farona's openness about sexual matters. The yan-kanat females were not shy about discussing sex and their lovers, nor about taking on casual partners—often more than one at a time. Though mating was for life, both males and females were quite promiscuous until they were sealed to their mate. This sort of thing wasn't openly announced on some public forum, but they had no sense of shame when speaking about it among their circle.

"I'll leave you to it, then," she stammered, her cheeks still burning.

She wished she possessed the coolness and unflappable serenity that Farona always displayed. There was something so worldly and glamorous about the other female that made Sarah still feel inadequate—like Jotaha was being forced to take a step downwards.

She left Farona to her worship, wishing she could stop in and visit Zan Cyall as she passed the door to his quarters, as if her presence could somehow help him, even though it might have ended up harming him.

Her trip back to the wing district was uneventful, but apparently, Jotaha had arrived home before her, and she realized that a lot of time had passed while she'd made her visit to Seta Zul. When she walked into their housing pod, she saw that he had already set out their dinner, poured a light, fruity fermented beverage that had become one of her favorite drinks, and had scattered flower petals all over the floor around his sleeping furs and over the bed.

She didn't get a chance to speak before he caught her by the arms and bent to kiss her. She moaned in pleasure as his mouth claimed hers, his tongue flicking along her lips until they parted to let him in.

She expected him to stop, as he always had to because of his arousal, but he kept their kiss going, plunging deeper, like he was consumed with hunger for her taste.

She shivered in his arms, her core heating up like the infernos the yan-kanat revered so much. Somehow, he seemed to sense her arousal, because he pulled his lips away from hers just long enough to tell her how good her desire smelled, his voice rough. Then his lips caught hers again.

His hands did not remain still while his kiss tormented her with lust they both knew he couldn't fulfill in that moment. They skimmed over her clothes, tugging at the wrap dress until she released his waist and held out her arms, allowing him to pull the layers of fabric away from her body.

She moaned with pleasure as his scaled palms finally slid over her bare skin. His lips caught the sound. Then he lifted his head to look down at her, his slit pupils almost fully dilated, as if he had drunk a whole jug of yanhiss.

"Jotaha, are you okay?"

She shivered with pleasure, her skin pebbling with goosebumps as his cool palms stroked over the naked flesh he revealed with each impatient tug on her dress. The last thing she wanted to do in that moment was remind him that continuing this would only end up hurting him.

"Your skin is so hot, my drahi. I can only imagine how warm your vessel will be around my salavik."

"Jotaha?" His name ended on a low moan as he bared a breast, his palm sliding across her hard nipple, the rasp of his scales shooting a delicious sensation through her body.

He lowered his head to nuzzle her hair as he stroked over her nipple again. "It is Jotahan now. Does this feel good to you?"

"Yes," she whispered. Then the rest of what he said broke through her fog of lust. "Oh, Jotahan! The chanu zayul have chosen a new guardian! I'm so happy for you."

"For us, my drahi. Soon, we will be bonded and begin our seclusion." He followed his words by pressing kisses down her face, nuzzling her temple before making his way to her neck.

Her head leaned to the side automatically, even though she now knew this was a sign of submission. She didn't give a damn about that when his tongue flicked over her throbbing pulse and his lips teased that vulnerable area.

"How... how are you doing this without pain?" she wondered aloud.

"I have taken some herbs to inhibit my arousal."

He lifted his head to look down at her, but his hand still teased her nipple, making it difficult for her to concentrate fully on his words. "Our ceremony has been delayed again, but I realized that I could still give you pleasure if I took the utiva mixture." His lips trailed over her collarbone, his tongue flicking out to stroke her skin. "I could learn your body, and how to please it."

"Is this numbing mixture safe to drink?" She clutched at his head, her hands skimming his prominent cheekbones as he dipped lower, his forked tongue finding the hard bead of her exposed nipple.

"For a short time." His lips closed over her nipple, teasing it without bringing his sharp teeth into play.

She gasped, the damp heat between her legs increasing to the point that Jotahan pulled his lips away long enough for his tongue to flick the air, barely brushing her heated skin.

"I always wondered what this would feel like," he said, his breath cool as it brushed over her sensitive nipple. "This mound is so soft," his claws dented her breast around her nipple as he gently squeezed it, "but this," his tongue flicked her nipple, "is stiff now, though it is only that way sometimes."

"It gets hard when I'm aroused... or cold." She struggled to pay attention to the words coming out of her mouth as his other hand pulled aside more of the dress fabric, most of which was now hanging off her. "The drug...it isn't going to hurt you, is it?"

"I don't care if it does at this point," he said, one hand skimming down her belly to dive beneath the last swath of fabric that still covered her pelvic area, while his other continued to massage her breast.

She tried to pull his head away from her breast, even as his tongue and lips continued to shoot delicious pleasure to her core, but he wasn't interested in stopping. "You're not telling me it's safe."

A soft cry interrupted her words as his fingers stroked over her folds, the texture of his scales raking over her clit in a pleasurable way that had her tensing. She fought the urge to pull him closer even though she wanted to make sure that this wouldn't ultimately harm him.

He did lift his head, but only to shoot her a dilated glance, a wicked smirk tilting his lips. "You like this." His hand shifted over her folds again, drawing a long moan from her.

"Jotahan," she said weakly when she could manage to speak.

His mouth cut off her next words when he silenced her with a kiss. His fingers moved over her clit again, as if testing her response. He learned quickly about her clit, and the next stroke of his fingers targeted it, drawing forth another moan that he consumed with his hungry kiss.

"Shhh," he said when he broke the kiss, his breath whispering against her swollen lips. "Let me please you. It's too late to worry about the utiva. Let's not waste it."

With that, he dropped to one knee, kissing his way down her body, one strong hand supporting her by gripping her waist just above the curve of her buttocks, the other still rubbing over her clit.

He pulled the last bit of fabric away from her folds with his teeth, then he nuzzled the manicured strip of hair that she'd very carefully cultivated using a sharp blade, since the yankanat didn't have razors. She was grateful now for learning to do that without injuring herself. The time and patience spent trimming those curls seemed worth it as he toyed with them.

She clutched the top of his head, feeling his spines shifting against her palm in response to her cry of pleasure when his tongue flicked over her clit.

"Your arousal is delicious." His tongue trailed down her clit as she gasped. It sought her slit, which was soaked with her desire.

He pressed his face against her mound, burying his nose in her curls. His tongue delved into her, making her stumble as her knees gave out from the pleasure.

He steadied her with both hands, withdrawing his tongue long enough to lift his head to look up at her face. "You *really* like this."

At her wordless nod, he rose to his feet in a blindingly fast movement, then swept her up in his arms and carried her to the bed. Once he had her on her back, he returned to his place between her legs, pushing her knees apart. For a long, breathless moment, he paused, studying her. Then his claws traced her slit seconds before he lowered his head and she felt his tongue delving inside her.

It didn't take long for him to bring her to an orgasm as she begged for mercy. She writhed on the bed as her hips bucked, until one heavy arm pinned her in place as he explored her with his tongue while his free hand teased her clit.

As she arched her back with a loud cry, her entire body tensing as her inner muscles convulsed with the waves of pleasure from her climax, Jotahan lifted his head to watch her.

She heard him call her reaction "vemazu", but had no idea at that moment that he intended to draw more "glorious" moments out of her.

In fact, he would do it for most of the night, exploring her body with a focused commitment solely to *her* pleasure that no lover had ever shown her before.

It was only after many sandfalls that the utiva wore off and Jotahan had to leave the housing pod because the scent of her arousal caused a powerful response from his salavik. His seal put out enough heat that Sarah had felt it burn next to her skin as he growled in pain right before he left the bed.

36

The only place Jotahan wanted to be in that moment was in his bed with Sarah. Unfortunately, a side effect of pleasuring her all night was that the scent of her arousal lingered after the utiva's effects wore off. Once freed of the numbing effect of the drink, his salavik responded with predictable eagerness to her scent.

He was driven from his bed and the warmth of his drahi because of the damned seal, and frustration filled him that he would have to wait even longer for the ceremony to bond Sarah to him. The evening they'd spent together—the things he'd done to her—made him hunger for more—made him want to claim all of her, in a way that his tongue and fingers couldn't.

Her body was as exotic and beautiful as he'd imagined, and her taste was the most incredible one that had ever flavored his tongue. Different, alien, and yet so perfect, as if she was created just for him. Everything about her felt different, from the silken softness of her skin, to the barely visible fibers that furred her body, to the way she behaved during climax.

A yan-kanat female practiced ir'meku—personal serenity—when making love, so their climax was always calm and sedate.

Traditional yan-kanat beliefs claimed that the Inferno lay dormant in their blood. After the Ajda had gifted the very first yan-kanat their divine blood, they had warned their chosen people that if the inferno was sparked to life, it would consume them and everyone around them, because their mortal bodies were not built to contain it.

Sex and violence were the two most likely sparks to the Inferno, so yan-kanat practiced meditative mantras to control their high emotions in both situations. Those mantras were how he was able to calm the glow of his body when he needed to be stealthy, using deep breathing and repetitive words to cool his emotions during violent encounters. The female yan-kanat were the ones who practiced the mantras during sex, afraid that revealing their passion might spark that of their lover and end up burning them both to ash.

As a result, even in orgasm, they laid nearly unmoving on the bed, sighing softly with their release. Sarah's reaction to her climax had been both beautiful and surprising, making him feel powerful in a way that none of his successful battles ever had. Watching her back arch as she screamed with the intensity of her orgasm, then feeling the muscles of her vessel convulsing around his tongue had been an almost spiritual experience.

If there was ever a chance that the Inferno of the Ajda could spark inside the yan-kanat, then it would have happened for him in that moment. His salavik might not have been able to respond, but his heart had felt the powerful emotions between him and his mate.

Younger generations were not so convinced that they would truly burn up if they experienced powerful emotions, given the fact that it had never happened before, and there had been many yan-kanat who had lacked full control over themselves. Yet old traditions died slowly, and most still practiced the rigid controls over their passionate feelings, feeling a certain sense of pride about their self-control—especially in the mating chamber. It was yet another reason to appreciate his nixir mate, who allowed herself to express her climax openly, without fear of being judged for losing control of herself.

He strolled the dark streets of the city, walking off the excess energy that arrived in the wake of the utiva wearing off. There were side effects. This was well known, which was why many males didn't use such a drastic method to control themselves while waiting for their sealing ceremony. Normally, he wouldn't have either, but having Sarah live with him while they waited—in close quarters intended for an unmated male—and then experiencing one delay after another, had made it impossible for him to resist any longer.

He didn't regret it, even as his body trembled from the after-effects of the concoction, and his salavik ached beneath his sealed slit as all the feeling returned to it.

Sarah had asked him if it was dangerous, and he hadn't wanted to tell her that it could be, because he was afraid she wouldn't allow him to take it again. He definitely wanted to do that again. Every night if possible, though he knew that would be pushing it, increasing the chance that the drink would cause permanent damage to his nervous system, even with the chanu zayul inside him speeding his healing and the rate at which his body flushed the drug.

His rambling walk carried him through the tail district, winding back and forth as he followed the switchback trail down the hill with no real destination in mind. He only knew that he had to remain a safe distance from Sarah or he would be too tempted to return to her and end up getting himself injured in the process. He passed the hunter's lodge, feeling his seal warming up with the distance he put between himself and Sarah. He was approaching the maximum distance he could travel from his drahi before the seal began to truly hurt him.

He turned to head back up the hill, glancing at the homes built for single sentils and hunters out of the vertebrae of

Draku Rin. Each hollowed-out bone structure housed several sentils and hunters, but they all had their individual quarters inside that space.

Sarah found it odd that the yan-kanat built so many things out of bone. He found it odd that the nixirs did not. He couldn't imagine why they would toss perfectly good bones into a waste heap instead of finding a use for them, but then again, nixirs created new materials to make things, never content with what nature provided them. Nixir alchemy was so arcane that it sounded like magic to many yan-kanat, even though they knew the species had lost all magical abilities long ago, when the Ajda abandoned Gaia entirely.

The bones of Draku Rin were considered sacred, and that also made Sarah surprised that they were turned into functioning buildings. Apparently, nixirs treated sacred things like decorations, setting them up somewhere just to look at them—or even locking them away so that only a few ever saw them—instead of making them useful to everyone, in order to honor those that had sacrificed to provide them.

His contemplation of the differences in yan-kanat and nixir mindset were interrupted as he passed one of the vertebrae and spotted movement in the shadows on the side of the building. He heard a familiar laugh and then recognized Farona's voice even though she spoke low enough that he couldn't hear her words.

He was confused that she would be this far from her home at this time of night. He changed the direction of his steps to greet her and offer to accompany her back to her quarters. Then he heard another voice that made him pause.

Kevos' deep voice was as low as Farona's, but Jotahan didn't need to hear their words to recognize the tone. He slowly withdrew from the area, hoping now that Farona didn't see him. It was clear that she had come to see her new lover off on his hunt, and Jotahan was happy for them both that they had found comfort in each other's arms.

He also felt a sense of relief, as if a weight was lifted from his shoulders as he escaped the area without being spotted. It was only then that he realized that he had felt burdened by his rejection of Farona. It had left a nagging guilt in his mind, even though the choice of his drahi had not been his—at least, not at first. Yet, his growing love for Sarah and the way it blotted out the feelings he'd once had for Farona—like the light of the sun blotted out the dim glow of the stars—had felt like a betrayal of his oldest and dearest friend. He understood now the difference between loving someone and caring about their happiness, and being "in love" with someone and needing them more than he needed air or sustenance.

Sarah was in his blood now. He could never walk away from her, or let her walk away from him without fighting to get her back. He understood now that it hadn't been that way with Farona. It had never been that way. He'd felt comfortable with his previous lover and content with the plans they'd made for the future. He'd never really felt like he wouldn't have a future if she wasn't in it. Such thoughts hadn't even crossed his mind. Whereas with Sarah, the fear of losing her was a constant concern for him, especially after the close call she'd had in the urvaka.

Now, understanding that Farona had moved on with Kevos made him grateful, rather than jealous or possessive of her. He couldn't imagine feeling as sanguine if Sarah even glanced at someone like Kevos with interest, much less moved on to the other male.

Seta Zul had been right to choose Sarah for him, rather than Farona, and he was glad that Farona had found comfort with someone worthy of her.

He did worry that she would grow too attached to Kevos, though. The male was notorious for having many lovers, being considered very handsome by most female yan-kanat, and where Jotahan had always seen his size as a hindrance while serving as Jotaha, Kevos' similar size had drawn many females to him as much as his pretty face. Most of the rings Kevos wore on his spines came from female admirers and lovers.

The hunter was both better-looking and more popular with the females than Jotahan, but he was also determined never to seal himself to a mate, and Jotahan knew that Farona wanted a family. She had told him that she shared his dream of many nestlings filling their family home, and they had spent many cycles discussing their plans for their offspring.

He wanted Farona to find a mate who could make all that happen for her, but Kevos had already made it clear that he would rather remain single and enjoy the many different females he was able to choose from, rather than settle with only one for the rest of his life.

In truth, whatever ended up happening between them was none of Jotahan's business, except when it came to providing support and comfort to his friend if Kevos broke her heart. Other than that, there wasn't anything he could do or say to help Farona realize her dream of having a mate with any other male. He was just grateful that she had found someone to distract her from the shock of him returning home with another female after they'd planned their lives together.

37

Sarah felt like she was floating the morning after Jotahan made love to her with so much intensity and focus on her pleasure. She had never had a sexual experience like that before. One where she didn't feel guilty about taking pleasure without giving the same amount in return. One where she didn't feel like her lover was just going through the motions to get her off so he could get down to business himself.

Her only regret was that they didn't get to spend the rest of the night snuggled up together as she enjoyed the afterglow of multiple orgasms. She understood why Jotahan had to leave, but it still made her feel slightly bereft to be alone after all those intimate moments.

Still, it had been worth it, and Jotahan had returned that morning to collect his things before heading off to the training grounds, and had even risked a kiss for her before heading back out. Despite her efforts to diminish her scent in the pod by burning more incense, he still struggled, and had to break off the kiss early, rushing out of his own home because of her.

After propping the door flap open, she finished braiding her hair, then pinning it up in a bun. Updos made her feel more comfortable when she was in a crowd because when her hair was down, she would often feel tugs on it as she moved among the yan-kanat. Not vicious pulls like they wanted to hurt her, but rather like they were curious enough to touch it as she was moving. Strangers were less inclined to accost her hair when it was on top of her head in a neat, braided knot, because it meant they had to be obvious about reaching for it.

She wondered how they would feel if she went around rubbing their head spines just out of the blue, then figured that could be a lot more painful than them touching her soft hair. Rub them the wrong way and she'd end up regretting it. Even with Jotahan, she'd found that out the hard way, accidentally stabbing her hand on the sharp tips of his head spines when she was rubbing them during a passionate moment that caused them to lift with his rising arousal.

She left the housing pod to make her way to the sky lift station that would take her to the temple. Farona waited at the station, which surprised her since the other female lived in the sternum district, in one of the expensive apartments carved out of the sternum itself. When she saw Sarah, she waved in greeting, answering Sarah's unasked question when she spoke.

"Hello, Sarah. I came here hoping to catch you before you left for the temple. I was hoping to lure you away from your... *hobby*," she smirked knowingly, well aware that Sarah could not call it a "job" without shaming Jotahan, "for a first turning meal. I hope you haven't already eaten. I know a delightful little place on the tip of the right wing district. The views are phenomenal. The best in the whole skilev—and the food is incredible. Some of our circle will be there as well."

Sarah debated the offer, feeling guilty about ditching her duties for that morning to hang out with a friend. The lorekeeper didn't treat her like an employee and told her she was more than welcome to show up whenever it was convenient for her during his shift. He was simply pleased that he had a fount of knowledge to draw from to round out his records about humans. It was only Sarah's own sense of responsibility and need for structure that had her keeping to a schedule.

"What's the occasion?" she asked, noting that Farona was dressed as always in a fashionable dress, this one a sleek shift instead of the luxurious wraps she often wore.

Farona sighed, waving one hand as if to brush aside an annoying insect. "I find myself at loose ends this cycle. I have taken the rest of it off from my craft-rooms, knowing I would be unable to focus, and now I realize I need something to do." She gave Sarah a sphinx smile. "I thought, what better way to spend my cycle than with my new best friend."

The compliment warmed Sarah, renewing her sense of belonging that had been chipped away over the weeks by every resentful glare or sideways glance or curious tug on her hair. She felt like an outsider, and she understood that she was still very new to this place and that made her an oddity among the yan-kanat, but she wanted it to be her home. She wanted to be as happy with Jotahan's world as she was with him.

Farona and her tight circle of friends had greatly helped in that regard by welcoming her into their number and making their acceptance of her very public so that other yan-kanat saw it, and hopefully learned from it.

"So, will you join us for the turning meal?" Farona asked, her emerald eyes twinkling in the morning sunlight.

Sarah couldn't resist an offer like that after such a welcome compliment. She agreed, and they hopped on the sky lift with a couple of other passengers, most of whom were already fairly familiar with Sarah's presence by now. They only briefly glanced her way before returning to their own conversations or contemplations of the views surrounding them as the lift moved along its cable to the skull district, where they could catch another lift to the right wing district.

The views really were incredible at the tip eatery, which was really more like a huge dining stall with open-air seating on a platform built over the edge of the wing. The place was crowded with diners. Many stared at Sarah as she passed, then turned to whisper to their companions. The warm welcomes from the females waiting for her and Farona to join them at a choice table right by the railing overlooking the ocean view helped to make her feel less self-conscious.

Rataka was the first to greet Sarah, and she rose to her feet to give her a hug. Sarah deeply appreciated the gesture even though she wasn't a big "hugger." Neither was Rataka, but the yan-kanat woman understood what it meant to the other yan-kanat to see Sarah welcomed in such a familiar way. In a way, their effusive greetings were a kind of theater, telling a story they wanted their audience to internalize. Letting the watchers know that the human among them was not a dangerous stranger, but a fellow citizen they felt safe befriending.

Her gratitude for these women swelled even further as they all took their seats, buoying up the floating feeling she'd started off the day with when she left her home.

She didn't know if she'd ever stop being amazed by the rapidity of communications in the skilev. Despite not having the ability to text each other, the women had been summoned from all over the skilev by Farona that morning for this turning meal. Word spread through the citizens themselves, messages passed as they went about their business, until they reached their intended destination. It was bizarre that perfect strangers could be trusted to communicate for each other, and do it accurately.

Jotahan said the yan-kanat did have scrying abilities, much like the wizards in a fantasy novel. At least, that was what his description of the process made her think. Yet this ability was rarely used within the skilev, since it took extensive training and focus. If there was a single other yan-kanat around, heading in the direction of the person you wanted to pass a message to, that was generally the most efficient way to do it.

The grapevine in a skilev might be slower than the internet, but it sure seemed to work effectively for the yan-kanat.

The day was beautiful and warm. The cool breezes coming off the sea just barely reached them this high above it, bringing the slight scent of brine that hardly shifted the delicious odors emanating from the kitchen in the back of the food stall.

That food was delicious and perfectly prepared. They even had one of Sarah's favorites—a Theian tear. The clear, spherical cake was similar to something she'd seen in an online video back on Earth that was made of agar. The Theian tear tasted sweet like sugar syrup, tinged with fermented liquor, and had a gelatin consistency. When the very center was pierced, a slightly savory flavor mixed in with the sweet. It tasted amazing on lightly grilled toast and left behind a light buzz.

Her charming companions topped off the experience, their conversation light, entertaining, and filled with humor and mirth.

Until Ane-ata approached them, her teeth bared in an angry snarl.

Two other females flanked her and several yan-kanat males still young enough to be almost indistinguishable from the slender adult females followed behind the group. Their expressions were avid, but it was Ane-ata's that froze Sarah's words in mid-conversation, causing the other women in her circle to turn to regard the approaching female.

Farona rose to her feet, her expression hardening into tight lines, her gaze narrowing on the younger female. "You were not invited, Ane-ata."

Her glass-hard glare flicked to the followers, and the other females in Ane-ata's group flinched when Farona met their eyes, shying several steps backwards.

Ane-ata continued to charge forward, undeterred by Farona's unwelcoming demeanor.

"Little idiot," Rataka muttered, just loud enough for Sarah to hear it.

"*You*," Ane-ata snarled, pointing a manicured claw at Sarah as she stalked right past the seething Farona. "You told Jotahan to send Kevos to his death because you know he sees right through your nixir lies!"

Farona grabbed Ane-ata's upper arm hard enough to make the younger female wince, before she angrily jerked it free. "You speak out of turn, Ane-ata."

Ane-ata hissed at Farona, her mouth opening and her tongue flicking out. The action caused the entire circle of females to gasp in shock, but Farona's expression only grew colder and more forbidding.

"*You* stay out of this! Just because you're willing to give up your male to this nixir filth doesn't mean I will let mine be sent off to his death because of her."

"What are you talking about?" Sarah said, jumping to her feet to move between Ane-ata and Farona, because her friend's expression looked deadly in that moment.

Despite Ane-ata's harsh words, she didn't want the younger female to end up flying off the ledge from a furious charge by the larger, older female.

She had never seen Farona get violent—had never seen any of the females get violent—but that didn't mean it wasn't a possibility. They always appeared fragile, elegant, delicate.

So did venomous snakes.

Ane-ata poked Sarah in the chest, causing her to slap aside the angry female's claw before it pierced her flesh. More gasps sounded at Sarah's rapid reaction.

"Kevos has been sent to hunt the deadly vislog stalking the baseland herds. I *know* you were the one who insisted on him being the hunter the elders sent. Your Jotahan would do anything for you—even send a good yan-kanat male off to die because you didn't like him."

"Ane-ata, I have nothing to do with who is chosen for a hunt. I don't even know what a vislog is, but I don't think—"

"You lie! *All* you nixirs lie!"

She tried to poke at Sarah again. This time Sarah caught her slender wrist and pushed it away from her. The strength of her shove sent Ane-ata staggering backwards a few steps, closer to the railing.

Dead silence hung like a heavy blanket over the crowd. A quick glance around showed Sarah that the yan-kanat diners were all watching *her*, not Ane-ata, with expressions of disapproval and even fear.

Even Ane-ata's followers had backed away rather than moving closer to help their friend. It was like they expected Sarah to shoot laser bolts out of her eyes or something. She was heavier than any one of them, and perhaps that additional mass would make it possible for her to do some damage to the clawed, scaled, wiry youths, but she couldn't take them all down.

Their fear of her was superstitious, and reminded her starkly of the fact that despite their less impressive natural weaponry, humans had chased the yan-kanat from Earth in a decisive and devastating victory. Of course, the fact that her skin began to glow probably didn't help either.

A hard hand captured Ane-ata's arm, dragging the female away from the rail. Sarah, feeling numb, turned to watch Farona pulling Ane-ata off the platform, towards the walkway. The taller female bent her head towards the Ane-ata, who tried several times to jerk away, her entire slim body tensed.

Farona's angry hissing could be heard all the way to the walkway in the silence of the crowd, though Sarah couldn't make out any words.

"Ane-ata has *completely* lost her mind," Rataka whispered to the other females in their circle.

A few light chuckles followed that statement as Farona returned alone. She caught sight of Ane-ata's followers, who seemed frozen with uncertainty. They glanced from Sarah to Farona, then in the direction of the walkway where Ane-ata had fled the area without a backwards glance.

When Farona opened her mouth to hiss angrily at the followers, they turned like one unit and rushed away, heading towards the walkway so quickly that they shoved aside some of the stunned diners.

At this point, Sarah had no idea who they were more afraid of—her, or the indomitable Farona. The elegant female managed to smooth her clothing and sink back into her seat with barely a ruffled head spine, but Sarah was completely shaken by the encounter. The beautiful morning had turned ugly in a single terrible instant. Now, even more of the crowd stared at her, making her feel like a zoo animal on display—a predator, if the fear in their eyes was any way to judge.

"Rataka," Farona said in her usual serene voice, "will you settle the bill for us?"

She rose to her feet again and took Sarah's arm, guiding her firmly away from the silent crowd, back towards the walkway that led down to the sky lift station. "Perhaps we should retire to a yanhiss den. I feel the need for a dark and peaceful corner."

Sarah let her lead them to the sky lift without protest, but demurred on going to a yanhiss den. All she wanted to do was go home and curl up on the bed and cry for hours until Jotahan got home. Farona told her not to take Ane-ata's words too personally, but must have realized Sarah didn't want to talk about it, and bid her farewell at the sky lift for the left wing district.

Sarah walked home with her shoulders bowed, her head

hung in despair. She feared that it would always be like this. That people would always stare at her like she was a boogie man that just popped up right in the middle of their city to feast on their children.

She had hoped that sharing everything she could about the human race would help increase the yan-kanat's understanding of her people and let them see that not all humans were bad, and that so much of what humans did could be truly good and benevolent. Maybe someday her hope for understanding would be true, but for now, it was a pipe dream. She was a stranger in hostile territory, and it seemed that she only had a few allies on her side. The fact that they were powerful and well-respected allies helped, but it might not be enough.

Jotahan walked into the door several sandfalls later to find her kneeling before the shrine of Draku Rin, incense smoking on both sides of the statue.

For some reason, despite not considering herself a spiritual person, Sarah found meditating in front of the statue strangely relaxing. She wondered whether the Ajda ever thought of themselves as monsters, or whether they had ever been bothered by the fact that humans had always seen them as such.

It was ironic, she supposed, that their chosen people now viewed humans as murderous beasts. It seemed such a shame that humans had looked upon such awe-inspiring dragons and had immediately hated them because they feared their power. If it was true that the Ajda had abandoned Gaia because they were offended by humans, then she could only mourn what humanity had lost with their small-minded bigotry.

She was slow to turn to face Jotahan when he greeted her, and that was enough to tell him something was wrong. He immediately set down his burdens and came to join her at the shrine. "Drahi, what happened? What's put that sad expression on your face?"

She turned back to stare at the statue. "Why would you

send Kevos to die because he doesn't like humans? That will only make things worse for me here!"

Her accusing question clearly caught him off-guard and he froze. When he finally spoke, his tone was chilling. "Is that what you think of me? That I would do something so dishonorable?"

Sarah jumped to her feet and spun around to face him, noting that he had crossed his arms over his chest, his eyes narrowed and his jaw so tight it ticked. "Ane-ata said you made the elders send him on a deadly hunt because of me."

"And you believed *her*." His voice was a low growl, dark with anger. "You immediately accept the word of a silly, hysterical female that impugns my honor."

Sarah had expected his support, his reassurance. Now, she'd even managed to make him angry. She should have asked him for an explanation of Ane-ata's thinking, rather than accusing him as Ane-ata did. Her emotions were so raw that she hadn't even considered what the implication would mean to him.

She hated herself for her weakness, but she couldn't stop her tears from coming. Words babbled out of her, broken by ugly sobs. She knew she wasn't making any sense as she tried to explain to him what had happened, and how terrible it had made her feel.

As soon as the tears started, Jotahan's demeanor shifted again. He quickly pulled her close to him, his hand stroking her back as he held her. "Shh, drahi. Calm yourself. Tell me what happened."

Once she managed to explain, with some difficulty, his body was hard with anger and his scales glowed unchecked. His softly whispered reassurances told her that anger wasn't directed at her any longer. He explained that now that he understood what had caused her question, and her distress. He realized she hadn't meant to insult him.

"Ane-ata has always been a fool," he said in a harder tone

than he'd used to soothe her, once her weeping slowed to short, miserable sniffles.

She hated herself for giving into this weakness, even though it meant that Jotahan could see how much the encounter had hurt her and show more patience and understanding than he might have otherwise.

"She's right. Kevos hates me. Lots of people here hate me."

He gripped her braided bun in one large hand, tugging her head away from his chest so she was forced to look up at him. "Do not surrender so easily, my drahi. It isn't in your nixir nature. You will win over the hearts and minds of the people of Draku Rin, simply by being yourself and showing them how good your people can be."

"I'm not the woman you think I am, Jotahan. I *want* to quit. I want to give up. I'm never going to fit in here. Not all humans are fighters."

He'd stiffened as soon as she said she wanted to quit, and she realized that was probably not the best choice of words when his arm tightened around her waist. "Do not make me follow you to Gaia, Sarah. I will, if you insist, but my people will not harm you here, no matter how unkind their words might be. Your people will kill me if they ever detect my presence in their land."

She shook her head, her arms clutching around his waist. "No, I would *never* put you in that kind of danger. Death wouldn't even be the worst fate some humans might visit upon you if they captured you." The thought of him being vivisected in some top secret research facility made her nauseous and terrified at the same time.

His hands freed the braided knot on her head, working it loose from its pins, then stroking the braid as if he could never get enough of the silky feel of her hair. "You can't mean to give up what we have between us. Is our love really not enough for you to want to fight to keep it?"

Sarah hugged him tighter, her sudden terror at the thought of letting him go nearly paralyzing her. "No! I will fight. I will keep fighting. We'll make this work. I'll find a way to convince your people to trust me."

She closed her eyes on a new wave of tears that she wanted to push back. "I pray that Kevos returns safely from this hunt, though, because Ane-ata has put it in everyone's heads now that I would be responsible for his death if he doesn't."

Jotahan huffed in amusement. "Kevos is more than capable of hunting the vislog. He will be deeply offended when he hears that Ane-ata suggested he would certainly die."

"So, it's not that dangerous?" Hope filled her. Perhaps everyone would realize this was all an exaggeration.

"A vislog? They are *extremely* dangerous. They are the size of... what are those odd, hairy beasts from your world with the tusks and the long breathing appendage? I have seen drawings in historical records from Gaia of them."

She pulled away from him just enough to look up at his face, hoping he was joking. "You mean... no... you can't mean a woolly mammoth! They've been extinct for ages."

He nodded. "Wool-e ma'am moth. That was probably what they were called. A vislog is that size, but has many rows of teeth in its massive head, long legs, sharp claws, and a crown of horns. Oh, and a venomous tail spine."

Sarah's jaw gaped open. "Please tell me Kevos has an army of hunters with him to take this thing down."

Jotahan snorted. "Hunters usually work alone. Yan-kanat males are very territorial about our hunting grounds. It is difficult to convince us to hunt together, even against the deadliest of prey." He cupped her face, his thumb brushing away the last of the dampness from her tears. "This is one reason why we lost to the nixirs and their armies. I have been trying to change that in the training grounds, and the younger hunters and guardians are learning to apply group tactics, but it is a slow process and not all trainers have willingly adopted the changes to our traditions."

She clutched his forearms, staring up at his face. "Jotahan, could Kevos die on this hunt?"

"He could." He gripped her chin gently, lowering his head to kiss her. "But he probably won't."

38

Four cycles after Ane-ata's baseless accusations towards his drahi, and himself, Jotahan still overheard the whispers talking about the confrontation. Those conversations always died when people recognized him, but he was aware they started back up again after he left the area. Well-meaning associates approached him in private to express their concerns about Sarah, and he tried to keep in mind that they were only acting out of good intentions so that he didn't end up hurting them.

He had made it very clear the cycle after Ane-ata's verbal attack on Sarah that it was completely false, and that Kevos had willingly volunteered to do the hunt. This fact was reiterated by the other hunters of the lodge, all of whom insisted that Kevos had looked forward to the hunt, viewing it as a welcome challenge of his skill and courage.

Sadly, the gossip was too strong for these facts to matter. There were rumors that Sarah had tried to shove Ane-ata off the platform, that she had attacked Ane-ata with physical violence, and that she had been the one to shout in the younger female's face.

Jotahan believed Sarah's recounting of the events. He knew she would fight back if she felt threatened, but she would never strike out first. The incident was being used by those who hated nixirs to turn the rest of the skilev against her, and it infuriated him that so many of his fellow yan-kanat were being swayed by such vicious propaganda. That was a nixir tactic, since the minds of their people were so easily swayed by those they followed, and it was easy for them to form unreasoning mobs. He never would have expected such a thing to work on the free-thinking yan-kanat. His people didn't even like to *hunt* as a group. He couldn't imagine why they were suddenly so willing to think as a group.

Turning the narrative back towards the truth was difficult, though he wanted to believe it was working, if far too slowly. When Kevos returned several sandfalls after first turning on the fourth cycle, Jotahan felt intense relief. He would like to believe it was for the safe return of one of the skilev's finest hunters, but in reality, it was because now Kevos himself could counteract the rumors with the truth. Perhaps people would listen to him, since it was well known that he had no love for Sarah and no other reason to defend her than to get the truth of the matter out there.

Jotahan knew that Kevos was honorable enough to defend her anyway, even though he might not want to. He would tell the truth.

Kevos was wounded when he was taken up the sky lift to the temple, but the tale of his battle with the beast was already spreading through the skilev. The vislog had managed to gore him with one of its horns, flipping him up onto its back. Despite the damage the horn that impaled his side had done to him, it had worked to his advantage, allowing him to ram his spear down through the base of the creature's skull and into its brain before it could scrape him off on the rocks that surrounded its lair.

Kevos had left the carcass in place for later retrieval, and as Jotahan made his way through the lobby of the temple, he saw the butchers drawing lots for the opportunity to travel to the lair and clean the animal. Tithes from the meat and hide would go towards the temple and the hunter's lodge, and Kevos himself would receive a payout in meat, bones, and skin—or in a comparable amount of kivan. Anything left would go towards the butcher lucky enough to draw the winning lot.

Jotahan found Kevos in the healing wing of the temple, surrounded by fawning healers' apprentices. The young females had eager expressions and gasped and sighed frequently and dramatically as Kevos again recounted the tale of his battle against the beast. The energy he displayed while telling his story seemed at odds with the severity of the bandaged wound on his side.

"Jotahan," Kevos said, catching sight of him hesitating just beyond the curtain that separated the hunter's healing alcove from the others that were currently unoccupied. He waved for Jotahan to enter, gesturing at the three healers' apprentices that they should leave. "I'll finish my story at a later time."

Disappointed groans were their response, and though they kept their heads bowed respectfully as they passed Jotahan to leave, he could tell they weren't thrilled that he'd arrived to spoil their fun.

"I wasn't planning on ending your entertainment, Sentil."

Kevos' nostrils flared, his spines bristling with amusement. "They are young and easily impressed with stories of action and adventure."

Jotahan shook his head. "I doubt that was what drew them to you like herd clingers."

Kevos smirked. "You have your drahi. Do not be envious of the fortunes of others." His expression sobered and he looked towards the curtain as if avoiding Jotahan's eyes. "I heard that the priests' council convened last cycle to advance one of Seta

Zul's acolytes to full priesthood without the final trial to earn their robes. Zan Cyall is comatose now."

Jotahan bowed his head sadly. "Yes. I cannot be happy for the news, though it means there will no longer be repeated delays to our ceremony."

"Are you certain this is the path you want to take, Jotahan?" Kevos glanced at him briefly before returning his gaze to the curtain, as if he needed to study the intricate designs woven into the fabric. "No one would judge you if you had the seal removed."

Jotahan snarled in irritation at the question. "I don't *care* what people will think. This isn't about anyone else but me and my drahi. I will love her forever, and I have no intention of letting her go simply because the yan-kanat are too small-minded to accept her among them. If I have to, I will return with her to Gaia, even if it means spending the rest of my life wearing the face of a nixir."

Kevos shifted his gaze back to Jotahan, his expression contemplative. "I can't imagine having such devotion to a female that you would cast away everything you have earned in your lifetime—and even abandon all that you are—for her sake."

"You want to play games for the rest of your life, Kevos." Jotahan gestured to the wound in the sentil's side. "But there will come a time when the horn gores you closer to your heart, and you will not recover. What do you leave behind? A string of sighing females who will move on to the next handsome male? A home filled with trophies that are meaningless to anyone else but you? Kivan paid out to the temple because you have no direct offspring to inherit it?"

Jotahan stepped closer to Kevos and rested a hand on the other male's shoulder. "Or perhaps you face a bleaker future. One where the females all move on as your head spines fall out and your muscles sag with age, and all you have left are stories of a past that is long behind you, with no one around you who is interested in hearing them."

Kevos shrugged off Jotahan's hand, his brows drawing together and his lips peeling back from his teeth in irritation. "I am not even close to retirement, Jotahan, nor interested in embracing it to begin a family I have never desired. There are still many more hunts ahead for me, before I even consider hanging up my spear." He shook his head. "I don't even know what I would do with myself if I gave up the hunt."

"Focus on creating life, instead of taking it, perhaps?"

Kevos sighed. "You've spent too much time alone in the dark, Jotahan. It has made you desperate for comfort and warmth. There are plenty of females who would have given that to you with enthusiasm, if you'd only glanced in their direction."

Jotahan shrugged, stepping away from Kevos. "You should think on what I've said, Kevos. Don't make the drahi intended for you wait forever, or Seta Zul might find another mate for her."

Perhaps his concern for Farona growing too attached to someone disinterested in starting a family motivated his words to Kevos, but he felt like the other male had come too close to death not to at least consider what he wanted to do with the rest of his life. The life of a hunter could not last forever.

Kevos was silent for so long that Jotahan turned to leave the alcove.

"Will you be attending the lodge celebration this evening?" Kevos finally said, causing Jotahan to pause.

"I didn't really want to leave Sarah alone for the night. Not right now."

"Jotahan." At the serious tone of Kevos' voice, Jotahan turned back to face him. "I have already heard about the lies Ane-ata has spread. She is foolish, but she is also young. Do not judge her too harshly. I will see to it that the truth is spread in turn, and in this, all will know your drahi had no part."

"Thank you, Kevos. I expected you would do the honorable thing."

"Come to the lodge this evening, Jotahan. It would honor me for you to attend. You know this. If you don't, it will look like a direct snub of me and my achievement."

This was true, and Jotahan had not stopped to consider what his failure to attend such a major event would mean to Kevos and the others of the lodge. His concern for Sarah could not completely override his duty to his people, especially since she wasn't in any physical danger. It was just that the whispers and rumors and hard looks from the yan-kanat were wearing on her spirit. He wanted to be there at night to comfort her—and to pleasure her. That always seemed to help her mood, though it made them both even more anxious for the ceremony.

"I will consider it, Kevos."

"WELL, of *course* you have to go, Jotahan," Sarah said that evening when he returned home from the training grounds and told her about his talk with Kevos. "The last thing either of us needs right now is for you to appear to be snubbing Kevos."

He stroked his claws through her long head fibers, never able to get enough of the feel of them running through his fingers, silky and warm from the heat of her body. "The lodge is only for members and honored guests. No females are permitted. I would have to leave you alone for many sandfalls." He lowered his head to bump her forehead with his. "I would far rather spend those sandfalls with you lying upon the bed while I—"

She pressed a finger to his lips, just as he caught the scent of her rising arousal. "Stop it, before you torment us both. You know you need to do this, and I can occupy myself tonight with those." She motioned towards the table where she'd set a sheaf of scrolls and a pot of ink. "I have some things I'm hoping to sketch out, some human tech I think I might be able to explain to those who have never seen its like before. I'm actually looking forward to the challenge. I've never been very good at tech writing, but it's been interesting learning it as I go, and it helps with the homesickness."

"Sarah, if you are truly homesick—"

"You're making a new home for us, Jotahan, and I love the changes we've made together on that home, but no matter where I am, it is always where I want to be as long as you're there with me."

He had never had the heart to tell her that he'd had to remodel the house he'd built with Farona in mind because he couldn't find a property matchmaker willing to work with him to rehouse a nixir drahi. It still angered him, but ranting at the matchmakers who were only representing the stakeholders themselves wouldn't help the situation. It was fortunate that he already had a property to work with, otherwise he might have had to get the elders involved just to have a place to settle with his mate. Throwing his title around to get things done against the will of others would only encourage more accusations that he was allowing a nixir to influence him to abuse his position.

He would do whatever was best for Sarah, but he wanted to do so with the least amount of friction against the yan-kanat people and culture. He could only hope that they would learn to put their biases aside once they grew more familiar and comfortable with having Sarah around.

He had considered the solution the mate of the previous nixir drahi had taken. There were good homes in the baselands, and the residents were more spread out and interacted with each other far less often. They also clung to their territorial ways even more than the hunters and sentils. He could protect his family even in that wilderness, and his half-blood nestlings would not face the judgement that he was beginning to fear they would face in Draku Rin, given the reaction of skilev citizens to Sarah's presence.

Baselanders were already considered strange by skilev standards. Practically wild creatures themselves in some ways, and they had mixed bloods among them, though it had been several generations since that nixir drahi had produced five nestlings for her mate—an astounding number when most yan-kanat females could only wish for more than two. Three was a blessing from Seta Zul. Five was a dream that very few yan-kanat couples could hope to achieve.

SARAH CONVINCED him to attend the lodge celebration, as much as he wanted to remain home with her. She was correct in this, showing wisdom about such things that he'd never had to consider before. He knew the nixirs were familiar with the ugly side of biases. They probably understood such things far more than any yan-kanat. He was disappointed that his people were behaving so much like the nixirs they had always believed to be inferior to them when it came to decency and honor.

The lodge was just as he'd expected it to be after such a successful and impressive hunt. The music was loud, the cheering and chanting even louder, and the boisterous speech the loudest as each hunter tried to outmatch the previous with the tallest of hunting tales. Liquor flowed freely, with not a single drop of yanhiss in sight. No one wanted to be calm and serene during a celebration like this.

Smoke from incense filled the large dining hall as the revelers partied, gorging themselves on meat and blood-based dishes from the kill. Many of them danced wild jigs, some even leaping onto the table.

The inevitable fight broke out, and the combatants were dragged to the small lodge arena to finish the bout to the cheers and hollers of their fellow revelers.

Through it all, Kevos sat in a well of silence at the head of the table, resting his cheek on his fist, his elbow propped on one arm of the giant, carved wooden chair designated for the master of the hunt.

When Jotahan had arrived, the crowd of hunters, sentils, and other Jotahans had cheered in greeting, and Kevos had also greeted him. Jotahan felt the others watching closely as they clasped shoulders and bowed their heads briefly in respect for each other, their spines flattened so that neither appeared to be more dominant than the other.

As soon as the greeting was completed, the tension appeared to ease among the crowd as they cheered again. Then many of the other males came to Jotahan to bow their heads, or slap him on the shoulder in greeting if they were Jotahans as well.

After his friendly and respectful greeting, Kevos had retreated back to the head of the table, seeming wrapped in his own thoughts, and they appeared to be dark ones. Thoughts that put a slight scowl on his lips and drew his brows together. His spines flicked and bristled as if he was agitated by something, and he spoke very little, even though his tale was the one the partiers wanted to hear most.

As the sandfalls passed, the revelers grew more erratic and intoxicated, until it seemed that only Jotahan and Kevos remained sober. Jotahan was studying Kevos, curious about his odd behavior, when the sentil suddenly rose to his feet, barely wincing at the movement despite the fact that it would take time for his wound to heal properly. Without a backward glance or a word to anyone, he left the dining hall, his tall form disappearing into the shadows of the corridor beyond.

39

A quiet evening at home sounded like a good idea at first, but Sarah's thoughts were in turmoil after recent events made her question if she could ever feel at home here in Draku Rin. She would do whatever it took to be with Jotahan, but she couldn't forget that she wasn't truly welcomed here.

Going through the records of the last human drahi to live in these lands only made her feel even less certain she and Jotahan could make a happy home in Draku Rin. Clearly, that woman—whose name she now knew to be Maggie Bennett—had decided she preferred living in the wild lands of heaths and thick forests and rolling hillsides to trying to live among the yan-kanat in the skilev.

She and her mate had been forced to withdraw from the city, perhaps not by any verbally-spoken decree, but simply because the yan-kanat didn't make her feel welcome. It must have taken great courage for a woman of that time to accept the drastic changes in her life that had happened when she was abducted from Earth by a male that must have seemed like a monster to her at first. Yet she had made a life here, by all accounts, as had some human women before her. Maggie had even given birth to five children—a fact that was noted in the records with great praise and admiration. It was also noted that she had been a fiercely protective mother who clearly cherished her offspring, making Sarah hope that she had ended up loving her mate as well.

The tale of the gunslinger was unknown. If Maggie ever knew the man who had apparently tried to retrieve her, there was no record of it. Frustratingly, records about Maggie herself were sparse and not written from her perspective.

Sarah had already begun journaling her own thoughts and experiences in the hopes that any future humans who came to this world would be able to make use of any knowledge she passed down to make this place feel more like a home. Perhaps even the yan-kanat would someday read her words and learn that humans were not heartless monsters devoid of feeling and emotion, but were actual people, capable of feeling love, and rejection, and grief, and hope—just like their yan-kanat neighbors.

She missed Jotahan as the sandfalls passed, wishing she could discuss these things with him. He had showed great interest and curiosity about Maggie's story too. He had also been forced to admit that he was happy Sarah was working at the temple now. He was grateful that she was sharing her knowledge in the hopes of increasing understanding for the yan-kanat when it came to humanity. She believed that their two species could someday find a way to live in harmony, if only both sides could acknowledge that the other side was not that different from their own.

They could even interbreed, and that alone should be enough to convince people that they were not incompatible. It was a pity that humans and yan-kanat did share one particular trait, and that was the fear of those who were different.

After several sandfalls passed and the evening grew into full night, Sarah gave up on her studies and set aside the pile of papers and the bottle of ink and quill. She rose to her feet, stretched, then made her way to the small shrine. After lighting some incense, she knelt on the pillow in front of the statue, studying the sinuous lines of the beautifully carved stone. The yan-kanat artisans truly understood how to bring life and motion to their static carvings. Draku Rin seemed to move in front of her as the smoke from the incense coiled between her and the shrine.

"What do you think, Wise One? Can humans and yan-kanat ever make peace? Or will people like me always end up being strangers in a strange land? An oddity to gawk at."

Despite the illusion of movement, she didn't expect an answer, but she still felt oddly disappointed that she didn't get one. By now, most humans had accepted the silence of their gods. She still couldn't understand how anyone could have faith in a being that remained silent while so many human atrocities were committed the world over, causing endless pain and suffering for their believers. It was little wonder many humans had made it their mission to kill their gods with logic and reason.

Yet there was something within the human soul that needed that spirituality, and that something had Sarah hoping against hope that the mysterious dragon god, Draku Rin, would actually speak to her in some profound and undeniable way.

But Jotahan had already told her that the Ajda had to leave Theia to appease the angry titans after Bal Goro slayed their sister. Where the Ajda had gone after they shed their mighty forms, even the yan-kanat priests didn't know, though they naturally hoped the Ajda would return one day.

The sound of the door flap pulling open interrupted her contemplation. Sarah leapt to her feet, turning to greet Jotahan. Her joy and anticipation turned to confusion as she saw the male standing in the doorway, towering as much as Jotahan did, but it mostly definitely wasn't her mate.

She recognized Kevos. It was difficult not to know the person who despised you the most. The male wore a tunic that was covered in blood and his eyes were dilated and wild, his lips peeled back in a snarl.

"You will come with me now," he said, striding towards her.

Sarah screamed, backing away until she bumped into the statue.

"Silence, nixir! Your scream will bring others."

He grabbed her arm, dragging her away from the shrine. Her hand flailed behind her, reaching, searching. Her other hand fisted, and in her struggle, she punched Kevos in the side.

He grunted in obvious pain, his grip on her arm weakening as he buckled.

She jerked her arm free, her other hand closing around the dart that was concealed among the incense sticks. Jotahan understood her need to have that little bit of protection close at hand, even though he didn't believe she could ever be in physical danger in the skilev.

She had known better, recognizing the rising darkness as public opinion of her soured, fueled by baseless rumors and accusations. The yan-kanat didn't even need social media to spread their poison and demonize someone. Of course, neither did humans. It was just more efficient to use the internet to destroy people. Why commit murder when someone could be tormented enough online to kill themselves?

Kevos growled, gripping his side as he grabbed for her again. She wasted no time in stabbing his hand with the poisoned tip of the dart. Jotahan had coated the tip with enough poison to drop a fully grown male yan-kanat, but she feared the coating would take time to rehydrate in Kevos' blood stream.

He didn't immediately go down, but he seemed to recognize

the dart. Realization widened his eyes as he looked from it to her.

"You *fool*! They will kill you for certain now. There's no escape."

Since he still seemed to be weakened by pain and surprise that she'd stuck him with the dart, Sarah picked up the heavy statue of Draku Rin and swung it at his head.

He turned just in time for the stone to strike his shoulder, but the impact still sent him staggering backwards, his steps unsteady.

Sarah took that opening, casting the statue aside as she raced past him and out the door.

"Come back here, nixir!" he said in a harsh cry as she exited the housing pod.

Sarah kept running, her feet carrying her rapidly down the walkway. To her frustration, no one seemed to be around to help her. Then again, she wasn't certain how many of the yan-kanat would stop Kevos from killing her.

She feared that the blood that had covered his tunic had come from Jotahan. Why else would Kevos be willing to risk attacking her, if he hadn't already put Jotahan out of commission?

She couldn't allow herself to believe Jotahan was dead. She couldn't bear the thought, so she kept running, torn between the urge to scream for help and the fear that it would only make her situation worse.

A growing sound reached her ears that she'd never heard in this skilev before. The sound of an angry mob, crying out for blood. Nixir blood.

She ducked into an alcove between two housing clusters, shocked by what the mob was saying as it drew closer to where she was, no doubt heading for her pod.

"Kill the murderer. Kill the nixir!"

She hadn't killed Kevos with that dart. She was sure of that.

Besides, she had only struck him in self-defense, and that had been only minutes earlier. There was no way someone could have discovered him and then formed an angry mob that quickly.

She didn't know what to do now. Breathing deeply and focusing on calming herself allowed her to quell the glowing of the chanu zayul that showed through her skin, but she still wondered if she could remain hidden in the alcove from people who could track her by her scent, or if she should make a break for it and try to get to the temple to beg her few friends among the elders to provide sanctuary to her.

Then she saw a familiar slender form walk hurriedly past the alcove, heading towards her pod.

"Farona!" Sarah hissed, trying to keep her voice low enough not to alert anyone else in the vicinity of her position.

Farona spun around, the bag slung over her chest shifting outwards with the movement before thudding back against the full fabric of her gown. "Sarah!" She put a hand on her chest. "You startled me!"

"Kevos is trying to kill me," Sarah said, blinking back tears of terror. "I think he's knocked out by now, but I hear an angry mob approaching, and I'm sure they're after me."

Farona's mouth hung open. "*Kevos*... he did what? I don't believe it!"

"Trust me, I was pretty shocked too when he stormed into my house covered in blood."

Farona's eyes narrowed. "Did he explain why he would commit such madness? What did he say to you?"

Sarah shook her head. "I have no idea what he was thinking. He just stormed in and grabbed me. I hit him with a dart. And a statue of Draku Rin." Her breath faltered as she relived the terrifying moments. "Then I ran for it. I need to find Jotahan."

Farona glanced from one side to the other, then turned

back to Sarah. "I agree. If anyone can help you, it will be him. But if there's a mob after you, then we can't risk taking you through the heart of the skilev to the hunter's lodge. There's a small hut on the beach where Ha-tah and I used to go for privacy. I can take you there through the mines, then fetch Ha-tah and bring him to you. Then we can figure out how to fix all this and see Kevos punished for his crimes."

Relief sagged Sarah's shoulders. "Then you think Jotahan is still alive?"

Farona smiled Sphinxlike. "You don't imagine Kevos could possibly take down Ha-tah? Of course he remains alive. He will be very worried about you. Come," she waved her hand, "we must move quickly! The mob is close enough that they will soon cut off our path."

Farona led Sarah through dark alcoves and alleys, making their way down the wing district until they entered the sternum district. They managed to avoid most of the yan-kanat and the few they passed seemed unaware of the growing anger of the mob, and its target, simply casting them curious looks as they headed to the mine entrance.

The main entrance to the mine was guarded to keep youths from entering and possibly getting hurt, but Farona knew about a side entrance and had a key. Soon they were inside the mine, inferno stones lighting the way for them, though the sight of the stone hanging above them made Sarah have flashbacks to the last time she went into a mine. She shuddered as she followed Farona deeper, towards the secret exit to the beach.

"Be careful here, Sarah," Farona said, speaking in a normal volume now, since she'd reassured Sarah that no one came into this part of the mine at night. "There is a vertical shaft nearby. It's covered, but the wood is old and brittle."

"Trust me," Sarah muttered, her eyes now adjusted to the inferno-lit mine so that she could spot the elevator apparatus of the shaft just up ahead. "I know how dangerous vertical shafts are."

"Poor Ane-ata. She was so obsessed with Kevos," Farona said, walking just ahead of Sarah.

"Yeah, news of his crime will probably somehow make her blame me even more."

"Do you know, she came to me in a rage once she discovered that Kevos was my lover," Farona said, her steps slowing.

Sarah was surprised by Farona's words. "*Ah*, so he's the mystery lover who has put that smile on your face lately. Oh, no," she shook her head, "I'm *so* sorry, Farona. Maybe there's some reasonable explanation for his behavior."

She doubted it, but Farona had already suffered one crushing heartbreak with losing Jotahan. She didn't deserve for Kevos to be the bastard he'd turned out to be.

"Ane-ata demanded I stop seeing him. She said he belonged to her. When I laughed at her ridiculous notion and explained that he had no interest in her, she threatened to expose some information that could have destroyed my businesses. What else could I do? I had no choice but to silence her."

Sarah froze, her eyes widening on Farona's back as shock filled her. The blue glow that lit up her skin in that moment brightened the shadows in the mine.

"But then I thought of a clever plan. After such a public confrontation with Ane-ata, Draku Rin's newest resident—the nixir—undoubtedly had good reason to stab the poor, young fool in the back. And," she turned to face Sarah, reaching into her bag, "that is the nixir way, isn't it?"

Sarah took a step backwards, but froze again when she heard a familiar click as Farona brought up the gunslinger's revolver to aim it at her chest. "Of course, thanks to all your useful notes, I have a far more efficient nixir way of dispatching a nuisance."

She tightened her grip on the gun, shaking her head as

Sarah shifted her weight forward. "Ah, ah. I assure you, I did a thorough study of your notes. Even the ones on the safe handling of this weapon. Especially the one that says, 'don't point the weapon at anything you don't intend to shoot.'" She bared her teeth. "I think that's excellent advice."

Sarah slowly held up both hands. "Farona, you don't have to do this! Ane-ata tried to blackmail you. I'm sure if you just explain things to the elders, they'll go easy on you."

Farona cocked her head. "Now, why would I do that? No one knows that I killed Ane-ata." Her brows came together over her eyes. "Except for Kevos, perhaps. He must have found her body just after I left, and made his way to your place to get you clear of the mob I was raising to drag you out and execute you."

She huffed in a chillingly amused sound. "He must have been *very* conflicted in those moments, feeling bound by honor to save an innocent female he despises from the one he loves." She shrugged. "I will have to dispose of him after I take care of you, but you've made things easier for me by incapacitating him, and I can even blame *his* death on you as well."

Sarah's eyes were fixed on the barrel of the gun, the hole at the end of it seeming to expand until that darkness threatened to blot out everything else. "Why, Farona? I thought we were friends!"

Farona scoffed, bringing Sarah's gaze up from the gun to see her expression twist into a snarl of anger and hatred. "*Friends*? Ha-tah is *mine*! He belongs to me. I claimed him from the moment I was old enough to speak. I don't care what Seta Zul wills, he is *mine*!"

She raised the gun slightly higher, aiming closer to Sarah's heart. "You were in the way. Nothing more. I knew that poisoning Seta Zul's priest was only a temporary measure to delay the sealing ceremony until I could convince Ha-tah to have the seal removed, but I was finding it difficult to come up with a plan that would free him from his obsession with you.

Killing you wasn't enough. He would never recover from that. He had to see you for the monster you are, and *hate* you for it. Ane-ata's death gave me the perfect opportun—"

Her words were cut off by Sarah crashing into her, one hand shoving the gun to the side. "Thanks for the monologue, bitch," Sarah spat into Farona's face. "Talking about your own brilliant plan always distracts a villain. Humans understand this very well."

Farona was taken by surprise, but she was also insane and strengthened by her rage. They wrestled for control of the gun, and Farona didn't drop it when Sarah put all her weight into slamming the slender female into the rock wall at her back.

Farona grunted as her grip weakened on the revolver, but when Sarah tried to shake it free from her hand, Farona slashed her face with the claws of her other hand, coming far too close to blinding her.

As she shied back, Farona rallied, tightening her grip on the revolver's pearl handle. She brought it down to slam the butt into Sarah's temple, then again as Sarah staggered. Her hold on Farona's wrist loosened even further as Farona pushed her backwards.

Sarah kicked at Farona's legs, trying to knock them from under her, but the other female was agile and easily dodged the move. She responded by turning her head to bury her sharp teeth into Sarah's wrist.

Sarah screamed as blood poured from the wounds in her flesh. Farona shoved her away, bringing the gun back up to aim at her again.

She didn't get a chance to pull the trigger before Sarah staggered onto the weakened boards covering the vertical shaft. Sarah screamed again as they shattered beneath her. Gravity that was so close to Earth's gravity that she never noticed much difference took hold, dragging her down.

The sound of Farona's huffing amusement followed, but

was cut off just like Sarah's scream when the fabric of Sarah's wrap dress that had unwound during her struggle with Farona caught on the shards of wood that remained of the broken cover. She now dangled over a deadly drop by the delicate silk length of her wrap.

Farona stood over the shaft, staring down at Sarah. "Curse you for being so damned *lucky*, nixir!" She aimed the revolver. "But it looks as if your luck has finally run out."

"Farona!" Jotahan's voice sounded like the music of angels in Sarah's ears. "Don't do this. Put the weapon down."

Farona's expression twisted to one of desperation as her head turned to look in the direction where Jotahan voice had come from. "Ha-tah! This nixir murdered Ane-ata in cold blood! She must be punished! I had to defend myself against her attacks."

"We were able to revive Kevos, Farona," Jotahan said, his tone saddened. "He told us he saw *you* leaving Ane-ata's home, right before he entered and discovered her still bleeding out on the floor. Please, my old friend, let us end this now. We can get you help. The priests can help you heal your broken spirit."

Farona screamed with rage, swinging the revolver up to aim in Jotahan's direction. Sarah shouted a warning, but it was too late as Farona pulled the trigger.

"If I cannot be with you, Ha-tah, then no one will," Farona shrieked, stumbling a bit from the kickback of the gun.

Sarah heard the ominous thud of something heavy striking the board closest to the shard that kept her from falling. She saw Jotahan's hand fall to hang motionless just over the edge.

"No!" she screamed, struggling to pull herself up the fabric. "Don't you dare die on me, Jotahan!"

Light blazed in the shaft as her chanu zayul glowed even brighter with her emotions, and she felt a burst of inhuman strength that allowed her to pull her way up the fabric.

But it wasn't enough. Farona had recovered from the shock

of shooting Jotahan, and now turned her focus back on Sarah. "You *made* me do it," she said in a shaking voice. "This was all *your* fault!" She cocked the revolver and her finger settled back on the trigger. "You made me kill my *beloved*!"

Jotahan's hand suddenly grabbed Farona's ankle. Sarah saw just the briefest glimpse of him as he struggled to pull his body up enough to put some weight into throwing Farona off-balance. She yelped in surprise and the gun went off, the bullet whizzing past Sarah's head to lodge into the stone below her.

Then Farona cartwheeled her arms as Jotahan put the last of his strength into a hard shove that sent her falling over the edge.

Her body plummeted past Sarah, knocking into her with just enough force to send Sarah spinning. The back of her head and neck slammed hard into the uneven rock wall as Farona's screams faded down the shaft, then cut off completely into dead silence. Sarah braced her feet against the stone to stop her dizzying spin. Agony filled her head, but her heart was in even more pain.

"Jotahan!" Sarah said, her voice quivering. "Please answer me! Please! Be okay." Her head blazed with pain and her arms shook as she clutched the fabric. The darkness of unconsciousness began to close in over her vision.

His hand had fallen again, lying motionless now over the edge of the shaft. She stared at it as her vision faded to black, willing it to move. It didn't so much as twitch, and he did not answer, no matter how loud and desperately she screamed his name.

40

When Sarah opened her eyes, she discovered that she was being consumed by fire. A fire that did not burn her.

"Wha?" She spun around, only then realizing that she hovered above an inferno, unable to feel the heat, nor the pain from the flames that licked past her feet and snapped around her legs like a pack of angry hounds.

"Where am I?"

"You are close to the Inferno, human." The voice was feminine, but strong and resounding, seeming to emanate from all around her.

The flames licking at her toes grew larger and larger, curling into a sinuous shape as they rose in front of her. A dragon formed from the flames, wings stretching, long neck curving as it swung its sharp triangular face towards her. A massive crown of horns crested from its skull, fading into a thick ridge of spikes that trailed down its back.

"You-you're Seta Zul!" Sarah recognized the shape of the horns, the slender build of the body in comparison to the heavier, more muscular male dragons depicted in the statues around the temple.

Smoke curled from the dragon's nostrils. "This is a name I am called, though I was once known only as Rin Troka."

"One Truth? That's a beautiful name." Sarah bowed her head, awed by the vision in front of her. "It's an honor to meet you."

"I have been curious to meet you as well, human called Sarah." The dragon's form curled into an S shape, the massive wings gently flapping as she hovered in front of Sarah, who still hung above the blazing inferno that roiled and spun below her like the surface of the sun.

"Humans have always fascinated me. Your people possess the arrogance of the titans without their power. This appears to make your kind irrational. As a species, you seek to distill all meaning—the entire essence of truth—into succinct words and concepts that define your reality. This mental prison your people have forged for themselves means that humans will never learn to walk with the titans, because your minds are not free. You will end up destroying yourselves before you can unmake your shackles."

"Are you talking about humans abandoning magic?"

Seta Zul chuckled, small flames slipping from between her sharp teeth. "Magic is what you humans have labeled those truths you cannot bring yourselves to accept. You try fruitlessly to explain chaos, so that you can put it into order. Like ignorant creatures, flailing in unfamiliar waters, humans search for meaning where there is none. You cannot accept when something simply 'is', you think it must always be explained." She swung her head so that one large eye studied Sarah.

Sarah shook her head. "I... I don't speak for all of humanity. I can't answer for anyone but myself."

This caused Seta Zul to nod her head briefly, almost as if she approved of what Sarah said.

"We once offered the gift of our blood to humans, and the power that came with it. Instead of venerating us, as the yankanat do, the humans branded us as demons and sought to slay us, because they saw within us a mirror of their own deepest desires—and they feared them. They abandoned the gods who walked among them for the same reason, and turned to a lie. A god they need never face to see their own reflection in its eyes. A god that would never interfere in their own plans for glory. A god they could control."

The dragon bared sharp teeth as flames spit from her jaws. "Mortal men used a god of words to control others, and in time, those words came to possess great power of their own. That power was used by corrupt leaders to channel the violent and destructive natures of humanity to suit their own petty purposes. They suppressed the harmonious aspects in human nature, creating an imbalance as words made virtue a prison with no key."

Sarah shivered at the hard tone that Seta Zul's booming voice took. "I can only say that I regret the choices made by humanity long before I was born. I would have made different choices."

Seta Zul cocked her head, tilting it so both her eyes now studied Sarah. "Would you? Then let me give you a choice and we shall see where it leads you."

Her heart thudded as she waited to hear the dragon god's next words, terrified of what they would be. Afraid that she would make a choice that would steal more from the future of humanity, just as those in the past had stolen from the present.

Seta Zul seemed to read her thoughts. "This choice will affect only you. Humanity no longer tempts us to share any gifts with them. They shed our blood instead of accepting it, and for that, we will not soon forget our anger."

"I'm sorry about that. Not all men are ruled by fear and loathing of those who are different."

Seta Zul snorted flames. "This choice is yours to make, Sarah. Let us see if it is the right one. My blood will heal Jotahan, but it will dissolve my seal and drain its power to grant him fertility. He will be forever sterile and his dream of having nestlings will die even as he goes on to survive. This, along with his guilt and heartbreak over being forced to kill his childhood friend will haunt him for the rest of his days. He will be honor bound to stay with you, but no longer compelled by his biology. He will suffer for his losses, and may someday come to resent you for punishing him by forcing him to return to a flesh prison, when he could have flown free in the Eternal Inferno, though he would never tell you this. Yet the decision is yours. Do you set him free, or do you demand I heal him and return him to you?"

Sarah shook her head violently. "No! You can't give me a choice like that! That's an impossible decision to make!"

Seta Zul's glowing draconic gaze was hard and merciless. "It is only difficult for a selfish human, too afraid of being abandoned and alone to set the one she loves free. Would you keep Jotahan from shedding his skin to find a new future? Will your fear bind him, Sarah? Or will you face your own future alone, with courage and hope?"

Tears poured down Sarah's cheeks as she sobbed in despair. "I... I have to let him die?"

"That is your choice to make."

"But you said he wouldn't be happy with me if he survived."

"Does that matter to you? He will still remain by your side. He will still give you his time, and attention, and love."

Sarah's head hung as she stared down at the flames crackling around her feet. She didn't want to meet that knowing stare any longer. "Is that what you chose? To set your beloved free? Is that why you're known as 'Wounded Heart' now?"

"Your questions are impertinent, mortal. In any other situation, I would destroy you for daring to ask such things."

Sarah looked up, feeling nothing at the threat. Not even the slightest tinge of fear.

"No," Seta Zul shook her head slowly. "I will not make it that easy for you. Your life will go on, regardless of what choice you make for Jotahan."

Sarah hovered there, numb to all sensation but the agony in her heart. "In that case, answer my question." She lifted her chin, glaring at the dragon. "If you won't kill me, then I see no reason not to demand an answer."

"I do not need to kill you to make you wish you were dead, Sarah." The dragon's body straightened out of its sinuous curve, tensing for a long, breathless moment, before it relaxed again.

"But, you make me curious, so I will indulge you for the moment. I am a powerful oracle, even among the Ajda. I foresaw the future for my beloved Bal Goro, and it did not include me. I believed that I could save him—that I could hold onto him so that he would not go to a place where his heart would be vulnerable to a mortal. A place where he would lose the will to go on burning when her life ended. He lashed out violently against my attempt to imprison him in his own flesh. I finally understood that I could not keep him from his destiny, but we did not part on good terms."

At Sarah's prolonged silence, the goddess spoke again. "You *can* learn to love again. The heart is resilient." She craned her neck, moving her head closer to Sarah. "I can send you another yan-kanat mate. Fertility is one gift human blood can give the yan-kanat, and you will be very fertile."

Sarah closed her eyes, her fists clenched. "I don't want someone else. I only want Jotahan." She sighed, reaching up to jerkily swipe away her tears. "Did you?"

She opened her eyes to meet the dragon's gaze, and she swore she saw sympathy on Seta Zul's reptilian face. "Did *you* ever love again?"

"My yan-kanat—my blood-touched children—became the

focus of my inferno after Bal Goro and the others left this world. I have no need for a lover at this stage in my existence. I bend my will and essence to protecting and enriching the lives of the chosen ones of the Ajda. Someday, when I know they will carry on without me and their blood will be fertile again thanks to my efforts, I will shed my own skin and perhaps rejoin the others."

She broke her steady gaze, glancing into the swirling flames that surrounded them. "Or perhaps I will forge a new path for the Ajda. Perhaps I will follow the heavy tread of the titans to some new reality."

Sarah's spine straightened, her chin lifting. There was no way she would ever learn to love another like she loved Jotahan. There was no way she could go on living without him as if he had never entered her life and changed it completely.

"I'm ready to make my choice."

PAIN SCREAMED THROUGH HER SKULL, and it felt like her brain was on fire. Her eyelids fluttered open as something suddenly jerked her upwards, causing the stabbing pain to strike through her head again. The sound of tearing fabric reached her, though it was muted and surreal. Her body slipped downwards, then jerked to a sudden halt.

She heard cursing, and shouts of warning. For several long minutes, she felt her body dangling, hovering, as though she still hung over the Inferno, but the pain of the flames had moved inside her and now burned through her mind.

Her vision was blurry, and her surroundings dark. Even her body no longer glowed, but she saw the shadow of a face coming closer to hers, just as she felt arms closing around her.

"I got her. You can pull us the rest of the way up now."

The voice was deep. Male. The arms were strong.

But it wasn't Jotahan.

"I think she's coming around," the voice said, close enough to her ear that she flinched as the volume of it shot more pain through her skull. "I just hope she doesn't struggle and end up punching me on my wounded side again," the voice muttered in a much lower volume.

Sarah closed her eyes tight, turning her head away from the one who held onto her as she was pulled out of the shaft. Tears spilled down her cheeks.

I'm so sorry, Jotahan. I will never forget you and I will always love only you. Fly free, and someday, my spirit will find yours again, even if I have to burn with you forever in the Inferno. I swear it!

41

"Sarah."

Jotahan! The sound of his voice made her heart break. Would she never reach a point where it no longer haunted her dreams?

"I need you to come back to me, Sarah. Please."

Oh, Jotahan! I will find you again someday. I promise. My soul won't rest until I do.

"I can't go on without you, my drahi. Nothing else matters to me but you."

Please, my love, please stop calling for me. I don't know how long I can resist the urge to follow you. She said you would fly free once you were in the Inferno, but you still cry out for me, endlessly, and I want to find you.

"Sarah," his voice seemed so close to her, ragged and hoarse like he'd been screaming for hours. "I don't know how to fight this enemy. I don't know how to get you back. I don't know what to do. I'm so lost."

No! She would find him. He needed her. They needed each other. Seta Zul had been wrong. Jotahan loved her as much as she loved him. Setting him free had not helped him. It was hurting him. How could the goddess have been so cruel? How could Sarah have believed her, when she knew in her soul that they were already bound to each other and would never be whole unless they were together.

She struggled to reach out for him. To cry out for him. It was like the dragon goddess herself was sitting on Sarah's body, paralyzing her limbs, weighing her down until she feared her heart would be crushed in her chest.

"I will follow you into the Inferno if I have to, Sarah. I promised you I would never let you leave me. I told you I couldn't let you go. I will fight to get you back, even if it means battling the Inferno itself."

42

When Kevos entered the sickroom, Jotahan was where he had been for the last three cycles. He heard the sentil walk up behind him, sighing heavily enough that even in his exhausted state, with his head lying on his arms, he couldn't avoid hearing it.

"You have to rest, Jotahan. You no longer have the chanu zayul to aid you in healing."

Jotahan didn't bother to lift his head, but his fingers tightened around Sarah's hand as if he feared it would be taken from him and he wouldn't have the strength to keep a hold on her. He felt no response from her. No response at all. Her eyes remained closed, her lips barely parted. Her chest rising and falling shallowly were the only sign of life left after the chanu zayul inside her died before they could leave her body.

Their toxins had poisoned her, and since not all of the chanu zayul's tendrils had been withdrawn when her impact with the stone crushed their almost completely mature bodies, there might have been some damage to her brain and nervous system.

Kevos had said she had cried out from hallucinations

before succumbing completely to her current comatose state. Jotahan himself had been in critical condition for over a cycle. His own chanu zayul had done what they could to heal him, but they had reached full maturity and needed to leave his body. Their grief over the loss of Sarah's chanu zayul was profound and lingered, even after they crawled out of him.

The healers had done a good job patching his wound, but they wanted him to remain in a sickbed, and he would not. He insisted on being at Sarah's side, begging her to return to him. Nothing else mattered to him but getting her back. If he couldn't—if there truly was nothing that could be done to draw her out of this state—then she would die. If that happened, there was no point in him healing completely, since he didn't think he could go on without her.

A hand fell upon his shoulder, and Jotahan knew it wouldn't move until he responded to Kevos. He finally lifted his head from his arms, his bleary eyes struggling to focus on the sentil, when he really wanted to look at Sarah's pale, slack face, praying to all the Ajda that he would see a return of life to her beautiful features.

"Just a little longer. I just need to—"

The hand on his shoulder tightened. "You have been speaking to her for two cycles straight. You haven't eaten or drank enough vandiz in that entire time. The healers are desperate for you to get some rest. You refuse to speak to anyone else, Jotahan. Not even the elders."

Kevos' expression was grim. "Don't make me drag a wounded Jotahan out of this sick room. Come with me willingly." He glanced at Sarah's unmoving form. "She won't slip away in the few brief sandfalls it will take you to eat and rest."

Jotahan snarled and flung Kevos' hand off his shoulder, surging to his feet as he turned on the sentil. "You're probably thrilled about all of this! You never wanted her here. You wanted to kill her yourself in the barrens! Maybe you'll finally get your wish, but you won't live to see it happen." He charged at Kevos.

Kevos met his charge, bringing up both hands to catch at Jotahan's wrists. Jotahan broke one hand free and swung his fist at Kevos' snarling face. He dodged the hit, then parried, striking lower to impact with Jotahan's unprotected side.

They exchanged blows, but it didn't take long for Jotahan's energy to sag, especially when he realized that Kevos was holding back, slowing his speed, pulling his punches. He was only playing with Jotahan, like the sparring partner of a newly recruited jotah.

"You feel better?" Kevos asked when Jotahan pulled away from him, staggering a few steps back to glare angrily at him.

"You know I don't," he growled, rubbing his wrists.

"What would your drahi have thought if she had woken up in the middle of that, Jotahan? Is this the state you want to be in when she awakens? Or would you rather be fresh and rested so that your haggard face doesn't frighten her back into a coma?"

Jotahan's spines bristled. "You think this is funny?"

"Do I look like I'm amused?" Kevos' expression remained as grim as when he'd entered the sickroom. "You are not the only one who must deal with what happened that night. I will never stop seeing Ane-ata's lifeless body in my nightmares, nor will I ever forget the moment when I realized that it was Farona who had murdered her in cold blood. I will never forget that flash of insight, when I finally understood the extent of her wicked plan and the madness that consumed her." His face twisted with a dark scowl. "I *wanted* it to be your nixir, Jotahan. I didn't want to admit that one of our own—a trusted friend—could be capable of such a thing."

Jotahan sagged, leaning back against the wall beside Sarah's bed. "My nightmares are haunted by Farona's screams after I shoved her to her death. They end in terrible silence, only to begin again in an eternal cycle."

"You did what had to be done. No one condemns you for protecting your drahi."

"I know," Jotahan said sadly, feeling as if the toxin of the dead chanu zayul infected his body instead of Sarah's. He tapped his chest. "But I will always feel the pain of her death, and wonder if there was something I could have done to help her before she went mad."

Kevos huffed. "She was always obsessed with you. Even when you were young. You allowed her to lead you around like her pet, so wrapped up in your training and duty that you never objected to her controlling ways as long as they didn't interfere with those. That madness was always in her. Her circle saw it, though I don't think even they truly understood how bad it had gotten."

Jotahan shook his head, not meeting Kevos' eyes, unwilling to believe his words. "If that's true, why would you have taken her to your bed? You told me she was the *perfect* yan-kanat female."

Kevos shrugged. "I imagine she *would* have been perfect for you, as long as she could manipulate you. I am not proud that I failed to see what she was until after I took her as a lover, but I was never serious about her, nor she about me. I understood what little I meant to her." He bowed his head, his spines flicking. "I also understood that she planned to convince you to abandon your drahi, and choose her instead." He looked up to meet Jotahan's narrowed glare. "I swear to you that I had no idea how far she intended to go to get rid of her rival, or I would have put a stop to her plans."

"You wanted her to succeed in changing my mind." Jotahan's spines rose. "You would have been happy if she had."

Kevos flicked a quick glance in the direction of Sarah's bed. "I believed that taking a nixir drahi would be a mistake for you. I thought that you were only doing your duty to Seta Zul, and that all you desired from this mating was nestlings. I did not want to see you bound in an unhappy mating for the rest of your life. Nor did I want an unhappy nixir living among our people, stirring up trouble."

"None of this is Sarah's fault," Jotahan snarled, straightening, even though his exhaustion made him feel weak.

"I know." Kevos bowed his head again. "I realize that. I underestimated her, and overestimated the yan-kanat. I never believed one of our kind would be so deceptive, and I assumed all nixirs were capable of such perfidy. But now, I have seen how much you love her, and I know that you would be incomplete without her. I also heard her profess her love for you, when she was too addled with hallucinations to lie."

He looked up to meet Jotahan's accusing glare. "I was wrong to object to her presence. Wrong to threaten her life. Wrong to assume I knew better than a goddess what was good for our people. I don't want your nixir to die, Jotahan. I hope that she will recover soon."

As Jotahan looked away, returning his gaze to Sarah's face, Kevos spoke again. "It will devastate her if she recovers only to find that you have fallen because you refuse to take care of yourself in your grief."

He knew Kevos was right. Knew that he needed sleep, and that his body needed food and fluids to heal. He wouldn't do himself or Sarah any favors by expiring at her bedside because he couldn't bear to walk away from her, even for a short time.

"Rataka has come to sit by Sarah's side in your absence."

Jotahan stiffened. "She is one of Farona's circle. How do I know she can be trusted with Sarah?"

Kevos sighed, running a hand over his spines to flatten them. "It is a tragedy that we must now question the motives of everyone we allow to come close to us. I fear we will end up living like the nixirs, always forced to watch our back, even among our own kin."

"Farona fooled us all. How can I be certain of any of the others she drew into her influence?"

Kevos shook his head. "Would you and your drahi live in the wilderness, hiding from all yan-kanat to avoid another betrayal? The healers will ensure that Rataka does nothing against their orders. I don't believe she or any of the other members of her circle were capable of what Farona did, and she appears to be genuine in her concern for Sarah."

Jotahan didn't want to trust anyone alone with his drahi. Not even the healers. But his body was failing him. Weakened, wounded, exhausted. He would end up falling out soon enough, and the healers would have him dragged out of this sickroom unconscious. Best to walk out on his own two feet and try to trust that they would be good judges of character and not allow anyone to harm his drahi.

He followed Kevos out of the room after one last kiss on Sarah's warm forehead. Her eyelids did not so much as flicker. Her hand in his did not give the slightest twitch. Hopelessness and despair pulled at his spirit as he rose to his feet and dragged at him as he walked away from her.

He barely noticed the healer pacing on the other side of the door when they left the room, his gaze zeroing in on the slender female who waited with the healer. Her eyes were bright with unshed tears, but she met his gaze with a steady one of her own.

"I will take care of her, Jotahan," she said, thumping her chest with her fist. "Farona's hate did not poison the rest of us. We should have recognized the signs of Farona's sickness, but none of us could imagine one of our own doing such a thing." She bowed her head, her spines flat. "Your drahi has more friends among us than you think. She has proven herself to be good people. We are all praying for her recovery."

Rataka seemed sincere. Jotahan wanted to believe. He wanted to regain faith in his people. He wanted to think that

Farona's betrayal was a once in a lifetime anomaly. The needs of his body for rest and healing gave him no choice in the matter, so he nodded to her without a word, then left the room with one last glance back at Sarah's sickroom.

Kevos kept his pace slow as he led Jotahan back to his own sickroom. He remained while Jotahan was served a tray, claiming he would ensure that Jotahan ate everything on it.

"I am not a nestling," Jotahan growled to Kevos in irritation as the food was set in front of him by a servant, who bowed at his thanks, then left the room as quietly as she'd entered.

"Then stop behaving like one. You think I want to act as your nest watcher? Unfortunately, the healers and servants would only submit to you and let you bully them into ignoring your failing health."

"You exaggerate." Jotahan picked up his eating utensil to poke without much enthusiasm at a slice of kirev bake. It jiggled in response.

"Like it or not, we are bound by this shared tragedy, Jotahan. I have always respected you, but I did not intend to become your keeper."

Jotahan stabbed the kirev bake, shooting a glare at Kevos. Then he sighed, feeling the exhaustion pulling him down onto his mattress. "I'm sorry about Ane-ata. Her death truly is a tragedy."

Kevos studied the tapestry hanging on the wall behind Jotahan's bed. "I went to visit her that night in the hopes that I could prove to her that she and I were not meant to be together. I believed that all I had to do was show her that she was not my mate, and that she would give up on her hopes of a relationship and move on to a male who could appreciate her the way she deserved to be appreciated."

"I never understood why you were so sure she wasn't your mate, Kevos," Jotahan said, ignoring the unappetizing food to regard Kevos curiously.

Kevos huffed softly, his expression regretful. "Some things you just know. I felt nothing but exasperation in her presence. I could not imagine being bound to her for a lifetime, yet I also recognized that she was as sweet as her name, though far too young and naïve."

He turned his gaze back to Jotahan. "When you spoke to me after my return from the hunt, I realized you were right. I didn't want to spend the rest of my life in empty pursuits. Nearly dying showed me that I didn't have much to live for. As soon as I was out of my bed, I went to the newly ordained priest of Seta Zul and asked for the seal. Ane-ata was going to be my first stop after the celebration party, but I decided during the party that I didn't want to wait to make certain she would not be the one to activate it."

Jotahan was stunned. He stared at Kevos, uncertain what to say.

Kevos smirked at his shocked expression. "I know. I was as surprised as you are now when I actually went through with having the seal painted on." He bowed his head to study the stone floor beneath his feet. "Instead of proving anything, I found Ane-ata lying in a pool of her own blood."

He glanced up at Jotahan briefly. "I passed Farona on the way to Ane-ata's pod, close enough that her scent should have activated my seal if she were my drahi. Even before I found Ane-ata's body and understood Farona's part in the murder, I was relieved my seal did not burn for her."

Seta Zul would not have been so cruel. Not even to Kevos, who had openly and heretically disdained her will in his objection to Jotahan bringing Sarah to Draku Rin.

"Has your seal activated?" He could not imagine what kind of drahi would finally tame the sentil.

Kevos shook his head. "Not yet, thank the Ajda. I instantly regretted having it applied, but it was already too late. The ritual was done. I would be dishonored if I removed it now."

Despite the grimness of their circumstances, Jotahan huffed with a brief spurt of amusement at Kevos' predicament. "You do realize that you have already angered Seta Zul by this point. She isn't likely to make your mating an easy one."

Kevos crossed his arms over his chest. "Which is exactly why I instantly regretted my decision. I curse the words you spoke that cycle that made me even consider the idea, and my own impulsiveness in my pain-addled thinking that had me actually going through with it."

Jotahan took a petty satisfaction in Kevos' unease. It served the sentil right to endure the seal and all of its uncertainties after how difficult he'd made Jotahan and Sarah's life with his bias against the nixirs.

A bias that Jotahan had once shared.

"Sarah will recover," Jotahan said aloud, as if the saying of it would make it so.

Kevos slowly nodded his head. "I'm sure she will, Jotahan."

Jotahan turned his gaze down to his plate, unwilling to look at Kevos' face any longer. He supposed it was a good thing that at least Kevos had not learned to lie convincingly, but this time, he really wished he could believe the sentil.

43

"Your willing sacrifice for love pleases me," Seta Zul's voice said, though Sarah could not see her. All she saw was darkness now. Not even the Inferno.

"It is time to wake up, Sarah."

Sarah's eyes opened to see a scaled face hovering over her. She recognized the high cheekbones, fine, delicate jawline, narrow, elegant features.

"Rataka?" Her voice tore from her throat, feeling like it carried shards of glass with it. Her mouth was so dry, she could barely move it.

The female yan-kanat's double eyelids flicked closed, opening to reveal the eyes of Seta Zul. "This one carries genuine affection for you in her heart. She can be trusted."

Her eyes closed again, and Rataka's normal yellow eyes returned when her lids fluttered open. She seemed to be completely unaware that anything odd had taken place, bending forward, the yan-kanat version of a happy expression crossing her face. "Sarah! You're awake!"

She turned her head to call for the healers, then reached for a mug of water that she helped Sarah drink. As water dribbled down her chin despite Rataka's assistance, Sarah decided that she needed to help the yan-kanat invent straws.

Then she remembered that Jotahan was gone, which meant there was no reason for her to remain in Draku Rin. In fact, she wasn't even certain that they would allow her to stay. She wasn't certain what her future held at all.

She couldn't even find it in herself to care.

Tears filled her eyes, despite the fact that she felt too dehydrated to shed any liquids. Somehow, they still managed to form, perhaps draining her of her last fluids.

IVs. She needed to help the yan-kanat invent IVs before she left Draku Rin. Maybe she could manage to do some good in this world before she left it. She couldn't help the feeling that all the tragedy was still her fault, even though it was committed by Farona. After all, if she hadn't come here, Farona would never have lost her mind and turned evil. Maybe the darkness that lived inside the human soul was actually contagious, like a virus. Maybe her coming here had spread it to the yan-kanat.

Rataka took the mug away from her when Sarah choked a bit on a sip of water. "Careful, my friend. You have been asleep for several cycles. The healers managed to force you to swallow fluids while you were unconscious, but they couldn't get much into you. I know you're probably thirsty, but you must drink slowly so you don't hurt yourself."

Sarah finished coughing, leaving her throat raw and even drier so she couldn't speak. Rataka stroked a gentle hand over her hair in a soothing manner. "I'm so sorry for what Farona did to you," Rataka said, her expression turning bleak. "All of us in her circle have known her for many passings, and understood her nature could become violent when her will was thwarted. We overlooked this failing, because none of us coveted what she had claimed as her own. Most of the time, none of us even went

against her wishes. It was just easier to allow her to lead us wherever she wanted us to go, and when we went along with her, she treated us *very* well."

She bowed her head, her eyes closing briefly. "I swear to you, my friend, we did not know the extent of her unethical business dealings, but now that they have been exposed with Ane-ata's murder we have come to question the disappearance of two former members of our circle who had expressed doubts over certain deals she had made. Farona told us they left Draku Rin to travel to other skilevs, and simply never sent a scry because they'd moved on. We had no reason not to believe her then. Now...."

Her tormented gaze lifted to meet Sarah's again. "We don't understand how we could have missed this, after knowing her for so long! How do *your* people handle betrayals like this? How do they learn to trust again, when those closest to them turn out to be the monsters they always feared hid in the dark?"

Sarah patted Rataka's hand where it rested on the bed beside her, propping the other female up as she leaned over Sarah. She tried to dredge up some emotion, though she felt dead inside, as though a part of her was lost forever.

"You learn to go on, Rataka, and try not to judge everyone you meet by the actions of those who have hurt you in the past." Her voice was still hoarse, and speaking was still a struggle, but it kept her from thinking about Jotahan and the deep, painful well of loss inside her that waited to drown her. "That's what humans have to do. It's not always easy, but it can be done. You can learn to trust people again—and to trust your own judgement."

She needed water after that, and this time, she managed to pull herself into a sitting position with Rataka's help as one of the healers entered.

It was clear Rataka was pondering her words, but they did not get to speak again after that, because she was shooed out by the healer, who then turned to Sarah and did an assessment on her condition.

Sarah went through the motions, struggling to find a reason to care about any of them. To care about her own condition. She drank water when she was told to, obediently ate as much as she could manage when a tray was brought in, and agreed without complaint to rest as much as possible, despite having been unconscious for so long.

Then the healer said he felt she was finally in a strong enough state to have a visit from Jotahan.

Hope and excitement filled Sarah, shooting energy through her limbs that had her straightening up from her dejected slouch against the headboard. Then she had a terrible fear that the healer meant some other Jotahan. There was more than one, after all. Somehow, that didn't seem to cause confusion for the yan-kanat, but she never wanted to hear the name Ha-tah again, even if Jotahan *had* been 'long awaited' in her life too—before she even knew she was waiting for him to enter it.

Joy and relief filled her when he entered the room. Her Jotahan. She sobbed, tears filling her eyes as he rushed to her side to kneel beside the bed. He gently enfolded her in his arms, cradling her close against his chest. His scent surrounded her as her body heat warmed them both.

He nuzzled her hair, his voice as hoarse as hers as he told her he loved her, and demanded that she never scare him like that again.

He told her he couldn't live without her. He told her that he would sacrifice anything to be with her.

Sarah had spent most of her life feeling like someone else's burden—a parasite draining her parents' best years away, or a runaway dragging her best friend into her problems. Jotahan made her feel wanted and loved unconditionally. Not because he had the seal. Not because he wanted children. He wanted her because he loved her.

After a long embrace, and a kiss so necessary that Sarah didn't even worry about the fact that she hadn't been able to brush her teeth in far too long, she could finally relax in his arms enough to learn all that had happened in the time she'd been comatose.

She learned that the chanu zayul in her body had been killed when her head hit the stone wall of the shaft. She was deeply saddened by this, as they'd saved her life once, though this time, their death had nearly taken it. She was grateful that she still understood the yan-kanat language. Jotahan had been right that the knowledge of it would remain in her mind after they left her body. She wondered if the yan-kanat understood how powerful such a connection to a hivemind like the urvak zayul could be, given their ability to share such knowledge. Humans would see the incredible possibilities of such information-sharing—and some would immediately think of ways to exploit them. For that alone, she understood why the urvak zayul wanted to keep humans out of the urvaka.

"You were having hallucinations from their toxins," Jotahan told her as he held her close. Though they had both relaxed in each other's arms, neither of them was ready to let go.

"I saw Seta Zul," she said. "I don't think it was a hallucination."

He stilled, then pulled away from her enough to look down at her face. "You think you saw the goddess?"

"I *know* I saw her." She reached up to stroke his prominent cheekbone, her eyes scanning his beloved face. She'd never thought she'd see it again, and she wanted to memorize every line of his features. "She told me I had to choose."

Jotahan was silent as she explained her conversation with Seta Zul—and confessed to the heartbreaking choice she'd been forced to make.

"You don't believe me, do you?" she asked when he continued to remain silent after she finished.

His expression was sympathetic as he lowered his forehead to bump gently against hers. "I could never have made such a choice, my drahi. You have more courage than I do."

"I thought you would be angry that I decided not to heal you. Or maybe hurt that I could let you go."

He huffed. "You made the choice you believed would make me better off. I know you made that decision out of love for me." He lifted his head again, his eyes intent. "You know that I want nestlings, but never more than I want you. I would give up any hope of offspring if it meant I could remain at your side forever."

She turned her head to blink away her tears, swiping impatiently at her eyes. "I'm so sorry you had to, Jotahan."

This caused him to stiffen again. "Sarah," he caught her by the chin, forcing her to meet his eyes again. "I still have the seal. The healers were able to heal my wound, with help from my own chanu zayul. Seta Zul's mark remains."

She hugged him, surprised that she could feel more happiness than she already did. "That is wonderful news!"

"So you will still accept the seal from me, even after all that this world has put you through?"

She chuckled, hugging his strong waist even tighter. "Are you kidding? You think I'm letting you get away from me *now*?" She snuggled against him. "Never again, Jotahan. If you leave me, I will follow you, even if I have to face the Inferno to get you back."

He gave her another kiss that began as a tender exploration and quickly turned into a scorching message telling her that the desire that burned between them still remained strong. Strong enough that he had to pull away before it hurt him.

As they both struggled to recover, she sought to distract them, and hoped to find an answer to a question that remained. Or perhaps just reassurance. "Do you really think my conversation with Seta Zul was only a toxin-fueled hallucination?"

Jotahan sighed, rubbing his hand over his head spines. "The yan-kanat know that our gods aren't dead. But the thought that Seta Zul might be speaking to her people again after remaining silent for so long concerns me. It would mean she is no longer dormant. If she has awakened, then something momentous lies in our future, and she must be moving her pawns into place on the game field to prepare for it."

Sarah laid her head against his shoulder. "I don't like the idea of being the pawn of *any* god."

He stroked his hand over her hair, running his claws gently through the tangles to straighten them out. "I love your hoo-man defiance. Your people always stand so boldly in the path of undefeatable forces. A yan-kanat looks at the impossible and accepts that it is so. A hoo-man looks at the impossible, and says 'all I need is time, and I will make it happen.' Such relentless determination is both fearsome—and admirable."

She lifted her head to smile at him. "You finally called us 'humans.' I never thought you'd use that word instead of nixir."

"I think it is time to change the way we view your people. Some of the yan-kanat underestimate hugh-mans," his attempt to correct his pronunciation gave further weight to his words, "and some rightly fear your people, but we have been wrong not to try to learn from you in all this time. With all that your species has already accomplished, and the relentlessness that you hugh-mans possess, you might finally achieve the ability to stride the cosmos with the titans. You're already reaching for the stars."

She snorted, shaking her head. "Trying to walk the path of gods is not always wise. You think the titans will welcome us beside them?"

Jotahan shook his head, his expression thoughtful. "I highly doubt it, but I don't think that will be enough to stop your people from trying."

She sighed heavily, leaning her head against his chest. "That's what scares me."

44

The time had finally come for their sata-drahi'at. Jotahan had experienced so much anxiety and frustration waiting for this moment that he had been afraid it would never arrive. They'd had to delay it another twelve cycles to make certain that both he and Sarah were strong enough after their ordeal to endure the ceremony. In that time, both had stayed within the temple while they recovered. This limited the activities he wanted to do with her, since they never seemed to be fully alone.

One positive of the delay was that the priest Zan Cyall was now recovered enough to lead the ceremony. Once the healers discovered he'd been poisoned, they'd searched Farona's home and identified the vial of poison, allowing them to successfully treat him.

Zan Cyall's death would have been yet another tragedy added to an already devastating one. Jotahan still struggled with his guilt and grief. He didn't grieve over Farona. Not anymore. Now that he understood what kind of person she was, what kind of person she had always been, he realized that he had loved a lie. He mourned the person who never was. The one he'd believed was his best friend.

His guilt came from the fact that he had never seen through her. He'd known that she was controlling, and always had been, but she'd been very subtle in her efforts when it came to him. On some level, he'd sensed that he and all her other companions were being manipulated by her, yet she'd done such a good job of it that he'd become complacent, focusing more on his duty than his private life. He'd allowed her to make decisions for him when he was too busy being Jotaha. After all, she'd known him best, and he couldn't be bothered with the small details in the skilev when he was serving as guardian in the urvaka.

That was not an easy thing to accept about himself and his judgement. He felt like a complete fool and was angry at himself for missing the signs when he'd been trained to sense danger. Support circles had formed in the wake of the tragedy, and he and Sarah attended meetings with Farona's former circle of friends. Yan-kanat he'd known all his life confessed their own guilt and anger and pain at Farona's lies, and also about their many passings of being used and manipulated by her. That was when he'd come to understand how deep her poison had sunk into the skilev of Draku Rin.

Sarah was there for him and her new circle of friends, always ready to offer wisdom and advice for the reeling yan-kanat, despite the trauma that she herself had endured at Farona's hands. It still bothered him that Sarah had grown up in a world where such betrayals and venomous people were commonplace, but only because he had not been there to protect her from those who had hurt her in her past.

He wouldn't allow those negative thoughts to encroach upon them on this cycle. They would finally be joined, after undergoing a trial that proved that darkness and evil would never separate them. Their love had been tested, and an even stronger bond had been forged in the flames of the Inferno. The passing of his seal to Sarah was a mere formality at this point.

A necessary one so that he could finally mate with his drahi.

They entered the chapel at the same time, coming from opposite sides of the room to step up to the dais. His drahi looked so beautiful that the sight of her stole his breath. She wore a sitak of orange silk in a sleek and simple design that brought to mind the flames of the Inferno. Her dark hair flowed over her shoulders and down her back in thick, shiny waves that he yearned to run his claws through. One side of her hair was pulled up and away from her face, a twist of her locks secured to the side of her head by the jeweled golden comb he'd given her.

Her eyes seemed to gleam in the candlelight as they came together in front of the mating mattress that had been made for them that now softened the dais beneath Seta Zul's statue. It would be taken to their home along with them for their seclusion, the herbs that filled it along with the stuffing adding a pleasant scent and hopefully increasing fertility.

They each held their offerings for the goddess, and after Jotahan poured his oil into the offering bowl, Sarah settled her flowers atop the liquid. As they knelt before the goddess and said their vows to Seta Zul and each other, the flowers sank into the oil until the two offerings were blended into a single harmoniously fragrant perfume.

The sharing of the mating pellet followed, and Jotahan lifted it from the plate beside the offering bowl and held it out for Sarah to take a bite. She pulled a face that made him want to huff with amusement, but dutifully chewed and swallowed. Then she took the pellet from his hand and held it up to his mouth. After he took his bite, he understood her disgust. The grainy, hard-packed pellet had a strong and somewhat unpleasant herbal flavor, but the ceremonial food was intended to increase their desire and enhance fertility during their seclusion.

That ritual finished, the time arrived as he rose to his feet again and turned to take his drahi's hand, drawing her up with him. He felt the fine trembling of her fingers, the dampness of her skin, despite it being cooler than normal for her. She was nervous, perhaps even frightened of what was coming. She'd been offered a potion to dull the pain, but she'd declined, saying she wanted to experience the full extent of the following pleasure.

He was worried that her pain would be greater than that of a female yan-kanat since she had no scales to guard her delicate flesh, but she'd insisted on no potion, determined to go through this last trial with him without aid.

He gently squeezed her hand in reassurance, and she shot him a grateful smile.

By the Ajda, he loved this female like crazy. He would do anything for her. If he could take all the pain of their sealing upon himself, he would.

They stepped onto the mattress, the soft scent of fertility herbs wafting from the fine woven fabric casing. Standing in the center of the mattress, they faced each other. He looked down at his beautiful mate, seeing the pale moon of her face looking back up at him, her head tilted back, the candlelight gleaming on the harzek he'd given her, sparkling in the faceted gemstones that nowhere near outshone her dark eyes.

The watching priests and acolytes were silent save for Zan Cyall, whose mellow voice guided them through the steps of the ceremony. He told them to remove each other's garments, and Jotahan felt his first moment of hesitation. Not because he didn't want to claim this female in front of the goddess and every servant of hers who watched, but because they were all males, and he didn't want to reveal the beauty of his mate's body to them.

But Sarah was already nervously tugging at the tie that bound his robe closed at his waist, her hands shaking. He dared not delay the ceremony because of his own possessiveness. No servant of Seta Zul would dare to covet another male's drahi.

With a few brief tugs on the straps of her sitak, it slipped from her shoulders, just as his robe fell from his. Their garments drifted to the mattress to pool around their feet, but he barely noticed the sensation of the silken fabric against his scales. His gaze roved over Sarah's body, taking in the alienness of her form, marveling at his own ignorance when he'd first met her and had not realized then how beautiful she was. Like Theia herself, Sarah stood before him in all her glory, her soft, warm skin finely dusted with very pale hairs. The coarser, curly hairs on her pelvis had all been removed for the ceremony, to decrease the possibility of them lighting on fire and causing even more pain for either of them.

He hoped she would be able to regrow them, as he enjoyed their unusual texture and the way they clung to her heady scent. Though they were not as silky as the hairs on her head, he loved to stroke his claws through them. Especially given how she reacted whenever he touched her there.

They were told to embrace, and a low chanting rose from the acolytes as Jotahan took Sarah in his arms. Because she was so much smaller than him, he had to lift her off her feet and hold her firmly against his body to align their pelvises.

The moment had come for the passing of the seal, and the volume of the chanting rose as he lowered his head to claim Sarah's mouth in a passionate kiss. This time, he would not have to stop. This time, he would be able to enter her heat and finally claim all of her.

He felt the temperature rising on his pelvis, going from bearable to scorching in mere grainfalls as his salavik eagerly shifted against his slit, seeking his drahi's vessel as it had since the moment his seal had first activated.

Sarah tore her mouth away from his, screaming in pain as her skin was burned. He held her as she struggled, stroking his hands over her back, feeling the tension in all her muscles as her screams turned to agonized sobs.

The pain was excruciating, but his focus was entirely on his mate's suffering. He wanted nothing more than to alleviate it, but he knew it was too late at this point as he smelled her flesh and his own scales burning between them.

The intense branding was mercifully brief, though the pain would linger until their pleasure swamped it.

His salavik was finally free to evert, and he shifted his hips so that it could find her opening, which was between her legs, instead of on the front of her pelvis like a yan-kanat female.

She was still whimpering as he moved into position, using his thighs to push her legs farther apart to expose her wet heat to his aching salavik. She no longer fought him, but he hated seeing her eyes shimmering with tears of pain.

Her hands clutched his shoulders as he entered her, and they both groaned as his length pushed inside her. Her inner muscles clenched tightly at first, despite the lubrication dripping from his salavik, but then the enhanced pleasure that the ceremony heightened began to fill them both, and her body no longer resisted his claiming.

He barely heard the chanting of the priests and acolytes as he filled her completely, until her legs were wrapped around his waist as she rode him with wanton abandon. Her head was thrown back, her neck exposed in complete surrender as he pumped into her heat, shocked by how different and incredible it felt to be inside her like this. Her vessel was so much hotter than her skin, and it felt as if he'd wrapped his mating spine with a warming stone—only, she was soft and supple inside, her muscles clenching and convulsing around him.

He moaned as she climaxed around his salavik, bending forward to nip at her delicate neck. She shivered in his hold, pressing her body forward so he could bite down on her neck where it met her shoulder. He was careful not to pierce any veins, but he could not resist breaking her skin, further marking her as his to show all yan-kanat males that she had already been claimed in the old way, as well as marked for him by Seta Zul.

This time, she appeared to feel no pain as he drew blood, because the euphoria was too strong for both of them. His climax came quickly after hers, and hers seemed to go on and on as his seed filled her vessel. He sank down onto the mattress, still holding her, her legs still wrapped around his waist. His thrashing tail brushed against her tantalizing calves with each flick.

Unconsciousness was coming for both of them as wave upon wave of pleasure swept through them, overloading their senses.

He welcomed the coming darkness, because he knew she would be in his arms when he awoke again.

45

Sarah awoke in Jotahan's arms. She snuggled closer against his huge body, noting that he was still sleeping soundly—or passed out. She recalled the incredible, euphoric sensations of what seemed to be an unending orgasm driving her into unconsciousness, so she wasn't surprised to see that Jotahan had also succumbed.

She sat up slowly, wincing at the ache in her inner muscles. It was an effort to push Jotahan's heavy arm off her so she could move freely. She immediately missed its comforting weight, but she was already feeling restless, unable to lay there quietly. Zan Cyall had told her that the aphrodisiac qualities of the mating pellet would not fade for some time, nor would her restlessness when she and Jotahan weren't mating.

She tried to distract herself from the big, enticingly nude body of her sleeping mate by examining their surroundings. As they'd requested, they'd been brought back to the house that Jotahan had originally intended for Farona. It had been drastically changed since Sarah's first visit, both outside and in. The exterior hide walls and scaled roof had been painted in dark greens and browns to blend with the grove of trees beyond. All of Farona's favorite things had been removed, including the plants she'd favored that were taken from their garden and donated to others who would appreciate them and not see them as a painful reminder. Sarah still had plans to plant her own garden but was in no hurry.

It was the inside of the house that had changed the most though. Large skylights had been carved into the scales of the ceiling and capped with crystals that spread their prismatic light across the tiled floor. They'd had wide windows cut from the hide walls to let in more of daylight and fresh ocean air. Most of their main living space and one entire wall in their mating room was formed of windows that could be shuttered if they didn't want the outside coming in, but Sarah loved having those windows opened, and she and Jotahan both loved all the light that now filled their home.

She also loved the bright paint that she'd chosen for all the walls, and the new furnishings she'd had made that more closely resembled a modern human style. The craftsman who'd constructed that furniture had been very interested in her descriptions of human contemporary styles, and had created some beautiful designs from them, even offering to pay her for the privilege of using them to make furniture for others. Jotahan had made her decline the offer, so the craftsman had paid in a roundabout way by gifting them some of the furniture instead.

Jotahan had indulged her every request to make this home hers, and she appreciated the gesture as they both worked to wipe away all of Farona's influence. Sarah loved this home now, because she and Jotahan had built it together for their future.

She looked down at her naked body, blushing a little at the realization that she'd been moved, along with Jotahan, through the skilev wearing nothing but the silken sitak to cover her nudity. She'd seen mating processionals before from a distance as the mattresses were carried through the town in a parade of family, friends, and servants from the temple, including the strong temple porters who bore the weight of the new couple upon their mattress.

Despite the fact that there had undoubtedly been a nice parade for her mating to Jotahan, since all of her "circle"—as her group of female friends were called—as well as many new friends she'd made since the tragedy, had promised to join the procession in celebration, she was grateful she'd been completely unconscious for the experience. The celebrants would have gone on to feast in their honor with many wishes for a fruitful seclusion.

She understood now how important nestlings and fertility were to the yan-kanat. Their population was declining rapidly, despite Seta Zul's efforts to increase their fertility. Theia was not the world they had evolved to live on, and for some reason, it seemed that it did not foster the same level of fertility they had once enjoyed before humans chased them from Gaia—though they had never reproduced at the rate humans did. This made every true mating a celebration for all yan-kanat—even a mating with a human.

Perhaps *especially* a mating with a human, since many of her new friends expressed hope that adding a human bloodline would increase fecundity among the yan-kanat, as it appeared to have done for other crossbreed matings with humans in the past.

She traced the brand on her stomach, flinching at the memory of the agonizing pain her searing flesh had caused her. The scar was still pink, but had been treated in a way that somehow sped up the healing process. She never would have believed she'd agree to such a thing before she fell in love with Jotahan, but now, seeing the matching brand on his pelvis, she felt a possessive satisfaction. He was all hers now, and she never had to fear that he would change his mind and have the seal removed, or ever want to leave her side. Knowing that he would never be tempted to be unfaithful to her—not that she thought his sense of honor would allow it—made the sacrifice of some of her skin worth it. She felt completely secure in loving someone, for the first time she could ever remember.

Her fingers switched from tracing her own brand to stroking the lines of his scarred scales. He stirred in his sleep but didn't awaken as she explored his body until she felt the movement of his erection beneath his slit. Aroused by the inhuman sight of this part of him, she traced along the slit, feeling it part as his tail flicked against her legs.

He moaned, his body tensing, letting her know she'd succeeded in awakening him. She smiled, dropping a kiss on his muscular abdomen that had him lifting his head to watch her, propping himself up on his elbows.

He hissed softly when she kissed him lower, closer to the opening slit. His whole body shuddered when she licked the ridge of his salavik that had begun to press through his scales.

"Sarah," he said in a harsh voice, his claws delving into her hair. "What—" The strangled sound of his voice cutting off rewarded another long stroke of her tongue along his exposed length.

It fully everted from his slit, bobbing in front of her face. She licked her lips as she got her first good look at his "mating spine."

It wasn't human. There was no mistaking the alien appearance of it, despite the distinctly phallic shape. Muscle bulged on each side of his organ, giving it a thick, girthy size that was rivaled by an impressive length. The rounded tip lacked the mushroom head of a human penis, and was tipped with a single slit that wept a slick, clear precum intended to ease entry into a yan-kanat female, who did not produce the same lubricant a human female did.

He seemed to be holding his breath as she studied him, but released it on a low moan when she trailed her tongue along the head of his salavik, licking away the salty drops of precum. Then she closed her lips around the tip and sucked, sliding her mouth down his length as her hand curled around the base of his salavik, right up against his parted slit.

He made guttural sounds that weren't words, bucking his hips upwards reflexively as she drew her lips along his length. The muscles of his salavik shifted, tensing as much as the rest of his body, tightening until she could feel them in her mouth vibrating like stretched rubber bands. Very large, thick rubber bands.

She loved having this power over him, and it was turning her on something fierce to see him so undone by her pleasuring him in this way. Not that she needed much help. She dripped with her desire for him.

She brought him to the brink of his climax, leaving him gasping, begging for her to let him enter her before he spilled his seed. She sat up, drawing her finger teasingly along her slick lips before slowly licking them. He shivered and closed his eyes. Then he pushed himself up onto his palms. She sensed he was preparing to grab her and pin her beneath him.

She quickly crawled onto his lap before he made his move, impaling herself on him.

He wasn't pleased with her more dominant position at first. His hands gripped her upper arms as though to pull her off him and roll her beneath him, but after a few slow pumps of her hips had him shuddering, he allowed her to continue riding him, though he growled in irritation. That growl got deeper and harsher as he orgasmed.

He pulled her hips down hard on his length as he came, then rolled her onto her back in one swift move while his salavik was still twitching inside her with each spurt of his seed.

"You will dishonor me and have me begging to submit to you, human," he growled in her ear as his salavik pumped into her. She knew he didn't grow flaccid like a human male and could keep pleasuring her until she begged him to stop, even after coming.

She smiled up at him as he pinned her against their mattress with his hard body. "I still have so much to show you, Jotahan. I promise you, you will love every minute of being conquered by this human."

He huffed and then lowered his head to nip at her neck, where he had bitten her during their ceremony. She recalled feeling nothing but pleasure when he did it, even though her blood had trickled down over her collarbone from his sharp teeth.

He didn't go that far this time, his teeth barely grazing the scarred skin that must have been treated, like the brand on her pelvis, to heal it so rapidly. Yet, his message was unmistakable. Jotahan refused to be conquered, but he could be loved, and she intended to spend the rest of her life doing just that.

THEY ONLY STOPPED MATING to rest and eat during their seclusion, and since they were supposed to spend the entire time naked and easily accessible to their mate's seductions, they didn't spend much time outside. Still, she did wear his robe a couple of times to walk outside onto the terrace with him, reasoning that she remained nude underneath it, so it should still count.

Jotahan had no problem being outside without a stitch of clothing on, claiming he was very proud of his new brand and had no desire to cover it until he had to.

If their neighbors or the fishermen far out in the harbor spotted them, there were no scandalized cries from them. Not even when they didn't exactly make it back inside before their passion overtook them, and Jotahan ended up pinning her against the railing to make love to her.

Friends and family and temple servants dropped off regular deliveries of food and supplies that were left on their doorstep, including many gifts in celebration of their sealing.

She couldn't argue with spending fifteen uninterrupted days with her new mate doing nothing but eating, sleeping, and making love in every possible way as she taught Jotahan exactly why humans probably had so many babies. She wondered if humans ever had a honeymoon this incredible, but doubted it. Life usually intruded before their time was up. Here in this world, the yan-kanat didn't allow it to.

As she lay in Jotahan's arms on their last night of seclusion, breathless from a spirited and passionate lovemaking, she felt thoughtful. Jotahan would have to return to his new profession as a combat trainer at the training grounds soon, and Sarah would eventually return to helping the lore-keeper at the temple, but they would still have their evenings together. Jotahan promised her those evenings would always end like this, together in each other's arms.

She prayed to the Ajda that her daughter would find a love like this someday. Prayed that there was a human out there who could make her feel cared for and valued and cherished as no one else could. She knew that she would never meet the child she had given away, but she would also never forget her and never stop wanting the best for her.

She also prayed that she had nestlings with Jotahan. Not just because it would make him blissfully happy to be a dad, but because she wanted a chance to prove that she could be a good mom. She knew she would love any children she had as much as she did the first, only this time, she finally had a home and a mate to help her give them the best life possible.

She also prayed that Beth had made it out of the mines safely, finally coming to an acceptance and understanding for

Beth running away and leaving her behind. There was nothing her friend could have done to help Sarah anyway. She had been smart to run. Expecting her to stage some sort of heroic battle to help Sarah fight the creature had been unreasonable and unfair. Even expecting her to drag Sarah out with her hadn't been reasonable, since Sarah had frozen in shock. Fear had affected them both in ways they could never have predicted before experiencing such a nightmare. As for Beth using the past to guilt Sarah into doing things for her, she had to admit she remained somewhat bitter, but she believed that—unlike Farona—Beth had genuinely cared about her and had simply allowed her own neediness and insecurity to affect her behavior towards Sarah.

Sarah knew the difference now, and because of that, she could forgive Beth and wish for the best for her, letting go of that last link to a life she wanted to leave behind. Though she could not bring herself to pray for her parents yet, that wound was healing, and perhaps someday she could find it in her to wish them well too.

46

Jotahan felt like he was floating through the temple at the side of his drahi. The news from the healers was promising. So incredibly promising. Already, Sarah's belly had hardened and her womb was enlarged, and the healers believed she was gravid with his nestling. If that was true, then she had undoubtedly conceived during their seclusion, though they had certainly continued to mate after they completed it.

She was more cautious in her optimism, telling him it might be too soon to get his hopes up, though the bleeding cycle that human females had to endure had not happened this last time, prompting Sarah to request a visit to the healers in the first place.

They had both studied what records they could find about cross-breedings between yan-kanat and human, and they were frustrated at how poor that recordkeeping was. What they did find assured them that the pregnancy almost always favored the development cycle of the mother, meaning their nestling would arrive sooner than if she were a yan-kanat female, who remained gravid for an entire passing before giving birth.

The healers were equally excited, and promised they would spend many sandfalls scrying with other skilevs to share information and prepare for the nestling. For the first time in his long life, Jotahan wished he could travel to a larger skilev, like Bal Goro, to meet other human/yan-kanat couples and discuss their experiences.

The yan-kanat did not "vacation" in other skilevs like humans did in their cultures. If one traveled to another skilev, it was generally for permanent relocation, because they were exiled or compelled for some reason to leave their own birth territory. The intensely territorial nature of the yan-kanat did not drive them to war among themselves the way humans did, but it did mean they didn't physically visit other skilevs often, unless they had good reason to collaborate in person.

He and Sarah stopped to make an offering to Seta Zul, and he could see his own hope reflected in his mate's eyes. They were both eager to start their family, though this time he had with her, when it was just the two of them together, had been the best in his life.

News spread quickly of their possible successful mating, which made Sarah blush as friend and stranger alike congratulated them during their journey through the temple. She shook her head, muttering something about a "Hipp-ah," and how she needed to help the healers invent that. She already claimed she had plans for a "strah" and an "eye vee."

Sarah had expanded her role in the temple, and he'd accepted that she needed this occupation for her well-being. Because she appeared to be volunteering her time, like it was a hobby, it didn't bring shame upon him. It was also good for her standing in the skilev, as she became a teacher of human history and technology, sharing information about her people freely and earning the respect of the yan-kanat for her willingness to do so. She possessed surprising wisdom that came from a lifetime lived among a culture so different from their own that some could not even comprehend it. Sarah was helping to bridge the understanding gap, and also helping to improve the recordkeeping in the temple.

She confessed to feeling guilt for sharing the knowledge about what she called the "gunslinger's revolver," but Jotahan reassured her that Farona would have managed to figure it out on her own, if necessary, or she would have simply used another weapon to commit her foul deeds.

They finally made their way outside, enjoying the shade under a buttress of the temple as they walked towards the sky lift. Jotahan felt Sarah freeze and turned to look in the direction she was staring, her mouth agape with shock.

He stiffened when he saw who her gaze had fixed upon.

"Kevos," he snarled, displeased to see his mate staring so fixedly at the other male, even if he was wearing human camouflage.

"What?" Sarah glanced back at him, her confusion clear in her eyes.

He recalled that she couldn't scent Kevos like he could, and probably believed she was looking at a human. In that respect, it was little wonder she appeared so stunned to spot him leaving the right horn tower.

Kevos strode up to them, his expression dour, even as he nodded in greeting to Jotahan. He knew better than to address Sarah directly until Jotahan acknowledged him back.

It was odd not to see the visual cues to Kevos' mood that were so familiar to him. Without his head spines and tail being visible, Jotahan had to rely mostly on his familiar scowl and snarl of irritation.

"I hate this skin," Kevos growled, explaining his irritable mood.

"I take it the training is going well," Jotahan said with a smirk.

Sarah held up a hand and both of them turned to glance at

her. "Hold up a second! *Kevos*?"

She studied him in a way that made Jotahan grind his teeth, his head spines standing on end.

Kevos slowly backed away a few steps, focusing his gaze on Jotahan. "I'm growing accustomed to the chanu zayul inside my mind, and they are eager to enter the human world and see for themselves what they have only experienced through Sarah's memories, but this," he touched his cheek with one hand, his fingers appearing to dent the soft flesh of his face, "I *despise*."

"Helloooo? Confused human here!" Sarah stood with her hands on her hips, tapping one foot and sharing her glare between them.

He realized that he had yet to introduce her to Elder Arokiv. He was surprised the elder hadn't sought a meeting with her as soon as he'd returned to the skilev, but he was very busy and probably hadn't had a chance to request a visit.

"Kevos is training to hunt in the human world. Elder Arokiv was able to successfully shut down the program that produced the twisted nixirs, but some of the people responsible for that program escaped the raid on the facility and went into hiding, taking a batch of the creatures with them. Those escapees are aware that certain levels of your government have been successfully infiltrated by the yan-kanat. They still want to war on our kind with their creations, and they don't intend to let our infiltrators put a stop to their plans."

"I have to learn how to *act* hu-man," Kevos said in a dour tone. "I curse the cycle I was declared a master sentil. It caught Elder Arokiv's attention."

"Wait," she pointed at Kevos, "don't tell me you're going to Earth looking like that."

Kevos glanced at her, noted Jotahan's low growl, then took another step away from her. "What is wrong with this disguise?"

Sarah tapped her bottom lip with one finger, eyeing Kevos

up and down, which made Jotahan want to drag him into the arena to beat him into the dust. "Let's see... a seven-foot tall man-mountain with the body of Mr. Olympia and a face that could have come off the cover of a romance novel? I can't imagine *why* that would attract attention from humans. Nope. Not at all."

"Then what is the problem?" Kevos asked, clearly unfamiliar with human sarcasm. He still had much to learn before entering the human world.

Still, Jotahan was more focused on Sarah's words. "You find Kevos attractive in his disguise," he said, his spines bristling as his tail lashed back and forth.

Sarah patted his chest, smoothing her hand down his shirt as she gave him a long, promising look. "Settle down, my caveman. I only have eyes for you, but I guarantee there will be plenty of people who *will* find Kevos attractive. He's going to have a hard enough time blending in at that size anyway, but if he wants to avoid getting swarmed by admirers everywhere he goes, he needs to look a little less...," she waved in the sentil's direction, clearly searching for a descriptive word that wouldn't raise Jotahan's spines higher, "like this."

She tapped her bottom lip again, but she didn't turn her gaze back to Kevos, showing Jotahan she was being considerate of his jealousy. "He needs to have less hair. A bald spot in the middle of his head. Maybe a nose that looks like it's been broken a time or two. Some crooked teeth. A spare tire. I'm sure we can come up with something less appealing than his current appearance."

"There won't be a 'we' for that task." Jotahan stepped between Sarah and Kevos so he completely blocked her view of the other male.

To his credit, Kevos was not smirking at Jotahan's obvious irritation. Instead he was frowning thoughtfully, his expression strange on a human face.

"Your drahi might have a point." Kevos ran his clawless hand over his thick shock of hair. "The last thing I want is to draw human attention, especially while I am hunting."

"I'm sorry but you're still gonna to draw attention, dude," Sarah said to Kevos, though she hugged Jotahan from the back, wrapping her arms around his waist so her affection for her mate was unmistakable to the sentil. "You're seven freaking feet tall and built like a terminator. That's pretty damned rare in the human world. Even some extra fat in the face and body will only increase your startling size. Still, changing your appearance to look less appealing and more intimidating would help keep people away from you, instead of falling all over themselves to talk to you."

"What is a 'dood'?" Jotahan growled, hoping it wasn't some human term of endearment.

Kevos huffed. "Human slang, according to the chanu zayul." Before Jotahan could demand a further explanation from either of them, Kevos spoke again. "I will discuss your drahi's suggestions with Elder Arokiv, and get his input." He nodded his head at Jotahan. "You have my congratulations, Jotahan, on the news of your nestling. I wish you and your drahi the best, since I doubt I will be here to see its arrival."

Jotahan clapped a hand on Kevos' shoulder. "Stay safe, Sentil Kevos." He glanced down at Kevos' groin area, concealed by an odd human garment Elder Arokiv must have brought for him that reminded him of Sarah's clothing when she'd first arrived in the urvaka. "Your seal... it clearly hasn't activated yet, or you would not be leaving without a satadrahi'at."

"No, thank the Ajda. It was a mistake to get it, and at least this is one bright spot in Elder Arokiv's plan to drag me out among the humans. I won't have to worry about bumping into my drahi."

"Um...," Sarah said from behind Jotahan.

He reached behind him to cover Sarah's mouth, cutting off any more words from her.

"Good luck to you, Kevos."

"And you, Jotahan."

They both nodded farewell, then Kevos spun on his heel and returned to the horn tower, no doubt to speak to the elder about Sarah's words.

Jotahan turned around to see Sarah glaring up at him, tapping her foot again. "You *do* realize his 'drahi' is probably human, right? Why else wouldn't his seal activate, even though he's gone all around the skilev sniffing at every single female?"

Jotahan crossed his arms over his chest. "How do *you* know this?"

Sarah chuckled. "Hey, my circle talks, and there are plenty of single females in it who were disappointed his seal didn't spark up at their scent." Her eyes widened as she noted his smirk. "Jotahan! You didn't warn him on *purpose!*"

"He might have refused to travel to Gaia if I put that concern in his mind."

She shook her head, a smile playing around her lips. "You are diabolical, my love."

"So is Seta Zul, at times," Jotahan said with a huff. "It will be good to see Kevos finally mated. Many males will breathe easier when he is sealed to one female."

"You *do* know he isn't a fan of humans, right?"

He ran his claws through her hair, dislodging the golden comb she always wore that was worth a fortune in kivan, without a single care for where it fell as he leaned down to kiss her, cutting off her protest for his treatment of the harzek.

When he lifted his head again, his drahi's eyes were glazed and a broad human smile spread her lips. "I did not like humans either, until I met the other half of my soul and discovered she *was* one. It changed me. In the best possible way. Made me happier than I have ever been. I have no regrets."

EPILOGUE

Ranaxe stood within the skull center of Draku Rin, that sacred place where the mighty Ajda's mind had once dwelled. She sought his wisdom. As one of the first of the female elders to ever serve the people of this skilev, she often found herself in this place, praying to a god that was long gone. She still found some comfort in the silence of the shrine, and the peace of it gave her time to think. Perhaps that in itself was the wisdom of Draku Rin—to give her space to find her own center and listen to her own thoughts.

Those thoughts were in turmoil on this cycle, as were all the citizens in every skilev crossing Theia. What was being asked of them might be too much for the yan-kanat to accept.

But Ranaxe could not help but try to convince her people that this must be allowed.

Seta Zul herself had left her mountain, roaring into the sky as her shadow swept over all the skilevs. She had let the people know that a storm was coming. One that could not be stopped by ignoring it.

Uncoupling their world from Gaia was unavoidable, and some of the elders had always known this decision would need to be made at some point. Humanity was doomed, and Gaia would soon fall to a new enemy that could only be stopped by the urvaka for so long before its forces found a way to counteract the machine-killing magic of the cave labyrinth.

They could not risk losing this world as they had lost Gaia. There was nowhere left for the yan-kanat to go, even as some of the humans managed to flee to the stars.

Many mourned the uncoupling, as the relationship between the yan-kanat and those humans who knew of her people had become better in the many passings since her grandmother had first arrived in Draku Rin, bringing with her extensive knowledge of the human world and a better understanding of their people—and adding six nestlings to carry on their family legacy.

All of Sarah's offspring had been very fertile, as had the offspring of the other human drahis that were to follow Sarah's arrival. This had given the yan-kanat hope that the decline of their species had finally come to an end, and more of them went to Seta Zul's chapel to request a human drahi when they were granted a seal.

Those of mixed bloodlines were suddenly elevated, and greatly desired. But it was the precedent that Ranaxe's grandmother herself had set that made it possible for her granddaughter to rise to the level of elder, even as a female—even as a mated drahi. The tradition still held that she was not directly paid for her service to the skilev, so that her mate would not feel shame at his drahi being forced to provide kivan for their family. Still, it was progress that no one in Draku Rin had expected, according to her grandmother.

To this day, she still loved to visit her grandparents and hear her grandmother's many tales about Gaia. She had hoped one day to be chosen to infiltrate the human world when Elder Hon'ra retired his post. Now, that dream would die.

The only real question left to ponder—the question that

caused so much conflict in the yan-kanat—was whether to allow the masses of humans still fighting to survive on Gaia to make their way to Theia before the worlds were uncoupled.

That was an answer they needed to come to soon, because many of those humans were males. If all of the resistance fighters still holding out against their inevitable doom had been female, there would be little debate, as the yan-kanat were eager to welcome more fertile females among them, but human males tended to be territorial, just like yan-kanat males. Fighting over females had already been a problem in those skilevs that had allowed small enclaves of humans to resettle in the past.

The humans would not want to lose their bloodlines entirely, especially since couplings with yan-kanat always favored their species over the human one. There would be males resistant to seeing their females claimed by a yan-kanat instead of remaining in an enclave to bear fully human offspring. There would be many conflicts with the warmongering species, and those conflicts would be brought to this world along with the humans.

Worse, the hubris of the humans could bring about another disaster like the one they had unleashed on their own world.

Yet Ranaxe wanted to save what humans the yan-kanat could save. She'd heard her grandmother spending many cycles passionately appealing to the elders in every skilev to allow those last humans to flee to Theia before their worlds were uncoupled. She'd heard the pleas of the other human drahis, and had even heard from a handful of the human males allowed to live in enclaves as they too cried out for their people to be saved.

Before leaving the skull center, she sent one more prayer to Draku Rin, begging him to give her the right words to say to finally convince the elders on this cycle, when the decision must be made.

As she lifted her head and opened her eyes, she swore she heard the faintest whisper, though it wasn't Seta Zul's voice. It was male, and deep, but so quiet she could barely hear it.

Still, she smiled as she turned to leave the skull center, saying one last thank you to the god who had reached out to answer her prayer, from some distance so vast that even the Ajda could barely make himself heard.

She knew the right words to say now. The ones that would convince the elders to do what was right, and save the last of humanity.

AUTHOR'S NOTE

I want to thank all of you who read this book, and I really hope you enjoyed it! If you did, please take a moment to leave a review as it is the best way to spread the word about my books to those who have never heard of me before and aren't sure if they want to take a chance on my stories. I know that time is the most valuable commodity we have, and I appreciate you spending yours to take a journey to one of my worlds! Your continued support and encouragement truly means the world to me!

At this time last year, I feared that I would never write again. I had hit a severe episode of writer's block that had nothing to do with a lack of ideas, but rather with a fear of sharing them. Every book I started to write with the intent of eventually publishing it caused me to falter. Sometimes at the beginning, sometimes as far in as halfway through. The fear causing this creative paralysis kept boxing me in, causing me to second-guess myself and even try to change the story I originally envisioned so it would suit a wider audience and avoid upsetting or disappointing anyone. The problem was that I couldn't write under those conditions. I couldn't complete a book that was bound by conventions, or expectations, or demands that were set by someone else.

I was ready to throw my hands up in the air and just give up writing altogether, because I felt like I had used up all my energy on putting out my last book by pushing past all my fears and insecurities to uphold my original vision. Each time I had to do that, I wore myself out. There is enormous pressure to conform and self-censor to please the widest possible audience, and fighting against that pressure in order to fulfill your own expectations and create the work that you initially dreamed of creating can be exhausting. I just wasn't sure I had it in me anymore to do that.

In fact, at the beginning of this year, when I finally sat down at the keyboard for the first time in many months and told myself that I was going to write again, I also told myself that I wasn't going to publish again. I wanted to write something that was unbound by anyone's expectations or constraints other than my own, and I wanted to do that without the added stress of worrying how it would eventually be received by an audience.

It turns out that when left to my own devices, allowing myself to be as crazy as I wanted to because I didn't have to worry about what anyone else thought, I ended up writing exactly the kind of book I normally write, only this time, without all the stress and worry that usually accompanied that experience. Oh sure, I'm working on some experimental stuff that will likely never see the light of day, but "Guardian of the Dark Paths" was the story that grabbed hold of me the hardest and demanded I finish it, and I was the most swept up in its world and characters, so it is the first one to be finished in all this time.

It was only after I finished it and realized that it would fit well into my list of published novels, and that I really *did* want to share this world and characters with my fans, that I decided to go ahead and publish it. I honestly don't know how it will do, even though I'm personally quite pleased with how it turned out.

I'm comfortable with writing again, no longer feeling the same pressures boxing me in, because I am willing to allow myself to fail, if need be, to see my true vision for the story come through. Of course, I really hope I don't, lol, but I won't let fear stop me anymore. I've discovered that the only way through something like that writer's block I went through is to face your fear and shove it aside to let your creativity through.

I hope sharing this story will help some of you who are also struggling with fear of failure. Know that you can push past it and find a new strength on the other side of the battle!

As for the story itself, I really wanted to return to the mythos I created in "Rampion", but I also wanted to write a book set on modern day Earth, and also visit a whole new world I had created that still had a little "magic" around it. I love sci fi, but sometimes, I miss writing fantasy, so I figured this story would be a good way to get a little of both into the story. If you aren't familiar with the name Draku Rin, he is a side character from my book "Rampion," belonging to the ajda-yan species, also known as "dragon-men" by most humans. For good reason, as you see in this book! :D Any time I can work a dragon into a story is a good time for me, because dragons were my first love, and my most enduring!

The yan-kanat themselves were inspired by conspiracy theories about the lizard people (of course, ;)) and also my love of anthropomorphic lizards. If you've noticed that a lot of my alien species are "scaly," now you know why. :D Why do I love them so much…? Well, I'll refer you back to the fact that my first loves are dragons, lol.

I still have plans for future books that are direct sequels to "Rampion," and some of those books will feature the Ajda (aka, ajda-yan), including Bal Goro (aka, the Overlord of the ajda-yan). I also want to feature some of the AI infiltrators, and I even have ideas for the titans themselves (those are gonna be so fun, and are also some of my more experimental works, as I have taken inspiration from Lovecraftian horror for the titans in my books). However, I am not going to make any promises at this point, because I really don't want to let anyone down by not meeting those promises. Let's just say that the ideas are there, and in some cases, the outlines are also there. Hopefully, someday, I will feel the inspiration to finish these stories!

Until then, I am playing around with a couple of different manuscripts, and I *can* say that one of them is the sequel to this book, which will be Kevos' story (if that wasn't clear by the end of this one. ;)) I know. He's a jerk. But reforming the antagonist from previous books is one of my favorite romance tropes, and I couldn't resist it with this particular character.

Thank you all again for taking the time to read my book. If you want updates on future books, you can sign up for my newsletter:

http://eepurl.com/gudYOT

You can also follow me on my Facebook page:

https://www.facebook.com/The-Princesss-Dragon-343739932858

Or you can check out my blog:

https://susantrombleyblog.wordpress.com/

You can also drop me a line at my email addy:

susantrombley06@gmail.com

Bookbub: https://www.bookbub.com/authors/susan-trombley

Goodreads: https://www.goodreads.com/author/show/3407490.Susan_Trombley

Amazon author page: https://www.amazon.com/Susan-Trombley/e/B003A0FBYM

Book Links:

Iriduan Test Subjects series

The Iriduans are up to no good, determined to rule the galaxy by creating unstoppable warriors using monstrous creatures found on their colony worlds. Can the courageous heroines captured by the Iriduans to be breeders to these monsters end up taming them and turning the tables on the Iriduans themselves? This is an action-packed science fiction romance series where each book features a new couple, though there is an overarching storyline in addition to each individual happily-ever-after.

The Scorpion's Mate
    The Kraken's Mate
    The Serpent's Mate
    The Warrior's Mate
    The Hunter's Mate
    The Fractured Mate

Into the Dead Fall series

Ordinary human women are abducted by an enigmatic force that pulls them into a parallel universe. They end up on a world that is in the aftermath of a devastating apocalypse and is now just a vast, inter-dimensional junkyard. There they will encounter alien beings from many different dimensions and discover the kind of love they never imagined, forming a life for themselves out of the ashes of a lost civilization. This series is an exciting reverse-harem, post-apocalyptic alien romance that introduces beings from many different worlds and includes a mystery that spans the entire series, though each book ends on a happy note.

Into the Dead Fall
    Key to the Dead Fall
    Minotaur's Curse
    Chimera's Gift
    Veraza's Choice

Shadows in Sanctuary series

The humans of Dome City have been raised to view the horned and winged umbrose as demons, but when their separate worlds collide, these brave heroines must face the truth that nothing is ever what it seems. Can love alone bridge the divide between human and umbrose and put a stop to the tyranny of the adurians, who are the enemies of both? This futuristic science fiction romance series features a new take on the demon/angel paradigm on a world where humans have forgotten their origin, but still cling to their humanity. Each book features a new couple and can be read as a standalone with an HEA, though there is an overarching story throughout the series.

Lilith's Fall
    Balfor's Salvation
    Jessabelle's Beast

Fantasy series—Breath of the Divine

When a princess is cursed and transforms into a dragon, she falls in love with a dragon god and sparks a series of events that plunge the world of Altraya into grave danger. Myth and magic collide with the cold ambitions of mankind as those who seek power will do anything to get it. The dragon gods work to stop the coming danger, but it might be the love of a human woman that holds the key to the salvation of the world. This fantasy series features a different couple in each book and a satisfying ending to each story, but there is also an overarching story throughout the series.

The Princess Dragon
    The Child of the Dragon Gods
    Light of the Dragon

Standalones or Collaborations

The well-known story of Rapunzel gets a science-fiction twist in this fairytale retelling featuring an artificial intelligence and a plucky princess determined to prove herself to be much more than a pretty face. This is a futuristic science fiction romance that introduces a new universe where humans live on colony worlds after being forced to flee a deadly AI on Earth centuries prior to the story.

Rampion

TRANSLATIONS

Translations from Yan-Kanat to English:

Vaka-iv, nixir. Zarken anzha xirak. —Calm yourself, human. Drink the xirak.
    Zarken, nixir. —Drink, human.
    Kiv'as shir, nixir. Zarken. —Don't talk, human. Drink.
    Iv-olar nixir. —You are human.
    Ris, Ir-olan yan-kanat. Iv-olar nixir. —No, I am yan-kanat. You are human.
    Vauteg, nixirs olar creta. —Curse [evolved in the language to be a generic expletive, original meaning lost], humans are animals.
    Hako ivkiv janata, nixir? —What [will] you do for now, human?
    Nata. —Now.
    Nata, iv tega drahi harzek. —Now, you take mate treasure.
    Drahi harzek. Iv hachek ver. —Mate treasure. You wear it.
    Sarah, drahi arxi Jotaha. —Sarah, mate to Jotaha.
    Dree. —Means the equivalent of yes or okay or "I got it."
    Ver-os voneill gemant. —It is scent-cleansing.

Sarah, akonrir. —Sarah, sleep.

Fanak auje. —Stay here.

Jotaha golex... Sarah fanak. —Jotaha hunts, Sarah stays.

Fanak. Vaelin gurez. —Stay. Be safe.

Sarah, Olar-iv zula? —Sarah, are you wounded?

Draho komin? — [Do you] Need help?

Mito olar-iv zula? —Where are you wounded?

Yan sutaz. —inferno stone.

Natna. —Close enough.

Trilneva. Ja neva'at Sarah. —Healing paste. For healing Sarah.

Vaelin rin itov Zigaro Yan, chanu zayul. —Be one with [the] Eternal Inferno, little spirit.

Rir draho ziga ita tizan arxi anzha skilev. —We need continue our journey to the city.

Kavaric oma, Sarah, iri drahi—Follow me, Sarah, my mate.

Ver-os troka! —it is true!

Made in United States
Orlando, FL
02 April 2025